PENGUIN BOOKS

THE LOVE DEPARTMENT

William Trevor was born in 1928 at Mitchelstown, County Cork, and he spent his childhood in provincial Ireland. He attended a number of Irish schools and later Trinity College, Dublin. He is a member of the Irish Academy of Letters. He has written many novels, including *The Old Boys* (1964), winner of the Hawthornden Prize; *The Children of Dynmouth* (1976) and *Fools of Fortune* (1983), both winners of the Whitbread Fiction Award; *The Silence in the Garden* (1988), winner of the *Yorkshire Post* Book of the Year Award; *Two Lives* (1991), which was shortlisted for the *Sunday Express* Book of the Year Award and includes the Booker shortlisted novella *Reading Turgenev*; and *Felicia's Journey* (1994), which won both the Whitbread Book of the Year and the *Sunday Express* Book of the Year awards. A celebrated short-story writer, William Trevor is also the editor of *The Oxford Book of Irish Short Stories* (1989). He has written plays for the stage and for radio and television: several of his television plays have been based on his short stories. Most of his books are published by Penguin.

In 1976 William Trevor received the Allied Irish Banks' Prize and in 1977 was awarded an honorary CBE in recognition of his valuable services to literature. In 1992 he received the *Sunday Times* Award for Literary Excellence. Many critics and writers have praised his work: to Hilary Mantel he 'is one of the contemporary writers I most admire' and to Carol Shields 'a worthy chronicler of our times'. In the *Spectator* Anita Brookner wrote 'These novels will endure. And in every beautiful sentence there is not a word out of place,' and John Banville believes William Trevor's to be 'among the most subtle and sophisticated fiction being written today'.

WILLIAM TREVOR IN PENGUIN

Fiction
The Old Boys
The Boarding-House
The Love Department
Mrs Eckdorff in O'Neill's Hotel
Elizabeth Alone
The Children of Dynmouth
Other People's Worlds
Fools of Fortune
The Silence in the Garden
Two Lives
Felicia's Journey

Short Stories
Collected Stories
Ireland: Selected Stories
Outside Ireland: Selected Stories

Autobiography
Excursions in the Real World

WILLIAM TREVOR

THE LOVE
DEPARTMENT

PENGUIN BOOKS

PENGUIN BOOKS

Published by the Penguin Group
Penguin Books Ltd, 27 Wrights Lane, London W8 5TZ, England
Penguin Books USA Inc., 375 Hudson Street, New York, New York 10014, USA
Penguin Books Australia Ltd, Ringwood, Victoria, Australia
Penguin Books Canada Ltd, 10 Alcorn Avenue, Toronto, Ontario, Canada M4V 3B2
Penguin Books (NZ) Ltd, 182–190 Wairau Road, Auckland 10, New Zealand

Penguin Books Ltd, Registered Offices: Harmondsworth, Middlesex, England

First published by The Bodley Head 1966
Published in Penguin Books 1970
7 9 10 8 6

Printed in England by Clays Ltd, St Ives plc
Set in Linotype Pilgrim

For Jane

I

Edward knew nothing about love as he sat in the back garden of St Gregory's playing draughts with Brother Toby. He was quite content at that moment, not worried about anything, not even the fact that, yet again, Brother Toby was proving invincible. He knew nothing then of the Bolsovers, or the Bolsovers' charwoman or James Bolsover's enemies, or his wife's, or of the Bolsovers' house in Wimbledon. He knew nothing of the woman with thick, square spectacles who was to hand him, one day, a pair of wash-leather gloves; or of the lover who created havoc. He did not know that in the near future he was to say with glaring anger and in an expert way: 'There's no love on the hoardings of Britain, Mr Lake.' He did not know that he was to call people the enemies of love, and know what he was talking about. Edward concentrated on the black and white discs, trying to see three moves ahead and not being able to. 'Excuse me,' he said suddenly. 'I must go and wash my hands.'

Brother Toby leaned back and smiled. Edward saw him looking around for his pipe, and heard the striking of a match as he walked away. He did not at the time consider why he had said that he must wash his hands: he did not look at them and see that they were perfectly clean, with trimmed nails and shining knuckles. He considered it afterwards, and discovered an explanation.

'Overwork and strain,' murmured Brother Edmund as he passed Edward on a linoleumed landing, referring to the condition that had brought Edward to St Gregory's, reminding him of it in case he should imagine some other idea. Brother Edmund carried a white bowl containing cream; he said in passing that he was on his way to do some cooking.

Edward ran a tap into a basin and wondered then if it was necessary, really, to wash his hands. 'You must simply try,' they had said to him, 'to be your age.' And then they had smiled, and packed him off to St Gregory's. But now, as he turned the tap off, he was aware that he had become weary of the prescribed quietude; he felt better in himself. 'I am my age again,' said Edward. 'I could take the posters in my stride.'

He had feared the posters on hoardings and had said so. He had complained of orange-and-black tigers, and old women drinking tea, of aeroplanes realistically in flight, and dogs and cats, cockatoos, parrots, giraffes, motor-cars drawn up by mountain streams, farmyard fowls, tins of spaghetti. He had feared most of all the men and women who played around with cigarettes or chocolates, people who eyed one another in a peculiar manner. Men leaned forward, sticking chocolates into women's mouths, or lighting cigarettes for them. They were the giants of the hoardings, standing in sunshine, in speed-boats or on rocks, up to their tricks. They performed on water-skis, balancing butter in the air; they ate and they smoked, they smiled over bedtime drinks or glasses of hard liquor. They had green faces or purple ones, and brown skins, and teeth as white as toothpaste.

Edward had complained of the size of the men and women and of their colours, and of their insincere teeth. He had complained, and for his pains had found himself at St Gregory's, a tranquil retreat, where he was trying to be his age. He quite understood that; he often felt three years old.

The water in the basin rushed away and Edward walked slowly to his bedroom. He moved in innocence, thinking that he could not go on forever being pampered simply because strain and overwork had caused him to complain about the posters. He put a few possessions into a green canvas bag, and on this cloudy August afternoon he walked out of St Gregory's when no one was looking.

As he strode down the quiet road towards the shops and the sea, Edward wondered if he had been wise in this abrupt action. 'No summer at all,' an old man said to him, interrupting his thoughts, and Edward smiled. He bought a bar of Cadbury's chocolate and walked by the chilly sea-front, eating and considering. 'I shall write to Brother Edmund,' he said. 'I shall thank him for all his kindness.'

Children played on the edge of the sea, dashing about, pretending to be soldiers. They fell down with cries of rage or despair, briefly simulating death. Edward understood how they felt, their irritation at being small and inept; he understood their wishing to be grown soldiers who could go their way, presenting arms whenever they felt like it and taking part in all conversation.

Edward walked on, nodding to himself about the children, and shifting from hand to hand the green canvas bag. At the railway station he bought a platform ticket and boarded the first train he saw. He entered a lavatory, where he remained until the train reached its ultimate destination. 'London,' said Edward, 'by the looks of things.' He planned to say that his ticket had been stolen from him by a tramp, but in fact no one asked him for it.

In an evening newspaper Edward saw that lodgings were advertised in quantity and that poorly rewarded work was available in all areas. *Young gentlemen catered for*, he read. *Convenient. 5 gns.* 'Five guineas,' said Edward. 'That's a lot.' He turned the page, and read again. *Lady Dolores Bourhardie requires another male assistant. Highly paid post, demanding intelligence, penetration and drive. Immediate interview.* The title of a famous magazine followed, together with a telephone number. Edward went away and dialled it.

After that, he walked to Clapham and accepted a room at the top of a large house. 'You'll be happy here,' the landlady said. 'This is an up-and-coming area.' Edward smiled, but when the woman asked for five guineas in advance he had to admit that he could not manage it. He reached down for his canvas bag and began to go away. 'Wherever are you off to?' said the woman, and added with a sigh that rent in retrospect would have to do. 'Have you picked up a position?' she asked, and Edward explained that he hoped to become another male assistant to Lady Dolores Bourhardie. 'Blimey,' said the woman.

Dear Brother Edmund, Edward wrote in his mind, *thank you for all your kindness to me. I have come to London and am staying in good digs. The posters are not on my brain any more: I have looked at them face to face and have not gone into an odd state. All of which is due to your wisdom and encouragement. I cannot say much else, except that I am aiming to go into the employ of Lady Dolores Bourhardie. Please give my regards to Bro. Toby and say I am extremely sorry about our game of draughts.*

Edward slept well that night, dreaming of the children playing soldiers on the beach, and of the back garden of St Gregory's, and his time in the train lavatory. He awoke refreshed, ate a breakfast of fried tomato and egg, and spent the morning walking from Clapham to Victoria, confirming on the way that the posters were no longer a worry. In the early afternoon he entered a building in the centre of London and took a lift to the fifth floor. 'Down at the end there,' a woman with a tea-trolley directed him, and he thanked her.

Edward passed through a door marked 305 and saw about him young and beautiful girls, working with typewriters, typing with all their fingers. These were girls who chattered as they worked, girls dressed gaily in the fashions of the time, with varying hair-styles. Had Edward paused long enough in Room 305, he would have discovered that they conversed on many subjects. They talked of experiences with men, of the hoodwinking of men in a harmless way, and the repulsing or encouraging of advances. They talked of evening visits to cinemas and restaurants, of clothes they had recently purchased, or clothes that some other girls had purchased, or clothes they coveted. They talked of what it might be like in the future, marriage and motherhood, a house in a suitable place, kitchen conveniences of every description. They talked of love and broken hearts and tears and happiness, but they lowered their voices when they did that, assessing the subject to be a private one. Some of them smoked as they chatted on, a few of them nibbled food: nuts and cheese, and confectionery that didn't cause fatness.

'Lady Dolores,' said Edward, looking around him.

'Not us,' said one of the beautiful girls. 'No, no.'

'Sorry,' said Edward.

'Straight ahead,' said the girl, and smiled.

Edward walked on, through a door marked 306, into a softly-carpeted room of immense proportions, with crimson curtains that reached the carpet and matched most elegantly, Edward thought, the subtleties of a pinkly striped wallpaper. *Love Conquers All!* said a framed embroidery that stretched the length of one wall, the coloured letters entwined with delicate leaves and flowers, and winged Cupids at play with arrows in the four corners. Around it, gay against the pastel shades of the striped paper, were very many smaller embroideries, in red and blues, greens, mauves, purples, yellows and a few in black and white.

Plants stood about on decorated saucers, on shelves and window-ledges and on the desks at which a number of murmuring young clerks sat. The plants were all green, ferns and palms, and exotic growths which had developed long, climbing tubers that advanced along the walls or wound their tendrils around the framed embroideries.

'Lady Dolores?' said Edward.

'She'll send for you,' said one of the clerks in a soft voice. 'Sit down, why don't you?'

Edward sat down. The clerk added:

'If you're interested, that frieze round the ceiling is by Samuel Watson.'

Edward looked up at the carved frieze. 'It is very lovely,' he said, and saw one of the other clerks shake his head. Edward examined the room more closely, his eyes travelling from embroidery to embroidery, along the frieze, and up and down the curtains and the stripes of the wallpaper. After ten minutes of this, fearing that Lady Dolores might have forgotten the appointment and aware that no one had informed her of his presence, he licked his lips and said:

'Where is her office?'

The clerk who had spoken before said:

'She'll send for you, you know.'

'I just wondered –'

'Gifts from the grateful,' said the clerk, pointing at the embroideries. 'She said she liked embroideries.'

'I was just wondering where her office was. I wasn't going to –'

'It's in there, actually: beyond that archway.'

Edward looked. Flanked by two immense rubber plants and an excess of fern and general greenery, he saw a door marked 307.

'That is the hub,' said the clerk. 'The heart of our love department.'

2

Lady Dolores Bourhardie, a woman of fifty, received more letters than anyone else in England. They came from women of all kinds and ages, women who had often only two things in common: the fact that they were married and the fact that they were in distress. Lady Dolores sat all day in her own inner sanctum, a woman who was four and a half feet high but had never been classified as a dwarf. She sat among grey metal cabinets, organizing and thinking, and drawing on her gifts. She deplored the follies and the horrors she read of in the letters: she replied with sternness or with gentleness, and often with both. *Why does he not realize,* Lady Dolores had read, *that he must make an effort? He makes no effort of any kind. His hair marks our wallpaper, and it is symptomatic, that, of a general malaise. The children have homes of their own now, and that being so I notice the details more. I am right to, I know; but how could I be happy, noticing the details?*

And again: *Dear Lady Dolores, why do we quarrel over the raw meat from butchers or food from tins. We quarrel over clothes we wear? We quarrel about what food to give our dogs, how to lay a table, and if powdered coffee has a drug in it. We think of separation, but now we are old: we are in our sixties now, my husband and I.*

Young wives wrote, sad and sometimes disillusioned, fearful for their marriages. The middle-aged feared the passing of time.

He says I've lost my looks. Wouldn't you lose your looks, with children and illness and hard work? He says my face was beautiful once. He shows me photographs of us taken on the Isle of Man. He sees women in magazines and says, 'There's good looks for you, that woman with the dog.' He says I should have a face-lift, but I'm frightened to have that kind of thing.

They sew the skin, you know. He tells me that; they pull the skin and sew it. His sister had it done. He says if she has had it, why can't I? He sits there, looking at me, saying I could do with a face-lift. He never stops.

Dear Lady Dolores, a woman in Brighton had written, we are polite and civilized, we do not quarrel, nor tell a joke. We simulate preoccupation, but are preoccupied only with the mistake we made in 1940. We are like funeral mutes in this house.

Lady Dolores had long since devoted herself entirely to her work. Three doors led from her small office: one to the luxurious place where all her clerks worked, one to her bathroom, and one to the room where she slept. Beyond the clerks' room, in Room 305, the girls typed out replies to letters, sorting out stamped addressed envelopes and keeping the details of the department in order. Some wag had once christened these rooms the love department, which was suitable in a way, for Lady Dolores' vocation was the preservation of love within marriage. She had powers, she said, and no one ever denied it, since she was the heart and soul of the magazine for which she wrote a weekly page, and on whose behalf she answered the letters: she had increased its circulation four-fold; her face advertised it nightly on a television network.

Lady Dolores often wept, thinking of the letters, of marriages that had hit hard times, of women confused or lonely or cruelly treated, of women who were foolish, or cruel themselves. She wanted there to be happiness, she wanted there to be love, love given and love returned; she wanted people to be patient one with another, and generous, and even wise. There were ten million lonely women in England, Lady Dolores said, and most of them were married. When they wrote to her, she did her best: she cobbled up what there was to cobble, she advised restraint and patience.

On this particular afternoon, while Edward Blakeston-Smith waited without, Lady Dolores smoked a cigarette and thought particularly about the women of Wimbledon. She knew something about them. She knew that many were the wives of men of business, that in the evenings their husbands returned and spoke, or did not speak, of the day they had spent. She guessed that the wives, if they were young wives, recounted a thing or two about the children, what the children had remarked upon, or how ill-behaved they had proved themselves. Older wives, she imagined, asked for a glass of sherry and turned on the television.

Marriages in that district continued under a strain, or ceased to continue, or continued in contentment: it was in that respect a district like many another. 'I have walked up there,' Lady Dolores often said aloud in the love department. 'I have kept my eyes open in Wimbledon, yet I cannot see anything different except that the place has a windmill. The air is much the same as elsewhere.' The air was pleasant, in fact: sharp in winter, balmy during the warmer months. Children played in Wimbledon gardens while their mothers sat and kept an eye on them, reading or sewing to pass the time. When it was cold, they kept an eye from their sitting-rooms, through double-glazed french windows.

Lady Dolores, in moments of great anger, used to clench her teeth together, and clench her hands too, thinking of the women of Wimbledon; for although it was a district like many another, there were marriages that had suffered there and need not have suffered, and there were women rendered low.

Lady Dolores thought of those marriages now, and felt frustration swelling in her breast. She recognized certain signs, and in order to prevent herself from losing her temper she rose and crossed the length of her office. She opened the door and spoke into the larger room outside. 'Where's this fellow?' she said.

'Me?' inquired Edward.

'Come on,' said Lady Dolores.

Edward followed the short, stout woman into her office, and closed the door behind him. 'Hi' said Lady Dolores.

'How do you do.'

Lady Dolores saw before her a young man who smiled at her with such innocence that she was obliged to bite hard on her jewelled cigarette-holder, fearing for his presence in a hard world. He stood before her, with his smile and his light-blue eyes, with red cheeks and fair golden hair, informing her that he had once, without distinction, attended a university. He had come in answer to an advertisement, he said, looking for employment since he had no money. She saw that his fair hair was short and neatly combed. She approved of that.

'Edward Blakeston-Smith,' said the new young man. 'My father was an Army man.'

'So you live with your mother, eh?'

'No, Lady Dolores. My mother died as she carried me into the world. My father never forgave himself. He tried to make it up to me.'

'I see,' said Lady Dolores. 'Very nice. And now you're here for work?'

'I'm hoping to find my feet, actually. I'm trying to be my age.'

Edward had determined that he would set out into the world and play again the game as an adult, disguising his conversation so that its shortcomings might not be noticed. For himself, he would have been happy playing draughts all day, but he knew full well that this was not the way of the world; he knew that excessive draughts-playing was not what his father had expected of him, nor his mother whom he had met in that rudimentary way. He could quite visualize the hurt look on his father's face if he discovered that his only son used up his time playing games of draughts with children or old men. His father had died four years ago, on manoeuvres on Salisbury Plain.

He has been sent to me, thought Lady Dolores, changing the cigarette in her holder; he has been sent through that door by Almighty God. She smiled at Edward, and told him that growing up was a difficult business. She told him not to be afraid.

'You have been sent to me, Mr Blakeston-Smith,' said Lady Dolores. 'Now why, can you imagine?'

'Sent? No, no: I rang up on the telephone. Yesterday afternoon.'

Edward was puzzled by Lady Dolores' conversation, and puzzled indeed by the woman herself. She was a person, he noticed, who seemed to be almost as broad as she was tall, attired in rough clothes, with black hair flowing down her back, thick-lensed spectacles that sat squarely before her eyes, darkly framed. Her teeth appeared abruptly when she smiled, and were unexpectedly long, pale rather than white. He was puzzled by the content of her speech, and by the intense way she fixed her deep-set eyes on him.

'It's difficult work,' Lady Dolores said. 'It's not all beer and skittles.'

Eager to accept any kind of paid labour, Edward said he understood that.

'You are aware of the extent of mail? And its unfortunate nature?'

'I've read about it.'

'There's never a let-up. Love goes on, Mr Blakeston-Smith. You follow me on that?'

'I think so.'

'Well, then?'

Edward looked about the room, at the walls and the ceiling.

'Don't do that,' said Lady Dolores. 'Let me warn you, Mr Blakeston-Smith: like the old song says, as a lovely flame dies.'

'I'm sorry?'

Lady Dolores lit another cigarette. The glowing end of it was quite near to Edward's face, because Lady Dolores' cigarette-holder was inordinately long.

'Smoke gets in your eyes,' said Lady Dolores. 'It's the marriages that count.'

'I see.'

'You couldn't see. You'd have to be here before you saw. I cry in my bath, Mr Blakeston-Smith, every day of my life.'

Edward wondered if this woman was still in her senses. He wondered if it wouldn't be quite a profitable act to walk out now and sell the story of this interview to the *Daily Express*.

'Take these letters,' said Lady Dolores, handing him a dozen, 'and sit yourself down at an empty desk. They are letters from Englishwomen in distress.'

Edward smiled.

'See what you make of them,' said Lady Dolores. 'We get people pulling our legs in this department.'

Edward took the letters, and paused. Lady Dolores made an impatient movement, waving her right hand in the air. 'Get on,'

17

she said snappishly. 'Get hold of a jotter and a ball-point.'

All the clerks in the love department were supplied by Lady Dolores with ball-point pens and jotters for making notes in. She warned them that she would tolerate no horseplay or discussion among themselves of the mail, threatening instant dismissal if her wishes were ignored. She had had youths in the past who had thrown the envelopes about and had eaten pies at their desks.

Edward sat down and asked the clerk at the next desk for a jotter and a ball-point pen. 'Open the drawer,' said the clerk, which Edward did, and discovered the materials within. He smiled, and murmured quietly some words of thanks, attempting to be discreet, since discretion seemed to be the order in the love department. He began to read the documents that Lady Dolores had given him, and was shocked beyond measure.

As he perused the letters, Edward was aware that his mind was registering words that the letters did not contain. The words seemed to be in the air, and at first he thought he must be imagining them. Then it seemed to him – an odd fact, he thought – that his colleagues were issuing them, muttering the words, or shooting them out in a soft, staccato manner that made Edward jump. As he listened, concentrating on what he heard, he reflected that a conversation among ghosts might be quite like this.

'His dog prowls,' remarked a clerk.

'Now, red mechanic!' said another.

Edward kept looking up and smiling when he heard a bout of words begin, but no one paid any attention to him. '*My husband has brought a woman in*,' he read, and then read on, and could hardly believe what lay before his eyes. He began to repeat it aloud, assuming that that was what the others were doing, but he was quickly asked to desist.

Two of the clerks began to argue about a king. 'Sweet king beribboned,' the first one said, but the other quietly objected, questioning the suitability of ribbons as a decoration for a king. 'Medals, surely?' he suggested. 'You don't put ribbons on the monarchy, I mean.' The first clerk narrowed his eyes. 'I put what I like on the monarchy,' he said. 'Any frigging object I fancy.' He spoke then of his veins, stating in a clear, low whisper that there were trespassers in his veins by night. 'Neck death,' said the other clerk. 'Eat your meat!' Both clerks laughed gently. 'Smiling mortician,' said one, and both were solemn again. Edward wondered if the afflicted clerk knew that the veins were a danger area, for it happened that he had known of a man in whom trouble with veins had proved swiftly fatal. The reference to a mortician had reminded him of this, and he wondered if the clerk had been wise enough to seek medical advice. He was about to mention that one couldn't be too careful with the veins when the words began again.

'Holy citadel,' said a third clerk, a worker who had not yet spoken, one with a black beard. 'Oh, cherished Roman!'

'Look here,' said Edward. 'What's going on in this joint?'

But the clerks ignored his plea. For many minutes no one spoke; the ball-point pens were poised and ready, eyes ran over yards of paper. A letter from Flintshire was put to one side for Lady Dolores' attention, and a pencilled missive signed *Joe from Bantry* was thrown away.

Behind a fastened door, Lady Dolores removed her stays and placed them in a drawer. She sat more comfortably then, her feet on a hassock that one of her assistants of the past had bought in a church furnishers' for her, and she read through the pickings of yesterday's mail.

Lady Dolores shook her head over it, finding nothing remarkable, and thought again of the women of Wimbledon. She saw them in her mind's eye, sitting down at writing-desks in their houses and starting their letters off. *Dear Lady Dolores, I am in a mess* ... She had once sent a private detective up to Wimbledon, to poke about and bring her back information, but all the man had done was to get drunk in the local public houses. That was essential, the man had said, in order to get to know the people, to discover the lie of the land. He had presented her with a bill for beer consumed by the gallon, by himself and by the local people, and in the end had presented her with nothing else except an address in Putney, which he claimed was relevant. 'Seventeen pounds for beer,' she had cried out in horror at the time, and handed him five shillings. The man had ambled off, with a cigarette sticking to a corner of his lips, not even bothering to protest.

Lady Dolores opened a drawer and withdrew the piece of paper on which this detective had written the address in Putney. She was regarding it, considering and wondering about it, when she was struck by a notion that seemed at first to be absurd and then to be of such truth and value that she threw her head back and ejaculated with a will. She curled her toes into the flesh of her feet; and having calmed herself down, she examined the notion and saw no flaw in it.

'Where's the new fellow?' said Lady Dolores, standing in her open doorway. 'Come in here, Mr Blakeston-Smith.'

Edward noticed, as he had noticed before, the contrast between the two rooms: Lady Dolores' was wholly businesslike, bare of curtains and embroideries, a room that was entirely grey.

Lady Dolores placed a cigarette in her holder and lit it. She said nothing. She picked up a large piece of paper covered with figures and began to read them, moving her lips. Edward watched her nostrils tighten and relax. He wondered if he should go away.

'You know the rules, Mr Blakeston-Smith?' said Lady Dolores eventually. 'Only marriages get on to the books. The unmarried I cannot help, and will not. They can go to hell for all I care. Letters from unmarried persons go straight to the wall.' She slipped a hand under her hair at the nape of her neck and shook her tresses wildly about, tousling everything, to Edward's considerable surprise. 'What I'm asking you now is, have you an aptitude for the job? Have you picked out any letters? Go out, Mr Blakeston-Smith, and bring us in what you've spotted this day.'

Edward returned to the desk where he had been sitting and picked a single letter from the waste-paper basket. 'Blood,' said a clerk, and Edward smiled at him, and conveyed the letter to Lady Dolores.

'Let's see,' she said, and read aloud: '*Dear Madam, my husband has brought a woman in, saying she is his daughter by a previous marriage, but I have never heard of any pre-*

20

vious marriage. They are always together, especially in the evenings, going out to the café or in her room. I have said to my husband that I had not known that the life had gone out of our marriage but he only stands there. He says that twice-cooked meat gives the girl heart-burn. We are a childless couple, which again is something that I feel, it being borne in upon me that this is definitely due to my inadequacy, if the girl is my husband's daughter. If she is some other man's daughter, that of course is worse. She calls me Mum, but I do not know where I am with the pair of them. Yours truly, (Mrs) Odette Sweeney.
An educated woman,' said Lady Dolores. 'Not a single spelling mistake. Things were better when Mrs Sweeney was a girl. Education was a living thing.'

'It was,' said Edward.

'Well, then?'

'Well, Lady Dolores?'

Lady Dolores's large chest heaved about as the air passed through her lungs and slipped in and out of her nostrils. She smiled at Edward suddenly, flashily; her eyes were fixed on him so intently that he was obliged to lower his. He examined the jewellery on her fingers: he had never before seen so many rings on a human hand.

'Well?' said Lady Dolores again.

'I threw the letter away, it being a put-up job. "A couple of lads in a public house," I said to myself, "trying to take the mickey out of Lady Dolores." '

Lady Dolores struck a match, but allowed it to burn without applying the flame to the point of her cigarette. She watched the flame die. She struck another match, lit her cigarette, and brought the palm of her right hand powerfully down on the surface of the desk. The thud of contact made Edward leap. Displaying signs of considerable anger, Lady Dolores shouted:

'You are a hopeless case. You are a handicapped person.'

Edward rose to his feet, but she told him to take his seat again. She added in a calmer voice:

'You are useless at the desk. Mr Blakeston-Smith, I'll warn you of that. You're sitting out there wanting a fat wage and the damn bit of good you are to me at all. Odette Sweeney writes from a tortured heart, maddened by the presence of a doxy in her house. "Here's a daughter of mine," announces Sweeney, coming home one night from the café. "Here's a young missy come to lodge with us." What happens then? I'll tell you, pet, what happens then. The hussy unpacks a suitcase, and two days later she's hanging out clothes on Mrs Sweeney's washing line. Two women can't live happily in circumstances such as those. Can you not see that?'

'Well, of course –'

'The girl cooks scrambled eggs and doesn't clean the saucepan. The girl abuses the electric iron. In no time at all Mrs Sweeney's house is smelling to high heaven of powder and bath salts. "What can I do?" she cries. "People are talking." She weeps and she moans, and eventually she takes her courage in both hands: Odette Sweeney writes a letter. A letter from her tortured heart, Mr Blakeston-Smith, that a certain person feels entitled to screw up into a ball and pitch into the nearest wastepaper basket.'

Edward blinked. He felt something clogging his throat and realized all of a sudden that he was going to cry. He panted slightly. He said:

'I was imagining two Irish labourers concocting in a pub. I couldn't believe a word that was written there.'

'Why not? Isn't it a perfectly genuine letter? You've proved yourself a failure at the desk.'

'I'm sorry, Lady Dolores. I don't know much about earning a living.'

'Have a good cry, then, and we'll forget the whole thing. Have you a hanky?'

Edward said he hadn't, and Lady Dolores threw him a few paper tissues.

'I have never cried before,' said Edward, 'in my entire life.' He looked Lady Dolores straight in the eye as he said that, and she knew by his gaze that he was speaking the truth. She knew as well, as though the heavens had opened and she had seen him emerge, that this was the person who would do the deed, who would cleanse all Wimbledon.

Lady Dolores screwed up her eyes and drew quantities of smoke into her lungs, considering how best to proceed.

'I think what I'll do,' said Lady Dolores casually, 'is put you on the outside jobs. Have you ever heard tell of Septimus Tuam?'

3

As Lady Dolores spoke his name in the love department, the man who was known to her as Septimus Tuam sat in the hall of a Mrs Blanche FitzArthur and devoted his mind to simple thought. Mrs FitzArthur had once written a letter to Lady Dolores, but Septimus Tuam did not know that, nor would he have been much interested had the news been presented to him now. Septimus Tuam, a young man of great paleness and gravity, was concerned with the present: with the fact that he and Mrs FitzArthur were about to set out to buy Mrs FitzArthur a rain hat, and with the more disturbing fact that five minutes ago Mrs FitzArthur had informed him that she had lost the capacity for thought. Sitting on a mahogany chair, Septimus Tuam reflected that a reconciliation between the FitzArthurs was in the air, and that in spite of it Mrs FitzArthur was behaving irrationally, announcing that she was in a dither and wearing out her husband's goodwill. Mr FitzArthur had laid down his terms in a straightforward manner, declaring quite clearly what he expected of her, while she, for a reason obscure to Septimus Tuam, repeated only that she could not bring herself to make certain statements.

Septimus Tuam sighed loudly and looked down at his hands. 'I cannot think,' Mrs FitzArthur had cried. 'I must go to New York.' What good would that do? thought Septimus Tuam. He examined his hands, and in his mind's eye he examined the future. He saw there a Mrs FitzArthur cut off with a small allowance, while her husband, piqued and out of patience, paired off with another woman. Alternatively, he foresaw the loss of Mrs FitzArthur's company for a passage of time while she recovered her thoughts in America. He recognized that one way or the other he might easily be taken unawares, and he had never cared for that kind of thing. He drummed his fingers on the mahogany of the chair, annoyed and out of sorts.

'I put a man on him,' said Lady Dolores in the love department, 'and he was no damn good. D'you get me? Septimus Tuam could spot a man like that a mile away. He's as fly as a granary rat.'

Edward nodded, understanding very little of the conversation. He wanted to ask what the words were that the clerks used, since they didn't seem to imply what their meaning implied. He wanted to repeat to Lady Dolores that he had never cried before, because she hadn't taken much notice when he'd told her the first time. 'Listen,' said Lady Dolores in a low voice, 'there's this person called Septimus Tuam who is a scourge and a disease. He lives in a room in Putney and takes a 93 bus up to the heights and off he goes, peddling his love. It's a scandal of our times.' Lady Dolores paused. 'I want you to put a stop to him, Mr Blakeston-Smith.'

'A stop?'

'You have been put on earth,' said Lady Dolores, 'for that reason alone.'

'Oh, surely not,' said Edward.

Lady Dolores closed her eyes and indulged in a vision. She dreamed that the wispy figure of Septimus Tuam was being pursued along a suburban road called Kilmaurice Avenue by the young man who sat before her; and as Septimus Tuam turned towards the garden gate of Number 10 she herself cried a command in the love department and the young man fell upon the ruffian, smiling at him and saying something. Up rose the women then, from the roads and the avenues, shaking their fists at Septimus Tuam and advancing upon him to tear him limb from limb. Lady Dolores opened her eyes and focused them on her visitor.

'Be ye as wise as serpents,' she said, 'and innocent as doves. Let me supply the wisdom, now.'

Mrs FitzArthur had written to Lady Dolores at a time of crisis in her marriage, not long after she had met Septimus Tuam. She had complained of her husband's ways, of difficulties she had experienced in extracting money from him. Her marriage, she wrote, had come to a full stop and she did not see much point in hanging on, especially since a younger man had entered her life. Lady Dolores had replied coolly. A younger man, she wrote, had no right to enter the life of a married woman. Mrs FitzArthur must attempt to see another aspect of her husband, she must develop subtleties in the business of relieving him of his wealth. *I trust*, wrote Lady Dolores, *that you continue to keep yourself attractive in the home? I trust you have in no way gone to seed?* She had added, with astuteness, that she recognized in Mrs FitzArthur's complaint a trouble that sprang, not from the parsimony of the husband, but from the upset caused by the advent of the other. She was not prepared to discuss this matter, she said, but gave it as her firm opinion that Mrs FitzArthur should remain by her husband's side. Two days later Mr FitzArthur discovered all; and having done so, he packed a bag and left the house, threatening divorce.

Mrs FitzArthur had been in a state ever since that moment: she had not known whether she was coming or going, and although her husband had recently held out an olive branch she felt she could not grasp it. Why can't she grasp it, thought Septimus Tuam, for heaven's sake?

Septimus Tuam, still on the mahogany chair in the hall, heard Mrs FitzArthur in her kitchen giving an order to her cleaning woman. He could hear only a word or two of this instruction, but he deduced that it had to do with Mrs FitzArthur's gas stove, for words came through which suggested to him that the merits of various oven-cleansers were being debated. He was idly thinking of that, of the cleaning woman down on her knees scrubbing at the oven, when the telephone rang by his elbow. He picked it up and spoke into the mouthpiece.

'Good afternoon,' said Septimus Tuam, in a way that suggested that Mrs FitzArthur kept a shop. 'What can we do for you today?'

'I beg your pardon,' said Mrs FitzArthur's husband from the other end of London. 'It seems I have the wrong number.'

26

'This is definitely the Blanche FitzArthur residence,' said Septimus Tuam.

'FitzArthur residence? Does Mrs FitzArthur live there? I am telephoning Mrs FitzArthur; who are you, by God?'

'Not Mrs FitzArthur,' said Septimus Tuam, and sniffed and clicked his fingers, and called out to Mrs FitzArthur, who came at once.

'Who is that man there?' demanded Mrs FitzArthur's husband, feeling intensely jealous and upset. 'I ring you up with forgiveness in my heart; you said you were going on the straight and narrow. Whatever's a man doing there?'

'He just picked up the telephone since he was passing through the hall. He thought to help, poor man.'

'I know. I know. But who is this poor man?'

'He is a Mr Spratt, come to repair the oven of the gas cooker. The wretched thing is all clogged up; I can cook nothing these days.'

'A Mr Spratt? I thought it was Septimus Tuam.'

'Mr Spratt is an employee in a gas shop. It is awkward saying this because the man is standing here. Do you want something in particular?'

'I am giving you a date so that you may come to me with a contrite heart. It is in me to let bygones be bygones.'

'Oh, God!'

'What's that?'

'You've taken me unawares. Date, did you say?'

'I am not an unfair man. I have thought and I have come up with a conclusion. Divorce proceedings may now be cancelled if you can offer me assurances that your heart is contrite. Is it empty of the blackguardly hound?'

'All is over between Septimus Tuam and myself,' said Mrs FitzArthur in a low voice.

'Maybe,' returned her husband. 'But do you come to me on your bended knees, spitting on the scoundrel's face? That is necessary before we can be secure again. Do not forget you are my seventh wife.'

'I cannot spit upon the scoundrel's face,' cried Mrs FitzArthur.

'Oh, I am on the straight and narrow, I grant you that, but the other takes time.'

'Tomorrow is the destined day.'

'Tomorrow, Harry? What's on tomorrow?'

'Tomorrow I come in person for my final answer. I am to hear from your lips, madam, whether or no the scoundrel is naught in your heart. He's run off from you, I dare say; they all do that.'

Septimus Tuam watched Mrs FitzArthur receive this news, knowing why she had told her husband that the telephone had been answered by a Mr Spratt from a gas shop. The suspicious Mr FitzArthur had put a private detective on them and had caused a bit of bother, but now, since the private detective had been called off, it only remained for Mrs FitzArthur to fall in with her husband's wishes. A reconciliation had first been mooted a month ago, and Mrs FitzArthur, on the advice of Septimus Tuam, had assured her husband that the lover had passed out of her life. In the future, Septimus Tuam promised, they would take more care.

'But I haven't it in my heart,' Mrs FitzArthur had cried, 'to abase myself and to spit upon our love affair.' She would have liked to hear Septimus Tuam say in reply: 'Let's go out and get married; let that be the end of it.' But she knew that she could hardly hope for that. 'Come, then, tomorrow,' she cried into the telephone. 'Come here to our house, boy, and let's just see. It makes my blood run cold.'

A pause, the work of Mr FitzArthur, registered along the wire. His wife felt sick in her stomach and sighed massively, and saw Septimus Tuam sitting a yard away from her, with his tongue lolling out of his mouth, examining the palms of his hands.

'I see no reason for your blood to run cold,' said the voice of Mr FitzArthur, 'unless you have been having me on.'

'Dear, I said that by mistake. I meant to say some other thing. Come tomorrow whatever you do. At eleven a.m.'

'Eleven a.m.,' agreed the man who had married seven times. 'All right, Blanche.'

'I feel an omen,' said Septimus Tuam, who didn't feel anything at all. 'Let Mr FitzArthur back into the house. Make up and be friends. Now is the time: I feel that thing.' He spoke from the mahogany chair, from the same position in which he had watched Mrs FitzArthur get into a state over her husband. He had sat there listening, endeavouring to think about nothing. He had relaxed as he had taught himself to relax, a gaunt young man with a face like the edge of a chisel and a mind that in some ways matched it.

'Oh God!' cried Mrs FitzArthur, looking down at the telephone receiver.

Septimus Tuam rose up from his lethargy then and whispered to her what she must do. 'Have him here,' he said, 'at eleven in the morning. Give him food and drink after his journey, and claim that Messrs Guilt and Shame have taken hold of you. Say you have loved him always, good fellow that he is. Say you do not understand the vileness that led you towards the vagabond scoundrel who led you a dance, who loved you and left you. Bury your head on his breast, Mrs Fitz; announce you are his forever. Cry mightily that you spit upon the vileness that carried you astray, that you spit upon the heart and diseased mind, upon the face and body of the evil Septimus Tuam. Tell him all that and he'll move back in with his suitcases and hand you a chequeful of housekeeping money. "Sit yourself down," say, "and I'll cook you a strudel." After which, why not suggest that he takes you out on the river?'

Mrs FitzArthur placed a hand on her brow and seemed again distraught. 'How can I think,' she cried, 'in the midst of all this? He must give me more time. He must let me go out to New York and be on my own for a while. Harry can be selfish.'

Mrs FitzArthur added that she was in too serious a state by now to go out and buy a rain hat, at which Septimus Tuam expostulated mildly, reminding her that he had come all the way to Wimbledon in order that they might go together to Ely's to see what rain hats Ely's were offering. 'And all that happens,' he complained, 'is that I'm obliged to borrow from you the taxi charge home again. I am a needy case today.'

Mrs FitzArthur, continuing to be vague and distracted, handed Septimus Tuam ten shillings of her money. 'Harry comes here tomorrow,' she said. 'What can I do but pluck up my courage and say New York to him?' Septimus Tuam nodded, stepping from the house, since it seemed the best thing he could do. He crossed a busy road and walked on to Wimbledon Common, thinking to himself that if Mrs FitzArthur was going to be in New York he'd better do something about it.

'I don't follow you, Lady Dolores.'

'Why not?'

'I don't understand in what way the man is a scourge and a disease.'

Lady Dolores reached behind her and grasped a cardboard folder containing several dozen letters. She handed the folder to Edward and indicated that he should read its contents. When he had finished she said:

'The women are of all ages. They are as old as seventy and as young as twenty-two. They have, in common, their riches.'

'He's after money,' said Edward.

Again silence developed. In the love department proper one of the clerks wrote idly on the back of an envelope: *Spine limp. Dead.* Another inscribed elsewhere: *His dog prowls.*

'They all say he is beautiful,' said Lady Dolores. 'That is the pattern that ties up the case against Septimus Tuam – for many do not mention him by name. They say, with no exception, that he is beautiful where others might say a lover is a bundle of charms or a fellow of excitements. They speak of him as beautiful, as though referring to an object.'

Edward would have preferred to have been given a place with the other clerks, reading letters and noting their contents, passing on the special ones to Lady Dolores Bourhardie. Now, it seemed, he was to get mixed up with some man called Septimus Tuam, whom Lady Dolores declared he had been put on earth to deal with.

'Is there no chance of a desk job?' Edward asked meekly.

'You are no damn good at the desk,' Lady Dolores snapped. 'You've completely disgraced yourself.'

'But the other –'

'You're perfect for the harder work; it requires the use of a fine brain. You have been sent to me to undertake this work, so's I can make a man of you.'

'I'll do my best,' said Edward. He was aware of a sudden flash of pride, hearing her say so confidently that he was perfect for work that required a fine brain.

'I'll warn you of this,' said Lady Dolores. 'Women have gone to their graves.'

'He hasn't killed them?' cried Edward, horrified.

'Three women of Wimbledon took to their coffins. Buried by love, Mr Blakeston-Smith.'

Edward shook his head in wonderment.

'Average age fifty-one and a half years,' said Lady Dolores. 'The three of them succumbed to a decline. D'you get me?'

'I don't know what to say.'

'You're sweet, Mr Blakeston-Smith,' cried Lady Dolores, jumping to her feet, pushing the hassock from beneath her desk and standing on it to clap her plump hands. The rings rattled together, sparkling in the artificial light that always burned in the room.

'Listen,' said Lady Dolores in an excited and urgent way. 'Listen to me, Mr Blakeston-Smith, my little baby. Are you listening?'

Edward said he was listening, and Lady Dolores told him at length about the suburb of Wimbledon. 'Close your eyes,' said Lady Dolores, 'so that you can imagine better.' She said that men from the business world had come to settle in Wimbledon, men from city board-rooms, who did good work by day and returned exhausted to spacious homes. They were men who were under pressure in middle age, because they sought to accumulate wealth – a process, so Lady Dolores advised, that brought pressures with it. She told Edward of the work the men performed, sitting about in offices in London, coming to decisions and being sharp about it. Lady Dolores went into considerable detail; she conjured up pictures of interiors of houses and of the men's wives; she spoke of the growing-up of children, of their accents and ambitions. 'S.w.19,' said Lady Dolores, 'is a suburban area like many another. It's a respectable, decent place.'

His umbrella dangled from his arm as Septimus Tuam walked and eyed the women; young mothers with children, nursery-maids and *au pair* girls, the middle-aged and the elderly, all strolling or moving briskly, Septimus Tuam wondered about them. He had read fantastic yarns of girls from Switzerland whose fathers, manufacturers of confectionery and the like, possessed great wealth. Girls from Switzerland, though, young things of seventeen and eighteen, would be looking for marriage more than anything else: the older age-groups interested Septimus Tuam more.

He passed the Bluebird Café and saw through the window a tall blonde-haired lady buying coffee beans from an assistant. She was about thirty, he decided, with a smart air about her, as though she knew her way about and had a use for money. As he watched, the woman paid for her coffee beans and then, instead of leaving the place as he had expected, she went farther in and sat down at a table. He at once entered the Bluebird Café, and although there were other tables that were empty he sat down at the one occupied by the blonde-haired lady, retaining his umbrella.

'Well, now,' said Septimus Tuam to a hovering waitress, 'I'll have a coffee, bless you.

With blood-red fingernails the blonde-haired lady placed three lumps of sugar in her cup and stirred the liquid until she was satisfied that all was dissolved. She drank some and glanced at her watch.

'I thought it would rain,' said Septimus Tuam. 'It is most unsettled, the weather we're getting.'

The woman nodded, without either speaking or smiling. She took a diary from her handbag and began a perusal of its general information.

'Extraordinary, the things they tell you,' said Septimus Tuam, his profile inclined towards her. 'Lighting-up time and all the information about the law terms. Oh bless you, Agnes,' he added, speaking to the waitress who had placed his coffee in front of him, whose name, in fact, was not Agnes at all.

'Yes,' said the blonde-haired lady, acknowledging the remarks about diary contents.

'I myself have a brewers' diary, given me by a certain Lord Marchingpass of whom you may possibly have heard. A little known fact about the life of Lord Marchingpass is that he sits on the boards of several brewery firms. Hence I have at my fingertips such information as the maximum pressure that may be applied to beer without gas being absorbed. Also, of course, the usual stuff about how to treat bleeding and wounds.'

Septimus Tuam drew from his pocket a diary he had found on the floor of a tube train. 'What would I do if you fainted?' he said, and read from his diary: '*Lay patient down and raise lower limbs. Loosen tight clothing. Turn head to one side, and ensure fresh air.* I think that's odd, you know, in a diary for brewers. Unless the fumes cause it. Unless fainting is an occupational hazard in the work, men falling unconscious as they approach the vats. I wonder now.'

'I know nothing of such matters,' said the woman at the table.

'Nor I. I know nothing of brewing beer, or fainting, or anything like that at all. It is simply that the generous Lord Marchingpass, a kind of uncle really, kindly presented me with this diary. Well, there you are.'

The woman rose, and bowed slightly as a form of leave-taking. But Septimus Tuam rose too, and when the waitress came along with her pad and pencil, said:

'Put them both together, Agnes, like a good girl.'

'Oh, no,' protested the woman.

'Indeed.'

'No, I'm afraid I couldn't allow that.'

Septimus Tuam, who had certain stances that were modelled on those of Spanish dancers, took up one of these now. He nodded in a firm manner to the waitress, who scribbled a bill and handed it to him. 'Bless you,' he said, and pressed into her palm a penny.

'Actually,' he went on, having paid the bill and accompanying the blonde-haired woman from the cash-desk, 'beer is a beverage I never touch. I am a Vouvray man myself.'

'I really must insist upon your taking this money. One and

threepence, I think my share was: I cannot have you paying for my coffee.'

'Ha, ha,' said Septimus Tuam without smiling, swinging his umbrella. The woman felt a prick on the calf of her leg and looked down and saw that the rough tip of the young man's umbrella had pierced her stocking and caused an instant ladder. Septimus Tuam looked down too. He said, aghast:

'My dear lady, what a thing to happen! Now, look here –'

'Please take this money at once. I have a great deal to do.'

'No, no. We cannot have that. I have accidentally ruined your stocking in a public place. Look, dear lady, have you time? Come straight across to Ely's with me and I'll replace the damaged article. It's only fair.'

'It was an accident, it doesn't matter. I shall put this money in the charity box.'

The woman placed one and threepence in a box that asked for alms. She said:

'Good-bye.'

'My dear, we cannot say good-bye like this. I have utterly ruined your beautiful stocking. I do insist, I really do, that you step across the road to Ely's and see what they have for sale. I'm well known in the store.' Septimus Tuam had taken the liberty of seizing the woman's elbow, while she, feeling herself propelled from the café and on to the street, was thinking that a hatchet-faced young man whom she had never seen before had paid for her coffee and was now about to buy her stockings.

'I must ask you to release me,' she said. 'Let go my elbow: I do not intend to go with you to Ely's.'

'Oh, come now.'

'Please. You are greatly embarrassing me.'

'Nonsense, my dear. My name is Septimus Tuam. And may I be so bold –'

'Excuse me,' said the woman to two men on the street. 'I am being annoyed.'

The men turned on Septimus Tuam and spoke roughly, while the woman, glancing haughtily at him, strode away. He felt humbled and depressed and then felt angry. He crept away with the sound of the men's voices echoing in his ears, hating momentarily the whole of womankind, and reflecting that his failure had cost him two and sevenpence. He knew that in order to retain his nerve he must succeed at once. He went to Ely's and found a lavatory where he rested for an hour, weeping a little and meditating. Then, considerably refreshed, he washed himself, checked that the tip of his umbrella was correctly adjusted, and set off for a round of the store's departments.

Septimus Tuam had learned to live with this pattern, with the flaw in his make-up which seemed to dictate that failure must always precede success, that success must of necessity rise out of the other. He couldn't understand all that, although he had occasionally given the fact some thought. He had never likened himself to a phoenix, or to any bird: he would have thought that quite ridiculous.

'They don't quite match,' a pretty woman was saying in the button department. 'Have you others?'

The assistant brought out further boxes of buttons, shaking her head, as though not sanguine about the outcome of the search.

'It's a devilish business,' said Septimus Tuam in a general way. 'An old uncle of mine, Lord Marchingpass, actually, has asked me to try for some extra-large leather ones. You know, I don't believe they make them any more.'

The pretty woman shook her head.

'Look,' said Septimus Tuam. 'Aren't those a match?' He stretched out to hand her the buttons that had caught his eye, but in fact they turned out to have too reddish a tinge about them.

'What a pity!' said Septimus Tuam.

The assistant then imparted the information that a great supply of buttons was expected any day now. 'I'll ring you,' she said to the woman, 'when they come.'

'Now, there's good service,' said Septimus Tuam.

'Just your name and number, madam,' requested the assistant.

The woman gave her name and telephone number, which were memorized accurately by Septimus Tuam. 'It's very kind of you,' she said to the assistant and felt at that moment a prick on the calf of her leg. She glanced down, and noticed that the thin young man's umbrella had laddered her stocking.

'Marriage is difficult enough without the likes of Septimus Tuam,' said Lady Dolores. 'He's been a thorn in the flesh for seven years.'

'Seven years is a long time.'

'Only innocence can match the black heart of Septimus Tuam. I knew that, Mr Blakeston-Smith; I said it often. What good was a drunk?' Lady Dolores, who had been intending to say more, paused. She closed her eyes and again tried to understand what the women meant when they wrote that their lover was beautiful, since they might as easily have imbued him with a more usual characteristic. They might have said that he was handsome or had strong arms, or was more agile of mind than their husbands were. Lady Dolores saw the beautiful creature standing still, but he was no longer the victim of assault in Kilmaurice Avenue: she saw now a greater vision, one inspired, she believed, by this youth in his innocence; she saw the defeat of Septimus Tuam, and she saw the part that was already there for her to play. Edward Blakeston-Smith, under her command and her influence, would do what was required of him, while she in the end would achieve her heart's desire.

Lady Dolores was aware of a human voice speaking nearby, and noticed that the young man who had been sent to her was inclining his head and moving his lips.

'How can I help you?' Edward was saying. 'Is it to check some facts?'

Lady Dolores asked Edward to repeat that, and when he had done so she issued her instructions. She said she wished him to find out all possible details about the man called Septimus Tuam; she wished him to track the man down, to watch him, and to spy upon him. She ordered Edward to read the letters from the women in Wimbledon, to digest them fully and then to return them to her. She handed him the scrap of paper with the address of the house in Putney on it. 'Note as well,' she said, 'the address of a Mrs FitzArthur who has written to us nonsensically. Mrs FitzArthur is the current interest. Keep an eye on her house and see what there is to be seen.' Lady Dolores reached behind her and brought forward a loose-leaf note-book, containing two hundred blank sheets. 'Fill this up,' she said. 'Mark it with his name. Make this your dossier. D'you get me?'

Lady Dolores walked to a cupboard and took from it a chocolate cake on a plate and a bottle of Scotch whisky. She cut a slice of cake and poured herself a small measure of the intoxicant. 'D'you get me?' repeated Lady Dolores, uncertain about whether or not the youth had replied.

'I understand everything.'

'Well, then?'

'Thank you, Lady Dolores.'

'Love falls like snow-flakes, Mr Blakeston-Smith; remember that. Look into people's eyes.'

Edward rose and moved towards the door. He felt tired. He would have quite liked to be playing a game of draughts with Brother Toby. He considered that thought, and then he banished it. Lady Dolores Bourhardie was a famous woman and he had just become her right-hand man: could he ask for more than that? He was about to become a person of the world.

'Septimus Tuam is an enemy of love,' said Lady Dolores, mingling whisky and cake on her tongue. She bent her head over the large piece of paper that was covered with figures, which earlier she had been absorbed in.

'We'll put him behind bars,' cried Edward, with a fresh flush in his cheeks, pink spreading to his ears. 'That Septimus Tuam.'

Lady Dolores laughed gently. The picture became clearer in her mind, but this did not seem to be the moment to talk about it; and as she thought that, she knew that there would never be a moment. What would happen would happen, with neither argument nor discussion. She waved her hand towards the door and said nothing further.

Edward passed through the room where the clerks sat and then through the one in which the young women worked with typewriters. He saw a lift at the end of a corridor. He entered it and found himself within the minute on the ground floor.

Edward walked out into London, on to streets that were

thronged with people. Love was on his mind, since he had been hearing about it, and as he passed through the people he wondered how love affected them. They were people in love, he supposed, since love fell like snow-flakes. Or they were people made bitter by love, or people aware of love but indifferent to it. Lady Dolores would have added that there were those who were afraid of it, too, who lowered their eyes and kept them low, moving them over objects on the ground; and those who worshipped it and then were at a loss.

He walked among people who had heard of Lady Dolores Bourhardie, who had read her word and even taken her advice. Some there were who claimed that their flesh was made to creep at the sight of her, others who saw eccentric beauty in her face, and others who thought of her as something of a joke. But all over England the marriages were cracking, as always they had cracked. Love came and went and left a trail, people wept, while Lady Dolores looked on with an expert's eye and often felt sick at heart. She spoke of the enemies of love and said she saw them everywhere, offering shoddy goods.

Edward walked on, jostled by the crowd, until he arrived at an ABC, where he had a cup of tea.

4

The Bolsovers lived in Wimbledon, and on the evening of the day on which Edward entered the employment of Lady Dolores they were not at home. Their children, sleeping in an upstairs room of 11 Crannoc Avenue, had both of them thrown off their bed-clothes, for the night was warm and sleep had not come easily. In the Bolsovers' sitting-room, sipping her favourite liqueur, sat Mrs Hoop, the Bolsovers' charwoman, baby-sitting with the television on.

The Bolsovers themselves, with purple-coloured menus in their hands, faced one another in a restaurant that was itself a purple-coloured place. Waiters hovered not far away.

'Well?' said James.

His wife said nothing. Once upon a time, a year or so before marrying this man, she had been voted the prettiest girl in the district in which she had grown up. Now, at thirty-seven, four years younger than her husband, she retained much of her beauty. She walked gracefully, and she was slim; her hair was dark and gathered with care into a knotted arrangement at the back of her head; her eyes were brown and had been called, in a complimentary way, extraordinary.

'I'm going to have turtle soup,' said James, 'and probably hazel hen.' He looked over the rest of the menu and saw on it *bruciate briachi*, which he translated as burnt chestnuts. He remembered, one Christmas when he was a child, his father entering the house with a bag of burnt chestnuts, offering them instead of a Christmas wreath, saying that Christmas wreaths that year weren't worth the cost, saying as well that he had been delayed. James saw quite vividly the image of his father holding the bag in the air and heard his mother's voice remarking sternly that burnt chestnuts were unsuitable for children at seven o'clock in the evening. James gave a small laugh. He said:

'I was thinking of the day my father came into the house with a couple of dozen burnt chestnuts in a paper bag instead of a Christmas wreath. He stood, poor man, considerably confused, while my mother scolded him most roundly.' James paused, doubting that he had succeeded in soliciting much of his wife's attention. He added: 'I was put in mind of chestnuts by seeing *bruciate briachi* on the menu here.'

A waiter displayed the label on a bottle of wine, and James nodded his head. He said to his wife:

'This is a good place.'

Eve looked about her and said that the place seemed good.

'The food is good,' said James. 'Food is cooked here in a rare way. Their hazel hen, you know, is excellent. You should have had the hazel hen, my dear.'

'I have never had hazel hen. To tell the truth, I've never even heard of it.'

'It's a cheap dish and yet a delicacy. They're charging about ten times too much for it.'

On to the television screen in the Bolsovers' house there appeared at that moment the still face of Lady Dolores: the long, bared teeth, flowing hair, eyes deep and cute, nostrils taut. Mrs Hoop smiled at all this, and a voice spoke to her, advocating immediate purchase of the magazine for which Lady Dolores wrote her page. 'Love within marriage,' continued the voice, not the voice of Lady Dolores, but that of a once-famous actor down on his luck. 'Happy,' said the voice.

'*Bruciate briachi,*' said Eve, and then nodded, and did not smile.

'My father is dying now,' murmured James.

'I know,' said his wife.

On this day and at this precise moment ten years ago, the Bolsovers had been sitting together in the restaurant-car of a French train, ordering a different kind of dinner and sharing a certain excitement. Eve was thinking of that. She was thinking of that and of all that had taken place before it: a service in a church, the Church of St Anselm, not far from Wimbledon, and the wedding reception that had been held outside and in sunshine, on the lawns of a hotel that overlooked the Thames. In the great heat of an August afternoon a bearded photographer had captured for ever the scene of celebration: he had worked fast and hard, beneath the beady eye of Eve's mother, who with peremptoriness had called for photographs of the newly-allied couple against banked blooms of delphinium and lupin. The photographer had hoped for champagne, but had not, in fact, been offered any.

'My father is dying slowly,' said James. 'He says he's in a hurry, but doesn't seem to be.' That morning he had had a letter from Gloucestershire, from the nurse who was seeing his father through his passing. *It is quite absurd*, she had written, *to think, that at this time of my life I should be sent out to weed flower-beds in the rain.*

Eve raised a forkful of food to her lips, thinking that his father's son was dying too. She did not say anything. She did not speak of that day on the hotel lawns, because she knew it could elicit no response.

'There's too much purple,' she said after a silence had developed. 'They've overdone things.'

'What?'

Eve did not reply. Silence formed again before she said, since she could think of nothing else to say:

'In ten years' time I shall be close on fifty.'

'You said something different the first time.'

Eve looked at all the purple and wondered why the papal shade had been so ubiquitously employed. Her eyes moved from the menus on the tables to purple walls and purple velvet on chairs and lamp-shades. Through a sea of the single colour the waiters walked discreetly, whispering in their professional way.

The diners, men and women of several generations, lifted food to their mouths and talked quite loudly, laughing or smiling to fill the gaps in conversation. Eve watched the people, thinking about their marriages, for marriage was on her mind. She saw a woman who might be fifty, her hair defiantly blonde, her head held up at an angle as though the position suited it particularly. Her companion was a man who did not speak at all. He ate his food while the woman talked into the air, eating little herself. Eve wondered what the woman thought as she spoke and gushed her smile across the table. Was the man her husband? They had the appearance of a married pair. Was he unused to speaking? Did he prefer to eat with a book propped up in front of him, or a newspaper? And had the woman become so accustomed to this circumstance that she failed now to notice it? Or perhaps the man was dumb.

There had been a time in the Bolsovers' marriage when Eve would have drawn her husband's attention to this couple. They would have wondered together about them, staring too much, as once they had been apt to do. Eve perceived the woman's talk fail to gain a response and she wondered if one day soon she'd be doing something like that herself, while James appeared to strangers to be possibly a mute. She wondered about the wedding of that silent man and his wife, what the man had said then, and whether or not they either of them cared to look back to it.

'You said something else,' James repeated. 'You didn't say the first time you'd be close on fifty.'

'No.'

'I don't understand you,' said James.

Old Mrs Harrap in sky-blue clothes, a woman who had once been her father's nanny, had wept that day on the hotel lawns, having drunk too much champagne. She had snatched a metal hoop from a flower-bed and brandished it at a waiter because, she said, the man had spoken rudely.

'When he goes,' said James, 'there'll be that awful old house, and the garden gone to pieces. What on earth am I to do with it all?'

'Why not sell it all?' said Eve. 'As other people have sold property in the past.'

'Bring me some Hennessy brandy,' James called out to a passing waiter, who bowed in a neat manner. He turned then to Eve, and said in a low voice: 'What are you turning snooty for? I made a civil observation.'

'You asked me a question and I replied. I should have thought it polite rather than anything else.'

'You know what I mean.'

'I can't help it if I'm straightforward. Don't blame me for that.'

'This is our wedding anniversary.'

'Here comes your brandy.'

The waiter placed a glass of brandy by James's right hand, but James frowned and said :

'I had meant you to bring a bottle, and two glasses. We may sit here for an hour or two, my wife and I. Drinking wine and brandy, sip for sip.'

The waiter said he was sorry and went away to fetch what was required of him.

'I think he made that mistake on purpose,' said James. 'There's impudence in those eyes. What were we saying?'

'Very little if you care to analyse it –'

'Listen,' said James, leaning towards her. 'Let me put to you the simple facts.'

Eve looked at her husband, wondering what prevented him from remembering that he had put to her the simple facts before. The simple facts were the story of his adult life, how he had started at the beginning and for twenty years had clambered from success to success. 'One ends up on the board,' he had said to her, explaining the ways of the business world, and Eve had nodded, assuming that he would end up where he wished to end up. 'He'll do well,' people who knew about such matters said. 'Keep an eye on him.' And those who had kept an eye on him saw the efforts of James Bolsover rewarded as he made his way. He moved his family from one house to a better house, as modest riches came to him. The Bolsovers' children grew and thrived, and eventually went to school, to be taught by Miss Fairy and Miss Crouch. 'I am dying,' said James Bolsover's father, six months ago, and that had been another landmark. He had lain since in a house in Gloucestershire, beside a market garden which once he had run but which had long since become too much for him. He had claimed to see his dead wife on a marble ledge, waiting for him and urging him to hurry up.

While his father was nodding his head over all that, James

had reached a fresh peak and couldn't believe what he found there. He returned one day to his house in Crannoc Avenue and said that he was now on the board. 'You have ended up,' said Eve in a joking way, and had often thought since of those words, for it seemed that, long before his time, her husband had in fact come to an end. In the months that followed he told her bit by bit, regularly repeating himself, about the eight who sat around the board. 'Eight fat men with glasses,' he said, 'whom I had imagined to be men of power and cunning, sit yawning and grumping over the red baize of that table. They're fifteen years my senior, and they're fair in this: they see I've done a stint and so reward me. I may now relax in my early twilight and talk with them of how I heat my house, and exchange news of meals eaten in restaurants, and tell them stories they haven't heard before. They do no work, yet imagine otherwise. They talk of painting all the building a light shade of blue, or of new appliances for the washrooms. Mr Clinger, maybe, speaks of his pet. Dogs are unclean, says Mr Clinger; he disapproves of dogs. "We'll rear an intelligent young monkey," says he to his wife, "whether you like it or not." She didn't like it, poor woman, but now, by all accounts, has grown devoted. There's many a story we hear about that monkey when we're not hearing some detail of the office buildings. It passes the time on a sleepy afternoon while the underlings do the work. It's my reward to say the underlings are worthless. Well, some of them are.'

Eve could not easily imagine what it was like in the place where James worked: she had never been there, she had never met his colleagues. She thought of a ten-storeyed building and of many corridors, some winding and twisting, a few of them straight and very long, with similar doors opening opposite one another. She saw a few people, as in a dream, secretaries and men with spectacles, hurrying along, carrying papers. Her own world was vastly different: the world of mothers and Mrs Hoop, lunch and tea, chatting to Sybil Thornton, and talking to people in shops. Morning and afternoon, the mothers settled into their motor-cars in a rush, to convey their children to school or else to fetch them home. Eve settled into her red Mini Minor – Eve who had dreamed of marriage all her girlhood; born out of her time, she sometimes thought. 'Bring the children to tea,' a mother strange to her would say. 'Bring them on Friday, and we can have a chat.' And on Friday another mother and another mother's children would become known to her, and later on, if it was considered a suitable thing, the mother, without her children but with her husband instead, might sit down to dinner in the Bolsovers' house, or stand around drinking sherry or cocktails.

'I'm not a success in the board-room,' said James. 'Incidentally.'

'Why not?'

'I don't quite know.'

Middle-aged women with drapes on their skirts and men smoking cheroots had stood about together on the hotel lawns in the heat of that August day, laughing and telling anecdotes and occasionally lifting their glasses to wish the young Bolsovers well. 'We're running out of fizz,' one waiter reported to another, and the second waiter cursed because he thought that, that being so, the three bottles he had himself purloined might well be missed. 'Go!' cried Eve's mother, hurrying to the bridal couple with a flushed face. 'Go for heaven's sake or you'll miss whatever it is you're catching.' Before that Eve had stood for the bearded photographer, feeling happy on her wedding day, like a character out of an old-fashioned story-book, happy because the man she loved had married her. He had taken her hand and had led her away from the lawns of the hotel, and later they had boarded a train for France.

'My father is eighty-one this month,' said James.

'You act as great an age as that. Your middle years are stifling you.'

'You see me as a species of a bore? You see me in our house, drinking Hennessy brandy and watching the television, and wonder to yourself why the wretched man doesn't go out and play a game of tennis? He couldn't, you say to yourself; he couldn't do that simple thing to save his life. Well, maybe not. Listen.' James paused, and leaned closer to her. 'This is the man who on a wedding anniversary tells his wife that hazel hen is an economical dish, who tells her, as though she cared, that he will now take turtle soup, who sees in a waiter signs of impudence and remarks on it. Is that the picture?'

'I didn't say any of that.'

'I'm busy within myself, growing a stomach like the other men, and pains to go with it. They look the same, you know, sitting round the table: sometimes you can't tell one from another.'

'You're trying to put some argument into my mouth.'

'I'm saying in the open what's in your mind anyway. Is there harm in being straightforward? Look, I'll admit it: I'm dry and boring in my middle age.'

James paused. He saw before him a woman who was disillusioned because once upon a time she had believed in living happily ever after. She had borne him two children and had treated him well. He loved her still as she sat there, dressed in black in the purple surroundings, but he saw her and he saw himself, too, together with her somewhere, moving towards bitterness. 'The man you married,' said James, 'is watching himself now. He's growing gross, and growing older than a pair of grandfathers, well before his time. He'll tire quite soon of most of life. He'll sit in an armchair and see the cigarette ash like snow upon his clothes and not raise a hand to help himself. "Bring me Hennessy brandy," that man shall murmur, but no one shall carry it to him because no one can be bothered to be around in the room. And so he shall rise, and the cigarette ash shall fall about, and he shall mooch hither and thither looking for a glass, and a bottle to go with it.'

'You're a successful person,' said Eve angrily. 'There's no need at all to go on in this ridiculous manner.'

'I'm an astute trader, Eve: I've been honoured for it early.'

A waiter came near, murmuring about coffee. When he had gone, James said:

'The days go by while an old man dies. He's playing merry hell with nurses.'

Eve sighed. She stirred sugar into her coffee. She had heard some part of this before. James said:

'The days go by, and at pleasant afternoon meetings the

men foam at the mouth, sucking effervescent stomach remedies with their cups of milky tea. After which, they may talk of the central heating in their houses. Sometimes they talk of the wives who are in their houses too, complaining wives, so they say, who never stop. They talk of cameras and of food, of holidays in Spain, and boots they have bought, of trade in Wales. They argue about those central heating systems, the size of pipes and boilers, of gas and electricity, oil and coke. They say they have taken the temperature in their rooms and found the temperature satisfactory. Their systems are trouble-free, they say, and clean, and cheap, and beautiful. They strike their fists upon the red baize of the table, battling about the systems, balancing merit against merit, one outdoing the next in praise and admiration. This is the theatre of my life. I am sorry for myself, and I despise myself for that.'

There was one of the eight men whom he had told her about, a man whose ambition it was to change the metal door-handles in the office building to door-handles that had been there in the past, door-handles of black china. There was another whose wife had not been outside her house for twelve years, who lay on a sofa in Purley; and the wife of the man who wished to change the door-handles was the wife who had become devoted to a monkey: Mrs Clinger. In that mystery place, with men such as these, she imagined her husband walking about the long corridors in his quiet clothes, or strolling into a lift, entering an office and saying something succinct. In spite of what he claimed, did all his soul go into that, she wondered, that he should return by night so strange a creature? That he should watch with fervour the programmes on television and say he could not play a game of tennis?

'Take any three of them,' said James, 'and let's here and now invite them with their wives to dinner.' He poured and drank some brandy. 'Why don't we do that?' A tart reply crept to Eve's mind, but was held there. She said:

'You're getting drunk with all that brandy, James. The last thing you want is to do this.'

'I want to see,' said James, and rose and went away. When he returned he said that he had telephoned three of the men at random. 'I invited them to dinner this day week,' said James. 'Now, there's an occasion for you.'

The voice of the out-of-work actor spoke again in the Bolsovers' sitting-room while Mrs Hoop poured herself more *crème de menthe*. 'Happy,' said the voice, and it said it in Gloucestershire too, in a small room occupied by the nurse whom James Bolsover had employed to see to the needs of his father. On the screen, Lady Dolores smiled her smile, and then went out like a light.

In the pale purple lavatory of the restaurant, grandly embellished with silver-coloured ornament of an ersatz material, Eve looked at her reflection in an oval looking-glass. In her right hand she held a powder-puff, while her left gripped the cool edge of a wash-basin. She thought of her two children sleeping in their beds, and of Mrs Hoop snugly downstairs, charging five shillings an hour. She thought for a moment that she might find some other way out of this restaurant, that she might return to her children and Mrs Hoop, and leave James where he sat, because she could not bring herself to walk across the restaurant floor and take her place with calmness opposite him, while a waiter held her chair for her. He would half rise to his feet to greet her. He would smile and then sit still, the brandy moving around in his glass. He would lick his lips in a businesslike way, and would then begin all over again: about death in Gloucestershire and the living men in London. She remembered old Mr Bolsover standing about, looking lost, on the lawns of the hotel, and disappearing rather early. She remembered Miss Cathcart, who once had taught her music, drawing her aside and wishing her happiness, saying, beneath the influence of heat and champagne, that Eve was the most romantic girl she had ever known. They had wished her happiness, all these people of assorted ages who had stood about on the lawns of the hotel, even the bearded photographer. She had felt the splendour of the occasion and had never quite forgotten it.

What Eve had forgotten, and had forgotten totally and naturally, was an occasion that was far more recent, an incident only six hours old. She had forgotten the face and voice of

Septimus Tuam, a voice that had said, 'Look, aren't those a match?' and a face she had hardly looked at. Had she remembered the man now, she would probably have remembered what she had thought at the time: that the man at the button counter who was telling her about some errand for an uncle was a figure of absurdity. He had chattered on, reaching out, fingering the buttons, and in his clumsiness had laddered one of her stockings with the point of his umbrella. 'Please don't worry,' she had said, but the man had gone on sillily, apologizing in a profuse way and saying the stockings must be immediately replaced. 'I have children to collect from school,' she said. 'I must go at once.' She left the man in the button department and went urgently away, feeling that perhaps she had been rude. As she climbed into her car, she remembered that the girl had said that when the new buttons came in she would personally telephone her. She remembered that and at the same time forgot Septimus Tuam, who had been attempting to offer her a brand of love, although she did not know it. At a party once, a few years after she'd been married, a man had said to her that he and she should get to know one another better. 'Better?' she had murmured, and the man had smiled and said they might meet one day and have tea. He smiled with confidence at her, and Eve had frostily replied, 'I see no reason for that. I'm happily married.' The man laughed loudly and squeezed her arm, and then had gone away. 'I don't believe they make them any more,' Septimus Tuam had remarked that afternoon, referring to extra-large leather buttons, and had he gone on to suggest that perhaps they might have tea together she would have stared at him in horror and amazement. But she had often since thought of that other man, remembering his height and his smile and wondering what they would have talked about over tea in a café. She believed, though, that not even now, as love grew less in her marriage, would she be seriously tempted to find out. James had once been full of life; he had thrown his head back and carelessly laughed, his eyes had had a vigour in them. Their marriage had been an easy thing then, with pleasure in it. It was hard to part with the past.

Eve left the sumptuously appointed lavatory but did not seek some back way out of the restaurant. She walked instead across a soft purple carpet and sat down again. A waiter moved in to hold her chair, and James half rose to greet her.

5

In the purple restaurant the waiter pushed forward Eve's chair in his expert way, and as he did so Edward Blakeston-Smith's father walked into the love department. In military attire, in his son's dream, he strode through the room in which the typists sat, smiling with confidence and touching his moustache. 'Oh, cherished Roman!' said Edward's father.

He came to where Edward stood, and told him of the sadness he had suffered in the past, when Edward's mother had died without a word in a maternity home; how Edward, that tiny infant, had looked at the sadness and at the bowed head of a father, and had not cried.

'Well, then?' said Edward's father in the love department.

'It's simple,' replied Edward, eager to explain. 'It's a simple thing. I'll soon be on my feet.'

'Well, then?' said his father.

'Listen, Father. I was learning about the whole panorama: the Goths and the Visigoths, Attila the Hun, Charlemagne, Joan of Arc. Let me tell you the lives of the Popes, Father: listen to me.'

'Well?' said Edward's father.

'I was a student of history, sir, until I looked up one day and saw the Goths and the Visigoths. The golden barbarians were there on the posters, larger than life. "Go down to St Gregory's," they said when I told them.'

'There are three rooms in this love department,' said Edward's father. 'Room 305, Room 306, Room 307.'

'Room 307 is the sanctum of Lady Dolores. There are two extra doors in Room 307, but that is not our affair.'

'Room 307 is the hub of the love business. Don't forget that, son. Do your work well.'

In the respectable suburb of Wimbledon Edward looked around him in his dream and saw what Lady Dolores had said he would see: the men of business and the wives of those men, and children, and motor-cars, and large red buses moving to and fro. Edward dreamed of the women of Wimbledon and of Septimus Tuam wandering among them, peddling love. 'I do not live in Wimbledon,' said the woman called Odette Sweeney. 'Septimus Tuam is not my problem.'

Edward wandered behind Septimus Tuam, haunting him, tracking him from one end of Wimbledon to the other. 'This is a respectable suburb,' said Edward; 'this man is a scandal to decency.' He entered the houses of the wives of the men of business and hid behind sofas and hall-stands. Septimus Tuam talked about love and Edward crouched away in a corner, making notes on his blank sheets of paper.

'You have done a good job,' said Lady Dolores. 'You have been your age.' But as she spoke, two soldiers came into the love department and took Edward by the arms, saying he was for the high jump. 'It's the hangman's noose for you, lad,' said the soldiers. And then Lady Dolores laughed, and the soldiers laughed, and Edward led Lady Dolores and the soldiers up to the heights of Wimbledon. He showed them all the people, the men and the women and the children, and the four of them walked about Wimbledon for many hours, until they found Septimus Tuam. The soldiers took him and put a rope around his neck, and hanged him from the branch of a tree. 'It should have been prison bars,' cried Lady Dolores. 'No need to hang the poor man.' But the soldiers only laughed and said that hanging was too good for the likes of that. They took off their helmets and cut down the dead thing from the branch of the tree, lighting cigarettes before they did so. They walked away, with the body slung between them, holding up the traffic in order to cross a road. 'Look at that!' cried Edward, and he and Lady Dolores saw the two soldiers and Septimus Tuam climb on to a hoarding and take their places in a poster that advertised tea.

6

On the morning after the Bolsovers' tenth wedding anniversary, the people of London went about their tasks in a drizzle. They awoke on this first morning of September, in outer suburbs or in the fashionable areas of Kensington and Mayfair, to find the soft rain already falling. They reacted in various ways: sighing, yawning, murmuring, nodding or shaking their heads. Some of them examined weather glasses, confirming the accuracy of their instruments. Only a few of these people, here and there, were surprised to see the drizzle; others said they had felt it in their bones. In his room in Putney Septimus Tuam sneered at the drizzle, and sighed, and spat, and shaved his face with an electric razor. Afterwards, he lay alone on his narrow bed, thinking of nothing and in love with no one, relaxing his muscles and his bones as he once had taught himself.

A man called Lake, who also inhabited a room in Putney but was unknown to Septimus Tuam and a different kettle of fish, did not mind the drizzle one way or the other as he whistled and poached an egg for his breakfast. He was reflecting that he would further his ambition one notch, as it were, during the course of this damp day. He ate his egg, writing speedily in an exercise book, planning the downfall of James Bolsover.

The secretary of James Bolsover, Miss Brown, a young woman of thirty, stood in her underclothes and her glasses, and thought about Lake. She, too, lived in Putney, living there because she wished to be not far from Lake, whom she adored. She closed her eyes and saw him clearly, smiling serenely, coming towards her with his muffler on and his right arm outstretched. He spoke to her and touched her, and she thought while the vision lasted that she must play her full part in the stoking of his ambitions and the achieving of his ends. She muttered unsteadily to herself, and sought about for a suitable jumper to wear.

In Gloucestershire it rained more purposefully, bringing down a weight of water and causing the nurse whose task it was to attend the dying of James Bolsover's father to do so with the mien of one displeased. 'Take a packet of seeds, if you would,' commanded old Mr Bolsover from his bed, 'and set them down in sieved soil in the west greenhouse. I am concerned lest when the demand comes we are unable to meet it.' The nurse said quietly that it was raining cats and dogs, and added some more, quite sharply, about the nature of her employment. 'Put on rubber boots, won't you?' cried the old man, causing the nurse to supply him with the information that she had written a further letter to his son because of all this new cantankerousness. She spoke, in fact, the truth; and in the moment that she spoke it, James Bolsover in his Wimbledon villa was perusing that very letter while eating a slice of toast and marmalade.

The Bolsover children were talking of the slaughtering of cattle, while their mother spoke to them in a routine way, drawing their attention to the passing of time, and urging haste if they were not to be late for school. James Bolsover sighed, and thought that he would have to go to Gloucestershire again, to give the nurse more money and his father a talking to.

Edward awoke at half past seven with many images still in his mind: the men of business, well-to-do fellows of varying ages, leaving their houses in the wide area of s.w.19 and setting the bonnets of their motor-cars towards mammon and the east; the women working in the houses, talking to charwomen and tradesmen, some of them attending to the needs of children and *au pair* girls, others ordering food for dinner parties. Edward had seen in the night what Lady Dolores had told him there was to see: the windmill on the common, and the men of business relaxing at the weekends, tinkering with their motor-cars, putting a shine on the paintwork. 'They have a hard life,' Lady Dolores had said. 'They grow unhealthy through work and worry. They buy cheap, maybe, and sell expensively, or organize others to do so: much money is involved; it is quite a responsibility.'

As he dressed, Edward had a clearer picture of Wimbledon and its people than ever he had had before. He saw the wives of the men strike a patch of loneliness, as Lady Dolores had said they did, sitting down in the mornings to drink coffee and smoke a cigarette or two. Their children were growing up, or had grown up already; their husbands were absorbed. Edward saw cigarettes with touches of lipstick on them smouldering in an ashtray while the women talked or sat pensive. Were they like the women of the posters? he wondered; had those cigarettes been lit for them by the men before the men had disappeared?

'What nonsense!' said Edward, pulling up a sock. 'I have come to grips with the poster people. At St Gregory's I was hiding my neck in the sand.'

Edward put his shoes on his feet and tied their laces. He watched Septimus Tuam come in among the women who were having morning coffee. The women were given fresh cigarettes, their cigarettes were lit in an expert way. 'He's wandering all over the hoardings,' cried Edward, 'with soldiers or sailors or what have you. He's tired of selling margarine.'

'Your breakfast, Mr Blakeston,' called Edward's landlady from the bottom of the house. 'Hurry up, now.'

'He's going behind bars,' said Edward to himself. 'Wait and see it.'

On the back seat of Eve's Mini Minor the Bolsover children, a boy and a girl, argued quietly about cattle while their mother drove them to school. 'Be good with Miss Fairy and Miss Crouch,' said Eve as they left the car, and they promised that they would, protesting that they invariably were.

Eve drove away, waving to other mothers in other motor-cars, who were smiling and seemed more joyful than she felt herself that morning. For no reason that she could fathom she recalled a period in the past, a couple of years ago now, when she had taken it into her head that James was having a love affair. On a morning such as this, having waved goodbye to her children and the mothers, she had been driving calmly along when suddenly the idea had come to her. She had stopped at once, beside a pastry shop which also served coffee, and had had some coffee, trying to think about the idea and trying to do so with a steady nerve. She sat at a small table and imagined James spending whole afternoons with a tall, thin girl, talking to her and making love. She saw them in a narrow room, with a low ceiling and a number of painted wood-carvings. The girl was wearing green and was taking most of it off. 'May I make a telephone call?' Eve had cried with urgency to the woman selling Danish pastries behind the counter, and the woman had replied that the place was not a call-box, but had led her nevertheless to a small office at the back of the shop. Eve was certain by now that he was having a love affair; she was certain that he had looked around and had discovered this girl in green clothes, or some different girl maybe, dressed in another colour, in some different kind of room. 'What?' said James on the other end of the line, and she had tried to explain.

Eve smiled a little sadly as she remembered all that. Again and again, while speaking to James on the telephone, she had seen the tall girl in green. She had noticed that her hair was almost white, and she remembered thinking that that was the kind of girl who belonged out of doors. Her husband stood near the girl, a glass of Hennessy brandy in one hand and the bottle in the other, laughing loudly and saying that he had never in his life before seen green underclothes. At which the girl smiled. 'Miss Brown is here,' James said on the telephone. 'She is standing by, waiting to take some letters.' And Eve in her confused condition cried out in reply that the girl in green must be Miss Brown, which was absurd, as she afterwards recognized. In the small office of the pastry shop there were a desk, and a calendar with a mountain on it, and above the calendar, held in place by the same drawing pin, a British Legion poppy. The scene had engraved itself on Eve's mind, and eccentric dreams had since, and regularly, taken place in that small office. She had entered it once to find James talking seriously to the tall girl in green, holding her hand, and on another occasion he had had his arms around the woman from behind the counter in the shop. Once she had been there herself, weeping into the telephone, and Mrs Hoop had walked in with a smile on her face and had shot her with a small revolver.

In fact, she had replaced the receiver and had heard a voice beside her asking her what the matter was. 'Whatever's the trouble?' said the woman from behind the counter. 'You've had an upset in our office.'

She had walked away, with pictures of her wedding hanging at angles all over her mind, and a new grief in her heart. 'Her maidenhead's all there,' Mrs Harrap in her cups had whispered to James. 'You're taking a clean young creature to your bed, sir.' With the cold tang of tears on her cheeks, Eve had remembered the heat of that day and the dinner they had eaten with excitement on the train in France.

'What nonsense!' said James that evening. 'You need a change.' His face and his tone caused her to accept her unfounded allegations as nonsense indeed, and she had never again imagined that her husband was having a love affair, with tall girls in green or with any other kind of girls. The episode in the office of the pastry shop had been the end of something, but she wasn't sure of what.

Eve parked her car and consulted a strip of paper on which she had earlier written a number of grocery items. The sight of them caused her to recall the dinner party that James had so abandonedly arranged the evening before. She stepped on to the pavement, wondering what they were going to be like, these men who worried her husband so very considerably.

Mrs Hoop, crouched on her haunches, filled an area of rag with Mansion polish and applied it to the parquet floor of the Bolsovers' dining-room.

This has once been his pyjamas, thought Mrs Hoop, referring to the rag, which bore still the faded marks of stripes. She laughed aloud, finding it amusing that she should be polishing a floor with part of a man's night attire. 'Ha, ha,' chortled Mrs Hoop, reaching towards a corner in a manner that caused her heavy skirt to travel upwards on her rump. 'Ha, ha,' she laughed again, aware of the movement of her clothes, but not caring because no one was in the house to observe what the movement revealed.

'Let's see,' said Mrs Hoop abruptly. She straightened up and sorted out her polishing cloth, anxious to detect the area of Mr Bolsover's pyjamas from which the piece had been cut. She turned the cloth this way and that, peering closely at it for the marks of erstwhile hems or buttons, but in the end she came to no conclusion. In anger she rose and moved her substantial form towards the Bolsovers' kitchen, intent upon an iced birthday cake from which, two days previously, she had already removed a heavy wedge.

'I may not be back to lunch,' Mrs Bolsover had remarked to Mrs Hoop. 'But help yourself to tea and biscuits.'

Jesus, Mrs Hoop had at once reflected, the cheek of it!

She set a kettle on the gas stove, and went in search of the new *Vogue* and a glass of *crème de menthe*. There was no wireless set in the kitchen – why, she could not imagine – so she was obliged, as often she had been in the past, to turn on the receiver in the sitting-room and leave the doors open. The noise came on powerfully: a pleasant male voice relating a story about a dog called Worthington.

'Well, here we are,' observed Mrs Hoop aloud. She stretched on a padded bench that had been built into the wall and on which, every evening, the Bolsover children partook of their supper. Propped up on a single elbow, Mrs Hoop sipped tea and *crème de menthe*, listening to the radio story and turning the pages of the magazine. In a moment she walked again to the sideboard where James Bolsover kept his alcoholic drinks.

Mrs Hoop had been in her time employed in an underground tube station. 'I have seen all sorts,' she was wont to remark. 'I've seen the world go by.' She often reflected upon the past, and particularly on her experiences at night, as she walked home after being on duty until midnight. 'Hanging about in doorways,' said Mrs Hoop, 'clicking their teeth at you. "Want a fag, love?" they'd say, holding out a packet of Craven A, doing their clicking again. I never made a reply: I wouldn't demean my mouth.'

Mrs Hoop had several times related her experience to James Bolsover when she attended at the house in the evenings, for washing-up after a dinner party or for baby-sitting. She would seek him out and tell him a thing or two about working on the railways, and she found him always sympathetic and interested. He did not interrupt her by telling her that he had other things to do, nor did he abruptly walk away.

Girls stared glassily at Mrs Hoop from the shiny pages. She did not care for them, their lips parted, garbed so absurdly, yet she could not help thinking about them, wondering what they were like to meet, what they would drink if taken to a public house. 'Thin as a straw,' she murmured, turning from a model who advertised some new, important girdle. She felt a prick of jealousy, remembering that she, too, had once been slender. Then she recalled the desire she nightly observed in the eyes of an old man she consorted with: old Beach had said he liked her as she was. Once he had managed to slide his hand beneath her cardigan, causing her to spill a glass of beer.

Mrs Hoop closed the magazine and held it to her bosom. Her mind was on Beach, a fact that caused a sly expression to tug at the corners of her mouth. She did not object to the man; she did not object to his company or the gossip he carried to her, though she did not always welcome his exploring hand. When she had told him that in her girlhood she had weighed only seven stone he had at once replied that he would not have been interested. Old Beach had money; five hundred and seventy pounds. 'You should make your will, old Beach,' Mrs Hoop often advised him in the corner bar of the Hand and Plough.

Mrs Hoop devoted much of her time to the consideration of two topics of thought: her dislike of Eve Bolsover and Beach's five hundred and seventy pounds. She felt less frustrated about the latter, because at least she had succeeded in interesting Beach in the drawing up of a will, but where Eve Bolsover was concerned Mrs Hoop found little to console her. The woman did not listen to her, she did not continue to murmur appreciatively and in horror over the men who had advanced on Mrs Hoop by night. 'In big cars sometimes,' Mrs Hoop would explain. 'Two or three chaps together. They'd follow on for miles along the dark streets.' But Mrs Bolsover said not a word, except perhaps that she had ordered a new supply of Ajax. Mrs Hoop had come to believe that her employer sneered at her because she was fifty years of age and her figure had gone a bit, because she was obliged to work for her living, her husband having died of a throat infection in 1955. She had told Eve Bolsover about that, how her husband had had to be cut up for a post-mortem, how it had cost her twenty-two shillings to have him brought back to her house afterwards, so that a funeral might take place in a civilized manner. 'How dreadful, Mrs Hoop!' Mrs Bolsover had said, and just as Mrs Hoop had been about to continue, to relate a fact or two about the funeral itself, Mrs Bolsover had considered it suitable to say, 'How are we off for dusters these days?'

In the Hand and Plough Mrs Hoop often held forth to Beach and the barman, Harold, about the nature of Mrs Bolsover. 'She is a whore and a bitch,' she reported, 'and given up to ridiculous ways. She's quite incapable for a man like that: there's not a brain in her head.' In the Bolsovers' hall there was a suit of armour, discovered by James and Eve ten years ago, in a provincial antique shop. On the walls were small pieces of metal that James had collected and said were medieval gardening instruments. 'The hall's like a junk yard,' said Mrs Hoop. 'She's soft in the head, I'll tell you that.'

It had once been the opinion of Beach that Mrs Hoop should cease to work for Mrs Bolsover since Mrs Bolsover was so ill-natured a person and her house, apparently, little better than a lunatic asylum. But Mrs Hoop replied to this that she stayed on for the sake of the two children, to whom, she claimed, she was devoted. In truth, Mrs Hoop's dislike of Eve Bolsover was something of an essence in her life: it had developed and spread over seven years, and without it Mrs Hoop might have found herself at a loss. At night she lay in her bed and thought of Mrs Bolsover, seeing her dressed to go out and disliking every inch of the image. Often when she was kneeling on the floor, polishing the parquet, the feet and legs of Mrs Bolsover would pass nearby, feet stuck into high-heeled shoes, legs in nylon stockings. 'I'll smash her,' Mrs Hoop would murmur to herself with venom when the legs had walked on. 'I'll tell her bloody fortune for her.' In the Hand and Plough she had said that Mrs Bolsover was as ugly as sin, with varicose veins all over her body. That, she said, was a judgement.

Mrs Hoop rinsed her tea-cup and set it to dry on a rack with a debris of sugar congealing within it. Music came on the wireless. She hummed in tune with it, flapping a duster over furniture and ornaments. 'I've brought them kids up single-handed,' she had proclaimed in the Hand and Plough. 'She don't give a damn.'

Mrs Hoop paused by a wedding photograph of the Bolsovers, staring at it with displeasure. Overcome by sudden anger, she spat at it and watched the trickle of saliva course down the glass, blurring and distorting the face of the bride. She relaxed then, sighing with her eyes closed. She opened them after a moment and continued to flap her duster, in a happier frame of mind.

As Mrs Hoop was concerned with the wife, so was Lake concerned with the husband.

'I have nothing against Bolsover,' Lake was saying to Miss Brown while Mrs Hoop was spitting on Eve Bolsover's face in a photograph. 'I wouldn't like you to think me vicious in my attitude, Brownie. Bolsover, God knows, is a decent enough mortal: he's always supported my demands for more salary.'

Lake, in soft black boots with elastic let into the sides of them, stood staring through the window of Miss Brown's office, while she sat silent before an enormous typewriter. Miss Brown, splendid in her passion, was endeavouring to convince herself that he was standing above her, stroking the nape of her neck with two of his fingers.

'The thing is,' continued Lake, 'he's not the man to be sitting on a board. He's not going places, Brownie, as I am going places. He's not all that interested.'

In Miss Brown's imagination the fingers ventured beneath the top of her red jersey. She stared through her spectacles, concentrating on the Q of her great typewriter, not saying a word.

'It's the way of the world,' said Lake. 'A young fellow like myself must make his way.' Lake was fresh of face, with a longish nose and a prematurely bald head: at thirty-four he boasted but a lump of reddish hair above and around either ear. He wore a hat for journeying about outside, but had not been known to say that his early lack of hair caused him to feel older, or in any way annoyed. He smiled constantly, on all occasions, as though obliged by nature to express all emotion in this single effusive way.

'I am a suitable person to go to the top,' said Lake. 'I am particularly well qualified for it. Who would deny that? There are few young fellows in London, Brownie, who are as endowed as I am. I have learnt every trick of the trade. As the saying goes, I know my onions.' Lake laughed. Miss Brown imagined his fingers cool on her back, and felt them there, traversing it and tapping her shoulder-blades. He said, 'My father used to remark that he saw me as Prime Minister of this country, but he was ambitious in the wrong direction. I am loyal to Church and State, Brownie, but beyond that I wouldn't like to go. I shall make my packet: I am qualified to do that.'

In his battle for advancement Lake was a saboteur. That very morning, noticing James Bolsover on his way to the board-room, he had sprinkled the back of his suit with a small handful of flour, carried to the office in a Colman's mustard tin for that very purpose. 'What on earth is the matter with your clothes?' one of the eight bespectacled men had demanded, and all of them had surrounded James in a single movement, murmuring and brushing at him with their hands. They had smelt the powder to ascertain its nature, and James said that he must have leant against something. The men had murmured further, frowning, puzzled that a man should come to a board meeting with powder on his suit.

'I have cause for optimism,' said Lake, speaking through a wide smile. 'I have mapped the future out. Where are the difficulties?'

Behind Miss Brown's spectacles Miss Brown's wide eyelids slipped over her eyes, blocking the Q of her typewriter from view. Her mouth was open, revealing the tips of her two front teeth and a fraction of her tongue. They spent their evenings and weekends together, and quite often Lake would fall asleep in Miss Brown's bed-sitting-room, lying on her bed with his clothes on. Miss Brown felt that it was an unwritten thing between them that they would marry when Lake began to make his way, and she was worried only because Lake had so far not embraced her and had not yet held her hand in his. Miss Brown had written quietly to the women on magazines who were there to give advice on love, explaining this situation, but the replies she received, unanimous in their suggestion that she should seek love elsewhere, were harsh, she felt, and unhelpful. One woman had written to her repeatedly, begging her quite forcefully to persuade her friend to get in touch with the magazine's medical correspondent, who was, the woman said, an excellent man.

'I well remember my father saying it,' said Lake. ' "Here we have a future Prime Minister," he remarked to a friend of his, a Jack Finch who owned a milk business. "He'll be hobnobbing with kings and queens," my father said, "African blacks and the wild Australian. You'll be proud you sat in this room with him, Jack. You mark my words." I must have been about six at the time, Brownie, and I can hardly tell you the thrill it was to hear my father say those words. "Is that so?" said Jack Finch, and pulled hard on an old pipe of his, for he was a man who delighted in a smoke. "This young shaver," said my father, "will surprise us all. You mark my words, Jack." "It's probably time the young shaver was in his bed," said Jack Finch and we all three laughed uproariously, although I can't quite remember why. I remember the occasion, though, the three of us laughing so good-humouredly and Jack Finch filling the room with smoke from his pipe. I remember the feeling of pride, Brownie, because my father had said that to Jack Finch; and when I climbed into my bed I was thinking of Jack Finch going home with his pipe, saying to himself that he was proud to have sat in that room in our house. And before I went to sleep that night I closed my eyes and I saw myself sitting down to a meal in the Royal Household. I remember it distinctly: Princess Margaret Rose was making quite a fuss because she wanted to sit down beside me. "Let's share the chair," I cried, and you know, Brownie, we did.'

Miss Brown opened her eyes and saw that Lake still had his back to her and was, in fact, addressing the window. Yet his fingers were real on her flesh, light and soft, and skilful in their touch.

'But it wasn't to be, now was it?' said Lake. 'For I felt no pull at all towards politics. I turned my back on politics, and on the Royal Household too. "I'll make my packet instead," I said. Could you blame me?'

The fingers moved again, and Miss Brown nodded, shivering slightly.

'In small ways, I shall achieve my ends,' said Lake, 'In a month or so's time I shall be sitting in Bolsover's office with my feet up on his desk, waiting for the call to the board-room. Bolsover is an over-educated man; he has learned not a thing in the school of life. In small ways, I shall topple the poor devil from his perch. And you'll be there to help me, Brownie.'

Miss Brown looked at the man she loved and saw a smile of delight splitting his face in half. She saw the gleaming white cuffs of his shirt and the gleam of the white collar and the small knot of his narrow tie. Within that shirt there dwelled the man to whom Miss Brown wished, as a life's work, to bring love and more love, and further love again. She wished to feel the reciprocation of her love, to feel love like a cocoon snugly around them, Lake and Mrs Lake.

In London that day there was no love anywhere as great as the love of Miss Brown for Lake. No letter was opened in Lady Dolores' department that told of a love as deep and as sure. Beach who loved Mrs Hoop with an eager passion, and Mrs FitzArthur who loved Septimus Tuam, and Mr FitzArthur who loved his wife, had none of them love to give as great as this, though their love was generous, and painful enough. Love dwindled in the Bolsovers' marriage and dwindled elsewhere as well, but the love of Miss Brown increased and gathered strength. *He is using your good offices*, a woman on a magazine had written. *Give this one his marching orders*. But Miss Brown only wished that Lake would come to her with the words of a marriage proposal on his lips.

Whenever he fell asleep in Miss Brown's bed-sitting-room, he talked and smiled as he did when he was wide awake. He spoke of the past, of a political career and of the Royal Household he might have known; but he did not speak in sadness, because he was a man who did not go in for regret. The future was merry before him and he polished his song for it. He would own a Jaguar motor-car, he whispered from his dreams: he would own a house in a rising place; he would ride on a horse in Richmond Park; he would give away money to charity. Miss Brown, hearing the voice coming out of his sleep, saw herself always by his side, choosing wallpapers and carpets, making their house a good place to live in, cantering behind him in Richmond Park.

Miss Brown had seen the face of Lady Dolores on the television screen and had wished that she might write to her, because she felt that this aristocratic woman might not be harsh; but it was known that Lady Dolores was concerned only with love within marriage, and marriage at the moment was one of the difficulties.

'I have young blood to offer,' said Lake to Miss Brown, standing by the window of her office. 'What can hold back the tide of my business success? I have business acumen of an unparalleled quality.' And Miss Brown's heart thumped and tumbled inside her, and her love was greater than it had been a minute before.

7

Edward borrowed a bicycle from his landlady and rode on it to Putney in the early morning. Chewing a piece of gum, he watched the house in which Septimus Tuam was said to reside and he discovered only that watching a house can be a dismal business. The women of Wimbledon had called Septimus Tuam beautiful, but no beautiful man emerged from the house, and after twenty minutes Edward decided to ride on to Wimbledon itself and watch instead the house of Mrs FitzArthur.

He stood on Wimbledon Common and looked to the left and to the right, but could nowhere see a beautiful man who might be Septimus Tuam. Milkmen moved their carriers from door to door, two postmen met at a corner as though by design and walked away together, their empty bags tied to their shoulders with pieces of hairy white string. It was a cool morning; the sky was all cloud.

Edward sat on the saddle of his landlady's bicycle and balanced himself there by allowing his toes to touch the ground. Ahead of him, on the other side of a busy main road, he could see the house of Mrs FitzArthur. Buses and lorries, motor-cars, vans, scooters, bicycles, motor-cycles, invalid cars, and a few pedestrians passed before his eyes, but he still saw clearly the house of Mrs FitzArthur, the house that, strictly speaking, was the property of her husband: the curtains were still drawn, a single pint of milk stood upon the step by the front door.

At five to eleven he observed a man with flowers arrive at the house, and his heart leapt in his chest, as leapt the heart of Mrs FitzArthur when she heard the door-bell. She opened the door, and saw her husband, his moustache freshly clipped, his rotund form darkly suited.

'Come in, do,' cried Blanche FitzArthur, gesturing with her arm.

'Here are flowers,' he offered, stepping in, 'and I have peaches in a bag.'

Three peaches he had, held close to his chest, their paper container hidden behind dewy roses.

'My dear, how absolutely sweet!'

Mr FitzArthur handed over the fruit and the flowers, and placed his hat on the chair in the hall that had last been occupied by Septimus Tuam.

'How are you, Harry?' inquired his wife.

'I have rented a flat. I live on stuff from tins.'

Mr FitzArthur entered their sitting-room and sat nervously on a sofa that had been manufactured in Denmark. His wife bustled off to the kitchen, to set the peaches on a dish and to place the flowers in water.

'What a sight!' she said, returning, displaying the roses in a cream-coloured vase.

'Well?' said Mr FitzArthur.

Mrs FitzArthur sat down and sighed and reddened. She lit a tipped cigarette and held the lighted match for her guest, who chose a cigarette of his own, an Egyptian Abdullah. She exercised every morning to keep her figure trim; she found her nourishment in the juices of vegetables and fruit. She had a horror of becoming bloated.

'I have thought and thought,' cried Mrs FitzArthur suddenly. 'I've looked at the thing from every angle. I have cried myself to sleep.'

'I don't ask much, you know,' her husband pointed out. 'Now do I? I'll accept a yes or a no; I'll hear you say the suitable thing and then the nastiness is forgotten. But how can I come tramping back to this house if I am uncertain in my mind?'

'I have been unfaithful to you,' cried Mrs FitzArthur.

'That is what we are talking about. I might never have known. I might yet be returning to this house day by day, none the wiser. I might never have heard the name of Septimus Tuam.'

'I have been unfaithful to you,' cried Mrs FitzArthur again, 'and you have shown me only kindness. You are a sweet, dear man –'

'I can be stern, as well you know. I am given to sternness in its place. I'll not be bamboozled a second time.'

'Have a Harvey's Bristol Cream. Dear, do.'

Mr FitzArthur nodded his head in a sideways manner, accepting this offer. Mrs FitzArthur poured two glasses of sherry.

'Cheers,' she said. How well everything would be, she reflected, if only she could bring herself to perform as she was required to perform. Until the private detective had arrived on the scene, she had had the best of both worlds; and she might have them again.

'Well, here's a luxury,' said Mrs FitzArthur nervously, wondering if she dared yet mention New York.

'Luxury?' he said, shooting up an eyebrow, the fingers of his left hand raised to his moustache. 'What luxury, Blanche?'

'Sherry in the morning, Bristol Cream at eleven-fifteen. Dear, what pleasanter thing?' She spoke quickly, running the words together, keeping the other subject at bay.

'I'm at sixes and sevens,' said Mr FitzArthur. 'You must see that. I know neither one thing nor the other, except that on your own admission young Tuam has taken himself off. How can I live with a woman who is constantly thinking of afternoons spent with a blackguard? I cannot understand you, Blanche. It is like being lost in an undergrowth.'

Mrs FitzArthur, genuinely sorry for the plight that her husband found himself in, reached out and grasped his hand. 'Oh, poor dear fellow,' she said. 'An undergrowth.' She felt a finger that reminded her, as it had in the past reminded her, of a plump stick of chalk. She felt no quiver of response in it, although she knew that a response was there if Mr FitzArthur willed it. She felt it cold in her palm.

'You must see my point,' said Mr FitzArthur. 'I must trust you, Blanche. You are my seventh wife and my favourite of all. Yet here you go and insult our marriage and now will not in turn renounce your episode. I had better go.'

'No, no; don't go,' cried Mrs FitzArthur. 'Take another glass. Take a slice of seed cake. Let me fetch some from the kitchen.'

She moved quickly towards the door, but Mr FitzArthur held up a hand and said he did not desire a slice of seed cake.

'I have arrangements to make,' he continued. 'Have you thought of that? There is this house to sell, for I will not live in it without you, and the machinery for divorce to be set in motion. I am tired of that: I thought I had seen the last of decrees and lawyers. I take it your answer is no, Blanche? I am to take it so?'

Blanche FitzArthur hung her head in silence. Her fair hair, caught in a sun-ray, was pretty beneath it. She said:

'I am a silly woman.'

Again there was a pause, until he said:

'No, no. No, it is hardly that at all. I shall go now. You are not a silly woman at all.'

'Oh, do not leave me, dear. I am a foolish creature to have made this hash of things with you. It is only that I cannot make up my mind if it is right for me to say what must be said.'

Mrs FitzArthur spoke the truth. It seemed to her that the deception now required of her was more than she could bring herself to weave; for it seemed that in the web of this deception she would in some way deceive herself as well.

'Let me go to New York,' cried Mrs FitzArthur. 'Give me a few extra weeks. Time sets things right.'

'You have had your weeks, Blanche. There is writing on a wall and it is up to me to read it. Someone will be in touch with you.'

At this, Mrs FitzArthur flung herself upon her husband and held him firmly in her arms, pinning his to his sides. She placed her head upon his breast and wept. Placed thus, she thought of Septimus Tuam. She wondered what he thought of her as he walked away from this house, as he had so many times, to catch a 93 bus. He must see her surely, in that calm moment, as a fluffy, silly thing, mutton dressed as lamb? Thinking of that made her weep the more; and then she reflected that she was fifty-one years old and that soon she could not even claim to be middle-aged. The lines would chase themselves all over her face, her nose would probably redden, her limbs would creak, and exercises become more difficult. 'Juices?' some wretched medico would cry. 'Woman, you need bread with butter on it, eggs, meat, and green things.' And she would protest, and he would laugh, telling her sharply that she was well beyond her prime: what use were juices now?

All this was going on in Mrs FitzArthur's mind as she shed tears into her husband's waistcoat. I shall broaden in the hips, my knees will disappear in fat: she thought those words, and thought, too, that illness might beset her. She saw herself moving slowly, with a black stick to lean on, crying out in pain to strangers on the streets. She would be by herself, she thought, in some small flat, a silly fluffy woman, well past her prime.

Mrs FitzArthur, a woman who had known men well, raised her tear-stained face and sought to catch with hers the eyes of her husband. Some instinct told her that he would not hold this dishevelled face against her and would not cease to care. Finding his eyes and gripping a handful of his clothes, she opened her mouth to issue the words, but found herself when the moment came unable to issue anything at all. A bell sounded in the distance, chiming from a nearby convent.

Edward, peering round the edge of a window, could hear the chimes of the bell, but had succeeded in hearing little else. Mrs FitzArthur's visitor did not at all fit the description he had of Septimus Tuam, in that the visitor could not with accuracy be described as beautiful. Yet Mrs FitzArthur had handed out drink to him and had wept her heart out, restraining his movement by clasping his body within her arms. And in turn the smallish, rather fat man had indeed behaved in the manner of a harsh lover, causing a woman to weep and to plead with gestures. 'I have no experience of this business,' said Edward in perplexity to himself, watching the couple in Mrs FitzArthur's sitting-room. 'I expected a younger man.' He saw the man rise to his feet as though about to go. Edward moved too, away from the window and back to where his bicycle lay on the common.

'Oh, why can't you say it now,' cried Mr FitzArthur, 'without all this palaver? Why can't you tell me a couple of dozen times that if you saw Septimus Tuam this minute you'd tell me to kick him on the backside and laugh to see it done? That's all that's necessary: we'd have a good giggle over the blackguard. "He caught you out," I'd say and you'd reply that Septimus Tuam is a dirty microbe who couldn't inspire love in a mortal. You'd say it was the change of life that turned your head; you'd confess you must have been unbalanced even to bear the sight of the weedy horror. Why not all that, Blanche? It's quicker than going to America.'

'I need to be alone. I need to sort things out in my mind. Pan-Am shall find me a seat.'

Mr FitzArthur sighed again. He felt the warmth of the hands that held his, and he agreed then that his wife should be given the time and the circumstances that she requested. 'Go,' he said, 'and I shall wait.'

Edward, alert by his bicycle, saw the hall-door open and saw the moustached man place his hat upon his head and take his leave of Mrs FitzArthur. He saw Mrs FitzArthur wave and saw the man nod his head in turn. The door closed; Mr FitzArthur looked about him, and then crossed the busy road and set off briskly across the common. Wheeling his bicycle, Edward followed him, and Septimus Tuam stepped from behind a tree.

In that same moment Lady Dolores in her love department drew on a lined pad a face that she imagined might be the face of Septimus Tuam. She read a letter from a woman who had known him, and as she read it she realized that she knew the letter by heart. She added an eyebrow, arching it quizzically.

In Wimbledon Eve Bolsover lifted a cup of coffee to her lips in the house of her friend Sybil Thornton, and heard Sybil Thornton say that marriage was a gamble and always had been.

Mrs Hoop found Eve Bolsover's birth certificate in a bureau drawer and decided to put a match to it; Miss Brown sighed; James Bolsover thought again about his father's process of dying, and his father, still alive, spat out a mouthful of cabbage in Gloucestershire.

'My dear, you shouldn't have come,' cried Mrs FitzArthur. 'The man's just left.'

'I saw him,' said Septimus Tuam, 'from behind a tree.'

He had stepped off a bus too late to see Edward at his vigil by the window. He had noticed the fresh-faced youth on the common but had not paid him much attention.

'Pan-Am?' said Mrs FitzArthur into her telephone receiver. 'Look here, I want a passage to New York.'

Behind the white, gaunt face of Septimus Tuam the mind that went with it was concerned with details. This woman had not yet mentioned leaving him a little present. He looked at her, to see if he could ascertain any sign of such a gesture in her countenance.

'Oh!' said Mrs FitzArthur, her eyes falling upon his. 'Oh, God above!'

'I shall try to be good,' said Septimus Tuam lightly. 'I shall do my best.' He had hoped that that might seem like a hint to her. He had hoped to see her hand reach out for a handbag. Mrs FitzArthur said:

'I feel it as a duty to all three of us.'

'Of course it is,' said Septimus Tuam, and he asked her for her handbag, saying that he had noticed a looseness of the clasp. 'You wouldn't want to lose your cash,' he murmured, fiddling with the silver fastener.

'Cash!' cried she. 'Dear, you must take a gift before I go. Please do, for I know you are often hard put to make your ends meet.'

'How kind you always are,' said Septimus Tuam. 'I shall keep an eye on your residence, dear. Let me come in when you're gone and do a little bit of housework. That woman of yours is useless.'

'Who's talking of being kind?' whispered Mrs FitzArthur, looking again at his eyes. 'I've never known such thoughtfulness.'

'I'll borrow your key,' said Septimus Tuam.

8

Edward Blakeston-Smith pursued the man he took to be
Septimus Tuam, wondering where the man was heading for,
assuming he was moving on to the house of another woman. He
wondered and assumed, and mingled his thoughts with a consideration of Lady Dolores and the odd words that were spoken
by the clerks in the love department. 'She has a forceful person-
ality,' murmured Edward to himself, remembering how he had
wept for the very first time in her presence and how she had
thrown a few paper handkerchiefs at him. 'She is a great lady,'
he said aloud, believing that she was that and more, and he
thought that one day, when he knew her better, he would ask
her about the words that the clerks so often emitted. 'That dog
on the prowl,' said Edward, and laughed.

Mr FitzArthur was going for a walk. He was trying to clear
his mind of the confusion placed there by his wife, and he was
thinking that he felt far from sanguine about this latest move
of hers, and wondered if he should simply go back on his word
and start divorce proceedings immediately. Although he loved
her, he felt she might well be bamboozling him again. For all he
knew, the young blackguard was waiting for her in New York,
or had run away from her to New York. Perhaps, thought Mr
FitzArthur, she was following him over there in a final effort to
persuade him to make a go of it with her. And if all that failed,
back she would come to accept the second best.

'Have you threepence?' said Mr FitzArthur abruptly to a
woman with two full shopping bags. 'I have an urgent call to
make.'

Edward drew an excited breath. He was too far away to hear
what it was that Septimus Tuam was saying to the woman, but
here, at least, in the broad light of day, was the lover at work.

'A threepenny piece,' snapped Mr FitzArthur, 'or a sixpence.'

The woman placed her shopping bags on the ground and searched in a purse, and Edward saw money change hands. He saw the man stride quickly away, down a leafy road, and he heard the woman call after him.

'What is it, madam?' demanded Edward, arriving at the woman's side. 'What did that man do to you?'

The woman said that the man had asked her for a threepenny piece or a sixpence, that she had given him one of both expecting to be handed coppers, but had received nothing at all. 'I didn't know the man was begging,' said the woman. 'Well-dressed like that.'

Edward gave the woman a shilling. He said he was employed to watch the man. 'What else did he say to you?' asked Edward. 'Did he make a suggestion at all?' But the woman shook her head, and Edward, fearful of losing sight of his quarry, jumped on to his landlady's bicycle and rode off in pursuit.

'All I am asking,' said Mr FitzArthur, 'is whether the blackguard is in New York. I want it on your word of honour, madam, that this Septimus Tuam is not featuring in your plans.'

Mrs FitzArthur, who happened to be in a state of undress, said that the whole idea of her going to New York was to be on her own, adding with a pout that she thought she had made that plain. 'What would be the point,' she argued, 'of meeting up with Septimus Tuam in New York if I take the trouble of going all that way to be alone?'

'Excuse me,' said Mr FitzArthur, and opened the door of the telephone-booth to speak sharply to a young man who had been leaning against it, trying to overhear his conversation. 'Go away,' he cried at Edward. 'This is a private chat.'

'Have sense, Harry, do,' said Mrs FitzArthur.

'What?'

'I give you my sworn word. Send your detective with me if you wish.'

Mr FitzArthur said that that would not be necessary. He apologized, blaming a rogue thought that had engendered the suspicion. He would rest assured, he said.

'Be good as well,' replied his wife, with a little laugh.

Mr FitzArthur walked out of the telephone-booth and saw at the far end of the road, hiding behind a bicycle, the red-cheeked young man who had been listening to his conversation. He considered approaching him and complaining further but he decided that no good could come of it. Nowadays, he supposed, one must expect ill manners on the street, and the constant invasion of all privacy. He walked ahead, and a moment later heard a crashing noise close behind him and looked around to see the young man depositing his bicycle by the pavement's edge.

'Look here,' said Edward coming forward and barring Mr FitzArthur's way. 'It's time we had a talk.'

'Talk? What talk?'

'I know all about you,' said Edward. 'I know who you are.'

'What the hell are you on about? You were listening in to my conversation. Stand out of my path, sir.'

'You stole money from a woman. It is against the law, you know, to go up to women and walk away with money just like that. You think you can do anything you like with women.'

'You young pup,' said Mr FitzArthur.

'We're warning you off,' said Edward, speaking breathlessly but with clarity. 'We're warning you off this district altogether, this or any other district, unless you want to land up in a prison cell.'

'Get to hell!' said Mr FitzArthur. 'Stand out of my way at once, sir. Are you a raving lunatic?'

'I am in all my senses,' said Edward quietly. 'Why should I not be?' He handed Mr FitzArthur the list of women that had been typed from Lady Dolores' file. 'These, eh?'

Mr FitzArthur read the names of a large number of women of whom he had never heard, and then, to his considerable surprise, he saw that his wife's name lay at the bottom of the list.

'What's my wife doing there?' he demanded. 'What is all this, for God's sake?'

Edward laughed. 'These are all your wives. Or have been, in a sense. You know quite well what I mean.'

It came to Mr FitzArthur then that the young man was

referring in some way to the fact that he had been married many times.

'You've got your wires crossed,' said Mr FitzArthur. 'I know only one woman on that list, although it is true I have been married several times. Are you a Jehovah's Witness or something?'

'You cannot outwit me,' cried Edward. 'There'll be none of that. You are forbidden to walk these streets. If I were you I'd take the next boat out of the country.'

'I have a perfect right –'

'You have no rights of any kind whatsoever. You bring misery into marriages. You leave a trail of disaster and unhappiness behind you.'

'My private life is no affair of yours.'

'Your private life is the affair of every decent man in the country. You're the sort who starts trouble in picture houses, edging up to women and messing them about.'

'Shut your mouth, sir,' cried Mr FitzArthur in a rage. 'Let me by at once.'

'If you insist upon more of the truth, I'll tell you this: I'm a Scotland Yard man in everyday clothes. We're cleaning up the area.'

'Now, look here –'

'You think of women in terms of money only. You can't pass a woman on the street without putting the bite on her.'

'I did not put the bite on any woman. I merely wished to make an urgent telephone call, to which for some reason you saw fit to listen.'

'I was doing my duty, sir. I am obliged to do that.'

Mr FitzArthur, certain now that the young man was insane, glanced around to see if he could see a policeman. But the road was a quiet one and was rarely visited by a constable on the beat. Mr FitzArthur said:

'I had better be getting on.'

'Where to?' demanded Edward. 'Look, will you come to a rehabilitation centre with me and let that be the end of the matter? There's a good place down in Clapham; I passed it this morning. They'll hand you out decent work and ask no questions about the past. Let me give you my address and I'd like you to report to me every three days. Really, you know, this has worked out splendidly.'

Edward imagined Lady Dolores' face when he walked into the love department and said that he had taken Septimus Tuam to a rehabilitation centre in Clapham and that the sympathetic people there had found him work immediately: in a television showroom, Edward thought it might be, or with a car-hire firm.

'How would you like,' said Edward to Mr FitzArthur, 'to try your hand at selling television sets? Does it appeal to you at all?'

He could just imagine Lady Dolores smiling at him and screwing up her eyes, delighted by the news. 'Well done, Mr Blakeston-Smith,' he could hear her saying in a low voice, and then, as soon as she had said it, he would ask her about the words the clerks used. As he thought of that, the words themselves invaded his mind, interfering with his thought processes. He saw the words *Neck death* gleaming in the air in front of him, as though lit up in fine neon writing.

'Now look,' said Mr FitzArthur, and did not finish the sentence because he saw no point in finishing it. He had never before in his life been subjected to treatment like this on a public street: a young fellow with a woman's bicycle who pressed his ear against a telephone-booth in an effort to listen in to a most private conversation, a young fellow who accused him of crimes against women and offered to take him to a rehabilitation centre, and then offered him a job as a salesman of television sets. 'Now look,' said Mr FitzArthur again, attempting to walk forward.

'Give up this awful old life,' pleaded Edward earnestly, 'I do assure you, it's for your own good that we work. Give up the bad life, battening on women, peddling your love about. Come with me now and we'll walk together to the rehabilitation centre. I think you'd like it, you know, in a television showroom. It's not an uninteresting life.'

'I do not wish to sell television sets, interesting though it may be. I do not have to.'

'What's the use of that silly old talk? It's much better to do as we say. Honestly, Mr Tuam.'

'What?'

'Do as we advise,' urged Edward, feeling himself to be a grown man, employed in an important way. 'Listen to what the folk have to say to you down at the Centre.'

'What did you call me?'

'I said I knew you. I said we had you all taped out. I showed you the list of the letters. We're well aware that the list is not complete –'

'Who do you imagine I am, may I ask?'

Edward laughed. 'You are Septimus Tuam,' he said, 'the slippery lover of Wimbledon.'

'Good God above!' said Mr FitzArthur. He stood in front of Edward, lifting his arms up and down, expostulating.

'Why deny it?' said Edward with a smile.

'Am I to hear nothing but the name of Septimus Tuam for the rest of my days?' cried Mr FitzArthur, feeling sore and hard done by to a degree. 'Is it not enough that I have to go through all the other without having people come up to me and saying that I commit crimes against women? Who are you, sir? Is this some mockery, for God's sake?'

Edward, still smiling, was suddenly struck by something in the other man's manner. He saw that the man was outraged, and it slowly became clear to him that some at least of the outrage might be genuine. With less of a smile on his face, he said:

'Who are you, then?'

'The name is FitzArthur.'

'FitzArthur?'

'My name, sir, is Harry FitzArthur.'

'You're never Mrs FitzArthur's estranged husband?'

'I am Mrs FitzArthur's estranged husband. I'm telling you that. Now, what I want to ask you –'

But Edward was already on his bicycle, pedalling hard away, with tears of shame biting his eyes. In his mind everything was jumbled and jostled together; his face was like a beetroot. 'What's she going to say to me?' he muttered dejectedly. 'I'm still a child.'

Edward passed from the leafy roads of Wimbledon and rode down into Putney. The posters, gay upon their hoardings, mocked him and made his failure seem the greater. He felt as though a balloon had been inflated in his chest. 'Oh, God,' he cried, looking towards the clouds, 'say I'm sorry to that man for me.' But the prayer was of little consolation to him, as he sorrowed and moped over his bad beginning.

'God guide you,' said Septimus Tuam in the departure lounge at London Airport, 'and send you safe.'

A flight number was called and Mrs FitzArthur rose and joined her fellow passengers in a queue, waiting to pass from the building to the aeroplane.

Septimus Tuam turned away from the window of the departure lounge. He had helped Mrs FitzArthur to pack and had enjoyed the chore, slipping the occasional item into one or other of his trouser pockets. In his stomach lay omelette, wine, tomatoes, bread, coffee, and two of Mr FitzArthur's peaches. Thoughts of how best to act still filled his mind. He had requested of Mrs FitzArthur, as well as her small gift, a loan of fifteen pounds, and had received twenty-one, making forty-one in all. He was determined, as he always was in money matters, that the sum should not be frittered away: it would be placed and allowed to accumulate due interest in Septimus Tuam's post office savings account. It would bring the total to four thousand, four hundred and forty-two pounds, seventeen shillings.

Septimus Tuam eyed the women in the departure lounge and decided to leave them alone. Some were smartly dressed, others more humbly; a few wore fur coats, as though about to fly away to the Antipodes. The women stood about, talking to men, smoking and laughing, or alone, or with their children, *en route* for Edmonton or Cairo, Brazil, Switzerland, Greece, Italy, Ethiopia, Spain. He wondered a bit about them all and supposed they were much like other women, in any crowd, anywhere: some married, some in love, some in love with their husbands, others with lovers, some divorced and living alone, a few in love with older men, rather more with younger ones, many loving hopelessly. Septimus Tuam passed briefly by these women of different colours and classes, Methodists, Quakers, Episcopalians, American Presbyterians, Baptists from Germany, Mormons, Seventh Day Adventists, Catholics, agnostics, atheists. Nuns walked by with canvas bags, Belgian nuns, or Irish; nuns going out to the mission fields of Africa and Asia, to feed the minds in the name of God, to do their best. Septimus Tuam, respecting the nuns, saw a girls' chorus from Minnesota, girls of sixteen or eighteen with long white socks that almost reached their knees, and box-pleated skirts, white also, and blazers of navy blue. They were together in a bunch, chewing and speaking. 'Two hours' delay,' announced the woman in charge of them, attired as they were. 'Why don't we have some coffee?' She hastened away and the girls followed her. One saw Septimus Tuam and whispered to a nearby friend, who turned to look at him.

In Mrs FitzArthur's aeroplane a voice said that seat-belts might now be released, that smoking was permitted. Hostesses offered drinks. Mrs FitzArthur, having wept a little, patted her cheeks with a powder-puff, thinking of her husband and thinking also of Septimus Tuam. She pressed a bell and said when the hostess came that she'd like a full-sized gin and tonic.

Edward, in a telephone-box, pressed a threepenny piece into the correct slot and spoke to Lady Dolores.

'It's not good,' said Edward.

'Who's speaking?'

'It's Edward Blakeston-Smith, Lady Dolores. I can't track down Septimus Tuam. It's like looking for a needle in a haystack.'

'You have a cute turn of phrase, Mr Blakeston-Smith. I'm standing here dripping water. What d'you want?'

'You told me to telephone you. I haven't seen Septimus Tuam. I can't find him.'

'Then what are you bothering me for? I'm dripping wet from a bath.'

Lady Dolores replaced the receiver and returned to her bath. Imagine that, she thought: the youth to ring up and to tell her precisely nothing.

Edward walked disconsolately away from the telephone-box.

For five hours he had been watching the house in which Septimus Tuam was reputed to have a room and had seen no sign of anyone who answered to his description. Probably the man was a figment of these women's imaginations, he thought, remembering that he had heard of things like that. He sighed and mounted his landlady's bicycle, and Septimus Tuam, still at London Airport, spoke in turn into a telephone.

'Mrs Bolsover?'

'Yes.'

'We met in Ely's,' said Septimus Tuam, 'in the button department. I was after an outsize leather one for an old uncle of mine, Lord Marchingpass actually, while you were on to something different. My name is Septimus Tuam.'

'Oh yes, Mr Tuam!'

'Look, I hope you don't object to my calling you up like this. It's about your stocking. I'm exceedingly sorry about that, and to tell the truth I've been worried over the whole incident.'

'Please don't, Mr Tuam. Please. It was all an accident. It could happen to anyone.'

'I was upset about two things, if I may for a moment be specific: firstly, that I had damaged your stocking and for all I know the calf of your leg as well, and secondly, that you refused point-blank to let me replace your stocking. I had a dream last night, Mrs Bolsover, in which I saw you as a case of blood-poisoning. My wretched umbrella was exhibit A.'

'My leg is perfectly all right. It was just the stocking, and as I said at the time I couldn't possibly allow you to buy me a new pair. Still, thank you for ringing. I'm sorry you've been upset like that. I assure you there's no need for it.'

'I've bought the stockings, Mrs Bolsover. We guessed your size: nine and a half. "She had slim legs," I said to the girl assistant, "shapely and of average length." "Try nine and a half," the girl assistant said, and went away and came back with a pair of Bear Brand. In Autumn Mist.'

'Oh now –'

'I know, dear Mrs Bolsover, I shouldn't have. Well, the deed is done and that is that. May I post them on to you?'

'It's extremely kind –'

'I have your address from the telephone directory: 11 Crannoc Avenue. No wait a tic, Mrs Bolsover: I happen to be going out to Wimbledon myself in a day or two. Look here, I'll drop the stockings in. I'll pop them through your letter-box.'

'Oh, please –'

'What bother is it, for the Lord's sake? I'm in Wimbledon anyway, out to see an uncle of mine. Old Lord Marchingpass, as a matter of fact.'

'It's most thoughtful of you, Mr Tuam,' said Eve, feeling puzzled and thinking that the man really was going on rather.

'Not a bit of it,' said Septimus Tuam. 'It's quite a pleasure.'

9

Eve walked away from the telephone, not thinking about Septimus Tuam. She watched her husband pouring brandy into a glass. She had heard of men, of his colleagues and of similar men, who returned at night to a hobby that absorbed them. Some kept birds in cages, delicate creatures from the equator that now had to be kept in a heated conservatory. Others reared tanks of fish, whose health and habits they read about, at length, in magazines.

'Have you no interest?' cried Eve accusingly, angered by the sight of her husband. 'Why don't you do something else when you come in? You're forever drinking brandy.'

'What would you have me do?'

Eve was silent. She wished to say something, a great deal in fact, but for the moment all she could think of was the breeding of tropical birds and fish. James said:

'Would you have me up on a ladder mending a ball-cock somewhere? I am not that kind of man.'

'You once were interested. We bought things for the house. We chose our wallpaper; we bought the armour in the hall and new materials for chair-covers. We did a few things together.'

'I will choose a wallpaper any day,' said James agreeably. 'I'll discuss furniture and fittings till the cows come home.'

'I don't mean that.'

'I could get into casual clothes, I suppose, and start in every evening, rubbing my hands together and making a village out of old cardboard. Is that an idea? Should I take it up?'

She tried to see his world again: she tried to see the building with ten floors, the offices within it, the eight fat men sitting with spectacles on around a table. She tried to see Miss Brown and Lake, but she failed completely.

'One of the eight,' said James, 'does remarkable things with matchsticks.'

In Gloucestershire that morning his father had remarked that there would be no nasturtiums if they weren't careful. 'Go out like a good girl,' he had commanded his nurse, 'and take a few cuttings. This is the time for it.' The nurse had taken his pulse instead, thinking about a story she'd been reading, by Jeffery Farnol. 'That'll do now,' she had said mechanically, but a conversation had ensued that had resulted in her telephoning James. In anger, she had reported to him a version of this talk, altering the facts here and there since it was necessary to do so in order to add emphasis, and being unable occasionally to remember accurately because her memory was not perfect. Coming on top of the letter he had read at breakfast-time, the nurse's report had weighed drearily upon him, remaining with him in detail during the day.

'Do?' his father had apparently inquired. 'What'll do? What do you mean?' The nurse replied that she wished he'd be a good chap rather than a bother to her, and heard her patient state again that for his part he wished she'd place some cuttings in a cold frame. A garden, he said, was not a garden without nasturtiums. He promised he'd lie quite happily in his bed while she worked with her hands in the soil; he'd close his eyes and be able to see the small cuttings laid out beside her, and her hands moving about, patting down the bed. He told the nurse it did her good to get out, and added that the job would suit her, crouched there in her black stockings, looking a picture. The nurse with patience had shaken his pillows for him. 'A garden's not a garden without them,' Mr Bolsover repeated. 'I said it to my wife.' The nurse saw him thinking about his wife and realizing for a moment at least that his wife was dead and that the woman with him now was a state registered nurse. 'I had a dream about our strawberries,' said he. 'I dreamed that she and I were cutting off runners. Bring me a leaf or two from the strawberry beds, Nurse, and let me see how good they are.' But hearing that, the nurse's patience had snapped. She told him that already she had written to his son, that his son this very morning would be reading a letter that listed all the complaints: the requests to go out to the garden and bring back vegetation for a sick man to inspect, the rudeness that was quite unnecessary, and the unbalanced talk that was on the increase. 'He'll be reading that letter now,' said the nurse. 'And I shall get on to the telephone as well, sir, if you are going to start. I'm not here to be spoken to like an agricultural labourer.' The nurse had brought her teeth together with a snap and had felt her face becoming red. She cleared up the plates from which Mr Bolsover had eaten his breakfast, banging them about. 'I am in love,' said Mr Bolsover, 'which is the cause of everything.' Mr Bolsover looked directly at the nurse and saw her rage increase, knowing that it would. 'I will not have it,' she cried. 'Why should I? I'm not here, Mr Bolsover, for unbalanced talk like this stuff.' But the old man had continued to look at her, intent upon saying what he wished to say, the words that she called unbalanced. 'I am in love with a dead wife,' he said. 'I am keen to join her. We will be together on a marble ledge.' Mr Bolsover went on to say that he had known of old fellows who had wished to rise from their beds and take their young nurses to the altar. He told the nurse to have no fear of that, for all he wished to do was to fall down dead and find himself on the marble ledge. 'Not that I dislike you, Nurse,' he said. 'I'm fond of you for your appearance's sake: you're a very pretty nurse.' Mr Bolsover had paused, giving weight to that compliment. 'I like a woman with a few years behind her,' he had added. 'You are mature in your way.' The nurse left the room then, and walked straight to the telephone and spoke to James in London. 'You have just received a letter from me,' she said, 'which is the second in two days. I regret I am obliged to ring you into the bargain, sir.' She complained that the old man's fantasies were becoming hard to bear. He was utterly confused in his mind, thinking half the time that she was an agricultural labourer employed in his derelict market garden, and thinking the other half that she was his wife. 'Have you come to get me?' he had said to her the previous evening. 'Take off those stockings, love, and leap into this bed. Have you died before? We'll die together this time.' The nurse said the old man's mind was in a torment of confusion. It was hard on her, she said, being called mature and talked to about a marble ledge. 'It's not right for a young woman,' she had said to James. 'I'm only saying I may have to move elsewhere. My nerves are torn.' The nurse spoke for a long time to James. She offered the theory that the old man was feeling guilty because he had allowed the market garden to fall into such a bad state, and would thus be able to leave his son neither money nor a going concern. 'Everything's squandered,' said the nurse, 'so he tells me himself. It's Freudian guilt, sir: he's escaping, see, when he says he's in love with the wife. It's back to mother really, all the stuff about a ledge.' Listening to the nurse, James had imagined her, although in fact he had never seen her: he imagined her eating a biscuit and drinking coffee, and talking on the long-distance telephone while she did so. 'I'll come down,' James had said, 'as soon as I possibly can.' The nurse replied that she was grateful to hear it. She could not be expected, she repeated, to do work in a garden and deal with a nerve case. She knew nothing whatsoever about gardening, she said, and never had.

James told Eve that the nurse had telephoned, and added that middle age was a time of pressure, it appeared. 'The old are dying,' he said. 'The young grow up. Both make a fuss to catch us others with. It has been said before.' He did not repeat in any detail the nurse's conversation; he did not say that the nurse had gone on at length about his father's love for a dead wife and his nostalgia for a garden; nor did he repeat that the nurse had discovered a pattern in the confusion of the old man's utterances, something she had seen as guilt. The nurse, James considered, was wide of the mark in that: he saw no reason for his father to feel a stab of guilt. It might be true, James thought, what his father stated: that he was in love with the soul of his wife. Why should he not be?

Eve said she was sorry to hear that there had again been trouble in Gloucestershire. She spoke politely. James said:

'Should trouble in Gloucestershire interest you much? I don't see that it should. You have enough to do, dear: you have a world of your own.'

'Of course it interests me,' cried Eve, not knowing whether or not she was telling a lie.

James smiled and shook his head. 'Still, you know, you are not too badly off. Nor am I. Though maybe you are right about cardboard villages.'

'I did not mention cardboard villages.'

'And rightly: what good's a cardboard village in this day and age?'

Cows dashed across the Bolsovers' television screen. Cowboys fired pistols into the air, their horses neighing and rearing beneath them. A few of the men shouted wildly and swirled lassoes about. James, watching closely, said:

'Other wives do not have Mrs Hoop, who will stay here all day whenever you want her to. Mrs Hoop has given you your freedom. You can spend the day more or less as you wish.'

'I am lucky to have Mrs Hoop. I know that. I am not complaining about the domestic side of things. I have an easy life in that way.' A burly cowboy said, 'Get back on that wagon, Morgan.' He stood with his legs apart, waving a pistol, while Eve thought about the mothers and their cars. She thought about Mrs Hoop and the children, and the day, years ago now, when she and James had found the suit of armour and had bought it on an impulse. 'We'll set a fashion in the suburbs,' James had said, and they almost had.

'Go to the pictures more often,' suggested James, 'if you need taking out of yourself.'

'I don't feel the need of that. I don't think the pictures would do much good.'

'Why not try? There are big cinemas all round, within a few minutes' drive. Why not take in an afternoon show now and again? They open early.' The cattle roared in the Bolsovers' sitting-room, and the guns cracked noisily. Men fell down dead. 'In a few years' time,' said Eve, 'my conversation will be all complaints.'

'The men say their wives complain. Linderfoot's lies all day on a sofa. Clinger's wife keeps company with the monkey. Captain Poache's puts the fear of God into him.'

'You've told me that before. I know about them well, James: the woman lying down, the other with a monkey, and Captain Poache and Mrs Poache.' In her mind the voice of Septimus

Tuam said, 'A pair of Bear Brand. In Autumn Mist,' and she frowned when she heard it, because she couldn't understand what the voice was doing there, returning to her mind for no reason at all.

James had discovered that his assistant, Lake, was attempting to undermine his prestige and the security of his position. James knew that Lake had persuaded Miss Brown to act in a treacherous manner; that Lake had spread items of nonsensical gossip about the firm; that Lake in his prankish way had even gone so far as to convey to the office a tinful of flour in order to scatter it over the back of James's clothes when James wasn't looking. Yet, knowing all this, James took no action: he regarded Lake as the carrier of his salvation. Not possessing the heart or the courage to organize salvation for himself, he possessed enough of both not to stand in the way of Lake's machinations, or whatever it was they were. He knew that there was now only the hope of Lake succeeding: the absurdity of his mad frolicking must harden into reality, and the eight men must finally be faced with it, and must shake their heads and ask James to go away. Failure, he felt, would surely have some pleasure after the tedium of the other.

'I'm sorry,' said Eve. 'I'm full of complaints already.'

'Look, take some brandy,' said James. 'We're all full of complaints these days.'

But Eve said only that he was becoming a soak with all his brandy. She saw him, as she said it, keenly holding out a glass to her. She raised the palms of her hands to her forehead and cried:

'Are we the same couple, James? Are we? Can we possibly be?'

'Well, after all,' said James, 'it's ten years later.'

Lake sat in an arm-chair in Miss Brown's bed-sitting-room in Putney, with his exercise book on his knees and papers spread about him on the floor. He had taken off his jacket and his tie, having previously explained that it was necessary for him to rest himself. Miss Brown, in a plastic apron, was stirring a saucepan on a gas-ring.

'Very interesting,' said Lake, on hearing from her that James's father was giving trouble again. 'Well done, Brownie.'

He wrote in his exercise book, checking the fact against previous information that James's father was an old man who had once worked in London in a respectable way and then had opened up a market garden on inherited money. He was a thorn in James Bolsover's flesh, Lake reckoned, a worry that was probably keeping Bolsover awake at night.

'Bolsover's driving them round the bend in the board-room,' said Lake. 'Apparently he goes in there covered in filth.'

Miss Brown stirred silently on. Walking with Lake that evening, she had drawn his attention to pictures of weddings in a photographer's shop window. She had hoped he would say, 'Our turn next, then?' or 'What about it?' but Lake had said nothing like that at all. He had looked closely at the photographs and said that they were poor ones, advising her that if ever she had a photograph to be taken, she should not approach the man responsible for these.

'It's an upright ladder,' said Lake from his arm-chair. 'I've recognized that for some time.'

He had suggested to her that she should take a tin of green pea soup and turn it out into a saucepan and add cooked potatoes and sausage meat. His mother had made this dish, he had said, but Miss Brown felt that he must somehow have got the recipe wrong. She repeated the ingredients to him now, but Lake laughed and said he couldn't remember quite. He added, with truth, that he didn't mind what he ate.

'I didn't come out top at College,' said Lake, referring to a school of commerce at which he had undergone brief instruction. 'But the man in charge was extremely pleased and didn't hesitate to say so. I asked him if I was suitable for the business world and he replied that I was suitable in several ways. I don't think you could claim that I had let that man down?' Lake laughed. ' "Well done, Lake," he said, and told me in confidence that there were some in my class who would spend their lives licking stamps. He was a Mr Timms; a man with a metal leg. He gave me a reference.'

Lake smiled, glanced at a few recent notes in his exercise book, and yawned, stretching his arms above his head.

'Look,' he said, 'it's the simplest thing in the world. When Bolsover says to you, "What about that letter to so-and-so?" all you say is, "Sir, what letter is that? Letter to so-and-so? You never dictated a word of it." '

Lake paused, laughing, allowing his intentions to crystallize in Miss Brown's mind. 'Well, Brownie? Does that make sense at all?'

Miss Brown, tasting from her spoon, nodded. Lake said:

'It's psychological, you understand. It's the attack used by the nation's spy department. I have nothing whatsoever against Bolsover,' he added.

Miss Brown tried to smile and, noticing the effort, Lake smiled more broadly still, happy that she was able to see his point of view. 'When it happens a couple of times – you standing up and saying the letters were never dictated – Bolsover'll begain to think he has trouble upstairs. D'you understand me?'

Miss Brown said yes, implying that she clearly understood, implying too that she would play with diligence any part he cared to allot to her.

Lake watched the stooped form of the woman who loved him. He watched her with a smile on his face, but the smile was not related to what he saw, for he was thinking of himself: he saw himself in various poses, dressed differently, going to race meetings and taking a seat in an opera house. Press photographers hung about him, snapping their cameras and asking him to look this way or that; reporters asked him what he had to say. He thought of this while Miss Brown stirred potatoes and sausage meat into the green pea soup. She stirred more tenderly because he had given her the instructions for the dish; and in her small bed-sitting-room that evening her love was everywhere, bouncing off the man like a ball off a wall.

IO

Septimus Tuam was opposed to haste and the appearance of haste. When he failed with women it seemed always, in retrospect, a degree of haste that had been the culprit. Two hours after he had telephoned Eve Bolsover he lay on his narrow bed, examining a calendar. A day had elapsed since the damaging of the stocking. A day had elapsed or, to be more accurate, twenty-eight hours. Further days would elapse before Mrs Bolsover would lay her eyes on him again: he sneered, reflecting that many a person in his shoes would be around at the woman's house within the next fourteen hours, with a package in an eager palm. 'Thank you very much,' was what Mrs Bolsover would say. 'You shouldn't have bothered yourself.' And that would be that.

Septimus Tuam marked a date on the calendar and placed the calendar on a ledge beside his bed, where he could see it easily, so that it would catch his eye. The date, neatly ringed in pencil, was seven days hence, Wednesday, September 8th, the day after the one on which three of James Bolsover's board-men were due to arrive for dinner in the Bolsovers' house. For two minutes Septimus Tuam eyed the calendar and thought about the woman who had given her name as Bolsover and had usefully added a telephone number. He wondered what she was up to now, and guessed correctly that she was engaged with her husband upon the perusal of a television screen, occasionally saying something to the husband, exchanging a view or two. He ringed a second date on the calendar – October 12th – and nodded his head over the choice of it. 'A Tuesday,' said Septimus Tuam. 'Nine hundred and sixty-four hours away.' Then he banished Eve Bolsover from his mind.

He relaxed his bones and his muscles and thought of neither

the past nor the future, nor of love, nor hatred, nor any emotion of any kind at all. He remained in this condition for twenty-five minutes, and then roused himself slightly to reach out a hand for an unexacting periodical. He read part of a serial story that he had read four times before, sniffing and sighing over the details.

He has the eyes of an animal with a soul. He brings me the joy that once I knew. Yet what can I do? He is a younger man; he has a life to lead. I am fifty-nine.

Lady Dolores read that about him, sitting at her desk in the love department, in a red silken dressing-gown. She expected the words before her eyes fell on them, for she knew the letters about Septimus Tuam off by heart. 'He has green fingers with women,' said Lady Dolores. 'I'll admit that.' Some of the letters were long, telling her everything, not seeking advice but sharing an experience; others sought help and comfort.

He went away, saying not to blame myself, saying he was more to blame than I. Yet I cannot see that I ever did anything to warrant any blame at all where he was concerned. Only blame in my husband's eyes, if you understand. What can I do now? How can I go on as if nothing in the world has happened? How can I cook food and see to my husband's needs? This has made a mockery of a marriage.

Lady Dolores shrugged, not remembering what she had recommended that this woman should do. What was there to do? She read further familiar words, on mauve paper that was slightly scented:

I looked at him, standing beside me in a shop, and I thought I had never seen so beautiful a creature. He did not seem a man at all, but some angel or saint, some being that had visited heaven and hell and brought back the best of both. He spoke to me and said that in shops nowadays service was poor.

Lady Dolores closed the file on Septimus Tuam, and recited from memory:

'I cannot forget his voice; his voice comes back. At night I awake with his voice murmuring in my ear and turn and see my husband, a much larger man, deeply asleep. I get up then and walk about the house that he and I walked about on those stolen

afternoons, and then I cry, standing in the rooms he stood in. He was the most sympathetic person God ever made, if God did make him.'

God had not made him, Lady Dolores thought: the Devil had made him when God's back was turned, fashioning him out of a scowling rain-cloud.

'He was like another woman,' said Lady Dolores. *'He was not rough. He did not cough and splutter. He didn't say he couldn't walk on the streets with unpolished shoes. He would listen and kindly reply. He wasn't always coarse, putting his hands on you. He wasn't like that at all; he wasn't out for what he could get. He was a perfect companion.'*

'I worry now,' said Lady Dolores, walking about, taking another part. *'I worry now because he may be dead. I can never forget his eyes. I sit in the afternoons for a special twenty minutes and think of him and wonder if he's still alive. He was delicate, he told me once; he nearly died in birth. There is nothing left of my marriage since I knew him; he has shown my marriage up for what it was, a hollow thing.'*

Lady Dolores returned to the file and held the letters again in her hands, trying to imagine Septimus Tuam. She drew on a sheet of paper a face that might be his, with staring eyes, as of a beast with a soul. But the face looked ridiculous, and Lady Dolores crumpled it up.

At nine o'clock on that same evening, September 1st, Edward returned to the house that he had earlier watched for five hours. A policeman took him to task for being mounted on a bicycle without a light, saying that that was an offence and ordering Edward to walk beside the bicycle, pushing it. This stern reprimand, combined with the fact that his heart was still heavy after his experiences of the day and with the further fact that his landlady had prepared for him a repast that was inedible, rendered Edward low, more so than previously he had been. He stood on the street in Putney and examined the house at the corner, but saw there no sign of life. 'How come you're on a female's cycle?' the policeman had asked him, and had been dubious when Edward offered his explanation. 'Excuse me,'

Edward had said when the policeman was well out of the way, speaking to a man who had just left the house in which Septimus Tuam was said to reside. 'Excuse me, sir, but do you know a Septimus Tuam in that house?' The man had shaken his head and had said that there were many people in the house, all the rooms being let. It was a rooming-house, he pointed out, in which he himself had resided for fifteen years without knowing, or caring to know, the names of his neighbours. It was none of his business, the man said, implying that it was none of Edward's either. 'Are you a foreigner?' he inquired, examining Edward's profile, and added, 'We get them here.' Edward said that he was English, and the man said that people from the Scandinavian countries spoke English so well these days that they could pass for natives. 'You cannot trust a soul,' he added. 'The Irish brought an empire down.'

Edward looked at a distant church clock and saw that he had spent a further seventy minutes watching the house, and realized that the task might be endless. Earlier he had walked up to the rooming-house and had examined the door, and had even been so bold as to glance through the letter-box. All this told him nothing, though: a few cards with curled edges were stuck to the door by means of drawing-pins, but none bore the name he sought, and few in fact bore a name that was still legible. He thought it was likely that he would be still loitering on this street in a year's time, on the lookout for a beautiful lover, repeating still the name to strangers. He remembered the good food of St Gregory's, and sighed. 'Be a man,' his father seemed to say. 'Let no one down.' Edward sighed again, and agreed to do his best.

Pushing his landlady's bicycle, he noticed a public house called the Hand and Plough and decided to have a glass of beer to cheer himself up. *It is not working out as nicely as it seemed to be at first*, he wrote in his mind, in a letter to Brother Edmund. *I am finding it hard to hold up my head, but I intend to persevere.* He placed his landlady's bicycle against the wall of the public house, put a lock on its front wheel, and entered a glass door marked *Snug.*

' "Help yourself to biscuits," ' Mrs Hoop was saying within.

' "Help yourself to biscuits," she says. And back she comes before her time. I'd just reached out for a Crosse and Blackwell's Cream of Celery.'

Her friend Beach drank his beer. He declared it was scandalous, the way these women treated Mrs Hoop. He said she was worthy of better things, and proposed a few.

'Get on with you,' said Mrs Hoop.

'Half a pint of bitter,' said Edward to the barman, 'please.'

Beach wiped the foam from the bristles near his mouth. Although he was old – almost eighty, he thought – he still worked, employed as a weeder of flower-beds. With considerable ceremony Beach would place wire-rimmed spectacles before his eyes, unfold a small carpet mat for his knees, and set to with a will, clearing away minor convolvulus, ragwort, dock and other growths. Beach claimed to be professionally renowned. Astute and businesslike, meticulous to a fault, he said he was known to be a clean worker and was still in demand in the parks of London by those who valued a craftsmanlike attention to detail.

'I mean it,' said Beach. 'I mean that, Emily.'

'They are that unsuited,' declared Mrs Hoop. 'What do they have in common? You should see their wedding portrait.'

'We know they are not suited,' shrilled Beach, excited. 'We know it because Emily says it. We know what we know, and maybe they will part.'

Mrs Hoop drew breath through her nose and abruptly released it.

'It is better so,' opined Beach. 'It be better that the husband finds happiness in another place. Married to another lass.'

'I would see him happy. I would rest then.'

'It shall come to pass. We shall watch and we shall see.'

'It is my heart's desire,' said Mrs Hoop simply.

'She shall have it,' cried Beach. 'Emily shall have her heart's desire. That is written in God's will.'

'Well, that is nice,' said Mrs Hoop, and added, 'My old dear.'

Edward heard this conversation and considered it singular. He sat on a stool by the counter, looking at the bottles arrayed on shelves, attempting to appear preoccupied. He was well aware that he had had enough trouble with strangers for one day, and dreaded the old man and the woman turning on him and accusing him of eavesdropping on their conversation. Yet he could not avoid eavesdropping, since the snug was small and contained only the three of them.

'How about that will, my dear?' said Mrs Hoop to Beach. 'Look here, I've bought you a form from Smith's.'

'What's that?'

'Your will, old Beach. It's all agreed on now; you'll write it out tonight. That's what we've settled on.'

'I don't remember settling that, Emily.'

'We settled it Friday. "Get me a will-form," you said, and now I've gone to the trouble of getting you one. I've been into the shop, and that embarrassing it is, a purchase like that. Wasn't you wanting it now?'

'By jingo!' said Beach.

'It'll have to be witnessed up,' said Mrs Hoop. 'It'll have to be made legal and proper in every department. D'you follow me?'

'You'll witness it yourself, Emily. What better woman? Give it here to me.'

'I couldn't witness it, old Beach, if you had it in mind to leave me a little bit. Benefactors are not in a position to witness anything. That's the law.'

'I'm going to leave you the sum of five hundred and seventy pounds,' said Beach, 'which is the sum I have. How's that, then?'

Mrs Hoop rose and carried their two glasses to the counter and ordered further refreshment. She handed the barman two shillings that Beach a moment before had handed to her. 'Would you witness a will, Harold?' she said, as the barman drew the beer. 'Only Mr Beach is keen as mustard to draw up his papers tonight.'

Harold nodded. 'Certainly,' he said. 'It's a good move, to make a will. I'd put nothing in your way.'

'Excuse me, sir,' said Mrs Hoop to Edward. 'Would you ever mind if we was to ask you witness an elderly person's signature on a document?'

'The gentleman's making his will?' said Edward.

'He is doing that,' said Mrs Hoop.

But when Mrs Hoop, Harold and Edward arrived at the table

at which Beach was sitting they discovered that he had already filled in the will-form, doing so incorrectly. Mrs Hoop made a small, angry noise.

'That'll require a fresh form,' said Harold, 'to be on the safe side. He has put his name where the name of the witness should be.'

'He has not made the right sign for pounds,' said Mrs Hoop, 'which is more important legally.'

'What's the trouble?' said Beach.

Harold returned to his position behind the bar, but Edward, in need of the solace of company, hung around Mrs Hoop, wagging his head and saying he was sorry.

'Look here,' he said at last, 'why don't you let me get hold of another will-form and I'll come in with it tomorrow night? My work keeps me out on the streets all day: I can easily pop into a Smith's. And I live myself not too far away from here.'

'Well, there's kindness,' cried Mrs Hoop. 'Did you hear that, old Beach? This young fellow's going to get another will-form for you. Is it a trouble, sir?'

'No trouble at all,' said Edward. 'Honestly. I'm out on my bike all over the place.'

'Will you take a beer, son?' said Beach. 'Harold, draw that man a glass of ale.'

'Join us,' said Mrs Hoop.

'I have faith in you, Mr Blakeston-Smith,' said Lady Dolores speaking to herself in the love department. 'I have faith in your Godsent innocence. Come on now, pet.'

She drank some whisky, soaking it into the icing of her chocolate cake. Her eyes fell again on the letters about Septimus Tuam.

I told my husband, she read. *I waited for him one day, unable to bear it a minute more. I said I needed a divorce. 'A divorce?' he cried. 'A divorce? What on earth would you do with a divorce?' So I told him how I had had a love affair, and that the love affair was over but that the love lingered on, and with such pain that I couldn't bear to look on my husband's face. He took it well enough, after he had pushed over a chair*

*and broken it. And then, somehow, when he had done that it
seemed to clear the air. I agreed not to have a divorce, because
as he said, what was the use? I would be alone. So we have stuck
together, making do as we can.*

Again, Lady Dolores attempted to imagine the man's face.
She drew on her lined pad, but again she gave up the attempt.
She wrote instead a list of questions. *What is his height? The
colour of these eyes they talk about? How does he talk to a
woman? Does he stand close? Does he lean over her? What are
his hands like? What clothes does he wear? What kind of ears
has he?*

She would give that list to Edward Blakeston-Smith and request the answers at once. Septimus Tuam entered the lives of
women with an abruptness. Forearmed is forewarned, Lady
Dolores opined: the devil you know has his work cut out. She
half-closed her eyes, looking out through her lashes. She saw
what she wished to see. 'I believe you breed bulldogs,' said Lady
Dolores, speaking privately and in an esoteric way.

'I've never known the like of it,' said Mrs Hoop. 'Hiding in
doorways they was, two and three of them at a time, standing
with their hands out, clicking their teeth. "Got a fag, love?"
they'd say, and before you'd know where you were they'd be
offering you a packet of Craven A tipped. "You won't always
be on the railways," they'd call out after you. You wouldn't
know what to say.'

'That's very interesting,' said Edward. 'It's interesting to hear
about the past.'

'They couldn't get men on the railways, see,' said Mrs Hoop.
'Right after the war. A lot of them fellas was killed in their
prime.'

'Will you have another drink at all? How about Mr Beach?'

'Old Beach is asleep. He drops off like a babe. I'll tell you what
I'd like, mister, if you've the money on you: a glass of *crème de
menthe.*'

'What?'

'*Crème de menthe,* son. A peppermint drink.'

'Ah, *crème de menthe.* Of course.'

Edward approached the bar and bought Mrs Hoop a glass of *crème de menthe* and himself a half pint of beer.

'Hoop the name is,' said Mrs Hoop when he returned. 'Widowed these days.'

'My name is Edward Blakeston-Smith.'

'What's the trouble?' said Beach, jerking in his chair. 'I've run out of beer.'

'Let me get you something,' said Edward.

'Don't bother yourself,' said Mrs Hoop. 'What happened was that Hoop got caught up with a throat infection. It cost me twenty-two shillings, Edward, to get him brought back from where they conducted what they call a post-mortem of the throat. Nineteen fifty-five; they cut the poor devil up.'

'I'm dry as old parchment,' said Beach, 'sitting here.'

'He didn't say a word for four years. It was that eerie, Edward, in a house with the speechless. Have you ever done it?'

Edward shook his head. He explained that he had had but a small experience of life. 'I often feel a child,' he confided.

'Draw me a pint, Harold,' shouted Beach to the barman. 'Isn't it this fellow's round?'

'Twenty-two bob,' said Mrs Hoop. 'I never heard the like of it.'

'Emily Hoop works for Mrs Bolsover,' said Beach. 'They don't get on.'

'I was talking about my late hubby,' said Mrs Hoop. 'Not that woman at all, old Beach. I have the misfortune, Edward, to be in the employ of a woman out Wimbledon way. I'm on the point of leaving.'

Harold placed a pint of beer on the table, and Edward paid for it. 'Wimbledon?' he said.

'Emily has a terrible time of it,' said Beach. 'A Mrs Bolsover out Wimbledon way.'

'A painted Jezebel,' said Mrs Hoop in a low voice, 'if ever you've heard the expression.'

'Jezebel of the Bible,' said Beach, 'an old-time tart.'

'I've heard the expression,' said Edward, 'and I'm against all immorality. I work for an organization that's against anything like that. We're cleaning up the south-western areas of London.'

'She's married to a decent man,' said Mrs Hoop. 'The whole thing should be pulled asunder.'

'I'm a Sunday church-goer, sir,' said Beach.

'She needs her face smashed in,' said Mrs Hoop.

In such circumstances did Edward meet the woman who hated Eve Bolsover and hear her say, at twenty-five minutes past ten on this Wednesday evening, that Eve Bolsover should have her face broken. In the moment that she said it, Septimus Tuam was fast asleep in the house that Edward had watched, dreaming of the ringed dates on his calendar: September 8th and October 12th. Eve Bolsover herself was reading a book.

Edward felt more cheerful. He didn't know that in a round-about way he had come closer to Septimus Tuam; he had tried while in the company of Mrs Hoop and Beach to forget about Septimus Tuam altogether. It was good, he thought quite simply, to have someone ordinary to talk to.

Edward walked from the Hand and Plough with Mrs Hoop and Beach, and parted from them at the end of the street. 'I must make my way homewards, Brownie,' Lake said at that moment in the bed-sitting-room of Miss Brown. He rose from Miss Brown's bed, where he had been lying in a respectable way, digesting the potatoes and the sausage meat and the green pea soup. 'Bolsover is suitable for simpler work,' he said, and went away.

Edward saw a bald-headed man leave a house and noted only the shining dome of his head. He did not know that the man was the enemy of the husband, as Mrs Hoop was the enemy of the wife. He did not know that here in Putney, within a stone's throw of the Hand and Plough, lived the people who were destined to cause confusion in the two worlds of the Bolsovers. He knew that Mrs Hoop and Beach lived not far away, and he suspected that Septimus Tuam did, but Lake and his habitat were mysterious to Edward, as were Miss Brown and hers.

Lake noticed a blond-haired youth wheeling a woman's bicycle and did not pause to envy the youth his hair, as in the circumstances he might have. He spoke to himself in his mind, mapping the same future. 'I am a young blood,' he was saying to the eight fat board-men. 'I have come to give you the benefit of it.' They listened to him with their heads on one side, while James Bolsover reported at a labour exchange.

In his conscientious way, Edward considered returning to the house of Septimus Tuam and watching it for a while longer, but decided that little good would come of it at this hour of the night. He wondered again if Septimus Tuam could not be a figment of the women's imagination: perhaps they had all read the name in a romance, or had come across it in a film. He thought of mentioning the theory to Lady Dolores, but decided against that too, imagining her hard reply. Slowly, he pushed his landlady's bicycle through a night that was coloured orange because the street-lights dictated that colour. He had an urge to ride the bicycle because of his fatigued condition, but he did not do so, being of a lawful disposition.

II

Five days passed by and turned a damp summer into a sunnier season by far. A newspaper predicted the finest autumn of the century, and was not entirely correct in that because rain came later. But for the first days of September there was no rain at all, and people all over England remarked upon the fact. Londoners said it gave them a new lease of life, meaning that it cheered them up after the disappointments of the months before. 'Well, you need it,' people said in shops, buying tobacco or soap or almost anything else. 'You need a few good days to set you up for snow and ice.' A child in London asked her father what autumn was, having heard it spoken of these days, and the father in explanation said it was a season, though not a major one. In cities, this father said, you did not feel autumn so much, not as you felt the heat of summer or the bite of winter air, or even the slush of spring. He said that, and then the next day sent for the child and said he had been talking nonsense. 'Autumn is on now,' he said. 'You can see it in the parks,' and he took his child for a nature walk.

Miss Brown, remarking that the season suited her, was contradicted with a smile by Lake, who informed her that spring was the better time for her in every way. In spring, he said, she got a flush on her cheeks which perked up her appearance. In summer, he explained, she was liable to sunburn and its peeling aftermath, and in winter there was the common cold which, he reminded her, she caught with more than usual ease. As for him, all seasons suited him, since he had never suffered from a cold in his life and took a tan if there was sun to tan him, and was equally at home in autumn and spring. 'That is life,' said Lake to Miss Brown. 'Some of us are made for it.'

The nurse in Gloucestershire telephoned James twice during those five days and wrote him a letter and a postcard. 'I think it better to keep in touch,' she said, 'although I've become more used to his nonsense.' James was glad to hear that, but was unable to prevent the nurse from regularly communicating. 'He swears he'll be pushing up the daisies, sir,' she said, 'by September the fourteenth. I've told him that's terrible talk. I've told him you're coming down to see him. He says he won't be here.' She talked to James of other matters, telling him about the house and gardens and what she imagined the place must once have been like. 'It's sad here in the autumn weather,' she said. 'As well he'll not see it.' James sensed in her voice a softness that had not been there before and thought that as well as becoming used to the nonsense she had come to feel pity for the man who could no longer walk about, whose property was falling into rack and ruin around him. James remembered the gardens as they had been in the autumns of the past: chrysanthemums stacked in the greenhouses, wallflowers and asters still in bloom, long rows of sprouting celery and cauliflowers, leaves swept up and leaves falling down, bonfires blazing in a mist. Now there were apples rotting in the long grass. There were thick layers of decay, and broken glass in the greenhouses, and wood that needed more than a coat of paint. Weeds were everywhere, sturdy still after the wet summer. 'Aw, it's terrible,' said the nurse. 'I think so when I see it. God alone knows, sir, what it'll be like in this house in wintertime.' It sounded more hopeful to James that she mentioned winter, as though she had resolved to stay that long. His father had stubbornly refused to be moved, saying he liked the place and asking that the wishes of a dying man be honoured in that matter. 'Mind you,' said the nurse, 'he hasn't ceased. He's not so bad about the plants as the days go by, but the other's on the increase. He says the passion for that wife is more intense: he's like a young fella out courting.' The nurse laughed and then was solemn. 'He says the hand of death has neither skin nor bone. I was repeating, sir, what I told you in the way of a diagnosis the other day; I was repeating it to the woman who comes in for the cooking. Well, she quite agreed. I mean, she couldn't but,' But James again thought that his father was dying in his fashion, and saw no cause for theories.

One afternoon James overheard Lake saying on the telephone, 'I'd best handle the whole thing myself, sir. Mr Bolsover is having one of his off days.' The man at the other end asked some question, and Lake replied, 'Oh yes, sir; a regular occurrence these times. We have to send the doorman round in a taxi to get the poor man home. I shouldn't mention it, sir; it's a secret shared between Mr Bolsover and his immediate staff.'

After a time, James began to enjoy acting the part that Lake had willed upon him. 'Where's the mail?' James would ask Miss Brown and she'd reply that he had already asked her to get Lake to deal with it. 'Oh, yes, I remember now,' James would say, causing Miss Brown to raise her eyebrows. He could organize the dismissal of the pair of them, on the grounds of poor time-keeping, stupidity, insubordination and, in Lake's case, a general and total inability to do the work he was required to do. It was not widely known that Lake's annual errors cost the firm a good deal more than his salary amounted to.

James didn't know what he would do when Lake struck his final blow, and he didn't much mind not knowing. He had heard of cases like this in the business world: men who one day were highly successful and were the next reduced to selling motor-cars in provincial garages, working out their commission on the backs of envelopes. He had heard of men who had taken to petty crime in order to keep up appearances, sacked men who left their houses every morning as though nothing at all had happened, and spent the day filching bicycle bells and small electrical fittings from the open counters of shops. He had heard of men with all the heart gone out of them, who cared no longer for their wives and children, who sold their houses and took on inadequate rented property, living on small capital and hanging about the kitchen all day, unwashed and drinking beer.

James supposed that the future might turn out to be something like that. He saw himself selling a second-hand Ford Estate car to a woman in a fur coat and receiving from her a hundred and forty pounds. He saw himself as a door-to-door salesman, interesting housewives in brushes and tea-towels and nylon gadgets, and he thought he'd be rather good at that. He thought he'd be good as a demonstrator of kitchen aids: vegetable dicers, garlic presses, frying pans that didn't burn. He saw himself selling racing tips at Epsom, and pouring petrol into people's cars, and working in a tube station, as Mrs Hoop had. He saw his children ill-dressed, with holes in their shoes, his wife exhausted, going out to work herself. 'The others don't take kindly,' one of the board-men said to him. 'They think you're being casual.'

James offered no explanation. He had never seen Lake throw the flour, but once he had seen the Colman's mustard tin on Lake's desk and had noticed a little flour fall from it when Lake hastily put it in his pocket. They'd have to sell the suit of armour in the hall, he thought, and the medieval gardening instruments, and the house itself, and quite a bit of the furniture. He thought they'd probably move down to s.w.17 and rent a basement flat. He saw himself returning to a basement flat one foggy evening in winter, in the company of a man with a wide R.A.F. moustache, who worked with James, selling washers and nails to ironmongers. 'He's been telling me all about it,' James said to Eve. 'Prospects are pretty good.' Eve smiled at the man. She told the man how bored she once had been, when they had lived in a large house in Wimbledon with a suit of armour in the hall. 'We bought it for fun,' said Eve, 'and sold it later for fifty-eight guineas.' Eve was going out to work, and was looking pale, but happier, James thought. 'Where's the lav?' asked the man with the wide moustache, and laughed to cover his embarrassment. Afterwards, many years later probably, the man rose to the top of the business, while James remained contentedly where he was, eliciting repeat orders for washers and nails from the ironmongers of s.w.17. Eve had learned how to trim poodles, and brought home twelve pounds ten a week from a pet shop.

James saw himself in a court-room, answering a charge. They said he had been drunk and disorderly, and had broken a shop window in order to take from it a tin of biscuits. He pleaded guilty, and walked away to prison. He saw himself lying on the ground in Victoria Station, pulled to one side so as to be out of the way. 'He's drunk on brandy,' a passer-by said, 'a man like that.'

During those five days Edward became a familiar sight in Putney. He watched the rooming-house at the corner of the street and was spoken to by people who wondered what he was doing. He asked in the local shops if a man called Septimus Tuam was known, but he met only with a negative response. 'A handsome man,' said Edward. 'I've heard him called beautiful.' The people in the shops shook their heads and referred Edward to the Hand and Plough and other public houses. 'Not known here,' said Harold in the Hand and Plough. 'Not known here,' said the barmen in the other places, too. 'I am becoming the idiot of the neighbourhood,' said Edward to himself. 'I've been taken for a ride.' Septimus Tuam looked from the window of his room and saw the loitering figure, and raised his eyebrows.

Edward telephoned Lady Dolores.

'I've been standing about Putney for five days,' he said. 'People are looking at me.'

'Why wouldn't they?' said Lady Dolores. 'Have you filled up that dossier?'

'I haven't even established the man's identity, Lady Dolores. I don't even know if he exists.'

'You're saying he's a spirit? You may be right. He drove three women to their graves: God knows what he is. Are you listening to me?'

'It's no good hanging about here. I'd be better off at a desk.'

'Who told you that? Listen, I have a list of questions I want answers to. Another thing: sneak up on our friend and take a snap or two. Get on with it, now.'

'I haven't got a camera. I haven't even got a bicycle. I have to borrow a woman's bicycle every day.'

'Listen, pet,' said Lady Dolores on the telephone. 'I'm going to read you a story. Are you ready now? Listen. *He always wore dark clothes and was neatly turned out in every way, though never a dandy. The tip of his umbrella swung against my stocking and laddered it, and then he apologized, and was determined to pay for what damage he had inflicted, which goodness knows was slight. He told me about Lord Marchingpass, his uncle, and wondered if I knew him, and somehow the name seemed familiar. But now he's gone and everything is empty once again. I* can't stop crying. 'See a doctor, for Christ's sake,' my husband says. I've come to dread it, hearing him saying that. What d'you think, Mr Blakeston-Smith? Wouldn't it affect you?

'An awful lot of people wear dark clothes,' said Edward. 'Should I not try to get hold of this Lord Marchingpass?'

'For heaven's sake,' shouted Lady Dolores crossly, 'will you be your age?'

Whenever I look at him I see my friend instead. My friend is there, sitting in Colin's chair, sitting quietly and nicely, not shouting out with laughter at something that's not the least bit funny, not telling me an obscene story picked up in a bar. When I see Colin for what he is, unbuttoning his shirt, I think of my friend, who did things beautifully. I cannot bear to see Colin eat now. There are certain foods that I will not serve; I never noticed anything before.

The sentences were there in front of her. They increased her wrath, but they coloured it, too. Edward said:

'I've been five days on it, Lady Dolores. It's no good at all.'

'What are you on for five days? Where are you, pet?'

'In this telephone-box opposite the house.'

'How's he getting on with Mrs FitzArthur?'

'Mrs FitzArthur's gone away. A note has been left for the milk to say that Mrs FitzArthur is in America.' Edward had not told Lady Dolores about mistaking Mrs FitzArthur's husband for Septimus Tuam; nor had he told her that he had mistaken several other men as well, that he had followed one of them across London to Wapping, and that the man had rounded on him, realizing that he was being followed, and without a word had struck Edward a heavy blow on the face. Edward, certain that this man was at last the right one, had wiped blood from his cheeks and had observed the man entering a butcher's shop and placing around his waist a butcher's apron.

'I'm in a terrible state,' said Edward, 'with loss of confidence.'

'We are all well in the love department,' said Lady Dolores quietly. 'We are all doing a good day's work. We are earning our wages, Mr Blakeston-Smith.'

'I've come across a case that might interest you,' said Edward. 'A Mrs Hoop and an old boy called Beach. This Mr Beach is deeply attached to Mrs Hoop, and wishes very much to marry her. Mrs Hoop, however –'

'Am I still speaking to Blakeston-Smith?'

'I thought there might be something in it for you –'

'Septimus Tuam is a creature of the devil, while you are standing in a telephone-box telling me about some man who wants to get married.'

'It's not that –'

'What is it then? Why are you delaying me half the day with old rubbish like this? What's on your mind, Mr Blakeston-Smith?'

'I don't know that I'm suited to this work.'

'I wonder if you go at it hard enough. We've all got our noses to the grindstone in here, you know. No fresh air for us boys.'

'But there's no sign at all of a beautiful man, Lady Dolores.'

'You see what I mean? You're not working your gumption. Beauty's in the eye of the beholder. Didn't you ever hear that one?'

'Yes, of course.'

'Make a round of the poor ladies who wrote in, and ask them the questions I've made out for you. See if you can get hold of a photograph. D'you know what I mean?'

'I couldn't do that. Whatever would they say to me?'

'Get into a disguise. Go out as a window-cleaner or a man from the North Thames Gas. Get into the women's houses and get into conversation with the women. Ask them about Septimus Tuam, as bold as brass; say you're his brother. "Are we talking about the same one?" say, and ask them to describe the chap they used to know, or to show you a photograph. They probably have a photograph in a locket. I'm surprised to have to tell you.'

'No, really,' began Edward.

'Nonsense,' said Lady Dolores.

Mrs Hoop, loitering about the kitchen, watched Eve making sauce *Béarnaise*. 'What's that stuff?' said Mrs Hoop.

'Sauce *Béarnaise*.'

Eve measured wine and vinegar into a saucepan and added

chopped shallot, tarragon, chervil, mignonette pepper, and salt. 'I have to boil this,' she said, 'and simmer it until it's reduced by two-thirds.'

'Boil it away?' said Mrs Hoop. 'There's people hungry, Mrs Bolsover, you know.' Still unsuccessful in persuading Beach to draw up his will, she wondered if she shouldn't approach the matter in another way: if she shouldn't quite openly make a bargain with him.

'I really had to see about a friend's troubles tonight, Mrs Bolsover. I shouldn't be here at all. The drawing up of a will, you know.'

But Eve, concerned with the mixture in the saucepan, didn't hear what Mrs Hoop had said.

'The drawing up of a will,' repeated Mrs Hoop. 'It was not the most convenient night to come out.'

'It was very good of you,' said Eve vaguely, aware that Mrs Hoop was complaining slightly. 'My husband and I appreciate it very much. You are always such a help, he says, when we have a dinner party.'

'I used to give a lot myself, when Mr Hoop was alive. We'd have quite a number of wines.' Mrs Hoop paused to consider that. After a moment she added, 'Not that I don't have a social life still, you know. Me and young Blakeston-Smith are out a lot these days. The cool summer evenings are ideal.'

'Peel twenty potatoes, please,' said Eve. 'Just in case these men are fond of them.'

Hatred thundered within Mrs Hoop when she heard Mrs Bolsover say that she was to peel twenty potatoes. Streaks of red swept over her face and neck, the calves of her legs tingled, her back arched with anger.

'Twenty potatoes?' she said, not moving.

'What do you think? Twenty for seven people. Just to be on the safe side.'

Mrs Hoop bent down and counted out a score of potatoes. She disapproved of this arbitrary number. She said:

'How many will each person eat?'

'Well, I don't know that. But the men may be hungry.'

Eve added three yolks of eggs to her sauce, and then, having stirred for a minute, dropped in small pieces of butter. 'I hope it's not going to curdle,' she said.

'Who's coming, then?' asked Mrs Hoop.

'A Mr and Mrs Clinger, a Captain and Mrs Poache, and a Mr Linderfoot.'

'I don't think I ever met them,' said Mrs Hoop. 'Everyone mixes nowadays,' she added. 'The barriers is down.'

'I have never met them either,' said Eve.

'Funny, that, having strangers in. They could be anything, I always say.'

'My husband knows them –'

'We have our own little social set: me and Blakeston-Smith, and Mr Beach, and Mr Harold.' Mrs Hoop sucked her cheeks in. She said. 'Young Blakeston-Smith was inquiring if I was interested in hunting at all.'

'Hunting, Mrs Hoop?'

'Hunting on a horse. Edward is that keen.'

'I see.'

'He says to me I should take it up. Anyone can, you know, nowadays.'

'Oh, yes.'

'We meet for conversation, every now and again. As was done in the olden days.'

'Of course. How are the potatoes doing?'

'They are doing all right, Mrs Bolsover. I have peeled seven potatoes. Is that a fast enough speed?'

'Gracious, yes.'

The Bolsover children entered the kitchen and asked for something to eat. Eve refused this request, drawing their attention to the fact that it was almost their suppertime. Mrs Hoop winked at them, and slipped them two biscuits which she had earlier secreted in the pocket of her apron. She placed a finger on her lips, indicating that their mother mustn't know about this. 'How's Miss Fairy and Miss Crouch?' asked Mrs Hoop, and the children said that they were quite all right, actually, and went away with their biscuits.

'I wish you wouldn't give the children food, Mrs Hoop. All this eating between meals isn't at all good for them.'

'I've brought up five,' lied Mrs Hoop, peeling potatoes and sniggering triumphantly.

'Hurt not the earth,' said Beach, 'neither the sea, nor the trees. I read of chemicals, sir, that are absorbed through the leaf and destroy the Lord's handiwork without a by-your-leave. I read it in the *Radio Times*. The name is Beach, sir.'

'I know you well, Mr Beach,' said Edward, disappointed that Beach should take him to be a stranger when every night for almost a week he had been sharing the old man's company. He was feeling melancholy in any case, after his conversation with Lady Dolores. He felt, as he had attempted to explain to her, that he could never go into people's houses dressed up as a window-cleaner or other such person; he felt that it was steadily being proved that he was not of the ilk to track down Septimus Tuam.

'I am a weeder by trade, sir,' said Beach. 'I am a weeder of flower-beds in London parks. They have found this stuff, sir, that the weeds take in through the leaves. It does not damage the flowers. Mister, I may never weed again.'

'A weed-killer,' said Edward. 'I'm sorry to hear it.'

'It goes through the leaf. It's a new invention, sir.'

With a heavy sigh, Edward rose and carried their two glasses to the counter.

'Untimely weather,' said Harold, drawing the beer. 'Not a shadow of a doubt about it.'

Edward agreed. He felt so small and so inept that he suddenly said, with brazenness, 'Do you stock whisky?'

He had seen Lady Dolores pouring out a glass of whisky. He had smelt the stuff on her breath. He had heard from others, listening to conversations, that it was powerful stuff. He had read the same in newspapers.

'Give me a glass of whisky,' said Edward, and added, as he had heard others adding in public houses, 'like a good man.' He felt better even before he tasted the liquor, even before Harold poured out the measure. He thought there would be nothing pleasanter than to spend his days in this small snug, drinking beer and whisky, and keeping out of the way of Lady Dolores.

'As well as the bitter?' asked Harold. 'Spirits on top of beer, is it?'

'Whisky,' said Edward, inclining his head. 'And whisky for Mr Beach.'

'Four bob,' said Harold, before pouring a drop.

'What's wrong with four bob?' Edward placed the coins on the counter. He said to himself that he had aged ten years in the last half minute.

'By the holy Lord,' said Beach, 'you're a generous man. Here's to your health, son.'

'I'm celebrating my freedom from the influence of a woman,' said Edward, 'if you follow what I mean, Mr Beach.'

'I'm influenced by Emily Hoop. I'd lay down on the floor for her.'

'You're in love, Mr Beach. It's not so with me. I'm employed by a woman who sets me impossible tasks. I spend my day riding around on a cycle, making a fool of myself with strangers. I'm the laughing stock of London, when I might be sitting at a desk. Deskwork's my ambition, but I see no sign of it. I'm got down, Mr Beach. Did you ever play draughts?'

'Where?' said Beach.

'Draughts. You have them on a board. You can play draughts all day and be perfectly happy. Maybe we would one day, Mr Beach?'

'Women is a problem,' said Beach. 'Take Emily Hoop.'

But Edward was thinking that first thing in the morning he would telephone Lady Dolores and tell her that he was resigning his post. He would do it and be left only with the regret that he would never see the love department again and would never now discover the true meaning of the words that hung about the air there. 'That dog,' said Edward to himself, drinking his whisky and feeling nostalgic already.

'Emily Hoop is all I ever want,' said Beach. 'I would live with the girl, wedded man and wife; we'd be happy as a pair of fireflies. Where's the harm in it?'

'No harm in happiness, Mr Beach.'

'I'd take her in,' said Beach. 'I'd take the girl in tomorrow. I'm keen on Mrs Hoop, son.'

'Put it to her,' said Edward. 'Employ a bit of cunning. You've got to be careful with women.' Edward laughed coarsely. 'Bring us two more of those whiskies,' he demanded in a loud tone, addressed to Harold. 'Have one yourself, Harold. It'll put a bit of lead in your pencil.'

'I know right well,' said Beach. 'I'm no fool, son. Women is all right, but you got to know your way. Where's Emily Hoop?'

'I'll bring in a draughts-board,' said Edward, 'and you and I'll play many a game, Mr Beach. That's the safer thing.'

'Listen to me, son,' said Beach, placing his glass of beer in the centre of the table and finishing his whisky. 'There's chemicals being absorbed through the leaf. Night and day. You're right in that, sir.'

'Drink up,' cried Edward. What would she say, he wondered, if she could see him now? What would she say if she could see him sitting about in a bar parlour with a gardener, telling the barman to put lead in his pencil, advising the gardener to play cunningly with women? Edward laughed. He raised his whisky glass above his head, winking his right eye.

'Hurt not the earth,' said Beach, 'neither the sea, nor the trees.'

'Hurt not the earth,' repeated Edward, coughing, and laughing the louder. 'Here's to Septimus Tuam.'

For five days Septimus Tuam had read the stories in magazines, and had relaxed on his bed. He had done some mental mathematics from time to time, working out the length of certain relationships he had engaged upon in the past, and working out sums of money that were connected with them. He considered that he had no brain, and so in his calculations he took great care, checking all results several times. He considered that his only gift was an instinct, and even that was flawed, as though as a punishment for having it.

As Edward laughed and spoke his name in the Hand and Plough, it happened that Septimus Tuam's eye fell on the calendar beside his bed. He saw the first ringed date, September 8th, and he knew that tomorrow was that day. 'Eleven Crannoc

Avenue,' he repeated to himself. He remembered approximately where that was, having been more than once in adjoining roads.

Septimus Tuam rose briskly from his bed then, and shaved himself. He left his room and walked out into Putney, where he caught a 93 bus to Wimbledon. He strode to Mrs FitzArthur's house and let himself into it, glancing about to ascertain that all was well there, since he had promised to keep an eye on the place. He made some coffee in the kitchen and, having drunk it and washed the cup, he climbed the stairs to Mrs FitzArthur's bedroom. She was a woman who bought stockings in quantity, Bear Brand invariably, and always Autumn Mist. He found a pair still in their box and, rooting around, discovered a piece of gay wrapping paper that bore as a design the flags of many nations. He noticed as he wrapped them up that the stockings were not the correct size; he shrugged his shoulders over that, thinking that this Mrs Bolsover couldn't expect everything. He left Mrs FitzArthur's house and instead of returning to Putney walked for half a mile in the other direction, to Crannoc Avenue. He looked at it from behind a pillar-box, establishing the nature of the place so that the lie of the land might be fresh with him when he made his first moves. He walked along it, since he had nothing to lose by doing that if he kept his face correctly averted. He passed by Number Eleven and saw to his considerable surprise that a man and a woman were approaching the house in the company of a monkey.

12

When Eve Bolsover opened the door to the Clingers and saw a small tartan-clad animal in Mrs Clinger's arms she was aware that surprise registered in her eyes. Had the creature been a Pekinese or even a kitten she could have thought little more of it, expecting only to hear by way of explanation some story of the pet's pining during the absence of its owners. But there was something altogether singular about the presence of a monkey at a dinner party, and Mrs Clinger, a stout, shy woman dressed in blue, with blue hair, was well aware of it. In a low voice she apologized profusely, saying that the man who usually came to sit with her monkey had caught a summer cold and was confined to bed.

'He'll go into a corner,' explained Mr Clinger. 'He'll be no trouble at all.'

'I'm sure,' said Eve.

Mr Linderfoot, the heaviest of the eight board-men, arrived without addition, without, in fact, his wife. He was a hearty man with a ready smile who had a reputation for hanging about the office corridors seeking the company of young girls.

While Mr Linderfoot was standing in the hall, the Poaches arrived, and James thought the opportunity a suitable one to explain to Mr Linderfoot and Captain and Mrs Poache that the man who usually sat with the Clingers' monkey was ill, a fact that had obliged the Clingers to bring their monkey with them. 'Oh, no,' said Mrs Poache, and made as though to leave the house. She and the Captain had once been invited to tea on a Sunday with the Clingers, and she had considered them socially inferior. 'That blue hair,' she had afterwards commented to the Captain, 'and the monkey wetting the cushions.' James said that the Clingers' pet had settled down in a corner of the sitting-room and would not be noticed. 'Are they in business with the thing?' said Mrs Poache. Mr Linderfoot laughed at this, shaking his head back and forth in a slow manner, saying it was amusing, the idea of the Clingers doing an act with their monkey.

In the sitting-room, James poured drinks and heard a desultory conversation develop around him. He was thinking of the past and of the future; of his childhood in Gloucestershire, and of the years ahead of him, striding into ironmongers' shops, drinking beer with the man who had the R.A.F. moustache. He wondered what kind of timing Lake had worked out, or what precisely the lay-out of his plans was; he hoped Lake wasn't going to bungle it. He saw himself lying again on the ground in Victoria Station, late at night, near a bookstand. He saw himself wholly discredited, a man who let his children go without essential clothing and allowed his wife to work in the trimming rooms of a dog shop. And then he saw himself pulling himself together.

'I must say,' said Mrs Poache to James in confidential tones, 'I consider it a peculiar thing.' She was a thin woman, firm of manner and of medium height, attired for the occasion in several shades of pink, with a string of small pearls.

James drew her attention to the weather, reminding her how poor the summer had been.

'To keep a monkey as a pet,' said Mrs Poache. 'And not only that, Mr Bolsover, but to insist upon bringing the thing into people's houses. Is it unusual? Or some new fad?'

'Mr Clinger has a theory about cats and dogs,' said James. 'He believes they carry disease.'

'And what on earth does this thing carry, I'd like to know? Monkeys are notorious in ways like that.'

Mrs Clinger asked Eve if she had heard of mattress ticking as an item of decoration. As a covering for lampshades, she understood, it was increasingly popular. Eve said that she had not come across this idea, and Mr Clinger wished to know what his wife was talking about. Mr Linderfoot was opening and closing his lips and scribbling something on the back of an envelope. Eve, noticing to her surprise that the Clingers were entering into an argument between themselves on the subject of mattress ticking, smiled at Mr Linderfoot, who said to her that he liked to make a note or two on social occasions, so that he could relay the details of the evening to his wife. He whistled as he wrote something further on the envelope. Eve asked him how his wife was, and Mr Linderfoot replied that his wife, he thought, would be a woman after Eve's heart. He was sitting beside Eve on a sofa, inclined towards her and looking closely at her head. 'You have very beautiful hair,' said Mr Linderfoot, moving his right eyelid. 'Quite charming.'

Eve smiled again, thinking that tomorrow she would tell Sybil Thornton every detail of this dinner party. She heard herself doing so, repeating parts of the conversation, sitting in Sybil Thornton's immaculate kitchen, drinking a cup of coffee and hardly smiling at all.

'Mattress ticking,' she heard Mr Clinger mutter fiercely to his wife. 'Wherever did you get hold of a screwy notion like that?' She heard Mrs Clinger whisper that she had read about it in a magazine, in an article to do with interior decoration in New York. Mrs Clinger was wriggling uneasily on her chair. She said it didn't matter, but her husband contradicted that: he said it mattered to him that she should suddenly begin a screwy conversation about mattress ticking. He thrust his jaw out and advanced it towards one of Mrs Clinger's ears. 'You've made a bloody fool of yourself,' he said with violence, 'saying a thing like that. This Mrs Bolsover is a sophisticated woman.' He rose and moved to another chair, away from his wife.

Eve listened to Mrs Clinger's modestly pitched voice relating more about her readings on the subject of interior décor. She lit a cigarette, keeping a smile on her face. 'It's tasteful here,' said Mrs Clinger, and Eve acknowledged the compliment. She was thinking that in the past, before the children had gone to school, her days had been full and busy. She had looked forward to the time when they were less so, but when that time had come it seemed that marriage itself was not enough. She wondered now if she should take on some other work.

Beside her, Mrs Clinger said, 'You have a suit of armour in your hall. Most beautifully polished.'

Eve wondered if these wives loved their husbands now; and

what the history of love had been in the marriages. She wondered if Mrs Linderfoot in Purley had woken one morning and seen that there was no love left, and had climbed on to a sofa and stayed there. She wondered if the Clingers ever spoke of love, or how Mrs Poache and the Captain viewed their wedding day. She looked across the room and saw her husband, his head bent to catch what Mrs Poache was saying. He was still a handsome man; the decay was elsewhere.

'I mean,' said Mrs Poache, 'supposing the Captain and I had walked into the house with a young giraffe. What then?'

James nodded. Mrs Poache reminded him that Captain Poache had once been in command of a vessel and had been all over the world. James nodded again, pouring Mrs Poache more sherry. Of the eight men, Captain Poache was the one he preferred. In the board-room the Captain slept a lot, and often stumbled when he walked about.

'He's lost all his nice naval manners,' said Mrs Poache sadly, and her eyes were drawn again to the corner that contained the monkey. She shook her head. 'I can't understand the mentality of it,' she said, 'people rearing the like of that.'

In the kitchen Mrs Hoop washed and dried an egg-beater. She was thinking that it was typical of the sullen character of Eve Bolsover that she should take exception to a few biscuits being given to her children. The children were hungry, they had stated so quite clearly: what harm in the world could two wafer biscuits do them? She worked out in her mind that two wafer biscuits at one and three the half-pound would probably cost a penny halfpenny. 'There's meanness for you,' said Mrs Hoop in a sudden temper. What business was it of the woman's if she gave them food or not? Why shouldn't she give them a bite of food if the children came and asked politely?

Mrs Hoop breathed heavily. She hung up the egg-beater, thought for a moment longer, and then opened the tin that contained the wafer biscuits. 'Two each,' she said in the children's bedroom, shaking them awake. 'Two little pink fellas from Mrs Hoop. Who's good to you?' The children stuffed the biscuits into their mouths, and Mrs Hoop kissed them and told them not to tell their mother. She returned to the kitchen and ate a spoonful of Eve's *Béarnaise* sauce. 'Not enough salt,' said Mrs Hoop, and added a quantity.

'I was saying to your husband,' said Mrs Poache in a low voice, 'that I cannot understand the mentality of people keeping a thing like that.'

'What's that?' demanded Mr Clinger. 'What are you saying, Mrs Poache?'

Mrs Poache replied that she had been saying nothing at all, and Eve passed from the room to see about the meal.

'What sort of food,' said Mrs Poache to James, 'do you imagine an animal like that would eat?'

James said he didn't know, but Mr Clinger, overhearing the question, said that the monkey ate solids like any other kind of animal, and an additional amount of nuts. There was no need at all, he added, for the tartan jacket that it was wearing now: the tartan jacket, said Mr Clinger, was simply and solely a screwy idea of his wife's. Monkeys, he claimed, didn't feel the cold.

Mr Linderfoot heard the remark about monkeys not feeling the cold and found it amusing, since, as he afterwards explained, monkeys came from the tropics. Mr Linderfoot laughed with spirit, bellowing out a noise that Eve and Mrs Hoop could hear in the kitchen.

'Whatever's that?' said Mrs Hoop, giving so violent a leap that a cigarette was dislodged from her lips. 'Lord!' murmured Mrs Hoop, looking around for a fork with which to retrieve it from a saucepan of asparagus.

'What is it?' said Eve.

'Lost me fag,' explained Mrs Hoop, 'with the shock of that damn noise.'

'I do wish you wouldn't smoke when there's food around,' said Eve. 'The ash gets everywhere.' And Mrs Hoop, angered by these words, replaced the fork and left the cigarette where it was.

In the sitting-room the talk continued. James listened and spoke a little himself, offering cocktails and sherry, whisky with soda, passing cigarettes and olives. In time, Mrs Linderfoot on her couch would remember what her husband reported of the

scene, and would attempt to visualize it. She would hear of the
Clingers' monkey, and of Mrs Poache taking exception to it.
She would imagine her husband's voice, louder than the other
voices.

Captain Poache surveyed the room and found it pleasant
enough: there were flowers in vases, and pictures upon the
walls, a green carpet, chairs and sofas quietly dressed. Beyond
the room, through french windows, lay a garden that seemed
in the increasing dusk to be a pleasant place too. Captain Poache
could make out the shapes of arched rose trellises and holly-
hocks aspiring, a long and narrow lawn, and a summerhouse on
a roundabout. Captain Poache was happy there, sitting on a sofa
beside his wife, watching the night creep into the Bolsovers'
garden and feeling warm in this pleasant room. He thought of
saying he would like to stay there while the others dined, but he
knew that such an utterance on his part would upset his wife
and probably his hostess as well.

Mrs Hoop watched Eve carry dishes of food into the dining-
room. She would wash up when the dishes were returned to her,
and then she would go her way, with extra money, and a meal
inside her. 'I'll open a tin of Crosse and Blackwell's,' she said to
Eve. 'I don't like the look of that stuff.'

Beach and Edward sat musing in the Hand and Plough, worrying about Mrs Hoop because she had forgotten to say that she
would not come that night.

'Only a king,' said Edward, 'can move backwards or forwards.
The ordinary piece must progress in the one direction only,
ahead.'

'It is the best direction,' said Beach. 'It's what the country
needs, son.'

Edward, having decided to resign his post the following morning, had come to feel melancholy again. In his whole short life
he had never known as beautiful a place as the love department.
He thought now of the beautiful typists, with hair that was dark
or blonde, reddish, chestnut, or subtle mouse. He considered
their clothes: chic little waistcoats over their linen blouses,
dresses starched and white, or dresses with miniature flowers on

them, primula and primrose, forget-me-not and aubrietia. The hands of the girls were pale and slender as they tapped with their pointed fingers on the keys of the typewriters. Pale necks curved elegantly, and their knees, in delicate stockings, were smooth and gently rounded, shaped with skill. Some worked with their bare feet displayed, naked masterpieces for all to see, like the feet of Botticelli's angels.

And when Edward passed through Room 305 and opened the door marked 306 it was like entering heaven itself. As the clerks strode to their desks, he imagined, their minds must still be full of that skin as pure as sunshine, and bosoms prettily heaving. There must remain with the clerks the scent that sprang from those bodies: *Apache's Tear, Blue Grass, In Love,* a modest *Chanel, Heaven Inspired.* All through the day, Edward imagined, as they read through the sordid letters, the clerks must draw strength from the perfumed beauty of the typists in their glory.

Sitting with Beach in the Hand and Plough and regretting that in a fit of pique he had drunk a measure of whisky to the honour of Septimus Tuam, Edward believed that after he had resigned, and for ever until he died, he would not forget the three rooms of the love department. He would never forget the harshly beautiful crimson curtains nor the indications painted on the doors: *Room 305, Room 306, Room 307.* For the rest of his life there would be one minute of every day in which he would walk between the rows of typists and pass into the sumptuous mystery of the love department proper. He would walk from the desk at which he had so sorrowfully failed and approach the sanctum of Lady Dolores, whose passion was love within marriage. She would talk to him again, explaining the words that the clerks spoke. She would smile with her long teeth and shoot her hand into her hair at the nape of her neck, and tousle it about in a surprising way. She would address him in her fashion and fit cigarettes into her bejewelled holder with bejewelled fingers; she would eat chocolate cake and drink whisky; she would say that Odette Sweeney was a genuine person. *Love Conquers All* were the words that came into Edward's mind, coming in a visual way. They came in the colours of the great embroidery, thundering out their message, as sweet as sugar candy.

'She taught me to cry,' said Edward in the Hand and Plough. 'I could feel her crying inside me; I had to cry too. I hadn't known it before.'

'Women is like that,' said Beach. 'Women makes strong men weep.'

'It wasn't like that. Not that kind of relationship.'

'I'd have a relationship with Emily Hoop. By the name of God, I would.'

'Have some more beer,' said Edward, miserably blowing his nose. 'Mrs Hoop'll be here in a moment.'

The guests ate melon, and then *tournedos* and the sauce *Béarnaise*, and some of the twenty potatoes that Mrs Hoop had peeled, and asparagus, and *petits pois*. Mr Linderfoot complimented Eve on her food, saying that it was excellent, and beautifully cooked. He said he had had a slice of chicken for lunch that you could have soled your boots with.

'We're having a fearful time,' said Mr Clinger to Eve, 'with door-handles. They've put on metal things. From Sweden I think they must come.'

'Arthur's most concerned about the door-handles,' said Mrs Clinger. 'I suppose your husband is too.'

'Yes, I suppose he is.'

'Another thing is WC pans,' said Mr Clinger,

'Arthur!'

'They've taken out the pedestal type.'

'Arthur,' said Mrs Clinger, her face the colour of a sunset. 'We're eating food.'

'What's wrong with it?' demanded Mr Clinger.

'No, no. I don't mean that.'

'What then?' said Mr Clinger cruelly.

'The sauce is far too salty,' said Eve. 'I can't think how I did that. I'm sorry,' she added in a louder voice, 'about this sauce.'

'I was saying about the pans,' said Mr Clinger. 'We were discussing the new look at the office.'

'It's hardly the subject,' said Mrs Clinger, bending her head over her plate, saying to herself that he always spoiled everything.

Farther down the table Mrs Poache heard Mr Clinger talking about the shape of lavatory pans and observed Mrs Clinger's discomfiture. She stared at Mrs Clinger, thinking how incredible it was that after a lifetime in the Royal Navy her husband should end up with a colleague who talked about lavatories at the dinner table, a man who kept an incontinent monkey as a pet.

'You have very attractive hair,' said Mr Linderfoot to Mrs Clinger. 'Did you know that?'

But Mrs Clinger did not immediately reply. She was experiencing a sour and unpleasant taste in her mouth and she could feel with her tongue something that was of the wrong consistency. Mrs Clinger didn't know what to do: she knew that if she attempted to extract whatever it was that was there her husband would note and remark upon the action. 'What have you got there?' he would demand. 'What's that, Diana?' Mrs Clinger identified the taste as that of tobacco; a matt of paper caught in her teeth. 'Look at that,' he would say. 'Look at what Diana's got hold of.' Mrs Clinger swallowed everything, sipping from her wine-glass. 'It's kind of you to say so,' she whispered to Mr Linderfoot.

Captain Poache ate his food and found it a little on the salty side. He drank some wine and found it much to his liking. He saw his wife listening to a conversation that was going on and noticed that she would have something to say about it all afterwards. She would keep him awake half the night with suggestions for his return to the ocean wave. He sought about in his mind for something to say that might improve matters, that might allow all present to develop a subject of conversation in a communal way.

'How about central heating?' said Captain Poache. 'Do you have it in the house, Mrs Bolsover?'

While Captain Poache was asking that question, Mrs Hoop, on the point of scouring a saucepan, remembered the waiting Beach. 'Lord above!' she cried, and rushed off into the sitting-room to telephone the Hand and Plough.

'May I speak to Mr Beach, Harold?' said Mrs Hoop, and then

she noticed that an animal, a kind of ape, as she afterwards described it, was sitting up in a corner of the room, looking at her.

'Who wants me?' said Beach in the Hand and Plough.

'The police,' remarked a bar-room wit as the old man made his way behind the counter to the telephone.

'Holy hell!' said Beach. 'Has Emily Hoop got into a bus accident? Hullo,' he said into the telephone. 'Is that a constable?'

'It's me,' said Mrs Hoop, watching the animal in the corner, wondering about it, and feeling nervous.

The monkey wandered from its position, quite slowly, and approached Mrs Hoop in a manner that alarmed her. It was breathing hard, wheezing through its nose and open mouth.

'Where are you, Emily?' demanded the voice of Beach in Mrs Hoop's ear.

The Clingers' monkey leapt swiftly from the ground into Mrs Hoop's arms, gripping her affectionately, biting her clothes.

'I'm being savaged by an ape,' cried Mrs Hoop.

'God bless you, where?' said Beach. 'You're never up a tree?'

'Who said I was up a tree? I'm here in the Bolsovers' sitting-room, attacked by an ape.'

'I'm coming on,' cried Beach, thinking that Mrs Hoop was alone, baby-sitting for the Bolsovers. 'I'll hire a taxi-car.'

The receiver slipped from Mrs Hoop's hand. She attempted to remove her clothing from the monkey's mouth, but the monkey, as had been its way from birth, held grimly on.

'Emily Hoop's attacked by an ape,' cried Beach in the Hand and Plough. 'Lend me a stick,' he demanded in a shout, addressing himself to Harold behind the bar. 'I'm going up there in a taxi-car.'

'I'll come with you, Mr Beach,' said Edward. 'Has the ape got out of a zoo?'

'The ape's eating her,' said Beach. 'He's savaging Mrs Hoop.'

In the Bolsovers' dining-room Mr Linderfoot was saying across the table:

'Small-bore gas is no damn good. That whole system is discredited.'

'Nonsense,' said Mr Clinger.

'Listen to me,' said Mr Linderfoot. 'I have temperature thermometers in every room. I gauge everything.'

'What's that got to do with it?'

'I have put in the best central heating I could lay my hands on. Oil-fired central heating.'

'You get the fumes.'

'You do not get the fumes, old friend.'

'The smell of oil would drive you crackers. I've seen it on the go.'

'There's not a single fume in the house. If the central heating was giving off a smell the wife would be the first to have a thing to say. So put that in your pipe –'

'I investigated the whole market. I investigated the whole market, Mrs Bolsover, and I can assure you there is no more efficient way of heating a house than by small-bore gas central heating.'

Mrs Clinger, in an agony of embarrassment because her husband was about to lose his temper at a dinner party, felt like crying. She tried to think of something to say, but no subject whatsoever came to her.

'It was discredited ten years ago,' said Mr Linderfoot to James. 'Don't ever have the stuff in the house, old friend.'

'It was not discredited,' said Mr Clinger. 'Small-bore gas central heating is the thing today.' Mr Clinger glared angrily across the table and thought that Linderfoot was looking smug.

'I remember reading about it at the time,' said Mr Linderfoot to the Bolsovers. 'Everyone was laughing at the whole thing.'

'It wasn't even invented ten years ago,' shouted Mr Clinger, standing up. 'That's a ridiculous thing to say.'

'Sit down, man,' said Linderfoot. 'Keep your hair on.'

'Arthur,' said Mrs Clinger, rubbing her right knee with her hand in a nervous way.

'Well,' said Eve, laughing, 'we haven't got central heating.'

'That's just it, old friend,' said Mr Linderfoot. 'Make sure when you do not to go for the gas job.'

'We have some other system,' said Eve quickly. 'Storage heating.'

'A total waste that is,' said Mr Clinger. 'Whatever inspired you, Bolsover?'

In the Bolsovers' sitting-room Mrs Hoop released a scream, and dropped to the ground in a state of hysterical terror.

13

'I don't know where they live,' said Beach to the taxi-man. 'The name is Bolsover. They're out Wimbledon way. Hurry on, now.'

The taxi-man explained that he couldn't drive to a house without more specific instructions.

'Go to a telephone-box,' suggested Edward, 'and we can look up the name in the book.'

'Drive to the house, can't you?' shouted Beach, hitting the floor of the taxi with a sweeping-brush which he had been handed in the Hand and Plough when he had called so agitatedly for a stick. 'What's this about a book?'

Edward repeated that they could look up the whereabouts of the Bolsovers' house in the telephone directory and thus save further argument.

'It's a scandalous thing,' said Beach, thinking of Mrs Hoop held at bay by an animal. 'I never heard the like.'

'If Mrs Hoop stands still and does not anger the creature, all will be well. It's when you try to edge away that they turn nasty.'

'Move the car faster,' cried Beach, poking the taxi-driver's back with the end of his brush.

'Leave off that,' said the taxi-driver in an annoyed way, 'or there'll be trouble.'

When Mrs Hoop had dropped to the floor the monkey had dropped with her, but in the fall it had seized some of Mrs Hoop's skirt in its teeth and had caused a portion of it to tear away. It was this scene that the Bolsovers and their guests beheld when they entered the room in a body, having heard the cry of anguish: Mrs Hoop prone on the floor, the telephone receiver dangling, and the monkey with part of a tweed skirt in its mouth.

Mr Clinger stalked forward and gripped his pet by the scruff of its neck, Mrs Hoop rose to her feet and looked down at the gap in her skirt, Eve asked her if she was all right, and James replaced the telephone receiver.

'What happened?' said Mr Linderfoot, and added, 'Tell us in your own words.'

'That woman needs brandy,' said Captain Poache and, finding some, pressed it upon her.

'I'm that ashamed,' were the first words that Mrs Hoop employed. She placed her hands over the damaged part of her clothes, hiding the sight of an under-garment.

'Sit down,' said Captain Poache.

'Yes, sit down,' said Mr Linderfoot, thinking that Mrs Hoop wasn't a bad-looking woman in her way. 'And try and tell us in your own words. I'm taking notes for an invalid.'

'Here,' said Mr Clinger, handing Mrs Hoop the area of her skirt that the monkey had removed. 'It should stitch in O.K.'

'It's ruined beyond measure, mister,' said Mrs Hoop.

'You'll have to pay, Arthur,' said Mrs Clinger.

'Nonsense,' said Mr Clinger.

Mrs Hoop, sitting in an arm-chair in the centre of the room, said she'd like her coat. 'A red one,' she said, 'hanging on the back of the kitchen door.'

The brandy coursed through Mrs Hoop's body, warming her, inspiring in her a touch of arrogance. She had hoped to see Eve Bolsover leave the room to fetch her red coat, but Eve Bolsover was tidying up some of the mess that the incident had caused. A woman with blue hair, the wife of the man who held the ape, she rather thought, slipped from the room instead, and returned with her old red coat. Mrs Hoop rose and put it on and then sat down again. James Bolsover, in his quiet, kind way, asked her if she was hurt at all, if she'd like them to call in medical aid.

'Shaken,' said Mrs Hoop, and heard Mrs Bolsover say that she'd make some coffee, and then saw her remove herself from the room. She was glad to see her go. She said, 'She needn't make up coffee for me. I never touch the stuff.' She held out her glass, saying the brandy had pulled her together.

'Who's this woman?' Mrs Poache asked Mrs Clinger.

'The char,' whispered Mrs Clinger. 'I suppose so.'

'How completely extraordinary!' said Mrs Poache, watching her husband filling Mrs Hoop's glass with brandy and reminding herself to speak to him about that in the car. He seemed to have taken leave of his senses, thought Mrs Poache, giving a charwoman glasses of brandy in somebody else's house. 'Where's the lavatory?' she said to Mrs Clinger, but Mrs Clinger replied that she really didn't know, and Mrs Poache thought that Mrs Clinger, as well as everything else, was a bit of a broken reed.

'Where's the lavatory?' said Mrs Poache to Eve in the kitchen.

'Oh, I'm sorry,' cried Eve. 'I'm so sorry, Mrs Poache.' She led the way, apologizing for everything.

'I never like an upstairs one,' said Mrs Poache on the way upstairs. 'They're uneconomical.'

Eve smiled, questioning that.

'Your stair-carpet gets worn out,' said Mrs Poache. 'It gets twice the usage.'

At that moment the monkey began to chatter hysterically, filling the house with the worried sound. 'Excuse me,' said Eve and rushed away, imagining that some new calamity had developed. But in fact the excitement was only the result of Mr Linderfoot's having abruptly and without warning clapped his hands together.

'Down, sir,' said Mr Clinger.

'Listen a minute,' said Mr Linderfoot. 'Could we have a second or two of hush?'

Eve, standing by the door of her sitting-room, forgetting about the coffee she had been making and Mrs Poache *en route* to the lavatory, watched Mr Linderfoot place his face close to Mrs Hoop's and say:

'Now then, ma'am, tell us in your own words.'

'I wouldn't know what to say,' protested Mrs Hoop, drinking from her glass. 'What can I say to you, mister?'

'Well, there's been an accident,' said Mr Linderfoot. 'It's unusual at a dinner party, this kind of thing.'

Mrs Hoop saw Eve standing by the sitting-room door and wondered what she thought she was doing there, since she had clearly stated that she was leaving the room to make coffee. She thought of pretending, just for the fun of it, that she was mistress of the house and that Mrs Bolsover was the woman who daily came to clean it and to wash up dishes after others had used them. It was on the tip of Mrs Hoop's tongue to ask Eve Bolsover if she had run out of Ajax, but she decided in the end that she'd prefer to ignore the woman. 'I didn't demean my mouth,' Mrs Hoop heard herself saying in her report of the incident, 'asking her any question at all.'

'A fine old brandy,' said Captain Poache.

'Have some more,' said James. 'We're all in need of brandy.'

'Thank you,' said Captain Poache.

'My wife's not here,' said Mr Linderfoot to Mrs Hoop. 'She's out in Purley.'

The Bolsover children awoke to find the light on in their room and a severe-looking woman in pink peering in through the door. 'Where's the lavatory?' said this woman, but the children, confused and sleepy, and thinking her to be part of a dream, told her to go away.

'I'm on the phone to old Beach, see,' said Mrs Hoop, 'minding my own business, and up comes this animal, see, and lays hold on me. Well, I was that terrified. "Get away, you old brute," I shouted at the thing. "Off with you," but the devil wouldn't budge. Up he comes closer and grips me in his jaws. "I'm attacked by an ape," I says to old Beach. "I'm being eaten alive." And old Beach says, "Are you up a tree?" Well, I couldn't understand that at all. I couldn't make head or tail of old Beach standing there in the Hand and Plough saying was I up a tree. Then the whole thing goes blank until I'm being helped up to my feet and given a drop to drink by kind friends. My clothes is damaged to the extent of a pound, and to tell you straight I feel unsteady on my pins.'

James said then that perhaps Mrs Hoop could manage the journey back to the kitchen, but Mrs Hoop shook her head and replied that she thought she could not. The big man was making a pass at her, she noted, keeping himself close to her. She lifted a hand to her hair to tidy it. 'I'm knocking them all for six,' she said to herself.

'Mr Bolsover,' said Mrs Poache, entering the room at speed, 'I must insist on knowing where the lavatory is.'

In the taxi-cab hired by Beach, Edward said:

'Did Mrs Hoop give details? She'll need the attention of a doctor.'

'A doctor, son?'

'Mrs Hoop may be injured. She may need a stitch.'

Beach again poked the taxi-driver's back with the end of his sweeping-brush. 'Here,' he said. 'Slow up at a doctor's place. We need a doctor.'

'Stop that immediately,' said the taxi-driver. 'What's the trouble?'

Edward leaned forward and explained that a woman had been attacked by an animal escaped from a zoo. He added that she was alone in a house except for children, and would need urgent medical attention. 'Draw up at the first brass plate,' he said. 'We haven't time to pick and choose.'

The taxi-driver drove slowly along the suburban roads, peering through the dusk for a doctor's sign. He halted his cab after about five minutes. Edward leapt out and pressed the night-bell.

A short man in a cardigan opened the door and looked tired in the brightness of his hall. He said, with a sigh:

'What's up, lad?'

Edward explained that an ape had attacked a woman and that the nature of the damage was not yet known. He explained what he knew of the circumstances.

'O.K.,' said the doctor wearily, and went to fetch his bag. 'Tell me what happens,' he muttered to his wife, referring to a television play they had been engrossed in.

'Who's this man?' shouted Beach as the doctor stepped into the taxi-cab.

'A medical doctor,' said the doctor with stiffness, 'since that, it appears, is what you require.'

'It's Mrs Hoop,' said Beach. 'She's caught up with an ape.'

'So I've heard,' said the doctor, closing his eyes. 'We'll do our best.'

The taxi moved forward, gathering speed, while in Crannoc Avenue the situation remained unchanged. Eve Bolsover, carrying coffee to her sitting-room, observed that Mrs Hoop was still occupying an arm-chair in the centre of the room and was surrounded by the dinner guests, who were standing up, drinking brandy or liqueurs, since they had felt the need of them. Captain Poache, she saw, was again filling the glass that Mrs Hoop drank from, while Mr Linderfoot was bending over Mrs Hoop, telling her something. James was leaning against a wall listening to Mrs Clinger's whisper. He seemed unaware of the social chaos; he seemed not to care.

'Now, Mrs Hoop,' Eve said. 'I think we could get you back to the kitchen.'

Mr Linderfoot smiled.

'I'm that shaky,' was what Mrs Hoop said. 'I'm that shaky, dear, I'd never make the kitchen.'

'Well, you can't sit here all night,' said Eve, smiling too. 'Now can you?'

'It's a very comfy chair,' said Mrs Hoop. 'I'll grant you that.'

'Come along now, Mrs Hoop.'

'What, dear?'

'She's as happy as Larry,' said Mr Linderfoot.

Eve smiled again and moved away.

'James, we must get Mrs Hoop out. She's had all this drink and says she can't move.' She smiled at Mrs Clinger. 'We can hardly sit down to our coffee with Mrs Hoop in the middle of the room.'

'You have lovely hair,' said Mr Linderfoot to Mrs Hoop. 'Didn't anyone ever tell you that?'

'Get on with you,' said Mrs Hoop. 'My mother looked a picture, mister.'

'I've tried,' said James. 'I've said to her she should go to the kitchen. I've asked her if she wanted a doctor.'

'Perhaps we should go,' said Mrs Clinger.

'Go?' said Mr Clinger. 'At this hour of the evening? Have sense, Diana.'

'Oh, no one must go,' protested Eve. 'Do sit down.'

'Look here,' said Mr Linderfoot to Mrs Hoop, offering her an arm. 'I'll help you out to this kitchen.'

Mrs Poache, descending the Bolsovers' stairs, had reached the last step when a loud knocking on the hall-door arrested her progress. 'Someone at your door,' said Mrs Poache, throwing her voice in the direction of the Bolsovers' sitting-room. She then stepped forward and opened it.

'Where's Emily Hoop?' demanded an old man with a sweeping-brush in his hand, scowling at Mrs Poache. 'What's become of her?' He pushed his way roughly past her, followed by a youth and a short man with a bag.

'That's Mr Beach,' said the young man to Mrs Poache. 'He's come about this ape thing.'

'Ape thing?' said Mrs Poache. 'The woman has been given drink by my husband.'

'Whoa up there,' cried Mr Linderfoot merrily, an exclamation that caused the monkey to chatter again. The door opened violently, and Mrs Hoop, sniggering on the arm of the heaviest of the board-men, uttered a cry. 'There's old Beach,' she shrilled. 'Whatever's he doing here?'

Attracted by this ejaculation, the monkey at once streaked to her side and gripped with his teeth part of her red coat. Beach, the only member of the company who was in any way armed, aimed a firm blow with the sweeping-brush from the Hand and Plough.

'Ah,' said the doctor, coughing. 'May I see the patient?'

Mr Clinger, seeing his pet molested by what in the confusion of the moment he took to be a street-cleaner, shouted loudly at the man with the brush, saying the animal was valuable and was not to be struck. Mrs Poache, who from the hall had had but a brief glimpse of Mr Linderfoot with the charwoman on his arm, tried to peer over the old man's shoulder to see what her husband was up to. 'I can't see,' she said to the young man who stood by her side. 'Can you look in there and tell me what a fat man with glasses is doing?'

Edward looked and said that there were three fat men with glasses. None of them, he reported, was doing much.

'Look here,' said the doctor. 'Where's this injured woman?'

'Who are you?' said Mrs Poache.

'I'm a doctor that's been called out. Where's the woman? Have they caught the ape?'

'Typical,' said Mrs Poache. 'You've been drawn out on false pretences. Mrs Bolsover,' she called, 'there's a doctor here, if anyone needs him.'

'Who are you?' said James to Beach. 'What do you want?'

'Emily Hoop rang me up on the telephone, saying about the ape. Here I be.'

'Down, sir,' said Mr Clinger to the monkey, whose teeth were still attached to Mrs Hoop's red coat.

'Would you mind repeating that?' requested Mr Linderfoot of Beach. 'Tell us who you are again.'

'Here's a doctor,' said Mrs Poache. 'Come to put down the monkey.'

Beach broke into obscene language. He prodded the monkey with the bristles of his brush. Mrs Hoop, having heard that a doctor had come, said nothing. She had a feeling that she was being fought over, that the big man who had held her by the arm and old Beach from the public house were coming to blows over her body. It didn't matter to Mrs Hoop: all she wanted to do was to sit in the middle of the room again and watch it going round.

'You are making matters worse,' said Mr Clinger furiously to Beach, 'with that sweeping-brush. You are maddening the animal beyond measure.'

'I'm being shoved at,' protested Beach, 'and Emily Hoop's the worse for wear.'

'I want to get into that room,' said Mrs Poache. 'This affair's an orgy. I've never seen the like of it.'

'Is it a joke?' said the doctor. 'I'd better go.'

'My husband's in there,' said Mrs Poache, 'drinking himself to death, if it interests you at all. He's never been happy on dry land.'

'I'm a doctor,' shouted the doctor.

Within the room Eve said:

'James, there's a doctor here. For Mrs Hoop.'

'Who sent for him?' said James.

Mrs Poache tried to push again, but Beach, still blocking the doorway, did not respond. He could not, for his own way was blocked by Mrs Hoop, held by Mr Linderfoot on one side and by Mr Clinger, who sought to ease the monkey's grip on her red coat.

'This is quite scandalous,' complained the doctor. 'I'm called out to attend an accident, and here we are with a lot of drunks.'

'Mind your tongue,' said Mrs Poache.

In the sitting-room Mr Clinger managed to persuade his monkey to release Mrs Hoop's coat. Beach stood aside, having no longer cause to brandish the sweeping-brush, no longer requiring space for the gesture. Mrs Hoop, held upright by Mr Linderfoot and sensing that the limelight was slipping away from her, demanded the attentions of the doctor.

'Hullo, there!' shouted Mr Linderfoot. 'Bring that medic back.'

'James, for goodness' sake!' said Eve.

'What?' said James.

'It's really singular,' murmured Mrs Clinger.

'Singular?' said Eve, having seen Mrs Hoop falling drunkenly about and a strange elderly man poking at the Clingers' monkey with a brush, and Mr Linderfoot trying to hold Mrs Hoop up and an innocent doctor shouting his head off. 'It is certainly singular.' She wanted to ask Mrs Clinger if this always happened when they took their monkey to dinner. She wanted to ask her why she kept such a monkey, if such a monkey was necessary in a world in which there was starvation. She wanted to ask James if the other five men talked of central heating until kingdom come, and were determined about door-handles.

'This is an absurd business,' remarked Mrs Poache to Edward. 'My husband and I were invited to dinner by these people, and trouble occurred at once.'

'It's the time of the year,' said Edward. 'I'm in trouble myself.'

Mrs Poache nodded, and then regarded this young man more closely. 'You remind me of a son of the Captain's and mine,' she said. 'Our name is Poache.'

'Poache?' said Edward. He repeated the word slowly. He savoured the word, rolling it over his tongue. He was silent.

Then he said, 'Not Mrs Poache of 23, The Drive, Wimbledon?'

'That is so. Married to a naval officer, as was.'

For Edward it was as though they had suddenly made him an emperor. The love department glowed before him, the ferns and the palms sprouted fruitfully to the heavens, the typists in their glory sang a hallelujah that was full of the mysterious words, Lady Dolores took her cigarette-holder out of her mouth and pressed scarlet lips to his forehead. She left the mark of her lipstick there and warned him not to wipe it away. The scent from the typists warmed his nostrils.

'D'you know who I am?' said Edward. 'I'm the brother of Septimus Tuam.'

'Septimus Tuam?'

'Did you know him?'

Mrs Poache did not reply at once. She again examined Edward closely; she said in a low voice, 'I knew Septimus Tuam. I knew him a few years back. Yes, I did.'

'Are we thinking of the same man? Listen, Mrs Poache, could I come out and talk to you about Septimus Tuam? I am trying to find him; he's come into a fortune. Could I come and see you?'

Mrs Poache nodded her head. She had forgotten where she was. She had forgotten her husband drinking heavily, sitting alone, talking to no one. She had forgotten the Clingers, the monkey, the Bolsovers and their strange ways, the old man with the sweeping-brush, the doctor, the young man who questioned her now. Mrs Poache went into a state of nostalgic fascination, which lasted for twenty minutes.

'There is nothing whatsoever the matter with this woman,' said the doctor. 'I was dragged away from my well-earned rest. Show me a scratch on this one.'

'I'm sorry,' said James. 'I can't think how you got here. I mean, who sent for you?'

'I'm going away,' replied the doctor, glaring about him. 'A childish display if ever I've seen one.'

Edward sat by Mrs Poache in the sitting-room and knew that at last all was going to be well. He would have to disguise himself neither as a representative of the North Thames Gas Board nor as a window-cleaner, nor as anything else. He would cycle out to Mrs Poache's house and hear from Mrs Poache's lips a full description of Septimus Tuam; he might even see a faded photograph. Then he would move in upon the man. He would spot the right figure coming out of the rooming-house. He would haunt Septimus Tuam so that Septimus Tuam's life was a misery; he would cause Septimus Tuam to commit a misdemeanour; he would see him incarcerated in a cell.

Captain Poache, who had not noticed the young man earlier in the evening, wondered what he was doing sitting by his wife, since his wife seemed to be struck dumb. 'He's like a son of ours,' said Mrs Poache after a time to Mrs Clinger, who nodded and smiled and thought that Mrs Poache, after all the havoc, appeared to be a changed woman.

'He's the Poaches' son,' said Mrs Clinger to Eve, 'come to fetch them home. Nice-looking boy.'

In the kitchen Eve made more coffee. 'I'm terribly sorry, Mrs Hoop,' said Eve.

'Where's that Linderfoot guy?' asked Mrs Hoop.

'Give Emily Hoop a hot coffee, ma'am,' said Beach. 'She's had an experience.'

'I've had an experience,' said Mrs Hoop. 'All me togs torn off.'

Beach explained how he had been waiting in the Hand and Plough and how Emily Hoop had telephoned through to say she was being savaged by an ape, how he and the young man had come at once in a taxi.

'The young man? He came with you, Mr Beach? They said he was the Poaches' son.'

'Oh, happen he is,' said Beach, 'but he come here in a taxi-car with me.'

'Tell the Linderfoot guy I was asking for him,' said Mrs Hoop.

'Excuse me,' said Eve in the drawing-room. 'Your friends are in the kitchen.'

'Friends?' said Edward, smiling.

'Mr Beach and Mrs Hoop.'

'Look,' said Edward with great new enthusiasm, walking to the door with Eve, 'what can you tell me about that couple? I belong to an organization. Resettlement, the elderly. Well, stuff like that. And love.'

'Love?'

'Love for all ages, Mrs Bolsover. Love for Mr Beach and Mrs Hoop. Love for the lady in pink.'

'I don't think I understand you.'

'Love in marriage, Mrs Bolsover. I may say no more.'

'Have some coffee in the kitchen,' said Eve, wondering about this well-spoken young man who was apparently a friend of her charwoman's. She didn't wonder for long, however, for she was beginning to feel immensely depressed.

'Thank you, Mrs Bolsover,' said the young man politely. 'I would welcome a drink of coffee.'

14

Once upon a time they might have laughed because they could not help it, or played some game they understood, communicating yet not seeming to. How could it be, Eve thought, that a tartan-clad monkey had leapt upon Mrs Hoop and that the Bolsovers would never come to laugh together over that ridiculous fact? Would they refer again to the arrival in their house of an elderly stranger with a sweeping-brush? Would they shake their heads over what Mrs Poache must have thought of the increasing pandemonium? Or wonder what tale had been borne to Mrs Linderfoot on her couch? She thought they mightn't.

The guests had gone their way, shaking hands in the hall, Captain Poache staggering, his wife seeming less vexed than she had been, Mr Linderfoot saying he'd like to come again, the Clingers quarrelling. Mrs Hoop and her friends had gone off also, the three of them in a taxi, since that had seemed the best way. The house had been silent then, for James had not spoken, nor had she. James had sat down and she had stood with an unlighted cigarette between her fingers, and James had fallen asleep.

Eve felt a headache beginning to thump behind her brow. She lit and smoked the cigarette, which made her headache worse. James slept in his chair, his mouth slightly open, his body full of brandy.

One by one, the scenes passed before her: moments of her marriage day, for she continued in her obsession about it and she knew the day well. She stood about, and walked and spoke; she was there in white, saying the right thing, moving among people: the scenes were like parts of a slow film. Would she, she wondered, take to a sofa like Mrs Linderfoot, when the children had grown up and gone? Would she lie there and dream all afternoon of the distant past, of a man she had married on a sunny day? What did Mrs Linderfoot think about? Or Mrs Clinger, come to that? Or Mrs Poache?

'Oh, James,' cried Eve, running across the room and putting her arms about the form of her sleeping husband.

James did not hear, nor did he move. But Eve talked on, speaking of marriage, saying that it was worth an effort. She said he must seek some work of a different order. She said that they must talk together, and she viewed them in her mind, talking together in the future, as once they had. They talked in her future, at breakfast and in the evening. They turned off the television set, saying the programmes had deteriorated, and not meaning that at all. They talked in bed and at the weekends. They sat in silence, knowing that the talk was there.

'Oh, James,' cried Eve, closing her eyes and feeling her headache. 'I never understood a thing.'

She believed at that moment that she had not raised a finger as their marriage had drifted into boredom. 'No marriage should be kept by children,' said Eve. 'We must stand on our own feet.' But her husband slept on, occasionally murmuring an agreement. Once he had opened his eyes and said, 'I thought of selling nails to ironmongers.'

'Sell what you will,' cried Eve. 'Only for God's sake, let's begin this thing all over again.' But James had returned to sleep.

Eve said that she knew it could be all right. Why could it not? she demanded, since now they were aware of all the flaws. 'Sell nails,' said Eve. 'We could be poor. Would it matter? Are we rich?' All their lives they would talk about the night the Clingers had brought their monkey out to dinner. In time they would tell their children about the monkey, about a Mrs Hoop who once had been their charwoman and had been given too much brandy by a Captain Poache, about a doctor who had come by mistake. They would relate the string of peculiar events and laugh over them, and she and James would remember that something of their farce had caused Eve to sense that she and her husband had but to take themselves in hand. Ten years ago they had chosen to marry, which was a fact worth holding on to. 'We made no mistake,' said Eve, 'and we haven't changed in essence. But marriage is not as easy as it looks.'

She stood in the centre of her sitting-room, in a black dress and in her stockinged feet, smoking a cigarette and thinking to herself that she would lie awake all night with her headache, considering and planning, allowing for all the flaws.

'I will tell you tomorrow,' said Eve to her husband, who had slipped by now into a deeper slumber. 'I will stand in front of you tomorrow evening and tell you that our marriage is in working order. At least as far as I'm concerned. Sell a bag of nails a day, James. Drive a dray. Serve at table. I too would be maddened by central heating and door-handles. We can at least share that.' Eve went to bed, and, contrary to her expectations, fell asleep at once.

Lady Dolores strolled about the rooms that Edward Blakeston-Smith had taken so passionately to his heart. She was thinking of Edward, attempting, in fact, to inspire him from a distance. She did not know that earlier that evening Edward had planned to telephone the love department and hand in his resignation but had later taken new heart through his meeting with a sea captain's wife. Lady Dolores would not have cared to know this kind of detail, the ups and downs of an evening, the lowering of a spirit and its subsequent revival. She was sanguine in the love department that night, which was enough for her.

She walked soundlessly, regarding without emotion the empty desks of the typists, moving on to eye the Samuel Watson frieze, and passing finally through the arch and into her own modest office. There, with cake and alcohol, she examined a lately arrived letter from Odette Sweeney: *I have done what you laid down. I've said the girl would be better off in digs, it being an embarrassment to have the daughter by a previous woman under my feet. 'If she goes, I go,' he said to me, standing up in his vest. What now?* Lady Dolores knew at once that Mrs Sweeney must wait: she must bide her time until a day came when the young girl saw some youth in jeans and preferred him with a fluttering heart to Mrs Sweeney's husband. That would be that: the girl would pack her traps and bit by bit the Sweeney marriage would take shape again, time being the healer. Yet none of that could be as bluntly put, lest Mrs Sweeney be tempted to offer financial inducement to youths in jeans.

Although Lady Dolores believed in being direct, she believed as well that the truth must be wisely delivered. She replied to Mrs Sweeney briefly: *Muster your patience. Your marriage will ride this storm. Stand firm with faith. Be calm, Mrs Sweeney.* It was advice that Lady Dolores often gave. She believed that love returned to marriages, even with Septimus Tuam about; she believed that there was more love available than was at all apparent. She would have found for Eve Bolsover evidence of love in the marriages of the Clingers and the Poaches and the Linderfoots. She would have pointed at small items and said they were enough. But she would have agreed with Eve Bolsover that marriage was not as easy as it looked. It was easier by far for Septimus Tuam to step in and cause all hell to break loose.

'Septimus Tuam,' said Lady Dolores, speaking his name since his name had come involuntarily into her head. 'Septimus Tuam.' She believed she had developed a nervous condition where that name was concerned; and as often as she warned a woman to wait and be calm, she feared the shape of the man entering that woman's life, urging her not to wait at all but to have a fling instead, offering her more than a box of safety matches. She saw him entering the lives of all the women who were depressed and tired, who felt an ugliness coming on, or who were young and felt that life was dim. *Take heart, be calm,* wrote Lady Dolores. 'I love you,' said Septimus Tuam.

Lady Dolores stared at the curved handwriting of Odette Sweeney. She whispered to herself that no woman in England received more letters than she did. She told herself that she had built the love department from nothing, that she had increased the circulation of the magazine fourfold. She recalled the letters of appreciation that poured in day by day, letters that need never have been written, that were written out of gratitude and the goodness in people's hearts. She remembered the gifts of the great embroidery and the embroideries that surrounded it. She remembered women who had clutched at her hands on the street, gabbling in excitement that her wisdom had saved them from a gas oven or a life alone.

Lady Dolores sat still. Behind her dark-rimmed spectacles her eyelids dropped: she saw a haze, and she moved her lips, practising the words she intended to say.

A mile or so away, just beyond the river on which London was built, Septimus Tuam slept and did not dream. In his large, bare room no single item was out of place. His umbrella hung from a hook on the back of his door. The cup from which he drank his daily milk and the plate from which he lifted his food lay neatly on a central table, with a knife and a spoon, ready for breakfast. Beneath the mattress of his narrow bed lay the fine corduroy trousers of Septimus Tuam, gaining a crease for the day ahead.

15

Mrs Hoop did not arrive at the Bolsovers' house on the morning after the dinner party. She stayed in her bed, trying to remember details, lifting her head up from time to time to assess the intensity of her headache. She recalled most vividly the antics of the man from Purley: she remembered his mentioning the beauty of her hair, and remembered finding herself being aided across the room by him, then being halted, seemingly, by old Beach. Afterwards, everything had quietened down again: she and Beach and Edward Blakeston-Smith sitting in the kitchen, she sending Beach in to ask Mr Bolsover if they could have a drop of brandy, and Mr Bolsover coming and saying that he would pay for a taxi home for her, and in fact telephoning for one. While they were waiting for it to come the big man from Purley had come into the kitchen to say that old Beach and Blakeston-Smith were to help with the ape in the garden, and as soon as their backs were turned he had said to her that she was an attractive woman. Then old Beach and Blakeston-Smith had returned and said there was no ape in the garden, and the man had announced outright and in front of them that he could fall in love with Mrs Hoop. And when the three of them got into the taxi-cab Beach had banged on the floor of it with his sweeping-brush and said he loved her the more, and the young man talked of love and happiness all the way home. Old Beach had been crying in the end, asking her for a kiss. 'Love falls like snow-flakes,' she remembered the young man saying. 'Forget about that will business and marry Mr Beach.' She had snorted with laughter at the very idea of it, marrying old Beach.

Mrs Hoop lay back on her pillows and dropped off to sleep again. She dreamed that old Beach was hitting the Bolsover woman with a sweeping-brush and that she and the man from

Purley were getting into bed together. 'Filthy dirty!' cried Mrs Hoop in her dream, waking herself up. She turned on her side, and slept again. She dreamed, more to her liking, of the will and its signing, of happy faces in the Hand and Plough, of Edward Blakeston-Smith and Harold shaking her hand as a signal of congratulation. She dreamed of the death of her husband, and of the death of old Beach.

'I rang the bell,' said Septimus Tuam, 'just to draw your attention to the fact that the package is in your letter-box. Look here.' He stepped over the threshold, around the door, and picked from the letter-box Mrs FitzArthur's Bear Brand stockings, wrapped in Mrs FitzArthur's gay wrapping paper.

'Oh,' said Eve, for a moment confused, and then remembering that this was the chattering man from Ely's who had later telephoned and whose voice had then roamed about her mind. 'Thank you very much.'

'Not at all, not at all,' said Septimus Tuam. 'This was no trouble to me at all. Why should it be? I was visiting Lord Marchingpass in any case.'

'It's extremely kind of you,' said Eve Bolsover.

Septimus Tuam bowed and said nothing, standing in the hall, looking about it.

'Would you like a cup of coffee?' said Eve, thinking that there seemed to be genuine kindness in the man.

'Oh, please don't bother, Mrs Bolsover.'

'It's no trouble at all.'

'No, no, I'd best be going.' He made as though to leave the house, and then heard Eve say:

'I'm making some, anyway.'

'In that case,' said Septimus Tuam, and closed the door behind him.

'I'm washing up,' explained Eve, leading the way to the kitchen. 'Mrs Hoop hasn't turned up.'

'Your charlady?'

'Yes.'

She lit the gas and placed a kettle of water on it. 'Everywhere's in a mess this morning. I hope you won't mind.'

'Why should I mind, Mrs Bolsover?'

'Some people might.'

'Might they? I live a simple life.'

Eve, finding it hard to know what to say to this man who was a stranger to her, began on the subject of the dinner party, since the chaos of the dinner party lay all around them.

'How odd,' said Septimus Tuam, hearing that guests had come with a young monkey.

'There's worse than that,' said Eve, laughing. She felt a warmth within herself. For an hour that morning she had lain awake, regarding the future and seeing that the future need not be grim. At breakfast she had heard her children chattering on in their usual way and had seen her husband's tired expression. 'I'll tell you,' she had said. 'It's going to be all right. It'll be all right.' James had moved his head slowly, up and down, his eyes half closed in a bloated face, glazed and watery, the eyes of a heavy drinker.

'There's worse than that,' Eve said again, and told of how the animal had leapt about the sitting-room, knocking things down and attacking Mrs Hoop. She told of Mrs Hoop's friends who had arrived, the old man, and the younger one who had spoken of love. 'Someone said the young man was the Poaches' son. He was a strange person, sitting like that and talking to anyone who happened to be around. Don't you think so?'

'It's certainly not what you would expect,' said Septimus Tuam. 'Did you say these people are your husband's colleagues?'

'The fat men are. The others, as I say, had to do with Mrs Hoop.' She measured coffee into a coffee-pot and poured in the boiling water.

'Sugar?' she said to Septimus Tuam.

'Two,' he said, thinking that she would get to know that fact well. 'What an extraordinary occasion it must have been.'

'It was indeed. I'm afraid it wasn't a success at all.'

'Why did they come, Mrs Bolsover? Why did you have these people come into your house?'

Eve paused. The explanation was a long one, difficult to present in a few words. Instead of saying that James had rushed away from a restaurant table to invite the three men and their wives, she said for some reason:

'I felt, actually, that I knew very little of my husband's life. Of what he did all day. Of the whole wilderness, or so it seemed to me, of his business world.'

'But, Mrs Bolsover, the business world is not a wilderness. It is full of palaces. It is a man-made garden of Eden.'

Septimus Tuam sipped his coffee, pausing only to say that it was very good coffee indeed, beautifully made. He was wearing a tie with the signs of the Zodiac on it, and a dark grey corduroy suit. His shirt was of a sober shade of blue, a shirt that had once belonged to another man who took a size fifteen collar, the husband of a woman whom Septimus Tuam had once known well. He felt quite confident within his clothes, knowing that no un-stitched hole was to be seen, that all hints of flamboyance had been thoughtfully eschewed. He said:

'You had forgotten I was coming, Mrs Bolsover?'

'I'm afraid I had forgotten for a moment. All that nonsense last night was enough to put anything out of one's mind. And then afterwards I came to a few decisions.' She smiled at the man, and he inclined his head in a grave manner. To her considerable surprise, she heard him say:

'Allow me to help you clear up the awful chaos. Your Mrs Hoop will not materialize today.'

As he spoke, Septimus Tuam rose elegantly from his chair and stripped off the jacket of his corduroy suit. He moved to the sink and immersed his hands in a basinful of soapy water. Eve laughed. She said:

'Of course not.'

But Septimus Tuam took no notice at all. He washed and rinsed glasses, saying:

'I know how it is for the housewife. She has a thinnish time of it; husband at work all day, kiddies to think about. I'm a bachelor, Mrs Bolsover: I help whenever I can.'

'But, Mr Tuam, you must have other things to do.'

'I am an idle case today, Mrs Bolsover. I haven't a thing on my hands at all.'

'Well, it's most kind of you.'

'I had thought to go down to the law courts to hear a case or two, but I'd as soon stand here talking, washing your dishes. I'm being frank about it.'

The house seemed quiet to Eve after the uproar of the previous night. Before he left, Mr Linderfoot had read some of the notes he had written down for his wife. 'I was on the phone to old Beach, see, minding my own business,' he had said, quoting Mrs Hoop.

'It is ending as it should be ending,' said Eve, 'with a strange man washing up the dishes.'

'Not a strange man, Mrs Bolsover. At least not as strange a man as the man once was, when he damaged your stocking in a button department, for instance. We are getting to know one another in a mild way.'

'Are you connected with the law, Mr Tuam?'

'The law?'

'You said that you might have gone to the law courts.'

'I take an intelligent interest in the law, Mrs Bolsover. That and other matters. Though I am not personally qualified to handle a case.' He lapsed into a meditation. 'Or indeed much else.'

'Oh, I'm sure –'

'Indeed I'm not. I take an interest in sacred things, Mrs Bolsover. I spend part of each day in the Reading Room of the British Museum.'

'How peaceful that must be.'

'It is peaceful indeed. There's a lot of peace about in the Museum. As the poet has it, it comes dropping still.'

'I don't think I've ever been in the Reading Room of the British Museum,' said Eve, drying a soup-plate.

'Today is September the eighth,' said Septimus Tuam. 'We met, Mrs Bolsover, on August the thirty-first, at four o'clock in the afternoon. I remember it well.'

'Yes,' said Eve, thinking that the man spoke peculiarly.

'Eight days have passed since then,' said Septimus Tuam, 'as simple mathematics proves. And in that time much has occurred. You, for instance, have had a dinner party. Your charlady had acquired a hangover. Men have been murdered, Mrs Bolsover,

148

during that time. Men here and there. In the Near and Far East, in the Middle East, and all over the world. New life has entered the world, and old leaves have withered. A lot can happen in eight days. I myself have been taking it easy, Mrs Bolsover. I was making certain of something in my mind.'

Eve nodded, not knowing how to comment.

'Time I find important, Mrs Bolsover: I keep a calendar. The passing of time is good to watch, though occasionally it is not so. It all depends, as so much else in life. It is one hundred and eighty-six hours since you and I first met, for instance, in that excellent department store. Do you have children, Mrs Bolsover?'

The conversation drifted on, its content influenced by the questions and remarks of Septimus Tuam.

'I'm a dab hand with a vacuum cleaner,' he said when the dishes were done. 'I'd love to, really.'

Eve wondered if the man was connected with a domestic agency and would in the end hand her a bill. Odd people penetrated suburban houses these days: Fairy Snow people, the sellers of encyclopedias, women offering dancing lessons, men with brushes made by the blind. It would not surprise her to discover that Mr Tuam had damaged her stocking in a deliberate way and then had telephoned to see the lie of the land and had come with his pair of Bear Brand, which he had said were nine and a half but which were clearly marked as ten. She wondered if the stockings were bought in bulk and if young men like this were working all over London, coming into suburban houses and helping with the chores. She wondered if Mrs Hoop's friend of the evening before hadn't been up to some game like this, although he had spoken of love rather than aid with housework. His face came back to her as a round misty blob, lit up by his expressive smile; angelic, she had thought. The face of Mr Tuam was not like that at all. It was stern in its expression, a serious mien. She watched it, five and a half feet from the ground, intent upon the cleaning of her drawing-room carpet, a face that seemed to reflect a total interest in that task; and a face that had become suddenly – as though some switch had been pulled – a thing of beauty.

Eve, with an orange-coloured duster in her right hand, stood still. Her hand was raised towards an ormolu clock on the mantelpiece, but the hand was motionless. The orange-coloured duster did not float over the ormolu clock, nor did Eve Bolsover's eye blink, nor was she aware of any physical feeling. The engine of the vacuum cleaner made the sound that such engines do; a sparrow in the garden chirped once, alighting on a crumb of bread, and the sound of the chirp came in through the open french windows but was not heard in the room because of the buzz of the vacuum cleaner. A postman poked two letters through the Bolsovers' letter-box and walked away from the house, whistling, not knowing what was happening.

Eve's mind worked again. Her hand, arrested in the air for what had seemed an hour but had been in fact seven seconds, pushed the orange-coloured duster over the ormolu clock; she moved her legs and bent to apply the duster to the surface of a small table.

The noise of the vacuum cleaner ceased, and Septimus Tuam walked to the french windows and said:

'Look, it's a beautiful day.'

She saw his head, held at an angle against grass and shrubs and a few flowers. His head was dark and thin, rather long, seeming as delicate as a doll's. He is a man, she thought, out of a black and white film: there's no colour in him at all; he'd make a good priest. She imagined herself telling Sybil Thornton about the head and the face, and what he had said about going down to the law courts, and the business about the stockings being size ten when he had explained so exactly on the telephone that he had ordered nine and a half on the advice of the girl in the shop. 'He tidied up beautifully, twice as well as Mrs Hoop. "Four pounds ten," he said in the end. "The Acme Domestic Agency."'

'It's a lovely autumn,' said Septimus Tuam.

Edward woke to discover new vigour in his body. He breakfasted quickly off an egg and a tomato, requested of his landlady that he might again borrow her bicycle and set off for the outer suburbs of London, for the house of Mrs Poache. Her written words echoed in his mind, for although they had been transmitted to paper almost seven years ago they retained still their urgent call. *Help me*, Mrs Poache had written simply, *to accept again the humdrum of my life with a husband who would buy me all I ask for, but who murmurs no more a word of love.* She had written much besides. She had written of the man who had stalked into her marriage and had then stalked out again. She had mentioned the philosophical ease with which her husband had tendered his forgiveness, confessing that he too, in those far-off sea-faring days, had wandered from the hard path of virtue. 'Take it easy,' the Captain had advised Mrs Poache, and had not ever again referred to the matter.

After riding for an hour through the sunny morning Edward arrived at his destination. With his bicycle clips still gripping his ankles, he hastened up a short paved path, rang Mrs Poache's door-bell, and prepared a smile for his face. Footsteps sounded in the house, and as he heard them it occurred to Edward that he had no idea of what he was going to say when the door opened and Mrs Poache appeared. Embarrassment at once overcame him, confidence fled as his heart beat wildly, the smile on his face felt false and stickly. 'I am inept,' he muttered, with red burning on his cheeks and a heaving in his stomach. 'Good morning,' said Mrs Poache, the woman who had been dressed in shades of pink and was now attired in a flowered house-coat. 'I'm afraid I don't ever buy at the door.'

'What?' asked Edward. 'Buy, Mrs Poache?'

'I don't buy anything at all.'

'Don't you know me, Mrs Poache?' said Edward. 'Don't I look like your son?' Edward, afterwards, did not know what had inspired him to say that: he should have gone away as soon as Mrs Poache had made the point that she did not purchase goods at the door. He should have beaten a hasty retreat, down the paved path, waving a hand at her and saying it didn't matter a bit. But something held him there, something that he took at first to be further evidence of ineptitude but then decided was the hand of Lady Dolores Bourhardie.

'Why, you were at that fracas,' said Mrs Poache. She felt as embarrassed as Edward himself. She had recognized him straight away as the brother of Septimus Tuam and had spoken as she had in order to give herself time to think.

'We had a talk,' said Edward, 'if you remember?'

'I have never in my life been present at such rubbish. I said to the Captain, "The people are nut-cases."'

'Poor Mrs Hoop was three-parts under.' He had told her he was related to Septimus Tuam; he had said he was tracing him, or trying to, because of a fortune. 'Describe the Septimus Tuam you knew,' was what he should say now. 'Describe every detail, show me a snap if you have one, so that we can be sure it's the same fellow.' But Edward knew that sort of talk would seem irrational and strange to Mrs Poache. 'Why?' she would probably say. 'What's the reason for my showing you a snap?' And all Edward would think of to reply was that all avenues were to be explored. After which, Mrs Poache would send him off with a flea in his ear.

'Well, come in,' said Mrs Poache. 'Don't stand there on the doorstep.'

She led the way into her house, which was a house that was not unlike the Bolsovers', though decorated and furnished differently.

'What a dump that was,' said Mrs Poache. 'Did you ever see the like, that ridiculous object in the hallway?'

'The armour?'

'What else?'

Edward smiled, admiring the details of the house he was now in. Perhaps, he thought, he could stand there admiring, and then just go away. He said he liked Mrs Poache's choice of pictures. She showed him some she had painted herself, adding that she had been guided by numbers.

'Well, bless my boots,' said Edward, shaking his head, not quite knowing what she meant by being guided by numbers.

'I used to be keen,' said Mrs Poache. It was Septimus Tuam who had suggested the pastime to her. They had gone together to a shop to buy her the materials. 'Cheerio,' he had said on the pavement outside, and had there and then walked out of her life.

Mrs Poache looked closely at Septimus Tuam's brother, re-

152

flecting that they did not appear to be much alike. There was
something mysterious about the behaviour of the young man;
she had thought so last night, and she thought so again. She felt
awkward in his presence, simply because he was the brother of
the man, and because she guessed that he had sought her out
with a purpose that was otherwise than his stated one: he had
come to her to deliver a message.

'It's my belief,' said Mrs Poache, 'that the drunken female
was Mrs Bolsover's mother or something of that nature. They
made her out to be the char when she hit the bottle in public.'

'No, no,' said Edward, 'that was Mrs Hoop all right.'

'The Captain gave her alcohol, of course.' In the car on the
way home she had mentioned that to the Captain, questioning
him about whether or not it was customary to go into other
people's houses and give drink to their servants. 'You gave the
charwoman brandy,' she had reminded him. 'What charwoman?' said the Captain, peering myopically through the wind-
screen of his motor-car. 'Look at the cut of you,' Mrs Poache
had cried. 'You're as whistled as a badger.' There the matter had
rested, another reminder for Mrs Poache of the change that had
been wrought in her life since the Captain had left his ship.

'He gave her alcohol,' repeated Mrs Poache. 'There's no escaping that.'

'Listen, Mrs Poache,' said Edward, 'I'm afraid I've been having you on rather. To tell you the truth, I'm not Septimus Tuam's
brother at all.'

'What do you want?' demanded Mrs Poache. 'Have you a
message?'

'How do you mean, Mrs Poache?'

'Have you come here with a message for me? Is that what
you meant? You were talking in riddles last night, you know.
Well, I understand that you had to. Naturally.'

'I work for an organization, Mrs Poache. Seeing to people,
helping them. We're interested in rehabilitation, and in love
within marriage.'

'Love?'

'Love, Mrs Poache.'

'I don't understand you. What's your name?'

'I am a nobody, Mrs Poache. I rode out here on a bicycle. Look here, we're trying our best to help Septimus Tuam. My job depends on it.'

'I don't understand this at all. Why have you come to me? Did you follow me to the Bolsovers' house last night? What do you want of me?'

'A snapshot of Septimus Tuam. I cannot trace him until I know what he looks like. I have stared at the window of his room but a face never comes there. Many people live in that house: how can I tell the one I'm after? I get depressed, Mrs Poache. I have not been well in the past.'

'I don't think I can help you,' said Mrs Poache, sick with disappointment. 'I would have you go away.'

'I've never had a job before, Mrs Poache. I'm trying desperately to take a place in this world, and to grow up into an adult. I feel a child, Mrs Poache: inept and suckling, three years old.'

'A suckling?'

'I need all the help I can get. I am brand-new in my department, Mrs Poache. I have been assigned the task of tracking down and killing Septimus Tuam.'

'Killing?' screamed Mrs Poache, on her feet in an instant, a hand to her lips. 'Killing?'

'Killing?' repeated Edward, wondering why Mrs Poache was talking in that violent way. 'Who said anything about killing?' He smiled and shook his head.

'You did,' screamed Mrs Poache. 'You said it yourself. You're out to murder Septimus Tuam.'

16

As it happened, Eve Bolsover did not ever tell her friend Sybil Thornton that a beautiful man had called at her house with a pair of size ten stockings and had helped with the washing-up and had run the vacuum cleaner over the carpet of her sitting-room.

'A lovely autumn,' said Septimus Tuam, his dark hair coming to a widow's peak at the back of his neck, and she had stood with her orange-coloured duster, feeling as though she would in a moment be again transfixed, unable to move or to think, or to feel anything at all in her body.

The dark head moved farther away from her, out into her garden, among the toys that her children had left there, away towards the sand-pit where the children had played once but where they played no longer, past the swing they never bothered with either. She wanted the man to turn his head so that she could see his face. She wanted him to turn and come back to the room and pick up the hose of the vacuum cleaner and ask her where else there was to clean. But she thought that none of that would happen: she thought that the man in the blue shirt, with the signs of the Zodiac on his tie, would walk away through the garden until she had to screw up her eyes against the autumn sun to see him at all. She would run to the french windows and move her head from left to right, looking all over the garden, and she would remember his corduroy jacket hanging over the back of a kitchen chair and she would run to it and find that it was gone.

'After this most unsettled summer,' said Septimus Tuam, standing in front of her, looking at her.

'Are you from a domestic agency?' She heard herself saying

that, very clearly, in a voice that didn't appear to have much to do with her.

'Domestic?' said Septimus Tuam.

'You've washed the dishes. You've cleaned the carpet. You're going to put your jacket on in a moment, Mr Tuam, and say I owe you four pounds ten. Aren't you?'

'I'm not going to do any such thing. I do assure you, you don't owe me any money at all.'

'Then why have you come?' cried Eve. 'Why have you come here with the wrong size in stockings? Why have you drunk my coffee and washed my dishes? Why have you cleaned a carpet?'

'Because I love you,' said Septimus Tuam, and the beautiful face came close to Eve's own, and the dark hair was there above her. 'Because I love you,' said the Celtic voice. 'Because I love you,' it said again and then again, and after that again. She imagined that she was dying, and she felt the arms of Septimus Tuam clasping her body. I am going to wake up, she thought .

'No,' said the voice of Septimus Tuam. 'We are together at last.'

I7

Edward moved from the outer suburb at a great pace. He felt the breeze bracing on the skin of his face, but he felt as well a swelling fear. Unable to think clearly in motion, he drew his bicycle to a halt. He placed a chain and padlock on it and proceeded to a café frequented by the drivers of heavy vehicles, where he ordered his favourite beverage, a cup of tea. Desiring above all else to be alone, he took it to a table that was empty of other customers and which contained in the way of comestibles only some pepper in a red container.

Edward stared ahead of him, beyond the immediate area, through a window. People were walking up and down, occasionally stopping to talk to one another in a friendly way. It was all very well, Edward thought.

He had denied the statement that Mrs Poache had attributed to him; he had denied it five times, as often as she repeated it. 'You haven't got it wrong,' he said, smiling. 'You've only put in a bit.' And then he had felt strange, and the smile had oozed from his face. 'Killing?' he said, and he remembered, afterwards, the sound of the words as they had come from him, the emphasis he had placed on them and the peculiar sensation that had strayed into his mind.

'You're not in your right senses,' Mrs Poache had said, quieter now and showing no fear in his company. 'I do not love him now,' she said, 'but I'll save Septimus Tuam.'

Edward felt worse than he had ever felt in his life. From the café window he could see posters on a hoarding, and he laughed ironically that posters on a hoarding should ever have upset him. 'The Brothers have made a thing of it,' he heard a voice say. 'Those Brothers down by the sea. St Gregory's is right for Edward Blakeston-Smith. Wouldn't you say so?' Another voice agreed, and added that the Brothers had done well to turn an honest penny in this way, measuring out tranquillity to those upset by the times they lived in. 'The hurly-burly of life,' said this voice, 'has got this youngster down. He is not at all dangerous.' Edward's father returned from the dead to impart a word or two on the subject. 'You are taking refuge in your childhood,' said Edward's father. 'Honour your Queen, sir. Do your job.'

Edward knew that he could not return to St Gregory's. He couldn't go now and sit in the autumnal sun, playing draughts with Brother Toby, buying quietude. Lady Dolores would winkle him out and draw him away towards his deed: she had made him her instrument and if he wished to escape her he must find himself a long way away, with a new identity. He must go into hiding; he must seem, to Lady Dolores and the Brothers at St Gregory's, and anyone else who mattered, to be well and truly dead. 'All this wretched love thing,' said Edward. 'Is it the cause of everything?' He remembered dreams about the poster people and the dream about his father in the love department, when Septimus Tuam had been hanged on Wimbledon Common and then had been hustled on to a hoarding. 'All this love,' said Edward again, thinking of Mrs Poache and of Beach loving Mrs Hoop, and the fat man saying he could enter a state of love over Mrs Hoop, and Septimus Tuam, and Mr FitzArthur, and Lady Dolores telling him to look for love in the eyes of all he met, referring to snow-flakes. 'We all set up a department of a kind,' Lady Dolores had said. 'As I have set up mine, though in a different way.' It would be best, he reckoned, to drink his tea and leave the café in a hurry. It would be best to get on to that borrowed bicycle and never appear in the vicinity of the love department again, to ride that bicycle in a northerly direction, far out of London, through woods and villages and country towns, by humming telegraph poles. It would be best to get away, to stop at some place and eat a cheap meal and buy a battery for the light, and then to ride on, into a cold night. He would offer himself for labour at a farm, and spend a day or two and then move on, and do the same again, until the tyres of the bicycle were shredded to ribbons and the spokes gave way beneath the urgency he was inflicting.

'I shall ride away,' said Edward in a soft voice. 'I shall ride to the north, and then north after that, and then north again. Why should I kill this Septimus Tuam?'

He drank his tea and felt a little calmer. He left the café and unlocked the bicycle and put the chain and the padlock in his pocket. 'I have come from the west,' he said. 'The north must be up there to the left.'

He aimed his bicycle in this adventurous direction, but he soon became confused and tired in a maze of suburban roads and avenues. 'I couldn't ride this bicycle up to some farm,' he said aloud, and then, since he had no money, he turned round and began to ride it into London. Afterwards, telling his story, he said he had been impelled to do that, as he had been impelled to do everything else, but nobody believed him.

At half past eleven that same morning James Bolsover took his jacket off and frowned at the white substance all over the back of it. 'You could bake a cake,' he heard one of the board-men say and he wished to hear the man say more, to say that, speaking for himself, he had had enough. Another man murmured that they were not in the granary business, and did not smile.

The men had discussed the events of the evening before, the ones who had not been present protesting that the others were exaggerating, the others denying the charge. They stood witness for each other, repeating the facts one after another: a drunken woman had set about the guests, a pet had been maddened by a road-cleaner with a sweeping-brush. 'Was it a joke?' one of the sceptics asked, but the men who had been at the Bolsovers' dinner party said that it was no joke at all. Mr Linderfoot explained how the drunken woman had attached herself to him, when all he had been doing was trying to help. He said that with an eye on Mr Clinger, fearing that Mr Clinger would recall that the facts had been different; but Mr Clinger, recalling or not recalling, held his peace. 'Eleven Crannoc Avenue,' murmured one of the men who had not been there. 'I must write that down in case I'm ever passing.'

The men thought variously as they watched James remove his jacket in the board-room. A few of them thought that it was all of a piece, dust on his clothes and the inability to organize a dinner party in a pleasant way. Captain Poache thought that there seemed to be poltergeists in this man's life.

James held his jacket in his left hand, brushing it with his right. He saw one of the eight men rise to his feet, which was unusual, for discussion did not demand this formality. He put his jacket on, knowing it was smeared. The man said:

'We do not come into this room in such a manner. We do not even enter this building in the morning in such a manner. Who does, even amongst the messenger lads? Mr Bolsover is newly elected to this board. I ask you, is he laughing at us?'

There was a silence around the table. The men thought of the error they had apparently made in inviting James Bolsover to join them on the board. They were prepared to give him every chance, but it seemed as though the eccentricities might go on for ever. He had been a man of outstanding ability, which made it, to the men of the board-room, a sadder thing. 'I offer no explanation,' said James. 'I do not know.'

The eight men saw James replace his jacket. They sighed and thought of what must surely have been an error, thinking as well, and at the same time, of glasses of gin and tonic water, with pieces of lemon floating on top, and cubes of ice. They sighed once more and spoke of other matters; Mr Clinger mentioned door handles.

James heard and did not say much. They noted that he did not say much, and wondered idly about that too, assuming that he was less interested than they in the organization and affairs of the firm. James could feel them assuming that and wished they would hold their peace no more. He imagined the future again: the basement flat in s.w.17, the man with the spreading Air Force moustache, the ironmongers' shops, and the cards of samples that he drew from a leather case, a case that was not a brief-case. He was aware of the voice of Miss Brown in his ear. He turned his head and saw her face and noted a sadness in her eyes. His father, she was saying, was dead.

'Turn left here,' said Septimus Tuam, 'and then absolutely straight.'

He had known, in similar circumstances, many kinds of houses: his senses had occasionally been offended by their interiors, but more often he had not noticed, because it wasn't his place to notice, or so he considered. He had become well used to admiring houses utterly without reservation, that being the easier course to adopt. In his pocket now was the key to the house of Mrs FitzArthur, a place he admired, most genuinely, in many ways. 'Who fancies the cheery voice of your Mrs Hoop all of a sudden?' he had said to Eve in her sitting-room, and had added that he would like to conduct her to a house that was half a mile away. 'I'm care-taking for a relative,' he said. 'I'd like to show you the garden.' And he had led the way to the car in which they now sat side by side.

'It's like a dream,' said Eve, 'in which a woman goes out of her wits. I feel I'm suffering from something.'

Her companion did not comment on this. He drew the corners of his mouth down. He said:

'These are super little cars, so nippy in the traffic. I have never owned a car. I've never had the money.'

The small red car cut among the traffic, outwitting ones that had to be careful of their long, luxurious bodywork.

'What did you think,' said Eve, 'that day in Ely's?'

'I thought a simple thing, as others have before: that I had never seen anyone so beautiful.'

'While I,' said Eve in a womanly way, 'I'm afraid I hardly noticed you.'

Septimus Tuam, who was used to everything, did not take offence at this statement. Why should he take offence, he considered, since she would notice him now, and notice no one else, for a time to come?

'Have you taken offence?' cried Eve, removing her eyes from the road to glance at him.

'Look where you're going,' he said. 'Who fancies an accident?'

'Aren't you offended?'

'I am offended,' he said in a sulky tone. 'I am offended beyond measure.'

The car passed along Cannizaro Road, and turned a corner sharply at the Rimini Hotel.

'Look out,' said Septimus Tuam. 'You nearly had that fellow off his bike.' He looked over his shoulder through the window by his left side to see that all was well with the cyclist. He saw a young man with red cheeks, arrested in his tracks; annoyed, apparently, that he had been stopped so abruptly in his progress by the swerving of the red Mini Minor.

'It was his fault,' said Septimus Tuam, shrill with anger, for this, he recognized, was one he had noticed before: the red-cheeked oddity who had been hanging about the rooming-house.

The traffic halted and Eve's car halted with it. The young man on his bicycle, with more room to manoeuvre, continued to progress. He looked ahead when he could move no farther forward and saw that a set of lights was the cause of this delay. To steady himself he reached out his right arm and placed a hand on the roof of the small red car that a moment ago had almost struck him. As he did so, he was aware of a rapping on the window of this car and, glancing down, beheld an angry face.

'What an ugly-looking fellow,' said Edward to himself, and then he saw, and recognized, the head of Eve Bolsover. He tried to attract her attention; he smiled through the glass. 'Go away,' said Septimus Tuam, waving with his hand. Edward looked into the deep dark eyes of the man with Mrs Bolsover. 'Hullo,' he heard a voice say, and saw that Eve Bolsover had recognized him in turn. What's she doing out in a Mini Minor with a chap like that? thought Edward. Why isn't she making something for her children's tea? Edward put a hand on the roof of the car again. The window was at once lowered and the man with Eve Bolsover again said:

'Go away.'

The man turned to Mrs Bolsover and reported: 'He has put his hand on the roof of your car. This one's a public nuisance. What do you mean,' said Septimus Tuam to Edward, 'by hanging around, staring at the house I live in? Take your hand off this car at once.'

'The house you live in? What do you mean?'

'You know well what I mean. You're a public nuisance, standing around with that woman's bicycle.'

'You're never Septimus Tuam?' whispered Edward in a frightened voice. 'You're never, are you?'

'You know quite well who I am,' said Septimus Tuam furiously.

'He arrived in my house last night,' said Eve. 'It's really all right, I think: he's apparently a friend of Mrs Hoop's.' She smiled, trying to keep the peace. The lights changed to amber and then to green. Septimus Tuam wound up the glass of the window, and the red car moved on.

'There's Septimus Tuam,' said Edward aloud to himself. 'There's the man I'm scheduled to kill.'

'Bolsover'll be away a day or two,' said Lake. 'Burials take a bit of time. Now is our hour.'

Lake probed the future and witnessed himself in his elastic-sided boots and sharply-cut suit, stepping into James Bolsover's office and sitting down behind his desk. While he did so, the men in the board-room were turning one to another and saying that Lake had better join them since Lake was rising so steadily within the firm and increasingly made so valuable a contribution. 'What if he left us?' he heard one board-man cry. 'My God!' cried out another, and there was a murmur around the table. 'Send for Lake,' the demand went up, and a moment later he rose from behind the desk once occupied by Bolsover and walked along the corridors until he arrived at the important room. He entered it, and displayed commendable calmness when the proposition was put to him.

Lake smiled more effusively as he thought of that, but then, with a familiar kind of nagging, he thought, What of Brownie? He thought for a while longer, in a most severely practical vein, and he believed when he had finished that Brownie would surely understand if he put the difficulty to her in a delicate way. He nodded briskly, and probed the future once more: he saw himself with a rising young starlet, strolling about a night-club frequented by royalty and sporting people.

'I am right for that,' said Lake, speaking to Miss Brown without explanation. 'I could take it in my stride, eh?'

Lady Dolores licked chocolate icing from her thumb, and asked Edward what the matter was. She remarked that he was flushed.

'Lady Dolores, I'd like once for all to be taken off the outside jobs. I am far from suited to the work.'

'Why not? You come here looking for work, Mr Blakeston-Smith, and all the time you're saying you're not suited. What's up?'

'I don't get on with people,' said Edward. 'I have a way of putting myself across them. I mistook a man for Septimus Tuam and ordered him to a rehabilitation centre. Another hit me, an East End butcher. I've had no success at all.'

Lady Dolores raised her eyebrows. She took her glasses off and rubbed them with a tissue, and then replaced them. Edward said:

'As for that list of women, I couldn't go up to their doors for all the rice in China.'

'Rice, Mr Blakeston-Smith?'

'It's a saying. It's vernacular speech.'

'I know it's a saying, old fellow.' She paused. She pressed a cigarette into her holder and applied a pink-tipped match to it. 'So you couldn't go up to the doors for all the rice in China?'

Edward shook his head, and then hung it down.

'Not even as the gas man? Or a window-cleaner, or a bloke with beauty aids? Someone must read the meters, you know. Someone must. And someone must clean the windows. Don't tell me that all the windows out there are left dirty. Don't tell me that, Mr Blakeston-Smith, for I won't believe you.'

'I'm not telling you that.'

'Well, then?'

'I'm not capable of any of it. I wouldn't have the stuffing for that kind of thing. I'd be afraid, Lady Dolores.'

'Afraid?'

'Yes.'

'Afraid of the women, is that it? You'd be afraid to go up to a door and ring a bell and ask to read the gas meter.'

'Am I dismissed?'

'As you wish now.'

Edward experienced relief. He experienced sadness, too, for he would go now and not ever again see the love department. He'd never again smell the mingled scent or hear the words. But he wouldn't have to kill Septimus Tuam. He rose and moved towards the door, feeling the tears that Lady Dolores had first of all inspired in him. He thought he could probably go and work in Foyle's. He said:

'Goodbye then, Lady Dolores. I'm sorry I was no good.'

Lady Dolores sat still, her cigarette-holder in the centre of her mouth, smoke coming from her nostrils. She watched the young man trying to go away, feeling his embarrassment as she had often in the past felt the embarrassment of other young men. They walked from her office when they had not been a success, and walked through the larger office in which they had sat at a desk. They heard for the last time the clerks murmuring their words, and they said goodbye beneath their breath, trying not to draw attention to themselves. They passed through the typists' room; they closed that third door behind them and left the love department for ever.

Lady Dolores took the cigarette-holder from the centre of her mouth and knocked some ash from the point of her cigarette on to the floor. She had not ceased to watch the young man. She said:

'Where are you going, Mr Blakeston-Smith?'

'I might get a job in Foyle's,' he said.

'Foyle's wouldn't give you a job,' said Lady Dolores, 'not for all the rice in China. Didn't you know that?'

Edward said he hadn't known that, and Lady Dolores said:

'Tell the truth, Mr Blakeston-Smith. Tell the truth and shame the devil. You've done a good day's work. You are frightened by worldly matters; you are frightened by success. Be your age, old chap: tell me the lie of the land.'

'I'm speaking through a layer of wool,' said the voice in the desk sergeant's ear, 'since I do not wish to be mixed up in anything. Why then do you imagine I'd tell you what my name is?'

'What is your name, please?' repeated the desk sergeant.

'Who cares about my name,' cried the voice, 'when a man is about to be murdered?'

'Well, we do, sir,' said the desk sergeant. 'Actually, we care very much.'

'Septimus Tuam is to be killed by an assassin. Act on that, can't you?'

'Come now,' began the desk sergeant.

'I've had a visit from an agent.'

'Now,' began the desk sergeant again, but as he spoke the telephone was replaced at the other end and he heard only a blankness on the line. The desk sergeant jerked his head and sighed. He pulled a mug of tea towards him and drank a mouthful before returning to a list of motor-car registration numbers.

'They'll move in fast,' murmured Mrs Poache, taking one of the Captain's socks from the mouthpiece of the telephone. She imagined the police cars surrounding Septimus Tuam's place, waiting for the young man to ride up on his bicycle with a weapon hidden beneath his clothes. She imagined them moving in on the young man, seizing him as she saw men seized daily on her television screen.

18

James saw before him the nurse who had written him so many letters and to whom he had talked at length on the telephone. He thanked her for all she had done. 'I was going to come down the week-end after next,' he said. 'I know,' replied the nurse.

She gathered all her things together, talking as she did so. She walked about the house with James, making certain that she had left nothing behind.

'I have left nothing,' she said, 'except my patient.'

His father would have said that this was the most significant nurse of all who had attended him because she was the one in whose care he had died. 'He said he saw the marble ledge before he went,' she said. 'And his wife sitting on it.'

'You did what you could,' said James. 'It wasn't easy.'

'I wouldn't know how to take cuttings of nasturtiums. I told him it was the wrong time of year, but he said who cared about that? In the end I went down to the greenhouses and put in a packet of seeds.'

She took James to the garden and showed him her handiwork. She had shovelled soil into a wooden tomato box and had sprinkled on top of it a packet of antirrhinum seeds. 'He was there in the bed,' said the nurse, 'and he hardly saw a soul. You'd feel sorry for him.'

James looked round the ruined greenhouse. Bits of flower-pots were everywhere, and white enamel pails with patches of rust and broken handles, and lengths of wood. He remembered the place in its heyday. The nurse said:

'I came into his room wearing an old pair of Wellington boots with leaves and mud all over them. "Where've you been?" he said to me and I told him I'd been out in the greenhouses planting snapdragons for him. He hadn't another bad thing to say, Mr Bolsover.'

James shook hands with the nurse and helped her to tie her suitcase on to the carrier of her bicycle. She said she'd borrowed a book by Jeffery Farnol and that she'd post it back, but James said not to bother about posting anything.

'I was cross with him often,' she said before she cycled away, 'but he died attended by love, Mr Bolsover. I'll promise you that.'

James waved after her, but she was looking ahead of her and couldn't see him. She had softened in her loneliness in the ugly old house. She had stepped out of her brisk manner because she had been moved in the end by the decay and the smell of death. She had carried a tomato box to a greenhouse to perform an action that she considered absurd. Others, who might have been less brisk in the beginning, might have been satisfied to make a kindly pretence by announcing that the action had been safely done.

The funeral took place in misty afternoon sunshine. A coffin slipped into its narrow slit, earth dropped on to it, words were spoken. James saw before him his father holding up a bag of burnt chestnuts on Christmas Eve, 1934, and heard his mother tartly say that the fare was unsuitable for children at seven o'clock in the evening. He remembered then the purple restaurant in which he and Eve had celebrated their tenth wedding anniversary, and the *bruciate briachi* that had stirred the memory in his mind, where it had lingered, apparently, ever since.

He walked from the graveside, nodding to people, recalling how he had gone on drearily that evening about the eight men in the board-room and the fact of his father's dying. Eve had been bored to tears, and really, he thought, he couldn't blame her. 'How about the garden, sir?' a man said to him. 'Will you be taking an interest, then?' James smiled, shaking his head. The man said he had once been employed in the garden, and simply wondered: he had been fond, he said, of Mr Bolsover, and had known Mrs Bolsover too. James remembered his parents working together in their industrious way, planning and purchasing, and talking about the vagaries of weather. He remembered the heart going out of his father when his mother had died; his sloping away on the day that he and Eve had been married, leaving the lawns of the hotel without a word to anyone.

The house would have to be tidied up and sold. There'd be an auction and his father's clothes would have to be got out of the way first, handed on to a charitable cause. As he walked about, passing from one high-ceilinged room to another and depressed simply to be there, James wondered who'd want a house like this nowadays. Who'd want a house with bad wiring and no modern kitchen arrangements of any kind, a place without central heating, that hadn't been painted or papered for thirty years? Who'd want a house with two staircases, and attic rooms that were full of damp, and rambling acres of garden wilderness? He wondered if workmen would ever come and set up the long greenhouses that he had played in as a child, if their shelves would ever again be covered in pots of flowers. Perhaps, he thought, the house might make a preparatory school or a lunatic asylum, and he visualized both sets of inmates.

'I've got a house to sell,' James said the next morning, standing in the office of an estate agent.

'Sir,' said a man in tweeds. 'And where would that be?'

James told him, and the man, who was, he said, new in the area, added that he didn't know the place and suggested that they drive out together to take a look at it.

'My father died,' said James in the car, 'having lived there alone, with a daily woman coming in, and a resident nurse. He had been an invalid.'

'Sorry to hear all that, sir,' said the estate agent, waving at a prospective client. 'Elderly, sir?'

'Eighty-one this month. He and my mother ran a market garden there in their time. That makes this more difficult, I think. The whole place is something of a shambles.'

'I have an aged dad myself,' remarked the estate agent thoughtfully. 'Gives us the hell of a time.'

'I mean,' said James, 'we couldn't try and sell it as a market garden. Nothing like that. Everything's far gone.'

'Not to worry sir,' said the estate agent, but when they arrived at the house he gave a whistle and kept his lips pursed for some time afterwards.

'I thought an auction of the furniture,' said James. 'Wouldn't that be best? And then just sell the rest as best you can.' He led the way around the rooms, and the estate agent wagged his head knowingly. From time to time he heaved his shoulders and sighed. He said eventually:

'You know, sir, it would pay you to tart this old property up a piece.' He dug his heel into a rotting board in the dining-room and twisted it about, powdering the surface of the wood. 'Fix up that kind of thing, put in a bit of heating and an Aga cooker, slap on a coat or two of paint.'

'No,' said James. 'I don't at all want that. I want it taken off my hands. I know it's large and inconvenient, but surely some institution would have a use for it?'

'It's large, sir, yes, but then not large enough to take an institution. A country club, maybe.'

'I thought a prep school. Or an asylum.'

'Oh, no, sir,' said the estate agent, and vouchsafed no explanation beyond the statement that though large in one way the house was small in others.

'I'll have the clothes carted off,' said James. 'I'll have that done before I return to London.'

'Personal effects. If you would, sir.'

'And leave everything else with you. Ask whatever price you think suitable, and release me as soon as possible of the liability.'

The estate agent drove away after a brief discussion of details, and James was left with his father's clothes, sorting them out and tying them into bundles. When he had finished, he lit a fire in the room that had been his father's study and sat down beside it with bundles of letters and papers, most of which he burnt.

In London, speaking to Septimus Tuam, Eve said that she should be with her husband. 'I should be with him now,' she said. 'There'll be a lot to do.'

'How could you?' murmured Septimus Tuam. 'You've got these kiddies to see to. You've got to go on as always, driving them off to school and preparing food for meals. I know a mother's drill, dear.'

Eve did not understand why she had fallen in love with Septimus Tuam as she had so clearly understood her love for James. More than ten years ago James had courted her in a conventional way, in a way that was agreeable to understand. He had stood beside her, a handsome man, and made a fuss of her; Septimus Tuam seemed still to trail absurdity. Septimus Tuam was a figure of fun almost, with his soft corduroy suit and peculiar speech. Septimus Tuam seemed to have a dimension missing – yet that, Eve felt, must in fairness be an impression gained because she didn't know him very well. She felt absurd herself when she was with him. She had felt that in Crannoc Avenue when she had stood with the orange-coloured duster, unable to move it; she had felt it when he had spoken about his uncle Lord Marchingpass. He had seemed like someone who might be in a circus, and he made her feel as though she belonged there too.

Eve tried to glimpse a future, but it came to her only in bits and pieces. She saw Septimus Tuam playing with a coloured ball, throwing it from one of her children to the other, as though employed to perform that task. She saw herself with him, without her children, in a country that appeared to be of the Middle East. Recognizing all the silliness in it, she beheld a romantic scene: a quiet wedding, attended by a handful of friendly Arabs, and a celebration at which the local food was consumed in quantity. 'Bless your heart, my love,' Septimus Tuam was saying in this scene, wearing a grey hat. He had some journalistic job; he was engaged upon sending reports back to England on some political upheaval.

'I am a seventh child,' her lover said. 'I am the runt of that family.' He spoke, it seemed to Eve, with that grey linen hat lazily upon his head, leaning over a typewriter that was gritty with desert sand. And it seemed, almost, to be as part of the wedding ceremony that he had offered the information that he was the seventh child and the runt of his family. She closed her eyes, and the friendly Arabs danced.

'I nearly died,' said Septimus Tuam, 'as a matter of fact. My mother had reached the end of her tether.'

Eve sat up and blew her nose. She smiled, and Septimus Tuam said:

'I should have dropped dead from my mother's womb: I

171

should have been the subject of a little funeral. I might have lived two hours.'

'Oh, my dear, please don't say all that –'

'Visualize this coffin, eight inches long. Fairies could carry it.'

'It's not a time to think of coffins.'

'I was an unwanted child. An error of judgement.'

Eve shook her head, but Septimus Tuam nodded his.

'My brothers and sisters threw tins and boxes at me. I was struck all over the head. The dog took exception to me. I invaded the dog's domain.'

'Well, you are wanted now.'

He spoke of love. He said that love, in its way, made the world go round. He repeated phrases he had heard on the wireless or had read in picture magazines. He said he loved Eve Bolsover; he said he didn't know how he had ever existed without her.

'I've been a bad lad,' said Septimus Tuam, 'I've been a bad lad in my time, with lots of ladies. I've led them up the garden path. I've done a naughty thing or two.'

Eve closed her eyes. Everyone, she said, had done a naughty thing or two.

'I don't mind admitting it,' said Septimus Tuam. 'I am making a confession, as I would make it direct to the Maker. I know what there is to know: I have never loved till I came to love you.'

Eve said she loved him in turn. She talked for a while about James, confessing that she felt particularly guilty, since she, as much as he, was responsible for the decay in their marriage. 'We were on parallel lines,' she said, 'and you know what happens with those.'

'Ah, yes,' said Septimus Tuam, thinking of something else altogether, of a character called Creeko, actually, whose adventures he was currently reading about in a serial story. Creeko, as far as Septimus Tuam could see, was destined to burn to death, since he had taken up a precarious position on the roof of a wooden building that ravaging Redskins had lit with an oil flare.

'Poor James,' said Eve.

Septimus Tuam nodded his head.

'I love you,' said Eve.

'My dear, of course you do,' said Septimus Tuam. 'Why ever shouldn't you?'

'Poor James,' said Eve again.

Lake wondered which of the eight men to approach, and decided in the end to take his tale to Mr Linderfoot, because he imagined that in conversation with Mr Linderfoot he might kill two birds with one stone. He reckoned that it was now only a matter of time before Bolsover was totally discredited, and as soon as that happened there would arise at once the problem of what to do about Brownie. He wished to hasten the discrediting of Bolsover and the dispatch of Brownie to other pastures, leaving him with a straight run to Bolsover's position and a starlet.

Mr Linderfoot took the wrapping off a Rennies tablet and slipped the medicine on to his tongue. He said:

'By all means have a word with me, Lake. Have two or three, Lake.' He laughed and Lake laughed.

'Confidential, Mr Linderfoot. A confidential matter.'

'Why not?' said Mr Linderfoot. 'Make it as confidential as you wish. Sit down, old friend. Take the weight off your dogs.'

'Thank you, sir.'

'I tell you what, Lake, I wish I was your age. There's some talent in the building these days, eh? Grrr!'

'Grrr, sir,' said Lake.

'I suppose a bachelor like yourself would be getting it from a different source every night? I can just see you, old friend, moving into action.'

Lake smiled enormously. He said:

'Mr Bolsover, sir, is a sickish man. We've been noticing, Mr Linderfoot, those of us who work close to him, and we decided it best to come into the open and pass on the information. For the sake of the company and its trading, sir.'

'When I was your age, Lake, I was out every night of my life. I used to know a girl by the name of Sandra Flynn. By gum, she could put it away. She worked for a solicitor down Epping way.'

Lake smiled and murmured. Mr Linderfoot said:

'There was another, I remember, who kept a confectionery kiosk. I was buying a bar of Crunchie off her one day and she gave me the green light. "Close up that stall," I said, "and come out for a spin." I was away, I said to myself. And so I was, Lake.'

'I was saying about Mr Bolsover, sir. He's a sick man, Mr Linderfoot.'

'The wife is a fine-looking piece of goods.'

'I've never met Mrs Bolsover.'

'Five foot five inches, good bones and skin, attractive hair. There was another woman in the Bolsovers' house. A Mrs Hoop who threw herself all over me, you know. I was being helpful in an emergency and up comes this creature with her green light going, as keen as a copper.'

'You were in Mr Bolsover's house, sir?'

'A few of us were: Clinger, the Captain and myself, with what wives we could muster.' Mr Linderfoot paused, thinking back. He shook his head and said, 'There's some, Lake, who wouldn't understand a passing attachment of any kind at all. "She was on to me like a leech," I was obliged to report when a few members of the board were discussing the incident afterwards. "I couldn't get rid of the girl," I put it to them, when the gospel truth was I was giving as good as I got. "Come out to the kitchen," I said, "till we see what it's like there." You mightn't believe it, old friend, but there's some in our organization who could be stuffy over a thing like that. Our Mr Clinger, for example, doesn't know one end of a woman from the other.'

'You had a pleasant evening at the Bolsover's house, Mr Linderfoot?'

'I wouldn't have said so at all, actually. More like a shambles. Clinger behaved badly, arguing like a street vendor and bringing a tropical animal into the house.'

Lake, who had feared that Bolsover had improved his position by inviting his seniors to his house, was relieved to hear that the occasion had not been successful. He said:

'Mr Bolsover could do with a break, sir. I was wondering about compassionate leave, sir. Miss Brown has noticed the same. The way things are at the moment it's only a question of time.'

'Who's Miss Brown?'

'Mr Bolsover's young secretary. The Welsh girl, sir, with the glasses.'

'Welsh, eh?'

'Miss Brown hails from Llanberis, sir.'

'Does she, by Jove?'

'Mr Bolsover's under an intolerable strain, sir. You understand, Mr Linderfoot, that Miss Brown and I are particularly devoted to Mr Bolsover? We would lay down our lives for Mr Bolsover, sir. We have come to know him, sir.'

'Llanberis, eh?'

'Miss Brown came to me, sir, feeling it was her duty. "Excuse me, Mr Lake," she said, and then paused, sir, as I did just now before relating the matter to you. She stood by my desk, sir, and said this was a delicate thing and highly confidential.'

'You've got her with child, have you? We can't have that, old friend. There are new ways, Lake.'

'I have not done any such thing, Mr Linderfoot. I'm not that sort of person, sir. "What's on your mind, Miss Brown?" I said, speaking in an informal way.'

'You are puzzling me greatly, old friend.'

'All I am saying, sir, is that Mr Bolsover is not well. Everyone who works near him has noticed it. "It's his memory," said Miss Brown, "his memory's failing him all over the place." Apparently, he stuffs the company's letters into his pockets and throws them into the river in the lunch-hour. "What can we do to help him?" I questioned Miss Brown. "How can we help?" "If we can, we must," cried Miss Brown. "That poor man." '

'Quite right of Miss Brown,' said Mr Linderfoot, wondering what all this was about. He found himself staring at Lake's head and thinking it odd that Lake should have no hair at his age. He wondered if he had ever had hair, but did not like to ask him.

'So Miss Brown said to me, "Go and see Mr Linderfoot. Mr Linderfoot will know what to do," Miss Brown, sir, has a very high opinion of you.'

'Of me, old friend?' said Mr Linderfoot quietly. 'Are you sure of that?' Mr Linderfoot narrowed his eyes. He drew his lips back from his teeth. He made a sucking noise before he spoke. He said:

'What else does Miss Brown say?'

'She agrees with me, sir. She thinks Mr Bolsover is under an intolerable strain.'

'I think I'd like to meet this Miss Brown some time.'

I am now moving into position two, said Lake to himself. *Watch this.*

'You would like Miss Brown, I think, sir. She has a very attractive figure. In the office she has the reputation of being a person of unawakened passion. Welsh girls are amongst the most passionate in these isles. I've heard that said.'

'What's her hair like?'

'A head of curls, Mr Linderfoot. Chestnut.'

'Ask her to drop by and see me,' ordered Mr Linderfoot in a low voice, not looking at Lake, already planning to take the girl to a public house and give her a few glasses of gin no matter what she looked like. But Lake was making a sound that was unusual for him to make. It was a protesting sound, a sound that suggested that for Mr Linderfoot it was not going to be as easy as that.

'If you'll pardon me, Mr Linderfoot,' he was saying, 'I think you'd need to advance with a certain caution where Miss Brown is concerned. She is not a girl to be taken unawares.'

'What d'you mean, old friend?'

'Let me prime the situation, sir. Let me drop a hint or two into Miss Brown's ear, explaining the advantages. Otherwise the manoeuvre might come to nothing at all. Which would be a pity, Mr Linderfoot, with so interesting a child.'

'A child, is she?'

'Little more,' said Lake. 'How about my having a word with Miss Brown while you, sir, look into the Bolsover business? Will you do that, sir, to please Miss Brown and myself? We would be happier in our minds, sir; Miss Brown would rest happier in her bed, sir.'

'In her bed, eh?' said Mr Linderfoot.

Lake clapped his hands gently together. He began to wink one eye and grin and laugh in a nudgingly familiar manner.

'What's the matter with you?' demanded Mr Linderfoot.

'I was just thinking about Miss Brown, sir.'

'Don't,' said Mr Linderfoot. 'I'll do the thinking about Miss Brown.'

Later that day Mr Linderfoot called a meeting of the older members of the board. He said:

'I am loath to say it, but I have no option. The presence of Mr Bolsover on this board has not proved to be a satisfactory thing. I said at the time that he was too young a man, and what I am saying now is that the strain has been too great for him. It is all very well for men of our maturity, men who have been through the mill of life and have experience to fall back on, but it's not at all so with poor Bolsover. Bolsover, I need hardly remind you, has repeatedly arrived in this room with powder on his clothes. We do not know why it is on his clothes; we do not know where the powder comes from; we do not know what this powder is. Someone said, at first, that it was Keatings' Powder, placed there for a purpose; and then the theory was that it was lime, that Bolsover for a reason of his own was involved with a kiln. Lately, some of us have come to believe that this powder is nothing more or less than common or garden baker's flour. So there we are. Bolsover offers no explanation in the world. He stands in his shirt and trousers, expecting us to wipe him down. On the face of it, it might seem to be a jest of some kind.'

'What are you on about?' interrupted Mr Clinger. 'We know all this, you know.'

'I am coming to my point, old friend,' said Mr Linderfoot. 'I have a revelation. Bear with me while I sketch in a simple background.'

'It'll take all day. He's as slow as a snail.'

'I am moving at the right speed for the purpose. I am speaking in confidence, you know.'

'All proceedings in this room are confidential,' pointed out one of the eight. 'Have you finished, Linderfoot? Is there to be undue delay?'

'I am merely saying what I have to say.'

'Well, hurry up,' snapped Mr Clinger. 'We'll be here all night.'

'It has now been borne in upon me,' continued Mr Linderfoot, 'that Bolsover is under a severe strain. Recently some of us were invited to Bolsover's house, to share a repast. We saw then, I think, that all was not well. We saw an occasion get out of hand. We witnessed one of our fellow guests attacked by a jungle animal, a development with which Bolsover proved inadequate to deal. Bolsover on this occasion summoned to the house three characters who better belonged on the music-hall stage. Now why did Bolsover do that? Why did Bolsover take it into his head to bring among us an elderly man with a sweeping-brush, a youth who claimed to be the son of the Captain's, and an unfortunate medical man who didn't know whether he was coming or going? Why, I say,' repeated Mr Linderfoot, leaning forward, his hands set firmly on the red baize of the board-room table, 'why did Bolsover do that?'

'For heaven's sake, Linderfoot,' exclaimed Mr Clinger. 'Are we to sit here and listen to all this? There's still this question of the door-handles and these wretched china pans –'

'I think,' said Captain Poache, 'that Linderfoot is going to make a point about Bolsover's behaviour. Some explanation, maybe. I could be wrong.'

'Quite wrong,' snapped Mr Clinger. 'We have problems enough without adding to them. That woman who interfered with my pet at the Bolsovers' house was not a guest: she happened to be the charwoman. Linderfoot should get his facts right.'

The men stretched their legs beneath the table, sniffing and whistling while Mr Clinger and Mr Linderfoot argued on. Peace was restored when Mr Clinger produced one of the older door-handles from his pocket and threw it impatiently on to the table for all to see. Ten minutes later Mr Linderfoot rose to his feet again and placed his hands on the red baize. He said:

'Bolsover, you might think, was having us on again. Bolsover, you might say, was up to more tricks, laughing his head off at his elders and betters. But with what has come to light, I would now report to you that the events fit a pattern. Here is the explanation for the powder on the clothes, the workman with the brush, the youth who was an impostor and the unfortunate medical man; Bolsover has developed a loose slate.'

'You mean he's mental?' said one of the men.

'I have been informed by those working with Bolsover that he throws unopened business letters into the River Thames. I am told his memory is in a frightful state. They are covering up for Bolsover in his department while our customers complain. His colleagues in their loyalty have come to me with the story that Bolsover needs compassionate leave so that he can pull himself together.'

'Why to you?' asked Mr Clinger. 'Why ever did they come to Linderfoot?'

'Because they'd get a hearing,' said Mr Linderfoot with heat, the fat on his body shaking with anger. Clinger was behaving like a cheapjack, he thought, interrupting and trying to make him seem a fool. 'They came to me because they knew they would find sympathy at home. They would go to some and get a mauling from a jungle beast.'

Mr Clinger protested, but the other board-men took no notice of the disagreeable squabbling between Mr Linderfoot and Mr Clinger. They shook their heads and devoured stomach powders, remarking that it was a bad business. They agreed that whether James Bolsover was playing pranks on them or was of unsound mind, he could not be allowed to continue in his ways, turning their board-room into a bake-house and throwing unopened business letters into the River Thames. 'We must investigate this more thoroughly,' one of the board-men suggested. His colleagues agreed with him: they decided to summon Lake to the board-room, for detailed questioning at an early date.

'Mr Linderfoot was saying to me,' said Lake, 'that he has noticed you about the place, Brownie. What d'you think of that?'

Miss Brown thought only that Mr Linderfoot had noticed many a girl around the place and had attempted to pour gin down the throats of as many as were willing to receive it. The sight of Mr Linderfoot's enormous body heaving along the corridors like a species of elephant had often repelled her, and she

was glad that he had never paused near her, or opened his
mouth in speech.

'Mr Linderfoot could do a lot for a girl,' said Lake. 'He's a
man of money and influence, Brownie.'

19

The sky, pale blue, was clear of clouds for days on end. Workmen on London's building sites, West Indians and Irishmen,
Londoners and men from Yorkshire and Wales, performed their
tasks with greater relish, recalling snow and frosty mornings,
and patches of damp on their boots. Edward on his bicycle,
riding from Clapham to Putney and on to Wimbledon, passed
through s.w.17, the area that James Bolsover had selected as
the one to which he would move when he fell from grace. Now
and again, Edward drew his bicycle in to the kerb to observe
more easily the workmen high above him on their scaffolds,
whistling and seeming from a distance to be idle. Idle, in fact,
they were not: more was built that summer and autumn in
s.w.17 than in any other similar period in the history of the
district, and more houses of an old-fashioned nature were des-
troyed. All Jubilee Road was levelled, and Dunfarnham Avenue,
and the corner of Crimea Road, and Fetty Crescent, and almost
all of Gleethorpe Lane. Edward watched the work of destruction and rebuilding, and felt sad to see it all, although he knew,
for he had read it in a newspaper, that new houses were necessary to keep pace with the increasing population. Occasionally,
he saw a single wall, all that remained of some old house, with
different wallpapers still adhering to the plaster, indicating the
rooms that had once been lived in. High up on such a wall there
was often a fire-grate with a mantelshelf still above it, seeming
strange and surrealist without a floor or a ceiling. After a time,
Edward used to look out for those fireplaces, and even developed a fantasy in which he came by night with a ladder and
climbed up with kindling and coal. In his bed in Clapham he
wandered in his fantasy all over the area of s.w.17, and Wandsworth and Putney, climbing up the ladders and lighting fires in

the fire-grates in the sky, causing a mystery that interested the newspapers and the nation. Before he dropped off to sleep the fires were blazing heartily, throwing a light on to the wallpaper that surrounded them, creating a ghostly cosiness.

The summer flowers faded in the Bolsovers' garden, and the scene from the french windows became one of fewer contrasts. Roses lingered in their hardy fashion, defying the chills that came in the night. The Bolsover children played less among them, thinking already in terms of winter. Edward in his skulking had seen those children and would have liked to talk to them. He had seen them in Mrs Bolsover's little motor-car sitting side by side in the back, jumping about and chattering. Once he had ridden past Mrs Hoop and she had called out to him, but he pretended not to hear her. 'I thought I seen you, Edward,' she said that evening in the Hand and Plough, 'riding your bike up Wimbledon way.' She attempted to elicit an explanation, but Edward had shaken his head and shrugged.

All through the fine warm autumn the clerks of the love department continued to read of sorrows and distress, pursing their lips over the marital tangles that confused the people of England. The clerks murmured on, writing and reciting about dogs that prowled, and death and blood, and whores and codfish, smiling morticians and red mechanics. The clerks sat by day in the love department, with their ball-point pens raised in the air, catching a mood or assisting a flight of thought.

Edward, still longing for a seat at a desk, saw no end to the drama that was playing around him. He saw forever old Beach and Mrs Hoop in the Hand and Plough, buying glasses of beer, Beach living in hope and the charwoman avid beside him. He saw the letters endlessly tumbling out of the large red sacks in the love department, letters that spelt out stories of bruised and broken hearts, pleading for comfort. He saw the dark eyes of Lady Dolores drilling through her thick lenses, and drilling through him as well, guiding his whole existence, like a puppeteer.

'Tell me about that face now,' said Lady Dolores, having said it before. 'Describe his whole face to me.'

Edward did that, and Lady Dolores sketched a sharp countenance on her pad. 'Does that resemble it?' she asked, and Edward said yes, it did.

'Are you ailing, Mr Blakeston-Smith, or worrying, is it?'

Edward sighed, and said that he was worrying.

'Don't do that, Mr Blakeston-Smith. Pack up your troubles in your old kit-bag.'

'I won't do anything wrong.'

'Who's asking you, Mr Blakeston? All you have to do is what you're told.'

Edward wondered how it would come: would he find without explanation a knife or a gun in his pocket? He had read in newspapers of people strangled with women's stockings or telephone wire, or done to death with cushions and pillows. He had read of a woman who had knocked the life out of her husband by striking him with a metal colander. He watched himself dragging the body of Septimus Tuam across Wimbledon Common and hiding it beneath undergrowth. Dogs found it the following weekend. *Pray for me*, wrote Edward in his mind to Brother Edmund. *Body on Common*, said the newspapers.

'Watch the destruction of this marriage, Mr Blakeston-Smith. Work yourself up on it. Write your notes fully, of this man at his work. We'll soon strike back.'

'Strike?'

'We are hunting dogs waiting, Mr Blakeston-Smith. Going in for a kill.'

'Oh, Holy Mother!' cried Edward. 'Oh God, release me!'

'What's up, Mr Blakeston-Smith?'

She had given him as a present a pair of wash-leather gloves with which, she said, he would always be able to remember the love department.

'I'm not going in for any kill,' cried Edward Blakeston-Smith, agitatedly on his feet, his fingers sweating in the gloves.

'You'll do as you're told,' said Lady Dolores, laughing; and Edward came to a decision.

'Hullo,' said the desk sergeant. 'Yes?'

'Nothing has happened,' cried a muffled voice. 'I've been reading the daily newspapers. What's holding you up?'

'Now then,' said the desk sergeant. 'What's the name, sir?'

'It's a female here,' said the voice, 'speaking through a layer of wool.'

'I've had you on before,' said the desk sergeant.

'Get your finger out,' cried Mrs Poache. 'Give protection to Septimus Tuam.'

'We are extremely busy, sir –'

'Why crack jokes? Earn your wage, you lazy peasant.'

Eve continued her life as best she could. She telephoned her grocery orders to the shops and later received the goods in cardboard boxes at the door. She made sponge cakes and other confections, prepared stews, risotto, pies, puddings, vegetables; she stewed fruit and scrambled eggs, and put butter on slices of bread. She roasted meat, and grilled it; she cleaned pans and plates and cutlery. She listened to the children talking to one another, she heard of their days at school, or their progress with Miss Fairy and Miss Crouch; she admired their paintings and gave them baths. And while doing all that she felt the presence of Septimus Tuam. 'How well you're looking,' one of the mothers said to her, a mother whose name she didn't know and didn't wish to know, a woman in a Volkswagen motor-car. She smiled at this mother, knowing she was looking well because Septimus Tuam had entered her life and desiring for a moment to relate this fact to the woman in the Volkswagen car. She wanted to say that she had found a tonic, in terms of a man who had the look of a priest about him. But she only smiled and said nothing at all, holding a door open for her children, and then driving away, listening to her children talking.

Watching on Wimbledon Common one afternoon, Edward saw Mrs Bolsover ring the door-bell of Mrs FitzArthur's house and saw Septimus Tuam open the door with a courtly bow of his long head. Mrs Bolsover entered the house, and Edward stood still, plucking up his courage.

Septimus Tuam was wearing his green tie with the signs of the Zodiac on it. In Mrs FitzArthur's drawing-room he took it off and looked at it. He said:

'When is your birthday?'

'June the first.'

'You're a Gemini. Queen Victoria was a Gemini.'

Eve felt herself embraced. She closed her eyes, and did not say what she had meant to say.

'We are in love,' said Septimus Tuam. 'We are made for each other. Could we do without it now, having tasted it already?' He stroked the pale skin of this woman he had come upon after his failure with the woman in the Bluebird Café. He had been lucky that matters had turned out as they had. Had the woman in the tea-shop not cut up so rough he would not be here now, about to mention that he was short of a pound.

Edward squared his shoulders on Wimbledon Common and thought of his father. 'I'm going straight up to the door,' he said, 'and I'm going to say, "My name is Edward Blakeston-Smith." ' A lorry carrying a load of cement blocks missed him narrowly as he crossed the busy road; its driver loosed a string of obscenities, but Edward did not hear them. He walked ahead, sniffing the agreeable air.

'Darling,' said Eve. 'I'm thinking about a divorce.'

Septimus Tuam felt a dryness in his mouth that he was not unfamiliar with. Oaths formed in his mind but were not uttered. He said:

'My dear. A divorce?'

'I don't like this deceit.' Eve heard herself speaking of divorce and deceit and felt more acutely like a figure in a dream. When she was with Septimus Tuam it seemed to her often that he was there almost specifically to dream what must happen to her. And when she wasn't with him she felt that he was dreaming from afar, causing her to perform her familiar tasks in a different way. When she spoke and made suggestions she was aware of bringing shutters down, as though she wished to close off half her mind and crush a part of reality. She saw him throwing the coloured ball to one of her children and then to the other; she saw him with his grey hat on his head, typing among desert sands. 'I have lived to become a figment of your imagination,' she had once exclaimed, but Septimus Tuam replied that he didn't understand such statements, adding that he possessed, in fact, no imagination to speak of.

185

Speaking to her now, he agreed that he didn't like deceit either, but said he could see little alternative. 'It's a question of cash, really,' he explained. 'A question of having a bit to live on.' He shook his head dismissively, and changed the tone of his voice. He said, 'We met, if you remember, on the final day of August. You have known me for approximately nine and a half hundred hours.'

'I make things in my oven,' said Eve, 'and all the time there is you to think about. All the time, no matter what I'm doing. Do you see?'

Her lover nodded sagely, saying that he saw. But he repeated his statement about finance. Vaguely, he mentioned a legacy that was tied up in a legal way. 'It isn't long,' he added, 'nine and a half hundred hours.'

Eve said:

'I couldn't lumber you with my children.'

She had planned that sentence. She paused where she had planned to pause, hoping that Septimus Tuam would shake his head and say that of course she must lumber him with children. But Septimus Tuam said nothing at all, and Eve, her tears beginning, said that maybe they would find a way, adding that she loved her children.

'The kiddies?' murmured Septimus Tuam. 'There's a bit of a problem there.'

'You'd like them. And they'd like you. I'm sure of that.'

'Indeed, of course. Still, let's not be hasty. Don't make it too unhappy for yourself, my dear, by mentioning divorce too soon to this husband of yours. Let's see the lie of the land; let's plan a few things first.'

What would James do, she wondered, after she had gone? She imagined him sitting in the house in the evenings, watching the television screen. She doubted that he would marry again.

'I wanted to be married,' said Eve. 'And all the things that now are smothering me once upon a time seemed pleasant: to be the wife of a successful man, and mother to his children: what more could I demand, especially since I loved him? I was an old-fashioned girl.'

Septimus Tuam made a noise with his lips that might have

been a sound of agreement, or might have been the opposite. He said:

'Does James bore you, dear?'

'He has been bored himself. One is more aware of that than of James.'

'It is a tale with many women. You can depress yourself thinking about it.'

'I would be poor with you, and not mind. I would work in a shop. I cannot ever see you being a shadow.'

'Nor I you. You are too beautiful for shadows.'

James had come back from Gloucestershire and said that he had arranged for the house to be put up for sale. He told Eve about the nurse's box of seeds in the greenhouse and how the estate agent had screwed his heel into a floor-board and caused the wood to powder away. Then he had announced that what he needed was a stiff brandy, and had poured one out. 'And how are you?' he had not said. 'How have you been, my Eve?'

Edward placed a finger on Mrs FitzArthur's front door-bell. He pressed it sharply twice.

'Who's that?' said Septimus Tuam. 'Perhaps we shouldn't answer it.' But the bell sounded again and then again, and in the end, with a sigh, Septimus Tuam was obliged to attend to the matter.

'Good afternoon,' said Edward. 'Look, can I come in? My name is Edward Blakeston-Smith.'

'Go away,' said Septimus Tuam.

'It's better that I come in,' said Edward. 'I can tell you something to your advantage, Mr Tuam. I really can.'

'I have warned you before. Why are you hanging about me?'

'I'm here to help. I want to talk to you and Mrs Bolsover.'

'Go to hell!' said Septimus Tuam in a low voice, not caring at all for the attitude of the visitor. 'There's no Bolsover here. This is the house of Mrs FitzArthur.'

'I know it's the house of Mrs FitzArthur. Mrs FitzArthur is enjoying herself in America.'

When Edward said that, Septimus Tuam threw his eyes upwards, assuming that the persistent young man was a private detective hired by Mrs FitzArthur to spy on him while she was abroad. Septimus Tuam, well used to detectives, sometimes saw them everywhere.

'Mrs Bolsover,' Edward called out loudly, still standing on the step, and noticed with pride that his hearty command had brought the lady forth. 'Good afternoon, Mrs Bolsover,' said Edward. 'Remember me, again?'

'I remember,' said Eve slowly, puzzled by several things. 'Who are you?' she said.

'I work for an organization,' said Edward. 'I come to warn you, and to help you in this moment of disaster.'

'Damn you!' said Septimus Tuam.

'No,' said Edward, 'I have things to say.'

'What do you want?' asked Eve. 'Why have you come here?'

'He's a private detective,' said Septimus Tuam. 'I've seen the like before.'

'I doubt it,' said Eve. 'He's something different altogether.'

'I work for a love organization,' explained Edward. 'And I will tell you this: I hold the trump cards.'

'Let him in, I should,' said Eve, and Septimus Tuam, much against his will, opened the door wide and allowed Edward to pass into the house. 'What a pretty place!' said Edward, looking around.

'See here,' said Septimus Tuam. 'Say what you have to say and then clear off. You're in the employ of Mrs FitzArthur, are you?'

'I am not in the employ of Mrs FitzArthur. Why Mrs Fitz-Arthur?'

'Who's Mrs FitzArthur?' said Eve.

'An aunt,' said Septimus Tuam, staring hard at Edward. 'An eccentric old aunt.'

'You have enemies, Mr Tuam,' stated Edward. 'But they are not the kind of enemies you might imagine. Your world is well beyond mine: I am being impelled beyond by desires.'

'He's queer in the head,' said Septimus Tuam.

Edward said:

'I'm not too bad in the head, actually. I went to a quiet house because I had a thing about the posters. But then I was impelled to come away in a hurry, and to do this work. I grant you I'm not entirely in control of myself.'

'I thought,' said Eve, 'you were a friend of Mrs Hoop's.'

'I met Mrs Hoop in the Hand and Plough. She and old Beach. I was feeling low one night.'

'Shove off then,' ordered Septimus Tuam, opening Mrs Fitz-Arthur's front door again, 'and stop following us about. Go back to the quiet house.'

'No,' cried Edward, banging the door with his fist. 'No, no, no: you don't understand a single word of what I'm telling you. What I'm saying is that I am engaged by a woman who has powers.'

'Go off to hell,' cried Septimus Tuam, 'or I'll put the police on you. Ring up the police, Mrs Bolsover, and say there's a raving maniac at large in Wimbledon.'

Edward drew a breath. Smoke rose from Eve Bolsover's cigarette and caused a tickle in one of his nostrils. He watched her lift the tipped cigarette to her lips and suck smoke through the tobacco and later emit it. He was aware of the anger and impatience of Septimus Tuam.

'God help you, Mrs Bolsover,' said Edward. 'God save your marriage. This is a slippery man: stick with your husband.'

'It is really no concern of yours,' said Eve.

'I suppose it's not,' agreed Edward sadly, knowing that he might speak for twenty-four hours and still not persuade either of them of anything. He had simply wished to say that Septimus Tuam should flee the country; he had wished to say that Septimus Tuam was scheduled for death. But the words stuck within him: it was an ugly statement to make.

'If I see you again,' said Septimus Tuam, 'I'll take official action. Be off down that road at once.'

Edward heard the door slam behind him as he walked despondently away. Once more, failure pressed hard upon him. 'I'm inept in every way,' he said. 'It's his only hope.'

Like James and Eve Bolsover, Edward often imagined the future he wished to know. He was not of the ilk of Septimus Tuam, who did not care to hazard too far ahead, whose trips through time were of a more local and practical kind. While Eve imagined deserts and dancing Arabs, and James thought wish-fully of the scenes of his disgrace, so Edward imagined the bung-ling of his crime. As he walked from Mrs FitzArthur's house and crossed the busy road, he thought of the telephone wire dis-integrating in his hands because of its indifferent quality. 'I had it on the neck of him,' he said to Lady Dolores. 'I was tightening it up.' He imagined rifles that were ineffective through rust, knives that were blunt or bladeless, and poison as innocent as milk. 'Run him down in a car,' commanded Lady Dolores. 'I couldn't drive one,' replied Edward.

But in his heart Edward doubted that the future would be at all like that for him. 'I want you to put a stop to Septimus Tuam,' she had said. 'You have been put on earth for that very reason.' Inept at all else, the truth might be that his genius was reserved for his violent task. *He is silent beside Mrs Bolsover*, he had written, *occasionally making a gesture. I have never seen him smile.* He had written that he was thin no matter how you looked at him, from the front or from either side. He had written that his black hair had a curl in it and that his feet were notice-ably small. He had filled the blank pages with a wealth of detail, but apparently that wasn't enough. He had no option but to go on weakly protesting; he would protest until he received his final orders and knew that he could not disobey. 'I'm useless with any kind of instrument,' he'd say to her. 'It's as much as I can do to butter a piece of bread.' She would shake her head, and for all he knew she might even be right. *A Very Fine Mur-derer*, a newspaper would pronounce; *Useful to the Nation*. The headlines dazzled Edward's mind and caused him to feel giddy. 'Is my leg being pulled?' he cried from the saddle of his land-lady's bicycle. 'Is this some joke?'

People walking on the pavements heard these questions and paused in their strolling to stare at the cyclist who had uttered them. A few raised their eyebrows; others laughed.

2O

'We can't have this, you know,' said the desk sergeant. 'You're snarling up all our lines, sir. The station's business is being interfered with.'

'What business, for heaven's sake?' shrieked Mrs Poache. 'Have you ever done an honest's day work in your life?'

Had she been able to, she would have telephoned Septimus Tuam himself, but Septimus Tuam was not, and never had been, on the telephone. He had explained to her that he did not care to have the dark and foreboding instrument anywhere near him, interrupting his thoughts, as by its nature it must. 'What's the matter with call-boxes?' he had asked her in his direct way, and she recalled with vividness being unable to say that anything much was the matter with call-boxes.

He had come to her at a time when she was feeling low. Just before a Christmas it had been, about ten years ago. 'What a lot of shopping you have!' he had said, sitting at her table in Fortnum and Mason's. 'Christmas is such a time.' They had drifted into conversation, in the course of which she had revealed where she lived. 'Well, here's a coincidence,' the young man had replied, 'I am making for that very area myself, my next port of call. Now, please do let me help you with that load.'

The next time, she had run into him in one of the local shops. 'Four thin slices of lamb's liver,' she'd been saying at the time. 'Why, Mrs Poache,' said he, coming up behind her. And then the following morning he'd arrived at the house, with a black glove, saying he thought she'd dropped it yesterday. But she had to confess that she had never seen this black glove before. 'So kind of you,' she said, and held the door wide, thinking of the Captain, who would probably have kicked the glove into the gutter rather than seek out the lady who had dropped it. She had given him a cup of coffee, and he, noticing all the work she had laid up for herself in the kitchen, had taken off his jacket and fallen to like a young Trojan. 'I'll wash these dishes,' he had murmured softly. 'You dry them if you'd like to, Mrs Poache; or why not take a rest from chores this morning?' But she, feeling she couldn't do that, had picked up a dish-cloth and had dried.

Mrs Poache could never afterwards remember at what point she had felt weak. All she knew was that she had suddenly sat down at the kitchen table, watching him and leaving him to do all the work. And then he had said that he'd fallen in love with her in Fortnum and Mason's and she hadn't been able to believe her ears.

Mrs Poache, ten years later, found the one photograph she had to remind her of him. It had been taken by a street photographer who had snapped his camera before Septimus Tuam could stop him. He had been angry about the incident, and had been even angrier when she gave the man her name and address and asked that a copy be sent to her. Septimus Tuam made her promise to bring him the photograph when it arrived so that together they might destroy it. But what had arrived was a small contact print from which she was to order the larger picture by quoting a number and enclosing money. 'Here's that photo,' she had said to Septimus Tuam, handing him the contact print. She had afterwards quoted the number and enclosed the money, and two days later the larger photograph had arrived. It was the only time she had ever deceived him, but she knew even then that a day might come when she would welcome the comfort of a memento. And when the time in fact did come, she often wondered as she looked at the faded photograph how much he had changed in the intervening years, and she guessed that he had hardly changed at all.

Mrs Poache sighed. She would have given a hundred pounds to be able to walk from the house now and take a bus into London and meet him for coffee in Fortnum and Mason's. She remembered his eyes. She remembered a way he had of running the tips of his fingers lightly over the palms of her hands. Angrily, she shouted into the Captain's sock on the mouthpiece of her telephone. She stamped her foot.

'He lived in your district,' she shouted at the desk sergeant, 'and may still do. You'll have a murder on your hands; I don't suppose you care.'

'Hullo,' said the desk sergeant.

She had never known his precise address, knowing only that he resided near the river, somewhere near Putney Bridge. He had told her that much one day, replying that he was a Putney man when she had called him a man from nowhere, a mystery man and an enigma. 'I am a seventh child,' he had said. 'I am the runt of the family.' He had almost died in childbirth, he added, reflecting aloud that fairies could have carried the miniature coffin. 'You might never have been born,' she had cried. 'Oh, my boy!' She remembered his taking a lace handkerchief from her handbag, on that occasion or on a similar one, and himself dabbing her tearful eyes with it. He loved to powder her face for her, and to smear on her lipstick. He said he had never known a woman like her.

'He lives nearby you, don't you see?' cried Mrs Poache. 'He's in your charge.'

'What's your name, sir, and address, please?' said the desk sergeant. 'Speak up a bit, if you would.'

'I am speaking through a layer of wool. I have no intention of making myself known.'

'In that case –'

'Listen to me at once.'

'What is it you wish to say, sir?'

'If no arrest takes place I am planning to report you to Scotland Yard. I am quite capable of telephoning friends at the Yard. I trust you appreciate that.'

The desk sergeant heard the line go dead, and blew loudly through his mouth, causing his lips to shake. 'That same old gin-and-tatters,' he said to a constable who was standing by with his helmet off, 'impersonating a dame.'

Septimus Tuam examined the calendar by his bedside and saw the pencilled ring around October 12th. He left his room and said to a man who was coming up the stairs of the rooming-house: 'Is it the twelfth?' The man replied that it was. 'The twelfth of never,' he said, and laughed very loudly.

'Mrs James Bolsover,' said Septimus Tuam in a telephone-box. 'Is she there and may I speak to her?'

'Who is that?' retorted Mrs Hoop. 'Who is speaking there?'

'The cutlery department of Harrod's.'

'Cutlery? The house is full of it.'

'Is Mrs Bolsover in? It would be helpful to have a word with her. I will not delay her long.'

'She is around certainly. I think she is trying to make some food in the kitchen.'

Septimus Tuam heard Mrs Hoop call out to her employer that there was a man about cutlery on the telephone.

'Yes?' said Eve.

'My dear, it's me.' He spoke quickly and urgently. He said, 'Something odd has arisen. I may have to go away absolutely at once, for six or nine months.'

'But why? Oh surely not!'

Septimus Tuam explained that all this was a considerable embarrassment to him. 'That legacy,' he said, and paused. He had mentioned the small legacy before, he continued, as being one that was tied up in a legal way. It was due to him from the estate of an elderly cousin and had been due for quite some time, while he, already counting on the money, had spent a portion of it in advance. 'A wretched creditor,' said Septimus Tuam, 'has taken it into his head to put on the heat. You may laugh, but what I am obliged to do is flee the country. It is more complicated than it sounds,' added Septimus Tuam, not sure himself what the law was in these matters.

'But surely nowadays –'

'Who fancies being chalked up a bankrupt, dear, when all the time there is this tied-up legacy? I've asked Lord March-ingpass, but alas, poor chap, he has over-spent himself on the Californian fig market. It is most wretched really; quite absurd –'

'How much is it? Surely I can lend you the money for a while?'

Mrs Hoop, polishing the floor of the Bolsovers' hall, heard her employer say that she was prepared to lend money to a man in the cutlery department of Harrod's. She ceased all polishing and edged closer to the half-open door of the sitting-room.

Septimus Tuam said:

'It is all of three hundred pounds, and I couldn't ever borrow three hundred pounds from you, my dear, or even more as may be. However could I?'

'Of course you could. It is only until you have the money yourself: it is the natural thing to do.'

'No, no: I could never allow it. No, I shall fly off as Lord Marchingpass suggested. He has a little financial aid stacked away in Barcelona, or some such: he kindly permits me to make free with it. Though I cannot bring it back to London: it is apparently quite against the law. So I am off tonight.'

'No, no –'

'Look, my dear, how could I pay you back? Three hundred pounds? If the cousin's legacy failed for any reason to materialize, what then, for heaven's sake? Cash gets nibbled up by legal men.'

'I'll give you the money,' cried Eve. 'Of course I must. I'll write you a cheque for three hundred pounds.'

In the hall Mrs Hoop entered a state of ecstasy, with her eyes closed and her polishing cloth idle in her hand. Well, this beats Bingo, thought Mrs Hoop.

'Give it to me?' said Septimus Tuam. 'But I couldn't ever let you. How could I?'

But Eve had already replaced the receiver and was searching for her cheque book, while Mrs Hoop, smearing on Mansion polish at a snail's pace, was telling her story to a judge in a divorce court.

'Anything like that?' enquired Lady Dolores, showing Edward another portrait on her lined pad. 'Have I got the eyes?'

'I want to speak to you, Lady Dolores.'

Lady Dolores blew smoke about. She used her pencil, watching the point of it moving on the paper. 'Yes,' she said.

'I'm useless at stealth, Lady Dolores, and I'm useless with any kind of instrument. It's as much as I can do to butter a piece of bread.'

'Who's talking about butter, Mr Blakeston-Smith? Look here,

I don't pay you to come in here talking to me about butter. I asked you about the eyes.'

'The eyes are deeper. They're blacker eyes. They'd frighten you.'

'They'll never frighten me. I'll warn you of that.'

'What about one of the clerks outside, Lady Dolores? They might be interested in this type of work. They're always on about blood.'

'They are poetic clerks, Mr Blakeston-Smith, which is more than you'll ever be. These are rising men in the world of verse, obliged to earn a living otherwise. Is the hair right?'

'The hair needs to be blacker. Is it poetry, all that? The dog and the mechanic? I never guessed.'

'It is of the avant-garde, Mr Blakeston-Smith. Poetry of an advanced nature.'

'Well, wouldn't it be a good experience for them?'

'The clerks have their work to do, as you and I have ours, Mr Blakeston-Smith. You appear to be trying to upset the whole organization.'

'They sit there reciting poetry,' cried Edward, 'while I have to go out and do the dirty work. It's hardly fair: they're as happy as sandboys.'

'You're a well-dressed man now, Mr Blakeston-Smith. Who gave you a lovely pair of gloves?'

'The clerks have the best of everything –'

'You are seeing life, are you not? You are growing up apace. While the clerks sit pretending.'

'The clerks are in their seventh heaven.'

'You are filling up the dossier well, Mr Blakeston-Smith: I like the details you are putting down. You'll be as angry as a cat when you see him at work in the Bolsover marriage –'

'I've seen it, Lady Dolores. I've written down just what happens.'

'You're doing frightfully well. Don't you like those gloves?'

'Yes, of course –'

'Well, then?'

'I'm terribly frightened, Lady Dolores. I don't think it's right, you know, following people around like this. It's against the law, that kind of carry-on.'

'It's not against any law, pet. There's nothing to say you shouldn't follow a man who sent three women to their graves.'

'You're making me act against my will,' cried Edward. 'You've got peculiar powers. You're a contemporary witch.'

'Don't be rude,' said Lady Dolores, and turned her back on him.

Edward left the love department and cycled straight to the Hand and Plough, thinking to himself that the woman was driving him to drink.

'I'm like the hands on a clock,' he said to Beach, who was already ensconced in a corner, and he sighed thickly, and talked to Beach about the playing of draughts. He drank beer for two hours and began to feel the effects of it.

'You could have knocked me down with a feather,' said Mrs Hoop when she came. Edward looked at her morosely. Beach said:

'What's happened to you, Emily?'

'"Have three hundred quid," she said. To a fellow in the knife business.'

'What's that?' asked Beach.

'The Bolsover woman,' explained Mrs Hoop to Edward. 'She's buying the men of London.' Mrs Hoop emitted a slow laugh. 'Did you hear that, Harold?' she called out to the barman. 'About what I come across this afternoon?'

'How's Mrs Hoop?' said Harold, wiping the counter with a damp cloth.

'That tired,' said Mrs Hoop. 'Honestly.'

'Septimus Tuam,' said Edward, 'is not in any knife business.'

'I was up at five a.m.,' said Mrs Hoop. 'I was washing clothes.'

'I'd like to have seen you, Mrs Hoop,' Harold said, 'up at five a.m.'

'Get on with you,' said Mrs Hoop. 'How's yourself? How's tricks with the Irish?'

'I have had a bad knee, Mrs Hoop. I'm after banging it on a barrel.'

'Three hundred quid handed out on the telephone. Get in on the act, Harold. Bad knee and all.' Mrs Hoop laughed loudly.

'Funny,' said Beach.

'You've got a wire crossed,' interrupted Edward. 'It's Septimus Tuam Mrs Bolsover was handing out money to. You can bet your boots.'

'I'm that tired,' repeated Mrs Hoop. 'I've had a fine old day, I can tell you.'

'You're too tired to concentrate. You've got the whole thing wrong. You misheard the whole caboodle.'

Mrs Hoop, suddenly aware that her report was being contradicted, repeated again what had taken place in the Bolsovers' house that afternoon. 'You're boozed,' she retorted, looked at Edward's loosened collar and wild, unhappy eyes. Edward said:

'I was telling Mr Beach about the game of draughts.'

'We was drawing up the rules,' said Beach, 'before you looked in, Emily.'

'It's typical of Septimus Tuam to say he's a man in a shop, you see. He's an angel of the devil.'

'What name is that, Edward? Tuam?'

'Septimus Tuam,' said Edward, forming a sentence that he would not have formed had he been sober, 'has become a friend of your Mrs Bolsover. There's no doubt about that at all.'

'We seen Mrs Bolsover that night, lad,' supplied Beach. 'That was Mrs Bolsover in the house with the ape.'

'I've seen her since, to tell the truth.'

'I seen her stripped to the skin,' said Beach. 'I seen the woman in her birthday suit.'

'What!' exclaimed Mrs Hoop loudly. 'By Jesus Christ!'

'In my bed,' said Beach in an attempt to make Mrs Hoop jealous, 'dreaming. She and me was walking through a garden.'

'Ha, ha. Did you hear that, Harold?'

'Septimus Tuam is in mortal danger. Listen, Mrs Hoop, why don't you pass that on to Mrs Bolsover?'

'She's a whore and a bitch,' snapped Mrs Hoop. 'Old Beach had a dirty dream. I'll pass on that, by God.'

'Tell her there's a plot to kill Septimus Tuam. Say a youth is being impelled.'

'Begin at the beginning, Edward,' said Mrs Hoop, interested. 'What's all this you're saying?'

Edward was feeling sick. He took the wash-leather gloves from his pocket and put them on his hands. He thought the action might distract his stomach, but it seemed to make it worse.

'I feel sick,' he said.

'Take a draught of beer, Edward. You're boozed to the gills.'

Edward took off his gloves, but didn't follow Mrs Hoop's advice. He said:

'I've been indiscreet in my speech. I shouldn't have mentioned Septimus Tuam.'

'He's mentioned now. Sexual, is it?'

Edward shrugged, saying he didn't know what to think. He said he imagined Mrs Bolsover was in love with Septimus Tuam. 'There's a lot of it about,' he added.

'We was made to be together,' said Beach, opening his eyes. 'We was made for a bit of love.'

'Have you brought another will-form, Edward? Old Beach is to sign on the dot tonight. He's promised on his honour.'

'Tell Mrs Bolsover. Tell her you heard it in a pub: death is after Septimus Tuam.'

Mrs Hoop, intrigued and joyful, was puzzled by Edward's repeated references to the death of the man to whom Mrs Bolsover had offered three hundred pounds. It was Edward who had got his wires crossed, she reckoned, confusing death with another story altogether.

'How come you're in on the act, Edward?' asked Mrs Hoop. 'Knowing all the dirt?'

Edward drew a deep breath and held it. He let it go gradually. He said:

'I shouldn't have spoken. It was a breach of confidential business.'

'It's safe with me,' cried Mrs Hoop. 'And old Beach doesn't know the time of day it is. What's the worry, Ed?'

'It's all a tragedy,' said Edward. 'It would make you cry.'

Mrs Hoop nodded her head.

'Pan-Am?' said Mrs FitzArthur in New York. 'Oh, this is Mrs FitzArthur here. Now can you book me a passage at once to London? I have made up my mind.'

The girl in the Pan-American Airlines office said to hold the line, please, and spoke again almost as soon as she had said it. She said yes, it could be arranged, and offered Mrs FitzArthur a choice of several flights.

'That early one,' said Mrs FitzArthur, 'sounds as good as any. And thank you most awfully.'

'You're welcome, Mrs FitzArthur,' said the girl in Pan-Am.

21

On the evening of Thursday, October 14th, two days after Eve had written a cheque for three hundred pounds in favour of Septimus Tuam, Mrs Hoop, her day's work done, waited for the return of James Bolsover at the corner of Crannoc Avenue. When his motor-car approached she hailed it with a peremptory gesture, holding up her open hand in the manner of a policeman at a crossroads.

'Hullo, Mrs Hoop,' said James, opening a window to talk to her. 'How are you?'

Mrs Hoop said that, considering everything, she was not too bad, adding that she could be worse. She was tired, she said, because once again she had risen early in order to do some washing. It was disgraceful, said Mrs Hoop, the amount of washing there was to do because of the fumes of London's air. James remarked that she was working late in Crannoc Avenue too, and Mrs Hoop pursed her lips and said that she had stayed on specially in Crannoc Avenue in order to have a word with him.

'With me?' said James in some surprise.

'I have to tell you a dirty thing, sir,' whispered Mrs Hoop. 'I'm that ashamed.'

'Why me?' enquired James.

'I'm sick with embarrassment,' confessed Mrs Hoop. 'I'm sick to my stomach, sir.'

'Are you in trouble, Mrs Hoop?'

'Your wife is having sex with a man, sir.'

'What did you say, Mrs Hoop?'

'Septimus Tuam, sir. Famous for it.'

James had never before heard of Septimus Tuam, and as Mrs Hoop spoke on about him he didn't understand how it could possibly be that his wife had fallen in with so apparently profligate a character. He had often considered her days in their house, and had seen them as days that scarcely allowed for a liaison with a lover. He imagined quite clearly the organizing of the children and Mrs Hoop, and shopping and cooking, and lunches with Sybil Thornton, and teas with the mothers of their children's friends. He thanked Mrs Hoop in Crannoc Avenue, looking past her at his house. It occurred to him as he spoke that she had never cared for his wife. He said:

'You're not confusing the facts, Mrs Hoop, by any chance? You're not thinking of another woman?'

'As God is my witness,' cried the charwoman, with bristling pride. 'Come down to the Hand and Plough, sir, and hear the facts from others.'

But James shook his head. He bade farewell to Mrs Hoop and drove on to his house, wondering if Mrs Hoop had invented the whole thing. It seemed most likely that she had.

'Who's Septimus Tuam?' said James after the children had gone to bed. He said it idly, crossing the room to sit in another chair. 'Who's Septimus Tuam?' he repeated.

Eve, not knowing what her husband knew or what his source had been, said:

'I'm having a love affair.'

James sat down. He looked at Eve for a minute without speaking. He knew that she was speaking precisely the truth, because she was saying what Mrs Hoop had said, and because her mind appeared to be elsewhere. He heard her say:

'Our marriage is without conversation. Our marriage has failed.'

James said he was sorry, apologizing in a general way about many aspects of their marriage. He had intended to speak at length, but Eve interrupted him. She said:

'I'm going to have to leave you.'

James shook his head. He walked to where his wife was sitting and put his hands on her shoulders. He did not say anything at all. Then he lifted his hands and left the room. When he returned, he said he had been sick with a vengeance.

'I am suggesting a divorce,' said Eve.

'We have two children.' James gestured above his head

towards the room where the children slept. 'What of all that?'

Eve said that in fairness to James the children should remain with him but that in fairness to the children they should go with her. It was a matter to arrange and discuss in a civilized way.

A scene occurred between the Bolsovers then. Eve watched her husband storming about the room, walking from one wall to another, and throwing questions at her about the nature of her love affair and the nature of the man she loved.

'You have deceived me in every way,' said James in anger. 'You have taken advantage of the money I make by the sweat of my brow. You have taken advantage of the trust I placed in you. I cannot believe that any of this is happening.'

'It has happened already,' said Eve. 'It happened before either of us could lift a finger. I don't understand it either.'

'It's all nonsense. It is rubbishy and silly.'

'Maybe, James. But it remains a fact.' She looked away from him, through the french window, into the twilight.

James remembered incidents in the past. He remembered the house when they moved into it, before their furniture was there. He remembered Eve bathing from a beach somewhere before their children had been born. She had walked out of the sea towards him, and he had watched her coming closer. 'It's not at all cold,' she had said.

James looked at his wife now and could not see her as she was; he heard her voice talking about the sea, he saw her standing with a bathing cap in her hand, her hair dishevelled and seeming damp. 'Your hair's wet,' he had said, looking up at her. 'That bathing cap is leaky.' There was a silence in his mind then: she stood before him, moving her lips and shaking out her hair. Her hair was long; the bathing cap had been white.

James saw his wife buying food in a shop. He saw her moving across the floor of a large room in which there were people that both of them knew. She should have moved more casually, with a glass in her hand, a glass of Martini since it was a drink she enjoyed, or a glass of wine. But Eve came oddly over the floor of the room, carrying in a basket the goods she had bought in the shop. She smiled at him, and he saw in her basket a loaf of sliced bread. She smiled at him again, in a quiet sitting-room in which they were alone, a month or two before their marriage.

'But I love you,' said James, not drinking brandy as she had imagined he would. 'I love you, and yet you do all this.'

Eve did not defend herself. She could think of no real defence and she could find no words to excuse her actions or even to promote them in a more favourable light. 'It is all too late,' she cried, seeing her husband in a new fury and hearing him make promises for the future. 'Oh, James my dear, it's far too late: I've met Septimus Tuam.'

But James said that the name was a ridiculous one, and reached now for the bottle of Hennessy brandy. She saw him note that it was three-quarters full and guessed his resolve to sit down in this room and finish it. He would remain there quietly in his chair, staring at the grey screen of the television set, drinking brandy until six o'clock in the morning; while she, above him, in their bed, would lie wakeful and watch the morning come, thinking of all the years she had been Mrs Bolsover, and murmuring to the image of Septimus Tuam.

James remembered Captain Poache sitting silently in this room, perched comfortably on a sofa and drinking. He remembered the presence of Mr Clinger and Mr Linderfoot. He saw them in the room, standing about, talking about the Clingers' pet; he heard Mrs Poache protesting that monkeys were notorious for carrying disease.

'We must have a divorce,' said Eve, but her husband made no reply. He opened the bottle of brandy and poured some into a glass. 'I shall sit in this room all night,' he said. 'I feel like dying.'

'A divorce,' repeated Eve. And James said:

'If I die, bury me in some graveyard. I will not be burnt, Eve: do you understand that? I am all against cremation.'

'James, please.'

'Sit with me here, if you care to. Look, have a drink.' He rose and fetched another glass, but Eve shook her head. 'Well, sit here anyhow, for by the look of things we'll be sitting less together in the future. Or can't you bear the sight of me?'

'Oh, don't be silly!'

'Then let's do other things. Let's make the most of this great moment, as we did of the moment of marriage. Let's go out laughing, Eve, why not? Let's walk about the house and bang on doors and wake our children and be hilarious over a joke or two. Let's burn things in the garden. Let's burn your marriage lines, and books and letters, the things that I gave you and all that you gave me: clothes and jewellery, fountain pens, and slippers. Shall we make a bonfire, Eve? Shall we burn our children's toys, the teddies and the gollies, Noah's Ark, old bricks and wooden horses, and plastic things that may go flaming away in a second, ships and submarines, racing cars and dolls? Let's smash that silly suit of armour into smithereens: I've often wanted to. Or shall we sit, Eve, more quietly here, and remember between us the day it happened, you and I in the Church of St Anselm, and afterwards on the lawns of that hotel, where Mrs Harrap hit a waiter? Did I propose this venture to you a month or so before? What did I say? I can't remember. I said I loved you: I must have.'

Eve murmured, but James didn't listen much. He said:

'I had thought, you know, that you and I would see old age together. I remember thinking that, seeing us on either side of a fire, talking of our children's children and being of comfort one of us to the other. Well, there you are.'

'I'm sorry, James.'

James Bolsover looked at the woman he had married ten years ago, and saw great beauty in her. He saw two people walking about in love, she and a man, planning a future, hand in hand.

'So you are having a love affair?' said James. 'So you are going round with some chap behind my back, making love and mocking me? You have broken our marriage.'

'It was broken already. It was as empty as an eggshell.'

'An eggshell? I didn't see it like that. Still, I've become so dull a dog I probably wouldn't.'

'No, no. We're both to blame for what has come about.'

'Well, off you go then: go out now and tell this fellow that you've broken all your news. Tell him I'm sitting here with brandy. Why not go out, Eve? Bring the fellow back with you.'

Eve said she didn't wish to go out.

'But isn't your paramour hanging about somewhere? Isn't he in a low-slung car, smoking feverishly and wondering how it's going?'

Eve said that Septimus Tuam was not like that. He did not smoke at all, she said, and did not own a low-slung car, or any kind of car.

'He's a lucky bird,' said James, 'to be cashing in on a girl like you. What shall I do when you go, Eve? What do you suggest?'

'Let's not talk of it now, James. Let's wait until we're used to this idea and have arranged for the children.'

'I could have Mrs Hoop come here as housekeeper, I suppose. Come to that, I could marry Mrs Hoop.'

He was smiling at her, Eve saw, but she saw his grief as well, and she knew in that moment what she had doubted: that this man who was still her husband loved her in his way, in a way that was inadequate.

'It is too late,' she cried out loudly, weeping herself. 'It's too late now, James.'

His hands pressed the glass he held, and pressed it harder until it cracked and broke into splinters. His blood came fast, and brandy stung his open flesh.

22

For two days James remembered his life with Eve, and considered what had come to pass. He sat silent in his office, watched by Miss Brown and occasionally by Lake, not caring if they watched him or how they interpreted his grief. In the end he came to a decision.

'He has seen the sign,' said Lake to Miss Brown on the evening of the second day. 'Straws are in the wind.'

Lake was stretched in an arm-chair in Miss Brown's bedsitting-room, well pleased with himself. He had been summoned to appear before the board-men at a time when James Bolsover was otherwise engaged. 'Tomorrow at ten,' he informed Miss Brown. 'It is the moment of my career. I feel well up to it: I am in tip-top trim.'

Miss Brown returned his smile, pleased that he was going ahead so fast, and that his dreams were coming true.

Lake thought that he had now better explain to the girl what he had been delicately hinting about for some time. He was about to begin when a picture flashed before him: he saw himself playing roulette with two members of the Italian aristocracy, a handsome middle-aged woman and her famously beautiful daughter. 'She can't sleep for thinking about you,' said the middle-aged woman in an Italian accent. 'And come to that, neither can I.' Lake stretched out his hand and collected a bundle of his winnings, chips to the value of twelve thousand pounds.

'There's a thing I've been meaning to say,' said Lake. 'Just a little point that I'm sure you'll understand.' He drew back his lips. He said that since he was now about to step into James Bolsover's position it would be difficult, unseemly even, for their association to continue. He would arrange, he said, for Miss Brown to be moved to another part of the building, to do work for another man. He mentioned Mr Linderfoot twice. He would feel proud, he said, if he were in Miss Brown's shoes, knowing that an influential person like Mr Linderfoot was displaying an interest. 'You see what I'm driving at,' said Lake, smiling widely now, and expecting of Miss Brown a sharp and wise nodding of the head. Instead, the girl hit him on his shoulder with a clenched fist. She struck him again, with the first object that came to hand, which happened to be a glass tumbler. She pushed him from the chair on which he was sitting, and his head struck the floor with an impact that caused him to lose consciousness and caused his teeth to leap from his mouth.

Miss Brown wept. She stood above the man, staring down at him, and comprehending everything. It had taken him forty-five seconds to betray her utterly. He had stated with a smile that they must go their separate ways, implying that there had never been love between them. Soundlessly, the tears flowed from Miss Brown's eyes as she stood in her gloomy bed-sitting-room and considered her ruined world. She had planned marriage with the man, she had seen them as a pair who might go far. She had often seen a scene in which there were children, the fruit of their congress, children who could also go far when the time was ripe for the journey, children who would heap credit on the credit already acquired.

Miss Brown in her emotion did not at that time care if she had killed Lake. She would say he had attacked her. She would say that he had terrified the life out of her, coming at her with a leer, without his teeth. She knelt beside the body and heard his breathing. She said to herself that she did not know what she was doing, that in a minute she would discover herself rushing to a cupboard and returning with a bread-knife to stick between Lake's ribs or to put to more grisly use. She saw the teeth on the floor where they had fallen from his jaws and she trod upon them, grinding them beneath the heel of a shoe. Violence flowed in her body: she lifted her small, neatly shod foot and drove it with power into the soft rump of the man who had used her ill.

Miss Brown filled a basin with cold water and poured it over her erstwhile lover. He groaned and began to move. Miss Brown, seeing the return to consciousness, quit the room.

Minutes later, utterly amazed, Lake sat up and shivered. He raised a hand to his head and felt a lump rising there, and wondered immediately how he would disguise it when he went before the board-men in the morning. He straightened his tie and looked about for his teeth. 'My God!' he cried, seeing the broken pieces of pink plastic all around him, and single familiar fangs buried in the carpet. 'My God alive!' cried Lake, thinking again of the board-meeting: he saw himself standing before the important men, his gums empty of teeth, a swelling the size of a billiard ball prominent on his head. The image caused Lake to moan with horror and distress: it caused him to pick the pieces swiftly from the floor and to run from the room and down the stairs.

'Quickly,' said Lake to a taxi-driver. 'This is top priority.' He gave the address of his dentist, thankful at least that the man was a local practitioner.

Miss Brown walked about Putney, thinking that it was going to rain and trying to prevent her hands from shaking. The face of Lake dangled before her, smiling at her with its gums exposed. She passed the house where Septimus Tuam lived: she passed the Hand and Plough. A man spoke to her, but she made no reply, not hearing the man and seeing him only as a shadow. She did not yet say to herself, 'This is the risk you run with love,' although later, and in a calmer moment, she said it repeatedly, adding that those who love most passionately have naturally most to lose.

Miss Brown climbed Putney Hill and walked on Putney Heath, and walked on until she came to Wimbledon Common. She passed the house of Mrs FitzArthur but did not know whose house it was, having never heard of Mrs FitzArthur. She did not walk as far as Crannoc Avenue, but turned instead and retraced her steps back to her bed-sitting-room. She would find there signs of the man who had been cruel to her: a plate from which he had eaten fish lay in a green washing-up basin, a fork that had been in his mouth lay with it, and a cup that retained the

remains of coffee he had relished. She thought she might keep
that plate and the fork just as they were, unwashed for ever,
and the coffee-cup with them. She thought she would cover them
with a light varnish to hold the debris of food in place: the fat on
the prongs of the fork, tiny flakes of fish on the plate, sugar
stained brown in the coffee-cup. She saw herself dipping a brush
into a jar of varnish and recognized an absurdity in the action.
So when she eventually arrived at her bed-sitting-room she went
immediately to the green washing-up basin and took from it the
objects that had been on her mind. She broke the plate with a
violent gesture, striking it with a meat-hammer; she struck the
cup a single blow and saw it shatter into many pieces. She wept
again in the quiet room, sitting on the chair he had sat on, holding his fork in her right hand, wondering what to do with it.
She rose after a minute, and threw it out of the window.

James Bolsover was on a train: he had felt in no mood for
driving. He had heard that the eight men had called a meeting
for the following morning at which he was not to be present, to
which Lake was to be called. The end seemed nigh, as the end
had come in another way too. He would telephone Eve and say
that he was instituting divorce proceedings, requesting her to
remain in their house with their children until something else
could be arranged.

An elderly woman sitting opposite read a copy of *Argosy*. She
placed it on the seat beside her after a while. She smiled at
James in a companionable way, and said:

'The stories they write nowadays.'

James smiled back. He was thinking about his children. He
recalled the man with the R.A.F. moustache who had been going
to show him the ropes, and the flat he had visualized his family
living in, down in the s.w.17 area. He shuddered when he
thought of all that now.

'How does one find a housekeeper, or someone like that?'
said James to the elderly woman.

'A housekeeper?'

'I have two small children. My wife's in the process of leaving
me.'

'I'm sorry indeed. We live in an age of change.'

'I was wondering about a housekeeper, someone who could see to their clothes and make a meal. I suppose it's the usual thing.'

'I suppose you put an advertisement in,' said the woman, 'asking for a friendly person.'

'I couldn't pay much,' explained James. 'I may not be well off.'

'No, well, I daresay all that's worked out. There's probably a kind of scale. You know.'

The train moved at sixty miles an hour through the dark countryside. The lights of villages and small towns appeared for a minute or two and then were gone. It was raining.

'Our fine autumn's gone, I see,' the woman said, rubbing the window with the palm of her hand.

'You wouldn't be interested?' said James. 'Or know anyone?'

'What?'

'I meant the housekeeper. Someone to keep house for the three of us.'

The elderly woman laughed. 'My dear man,' she said, 'you're paying me a nice compliment, but take a closer look: I'm much too old to keep much of a house for anyone.'

James said he was sorry, but the woman assured him that she had been cheered by his assumption. 'I'm afraid I know of no one,' she said, and James thought then of the nurse who had attended his father at his death. He wondered if a nurse would become a housekeeper, and rather doubted it.

'At this hour of the night?' said the dentist to Lake. 'No chance at all.'

'I must have teeth,' cried Lake. 'I have an important occasion at ten o'clock tomorrow morning.'

'I cannot help you, sir. I can repair nothing. You need a new set of dentures: an impression must be taken and the dentures constructed. It all takes time.'

'Repair what I have here,' said Lake, holding out the pieces in the handkerchief.

'I could not repair that. It takes a dental mechanic. You will appreciate, sir, that there is no dental mechanic on these premises at this hour of the night. Come in the daytime, please. Good night, Mr Lake.'

'No,' cried Lake, placing a foot across the threshold.

'There is no point in arguing,' returned the dentist, 'or becoming excited. You need a new set, in any case. No dental mechanic, however great his skill, could render a satisfactory repair. Your teeth are smashed beyond repair.'

'But surely you have other teeth? Surely you have a set about the place that would do for the time being?'

'A set about the place? What do you mean by that?'

'A dentist has teeth,' cried Lake. 'A dentist's job is to do with teeth, taking them out and putting them back. Haven't you a set that's been repaired by the mechanic and is awaiting collection?'

The dentist stared at Lake in some horror. 'I must ask you to go,' he said quietly.

'You're my dentist, aren't you?'

'I am the dentist of others also. I cannot do what you're suggesting.'

'I would let you have them back. At eleven tomorrow morning.'

The taxi-driver whom Lake had employed called out from his car that the meter was ticking over.

'What about it?' said Lake to the dentist.

'I cannot possibly allow you to take away the teeth of another patient,' said the dentist. 'The teeth wouldn't fit you, for a start. Untold harm might be done. The idea is ludicrous.'

'Look, I'll make them fit,' said Lake. 'Give me dental adhesive. A strong adhesive, a bit of padding –'

The dentist brought the door forward with force and drove the edge of it over Lake's toes. Lake cried out in pain and withdrew his foot. He returned to the waiting taxi-cab, muttering and sweating. It was just beginning to rain.

'Perhaps it'll be O.K.,' said Edward in the Hand and Plough. 'Perhaps they'll stick together. Perhaps Mr Bolsover'll forgive her.'

'Why should he forgive the woman?' demanded Mrs Hoop,

angry to hear the thought expressed. 'Be your age, Edward.'

'I fancy you, Emily,' said Beach. 'I was in a dream last night with you.'

'Sign the paper,' snapped Mrs Hoop. 'You're a right pair, the two of you.'

Harold shouted that it was closing time, and the three companions left the public-house soon afterwards. They walked together along the pavement, Edward wheeling his bicycle, Beach attempting to take the arm of Mrs Hoop. Rain spattered their faces. 'The good weather's gone,' said Edward. 'God damn the rain!' said Mrs Hoop, tying a scarf over her hair.

'Do you know a dentist?' said a bald-headed man to them, leaning out of a taxi-cab.

'Take no notice,' said Mrs Hoop, walking on.

'I need a dentist urgently,' said Lake.

'Dentist?' said Beach. 'We could lead you to a doctor, sir. We called in upon a doctor the other evening when Emily Hoop here was savaged by an ape.'

'What's the matter with you?' said Mrs Hoop, walking back again.

'I need a set of teeth,' said Lake in a low voice. 'My dentures have become smashed and it happens that I have an important engagement at ten o'clock tomorrow morning. I'm scouring everywhere for a sensible dentist.'

'False teeth?' said Mrs Hoop.

'Look here,' said Lake, lowering his voice still further. 'You don't know anyone who'd loan me a set of teeth until eleven o'clock tomorrow? It's a matter of the utmost urgency.'

'Will you lend the man your teeth?' said Mrs Hoop to Beach. 'He's distressed in himself.'

'What's going on?' said Beach.

'We'd have to make a charge, sir,' said Mrs Hoop to Lake.

'Naturally,' said Lake, emerging from the taxi-cab. 'Of course you'd have to.'

'Would five shillings be all right?' said Mrs Hoop. 'Just something to make up for the discomfort of the old man during the night and morning.'

'Isn't it lucky I met you?' said Lake.

Mrs Hoop allowed the three men to enter her house. She boiled some water with which to make tea. She arranged biscuits on a plate. 'I'll stay on after the other two johnnies have gone,' said Beach to himself in a mumble, and winked at Mrs Hoop whenever he could catch her eye.

'We'll take a cup of tea,' said Mrs Hoop, 'and then we'll get down to business.' She would arrange for the teeth to be returned personally to her when the man had finished with them, and she would hold the teeth until old Beach signed a will without making a mess of it. She was becoming tired of it, night after night in the Hand and Plough, begging and persuading, promising and cajoling. Beach was a wily bird, she had decided: a little touch of pressure of another kind would do no harm at all.

'Nice to meet you,' said Mrs Hoop, handing round cups of tea. 'This here is old Beach, and the younger man is Mr Edward Blakeston-Smith. I myself am a Mrs Hoop.'

'Mr Lake,' said Lake. 'It's very good of you.'

'Had an accident, have you?' said Mrs Hoop. 'A biscuit?'

'An extraordinary occurrence,' said Lake. 'Look at the lump on my head, Mrs Hoop.'

Mrs Hoop looked at the lump on Lake's head and gave it as her opinion that the lump was a bad one.

'That's another thing,' said Lake. 'That lump will be black and blue tomorrow, and I have to go in to a board-meeting. That's why I was concerned about the other matter: tomorrow is my big day.'

'We'll see you right,' said Mrs Hoop.

'I'll tell you a thing about myself,' said Lake. 'When I was a child of six my father remarked to a friend of his that he thought we had a future Prime Minister in the family.'

'Well, I never,' said Mrs Hoop.

'But when the time came, Mrs Hoop, I decided to enter the business world. My mind is made up about it: I am going to the top, I'm well-qualified for that.'

'I worked on the Underground myself,' said Mrs Hoop. 'I seen the world go by, Mr Lake.'

'Yes,' said Lake. 'Indeed. In my own case, I set out early to learn the tricks of the trade.'

'Tricks?' said Mrs Hoop. 'I could tell you a thing or two, as I've told these gentlemen here. "Got a fag, love?" they'd say to me as I passed. They'd follow me in cars, Mr Lake, two and three of them at a time.'

'That sort of thing's terrible,' said Lake. 'Really atrocious.' He paused. 'Tomorrow I hope to take over the work of a man called Bolsover, who is quite unsuited. I am to address the board at the invitation of Mr Linderfoot. You will understand now why I'm creating a fuss about the dentures and the lump on my head. I am not by nature a fussy person: I'm the most unfussy person you could care to imagine. In two years' time I'll be unstoppable, Mrs Hoop.'

'Bolsover and Linderfoot,' said Mrs Hoop. 'It's a small world.'

'We know the Bolsovers,' said Edward. 'Mrs Bolsover in particular.'

'Mrs Hoop got caught up with the ape,' said Beach. 'The lad and I fetched out a doctor.'

'How's Linderfoot?' said Mrs Hoop. 'There's a filthy man for you.'

'How come you know Mr Linderfoot and the Bolsovers?' said Lake, surprised; and Mrs Hoop told him. 'Well, I'll be jiggered,' said Lake.

'The Bolsover marriage has come to a halt,' said Mrs Hoop, 'owing to the woman being a whore. There's a Septimus Tuam who works in a shop messing it up with Mrs Bolsover, leaving the man with the kids. All Wimbledon is talking.'

'Oh dear, oh dear!' said Lake, and shook his head. 'Well, perhaps I should be off.' He glanced towards Beach's mouth. He rose and smiled toothlessly at the three of them.

'Stay awhile,' said Mrs Hoop, and Lake sat down again.

Thus it was that Edward witnessed these two people, the enemies of the Bolsovers, meeting in the small world. They sat and talked while Beach slept and snorted. Mrs Hoop explained how she had spoken to James Bolsover, saying that his wife was running around; Lake explained how he had cleverly planned the overthrow of James Bolsover, employing the usual and accepted business methods. Mrs Hoop made arrangements for the returning of Beach's property. 'Best hand them on to me,' she said, 'and I'll pass them to him in the evening.' She would put them in an empty tin box and strike her bargain in the Hand and Plough. 'I always got on with Bolsover,' said Mrs Hoop to Lake. 'He was unsuited to his work,' said Lake. 'There's no doubt about that.'

Edward, listening to this conversation, said to himself that Mrs Hoop and Lake were villains. Mrs Bolsover had shown him kindness whenever he had met her. She had calmed the atmosphere that day in Mrs FitzArthur's house when he had tried to warn Septimus Tuam and Septimus Tuam had turned nasty. She was a beautiful woman, the only beautiful person he had come across in London. He had been taken in drink and had accidentally said that Mrs Bolsover was meeting Septimus Tuam, and now Mrs Hoop had caused a havoc by passing on the information to Mrs Bolsover's husband. Mrs Hoop knew quite well that that was the last thing that should be done in such circumstances. Edward looked from one face to the other and saw that Mrs Hoop and Lake were twin souls. They were getting on like a house on fire, discussing the destruction of other people, exuding evil.

'You are crooks,' cried Edward, jumping to his feet. 'You're a disgrace to the human race.'

Mrs Hoop touched the side of her head. 'He's deprived,' she murmured to Lake. 'Like a babe in arms.'

'Wake up,' commanded Edward, shaking Beach roughly by the arm. 'You're not to lend that man your teeth, Mr Beach, and you're not ever to sign a will in Mrs Hoop's favour. D'you hear me now? They're out to get what they can. They've ruined the lives of innocent people.'

'What's the trouble?' said Beach.

'These two are wicked in their ways. They're up to no good. Don't do anything against your will, Mr Beach, while you still have a will to command. I'm impelled myself. There's good left in the world, Mr Beach: don't be a party to evil.'

'Listen to His Holiness,' said Mrs Hoop.

'If you could oblige me, Mr Beach,' said Lake, holding out his hand.

'What does he want?' said Beach.

'The borrow of your teeth,' said Mrs Hoop casually, glancing at Edward.

'Don't lend them,' said Edward. 'And don't sign a will as long as you live.'

'You bought the will-forms yourself,' Mrs Hoop reminded him, with bitterness in her voice. 'You're a Judas Iscariot.'

'That traitor,' said Beach. 'What's this bald-headed man want?'

'The loan of your teeth, old Beach. He's got a big engagement on tomorrow in the a.m. You'll have them back in no time.'

Edward saw Lake with his hand held out, colour beginning to mount in his cheeks, and Mrs Hoop looking angry, and Beach glancing at the pair of them. He knew that he would never now return to the Hand and Plough and sit with Beach and Mrs Hoop. He had made an enemy of Mrs Hoop, and he felt a certain guilt that he had not previously warned Beach with the vehemence that he had found tonight.

'Don't ever marry her, Mr Beach,' he exclaimed with passion now. 'She is an enemy of love, like Septimus Tuam. What happened to your teeth?' he demanded of Lake, staring intently at him. 'How did you get that lump? Who hit you?'

'An ungrateful person,' said Lake. 'Not that I see it matters.'

'Was it your wife?' Do you call your wife an ungrateful person?'

'I am not married in any way whatsoever. I was assaulted by a strong-limbed girl who surprised me.'

'I knew it!' cried Edward. 'I saw it there in your eyes: you are an enemy of love, like Mrs Hoop. You and she and Septimus Tuam. You ill-treated some beautiful woman.'

'Brownie is hardly beautiful,' said Lake, and laughed.

'That is in the eye of the beholder. Don't you know that?'

'It is time you went home, Edward,' said Mrs Hoop, 'sounding off like that. Mr Lake came here as a guest. More tea, Mr Lake?'

'You are an enemy of love, Mrs Hoop.'

'Go home and rest, Edward.'

'That is what I learned. I was sitting in the back garden of St Gregory's playing draughts with Brother Toby and I felt impelled to go into the house, to wash my hands actually. Before I knew where I was, I was walking down the steps with a bag in my hand, thinking I was a great fellow and could take the world in my stride again. There was love for his fellow-men in the heart of Brother Toby as he sat there waiting for me, and in the heart of Brother Edmund too, and in all other hearts. There's love in the heart of Lady Dolores and Mrs Bolsover and Mr Bolsover, and poor Mrs Poache. Love is everywhere, Mr Lake. There's love in the heart of old Beach there, and there's love in all the letters and the files, all over the love department. But there's no love at all where Septimus Tuam belongs: there's no love on the hoardings of Britain, Mr Lake.'

'Quite,' said Lake.

'There are people who are the enemies of love,' said Edward. 'As Mrs Hoop is, and Septimus Tuam. You too, Mr Lake. Maybe you all should die.'

'I'm not giving anyone my teeth,' said Beach, rising to his feet. 'I'm surprised at Emily Hoop.'

'I'm scheduled to kill Septimus Tuam,' said Edward in a meditative voice. 'I might as well be hung for a sheep.'

'You've been wasting my time,' exclaimed Lake, frightened to hear a youth speak so casually of murder, and ill-disposed to all members of the company since it was now clear that the old man did not wish to part with his teeth.

'Why do you think I have time to waste?' shouted Lake, leaving the room and banging the door behind him. He rushed from Mrs Hoop's house and ran along the narrow street outside, not knowing what to do, since it was now past midnight.

Lake walked the streets of Putney without thinking of a solution to his problem. He rang the bells of several dentists' houses, but achieved no success in his conversation with the men when they appeared in their night attire. Eventually, tired and full of spite against the three people who had misled him, he turned into a police station to report the threats that had been issued.

'A man called Septimus Tuam is threatened with murder,' said Lake. 'I'm reporting the matter as a citizen should.'

The desk sergeant, dozing over a dossier, thought he was

dreaming. 'I'm getting right fed up with you,' he cried in his sleep, and then woke up and asked Lake what he wanted. He heard the statement repeated in lisping tones and said to himself that he'd recognize that voice anywhere.

'Name and address?' snapped the desk sergeant, and Lake supplied him with both. 'I'll want proof of that,' said the desk sergeant. 'Letters, papers, driver's licence.'

'Certainly,' said Lake cooperatively. 'And here's a business card with my daytime address and telephone number. I am always pleased to assist the police in any way whatsoever. The law must be kept, and seen to be –'

'Thank you,' said the desk sergeant. 'Good night now, sir. And lay off the phoning.'

'Phoning?' said Lake and went on to tell the story of a meeting with three people and how the people had turned threatening. 'It's atrocious,' said Lake, 'things like that.'

'There's lots of atrocious things,' said the desk sergeant in a sour voice. 'Off you go then.'

'I'm in a bit of a predicament, actually,' said Lake.

'We'll look into the matter as best we can. It's all extremely vague, with not a clue or a word of evidence that might be used. On no account telephone us, sir: the entire station has been at sixes and sevens –'

'I don't suppose you have such a thing as a set of dentures about the place?'

'Dentures, sir?'

'You wouldn't have anything taken off a body or the like? What's below in the cells tonight, sergeant. If there's any criminal who'd –'

'I've had a hard week,' replied the desk sergeant, 'ending up with a bit of night duty. Do you understand that? You've given me your information, sir, and I'd now be obliged if you'd move along. If a single further call comes through on the subject of your friend Septimus Tuam, there'll be a load of trouble for you, Mr Lake. It is an extremely grave offence to hamper the police in the dispatch of their duties.'

'I don't know what you're talking about.'

'Impersonation on the telephone. False reports and insulting language. Coming into a police station in the middle of the night asking for false teeth. Get the hell out of here.'

Later that night Miss Brown's eye fell on a small white object on the floor. That object she kept, placing it in a box full of childhood treasures: sea-shells, pebbles, and old, oddly shaped keys. In the days that immediately followed, Miss Brown often opened that box and held between her fingers the tooth that had so often smiled at her, a memento of deceit, a lesson in itself. At first she grieved over the tooth, but in time her eyes stayed dry as they stared at it. And then one day, years later and in a different place, Miss Brown laughed at the tooth and at her own great folly. She threw the tooth into a fire that burned beside her, and she said to herself that she had lived and learned.

23

Edward ate his breakfast gloomily. He was sorry that he had never taught old Beach to play draughts properly, and he was sorry too, despite his reservations about Mrs Hoop, that there was nobody now except his landlady and Lady Dolores whom he knew at all well in London. He couldn't visualize his future. He didn't know whether his future lay in the love department or back in St Gregory's, or out in some friendly colony, planting roots in the ground, and he supposed that if he faced facts he would recognize that his future lay within the hangman's noose. He had dreamed in the night that he was being born all over again, and wondered what that meant. He had seen his mother's open mouth, gasping for breath, and he had felt her slipping away from him as she died.

'All right?' said Edward's landlady.

'All right,' said Edward. He rose from the table and went to his room. He put his bicycle clips on his ankles and his gloves in the pocket of his jacket. He descended the stairs and wheeled the bicycle out of the hall, down two steps and on to the street. He sighed, and rode away on it.

Septimus Tuam lay quietly on his bed, reflecting that his post office account had reached the total of four thousand seven hundred and forty-two pounds seventeen shillings. He had thought of that the night before, and been pleased. He had thought of it again that morning when the cablegram had arrived from Mrs FitzArthur. Blanche FitzArthur was returning: Blanche FitzArthur would be in London tonight and had said in her cablegram that she wished to see him as soon as she arrived. Twice a year, at Christmas and on his birthday, Septimus Tuam reflected that Mrs FitzArthur was arguably the most generous woman he had ever known. He tapped his teeth with his right thumbnail, considering how best to act.

'I think a tea-shop would be best,' he said into the telephone an hour later. 'I have very little time, as an old aunt of mine is returning from the United States. She demands my instant attention, so she says. The elderly –'

'I have something to tell you, too,' said Eve.

'Tell me at four o'clock,' said Septimus Tuam. 'Why not do that, dear?'

Eve replaced the telephone receiver, wondering about James, and then the telephone rang again and James said:

'I am here in Gloucestershire. I have written a letter of resignation. It only remains to file a suit for divorce, if that is the expression.'

'What are you doing, James?'

'I am talking to you from a public call-box. I am going to start up this market garden again. It's as good a thing to do as any other.'

'You are doing nothing. You're clowning around while a man is going to his death-bed.'

'Now look here, sir –'

'Look nowhere,' cried Mrs Poache. 'Why hasn't there been an arrest?'

'I warned you last night,' said the desk sergeant. 'I've given you fair do's. We're coming to get you.'

The desk sergeant replaced his receiver and ordered that a car be sent for the female impersonator who was disrupting the business of the station. 'I have the gen on him,' he said. 'Voluntarily given. Though God knows, he's probably moved up to Scotland by now.'

'Was it a trunk call, Sarge?' said a young constable.

'How the hell do I know if it was a trunk call?'

'Better come with the car, Sarge,' said an older man, 'for purposes of identification.'

'Maybe I had,' said the sergeant.

Mrs Poache, believing that the police had somehow managed to trace her telephone calls and were now coming to arrest her, put on a hat and left her house. She stood at the corner of the road, glancing this way and that, feeling a little frightened. She imagined she'd see the police car draw up by the house and policemen swarming all over the place. But she walked about for half an hour, keeping an eye on the house, and nothing happened. She returned apprehensively and with a lowness of spirit, and, feeling that she had betrayed Septimus Tuam, she resolved to make no more telephone calls to the desk sergeant.

'We have this morning received the resignation of Mr Bolsover,' said Mr Linderfoot, 'so we can in fact dispense with what you were to tell us, Lake. Thank you for your help.'

The board-men were relieved that matters had turned out as they had: all awkwardness, embarrassment, and effort had thus been avoided. James Bolsover, being unfit to cope with the pressure of his work, had chosen wisely and well. What use, the board-men thought, in hanging on when all was in clear and simple disarray? What point in being captain of a sinking soul? They had all felt, at one time or another in their rise to the heights of the business world, that the journey might be too much for them; and they sympathized briefly with the one who had fallen by the wayside before their very eyes.

'What of this Lake?' Mr Clinger had asked before Lake's arrival in the board-room. 'Is he a likely successor?'

'He's a lively wire,' said Mr Linderfoot. 'I'll certainly say that.'

'He has balded early,' said another man.

'Do we hold it against him?' asked Mr Clinger.

'Baldness is hardly a flaw,' said Mr Linderfoot. He was thinking of Miss Brown; in his mind he had just composed a note to her, not knowing that she had already telephoned the office to say that she would not be returning to it. 'It's not a chap's fault,' said Mr Linderfoot, 'if he hasn't any hair, is it?'

'I merely remarked upon the fact,' the other man said. 'May I not?'

'It has nothing to do with the issue,' said Mr Clinger firmly, 'whether or not the man has balded early. We do not hold it against Linderfoot that he is uncommonly fat, or against Poache that he is silent.'

'We held it against Bolsover that –'

'Bolsover was a different case,' cried Mr Clinger. 'He came with white stuff on his clothes. His ways got on to our nerves. The fellow was driving us to an early grave.'

At that moment Lake tapped on the door of the board-room. He entered and stood before the eight men with his mouth closed; and when he heard what Mr Linderfoot had to say he closed his eyes as well, with relief. He had heard of fortune favouring the brave and of Lord Luck being on the side of businessmen who did not flinch. 'Thank you,' he said, keeping his lips as close together as possible. So Bolsover had read the writing on the wall, had he? Well, it was only to be expected, really. He thought to himself that he would walk from the board-room and go straight to a good dentist and have his predicament attended to. In an hour's time he would be able to smile as he was used to smiling; and he would go along then and say a few words to Mr Linderfoot in private, and see if perhaps Mr Linderfoot had a few words to say to him. Afterwards, he would stroll into the office that had once been Bolsover's and see what changes he would make when the time came. Brownie, it seemed, had gone for ever, which in the circumstances was understandable enough. Nostalgically, Lake remembered the words of his father and smelt again the smoke from Jack Finch's pipe : he wished they could see him now, with his cup brimming up so nicely, fulfilling his promise.

Three policemen then entered the board-room and crossed to where Lake was standing. Two of them stood on either side of him, while the third read out a charge in a rapid voice. They arrested him and led him from the room.

Afterwards, Lake reflected that the promised land he had prepared for himself over several years had evaporated in a matter of seconds, like a mirage. The board-men, hearing a charge that was difficult to understand, witnessed the sensational removal of one of their employees by uniformed officers, and at once saw Lake as a criminal. They thought of fraud and embezzlement, confidence trickeries, theft, devious financial manipulation of many kinds. Within thirty seconds Lake became an outlaw in their minds, an untouchable in their world of business.

Edward followed Mrs Bolsover from her house to the tea-shop called the Bluebird Café. He saw the little car bobbing ahead of him through the traffic, but he had little difficulty in keeping up with it, or in finding it again when it passed from his sight. He followed Mrs Bolsover into the Bluebird Café, and sat at a table close to the one she chose herself. He hid behind an old copy of the *Daily Telegraph* which he carried with him for that purpose, guessing that Septimus Tuam would shortly appear and knowing that Septimus Tuam possessed a swift and sharp eye. Septimus Tuam did in fact arrive, but Edward heard little of the conversation that followed.

'This aunt of mine is coming back. Mrs FitzArthur. I haven't much time, dear.'

'I've told James,' said Eve.

'James?'

'My husband. I've told him all about us.'

Septimus Tuam sighed. He wished they wouldn't do that. He said:

'Why did you do that, dear?'

'So that I could ask him for a divorce.'

'Divorce? What on earth do you want to divorce the man for?'

Eve looked surprised. 'Tea,' she said to a waitress who had come and stood by the table. 'Nothing else for me.'

'I'd like an éclair,' said Septimus Tuam.

The waitress went away. Eve said:

'I want to divorce James so that you and I can get married. Is there any other reason for divorce in such circumstances?'

'But what about those kiddies of yours for a start, dear? How can we organize all that?'

'We must work all that out. Divorce takes place every day.'

'Divorce is not good for children. You must surely know it. Thank you,' added Septimus Tuam to the waitress, who had placed four éclairs within his reach. 'Is it real cream?'

'Indeed it is, sir,' said the waitress.

'Divorce is a modern thing,' said Eve. 'There are children everywhere whose parents have been divorced, who live quite contentedly with one or the other. Anyway, why are we arguing?'

'Why indeed?'

'Of course I had to tell James. I couldn't go on, not having James know. I'm not that kind of woman.'

'That's why I love you,' said Septimus Tuam, with cream on his stern lips. He said it automatically, and regretted the words at once: they were words ill-suited to the occasion.

'I am faithful at heart,' said Eve. 'As I have said before, I believe in marriage.'

Septimus Tuam nodded.

'Don't worry,' said Eve, 'Honestly, it'll be all right. Something is on our side. I'm sure it is.'

She had never before met him in a tea-shop like this, in so open a way. Probably the place was full of mothers. Someone might tell Sybil Thornton; and then she remembered that she would have to tell Sybil Thornton herself.

Septimus Tuam looked at his wrist-watch. He saw that he had ten minutes in which to break the news to this woman. He wished there was some way in which they might be given injections before occasions like this, to brace them for the worst. It was awkward having to do the thing in a tea-shop.

'James has gone away,' said Eve. 'He has gone to Gloucestershire to start up a market garden.'

Septimus Tuam wondered why she was talking suddenly about her husband's methods of earning a living. What was it to him if the man ran a market garden in Gloucestershire or if he didn't?

'He resigned his job and walked away. He telephoned this morning, asking me to look after the children for the time being, until the divorce was organized and –' Eve paused. She saw Septimus Tuam place the end of a coffee éclair into his mouth. She said, 'I want to keep my children. My dear, I want somehow to be able to live in the same house as we live in now, and have the children continue with Miss Fairy and Miss Crouch. Don't

226

you think we could make it possible? Or would it be too much?'

'Who on earth,' said Septimus Tuam, 'are Miss Fairy and Miss Crouch?' He tightened the knot of his pale green tie. He prided himself on being punctilious to a fault: he had no wish to be late at the air terminal.

Eve said that Miss Fairy and Miss Crouch were the women who taught her children.

'What would we do for cash?' said Septimus Tuam. 'You're indulging in a bit of a fantasy, dear.'

'But we'll be together?' cried Eve. 'I mean, no matter what happens?'

Several people in the tea-shop heard that cry and turned to regard the woman who had uttered it. Edward heard it, and peeped around the edge of his *Daily Telegraph.*

'Shh,' said Septimus Tuam.

'James has gone away. He's miles away, in Gloucestershire. He knows what there is to know: he admits our love, your love and mine. He has felt our love about him, all over the house. My face is different these days; my eyes are different; I am a different woman. James is no fool. Nothing is holding us back, darling. We'll manage somehow.'

Septimus Tuam said nothing. He considered the words just spoken and reflected that he was not the one to manage somehow. In three minutes' time, he knew, she would be weeping, here in a public tea-shop, and he would be obliged to go, utterly without option, because Mrs Blanche FitzArthur would be cooling her heels at the air terminal.

'The children shall not suffer,' said Eve. 'I am as keen for that as you are. James could not ever manage the children alone: they are bound to come to me. Can you face two children, darling? If you can't, I'll come to you anyway.'

Septimus Tuam saw the tears come, before he had spoken a word. Children caused tears; he had noticed that before.

'I really must be off,' said Septimus Tuam.

'I'll drive you.'

He shook his head. He said he'd rather she didn't drive him. His aunt who was just flying in would want to know all about her; his aunt, he said, was a stickler for detail.

'Let me drive you so that we can talk. I'll drive away again. I won't even meet the woman.'

But Septimus Tuam said that he didn't think that was a good idea. He shook his head slowly from side to side, like a pendulum. For many years afterwards, Eve was to remember that moment in the Bluebird Café, the lean head going from right to left and back again, swaying rhythmically in front of her like the pendulum of an old clock. She thought that in after years this would be the kind of incident with which to regale grandchildren; she looked ahead and caught sight of herself in the future, telling three grandchildren of an incident in the Bluebird Café in Wimbledon, a place long since demolished.

Eve saw the movement of her lover's head and thought of everything at once; she heard herself telling James that she was in love with a man called Septimus Tuam and that Septimus Tuam was in love with her too; she heard James's voice on the telephone telling her that he was in Gloucestershire, about to open up his father's market garden; she heard the voice of her lover telling her that he must leave the country or else produce three hundred pounds; she heard him saying that he would wash the dishes and run a vacuum cleaner over the carpet in the sitting-room.

The head of Septimus Tuam continued to move from left to right and back again, in a slow easy movement. Edward, glancing again around the edge of his newspaper, saw the moving head and wondered what Septimus Tuam was up to. The waitress saw it, and looked to see if there were sufficient éclairs on the table.

For no good reason that he could think of, some words from Hymn 27 came into the head of Septimus Tuam as it moved in the Bluebird Café. They caught there, so that he was obliged to repeat them under his breath in order to get rid of them. 'Swift to its close ebbs out life's little day; Earth's joys grow dim, its glories pass away.' He said all that, and could think of nothing to say to Eve Bolsover.

Edward noted that copper prices were firmer, and that those of shellac were dropping. Jute was steady; coffee was easier. The turnover of E. Wykes of Leicester, manufacturers of elastic yarn, amounted to £1,028,000, which was a record for the company, and an increase of 26 per cent over the corresponding figure for the previous year. The increased profits, he read, had been achieved in spite of increasing costs, constant pressures on profit margins, and the more exacting standards demanded by E. Wykes's customers.

'Is it the children?' cried Eve. 'We talked of my children before, darling: I said you came before them.' Eve sobbed, hearing herself say that. Her children had often themselves driven her to tears with their wayward ways and intractability. They had refused to eat fish and vegetables and certain kinds of meat, they had coloured in the outlined patterns on wallpaper, they had pushed one another all over the house, off tables and sofas, down steep flights of stairs. 'I love my children,' said Eve, 'but I'll come to you without them.'

The head of Septimus Tuam ceased to sway. 'My dear,' he said, 'it's all right. It's nothing whatsoever to do with your children. I'm certain they're delightful people.'

For a moment Eve thought that everything was going to go well for them; that her divorce would come through in time, and that they'd marry quietly.

'It's not real cream,' said Septimus Tuam, 'no matter what she says. You're wrong, you know,' he said to the waitress. 'This stuff isn't real.'

'It certainly is, sir,' retorted the waitress.

'I must go,' said Septimus Tuam, finishing his cup of tea and beginning to rise. 'What they do, you know, is to whip cream up to about ten times its volume. They introduce gas into the stuff: it tastes like nothing on earth.'

'May we meet again soon?' said Eve. 'Tomorrow morning?'

'Shall we shake hands?' said Septimus Tuam, and Eve looked up at him, standing there gaunt and unsmiling, his thin face seeming more than ever like a sacred thing, his body bent at an angle. 'Shall we shake hands?' he repeated. 'For you know, dear, it's nobody's fault in the world if all these weeks we've been at cross purposes.'

Septimus Tuam's hand was stretched out towards her, coming down from above, on a level with her head. He was thinking as he held it there that perhaps, in fairness, he should have explained that the extreme brevity of their love affair was to do with the part that Mrs FitzArthur played in his life.

People taking tea in the Bluebird Café heard weeping that afternoon such as many of them had never known could occur. A dark, narrow-jawed young man stood above a table holding out his right hand, while the woman at the table, a beautiful woman who was dark also, sobbed and moaned. She spoke some words – a plea, the people afterwards said – but the young man seemed not to be able to distinguish what the meaning was. The woman's body shook and heaved. A tea-cup was overturned on the tablecloth.

The people in the Bluebird Café saw the narrow-jawed man leave, looking at his watch, and they assumed that he was running off to fetch aid of some kind. And then they saw another man, a fair-haired person with the pink cheeks of a baby, come and sit beside the woman, and say something to her.

The woman left soon afterwards, guided by the fair-haired person. The waitress dashed after them, crying that not one of the three had paid a bill.

Edward led Eve to her car, telling her not to cry and not to worry. He said it was all for the best in the long run. 'Where has he gone to now?' he asked quietly, and Eve replied that Septimus Tuam had gone to the air terminal to meet an aunt who was flying in from America. 'It'll be all right,' she said. 'Just a love tiff.' She tried to smile, but wept instead. She sat before the steering wheel of her car, her head bent, crying her heart out like a character in a book.

Edward looked at her and felt the anger that Lady Dolores had said he would feel. He felt anger throbbing in his chest and upsetting his head so much that it caused a pain. He stood by his landlady's bicycle and felt rain beginning to fall on him. The anger made his hands shake.

24

Mrs FitzArthur stepped out of the Pan American DC-8. 'A lovely trip' she said to the air hostesses at the door of the aeroplane.

'A lovely trip' repeated Mrs FitzArthur in the air terminal an hour later. 'It really was.'

'So here you are,' said Septimus Tuam.

'Here I am,' said Mrs FitzArthur.

'I looked in once or twice at your house,' said Septimus Tuam, 'to see that all was well. I tidied up a bit.'

'Dear, how kind of you!'

'I enjoy a bit of housework. I like to see things all in order.'

'I remember that,' said Mrs FitzArthur.

The two talked for a while of other matters, matters relating to Mrs FitzArthur's stay in New York, to her two flights over the Atlantic and how one had compared with the other. Eventually, Septimus Tuam said:

'So you've come back with a decision, have you?'

Mrs FitzArthur did not at once reply. She fingered the silver clasp of her handbag, her eyes following the movement of her fingers. She said:

'I've brought myself to do it.'

'Good girl,' said Septimus Tuam.

Mrs FitzArthur glanced around her, and dropped her voice somewhat. 'I've brought myself to do it,' she said, glancing again. 'I'm going to return to old Harry FitzArthur and make the statements he wishes of me. That's what I wanted to tell you immediately.'

'I'm delighted to hear it,' said Septimus Tuam. 'It's much the wiser course. To have been cut off with a penny by Mr Fitz-Arthur would really have been no joke. You'd have got lonely, my dear, in that big old house of yours.'

'That's what I thought,' said Mrs FitzArthur. 'I'm going to get old Harry to do the whole place over.'

Not far from where they sat, Edward was speaking in a telephone-box. 'He came straight here from the Bluebird Café,' reported Edward. 'He's sitting talking to Mrs FitzArthur. Mrs Bolsover's in a terrible state.'

'And how are you, Mr Blakeston-Smith?'

'I am feeling ill. It made me ill to see Mrs Bolsover.'

In the love department Lady Dolores doodled on her lined pad, drawing another face.

'You've done terribly well,' she said. 'The entire department is proud of you.'

'But I haven't done anything at all,' cried Edward. 'Septimus Tuam is sitting here alive, not ten feet away.'

'I can see you're in a paddy. I suppose your face is red.'

'My face is hot, certainly it's red.'

'Well, then?'

'What am I to do next, Lady Dolores? What d'you want me to do for you?'

'Do? In what way?'

'I thought I might move in now –'

'You are a man of action, Mr Blakeston-Smith: you've proved it. Leave thought alone.'

'Mrs Bolsover's heart is broken. Her marriage has gone for a Burton.'

'I know all that, old chap. We'll never forget you.'

'What?'

'You'll be remembered for ever in the department. We'll talk about you, mentioning you by name.'

'I don't understand what you're saying, Lady Dolores. Have I done wrong?'

'You have done extremely well. Amn't I telling you? You have allowed us to fill up a file on Septimus Tuam that is beyond all value. We know the man's habits and methods, for which all thanks is due to your surveillance. We have noted down the evidence of your Mrs Hoop: how Septimus Tuam lifted three hundred pounds off Mrs Bolsover, how he posed as a shop assistant. We have noted how he uses the house of one woman in

232

which to conduct himself with another. We have noted that he favours buses rather than another form of transport, and how he's never without an umbrella. We have a fine description of him. We know now that he will leave a woman in distress in a tea-shop and walk out straight out of her life without a by-your-leave. He walked out of the life of Mrs FitzArthur and into the life of Mrs Bolsover, and now he walks back again as Mrs Fitz-Arthur flies in. You have observed from beginning to end Mrs Bolsover's love affair: you have done your stuff. This kind of information is perfect. There is a pattern of behaviour: I am studying it at this very minute.'

'But what about me?'

There was a pause before Lady Dolores repeated:

'You have done extremely well. If ever you're in the area –'

'You are giving me the brush-off, Lady Dolores. Let me tell you my side of things –'

'Pet –'

'No pet about it, Lady Dolores. You're there in your office insulting people and trying to be as tall as a house. You're living on your imagination, Lady Dolores, with your nerves and a bottle of old whisky: you've no idea what's going on in the outside world. All you do is read the written word: what good is that, for the sake of heaven? I'm the one that's seen the enemies of love. All you ever do is draw faces on a pad of paper.'

'You're in a great old paddy, Mr Blakeston-Smith.'

'Forget about the paddy. You put me in the paddy as well you know. You've arranged for the paddy, Lady Dolores, and now you're saying that if I'm ever in the area ... You're giving me the brush-off because maybe I'd make a bungle of it.'

'What are you talking about?'

'All I asked you for was a desk in the love department.'

'You're a man of action,' said Lady Dolores. 'You're useless at any desk. Remember Odette Sweeney?'

'That was a mistake. Anyone could make a mistake like that the first day.'

'You threw the letter away. You said it had been written by Irish labourers in a four-ale bar. I remember the sentence you used.'

Edward felt his anger increase. His anger became a greater thing, spreading from the scene he had witnessed in the Bluebird Café, from the tearful face of Mrs Bolsover and the face, unmoved, of Septimus Tuam. Edward's anger was directed now against everyone he had met in London except old Beach and Mrs Bolsover. What right, he thought, had that landlady to give him the same breakfast every day, a fried egg and a tomato? What right had Mrs Hoop to tap her forehead in his presence, whispering that he was mentally deprived? What right had Lady Dolores to use him as she had, and then to drop him entirely? Edward could see some other man stepping into his shoes, a hard-handed man of forty years or more, who was used to the work of tracking people down and putting a knife between their ribs. 'We had another chap on this,' Lady Dolores would tell this man, 'but he turned out to be a child. He was afraid of the posters on the hoardings.'

'You have been unkind,' shouted Edward into the mouthpiece of the telephone. 'I'd never have thought it of you.'

'That's a lovely paddy you've got hold of, Mr Blakeston-Smith –'

'Oh, for heaven's sake, give over about the paddy. What about the sins of Septimus Tuam? Isn't he to go before the face of God, abasing himself in his guiltiness? There's none can stand up to that, Lady Dolores.'

'He'll abase himself in his guiltiness, don't worry about that. And he'll go before the face. I've said it before, Mr Blakeston-Smith, you have a fine turn of phrase. You're a joy to know.'

'I'm awaiting an instruction.'

'I like the holy way you talk, Mr Blakeston-Smith. I could listen for ever.'

'What am I to do?'

'Go back to St Gregory's, pet. Go down there, and I'll send you on what little there's owing to you, and your card stamped up to the end of next week. You're a man of the Almighty: you don't have a place in this wretchedness at all. It is I who take over now, since you have paved the way. I can draw the face of Septimus Tuam. I know what to expect: I know every move he makes. I'm saying a thank-you, Mr Blakeston-Smith.'

'You wanted me to put an end to him. I had an itch in my hands, and it's stronger than ever.'

'You're a holy terror,' cried Lady Dolores.

'I don't think I can stop myself.'

'Do no such thing,' shouted Lady Dolores. 'D'you hear me now? Don't lay a finger on the fellow. That's an instruction, Mr Blakeston-Smith. Are you there?' Edward could hear that Lady Dolores had gone into a panic. He could imagine her gripping the telephone receiver, blowing smoke into it, flints of anger in her eyes. 'Are you there?' repeated Lady Dolores.

'I'm here all right. You've led me a dance.'

'Give me a promise now.'

'I am totally confused. Someone was on to me to kill Septimus Tuam. Someone was impelling me all over the place.'

'There's many an injured woman who's said in her time she'd like to see the blood flow out of Septimus Tuam. Injured unto death,' said Lady Dolores, and paused. 'Are you listening to me?'

'I'm standing here listening. Septimus Tuam is chatting up Mrs FitzArthur.'

'There are women in their graves, buried by the love of Septimus Tuam. Aren't there three who went into a decline and died within two years? I've told you, pet. It's in the letters. They couldn't eat their food, they had a taste for nothing at all. Women meet up in heaven and compare their notes. "We'll impel a holy man towards Septimus Tuam," said one to another. How about that?'

'I cannot accept it.'

'Dead women sent you to the love department. The dead inspired me to put you on the track of Septimus Tuam.'

'No.'

'The dead are devils when they get going. Give me the promise now: I'm a match for three dead women.'

'I don't know what to think.'

'I'm telling you what to think, Mr Blakeston-Smith. The dead sent you: I wondered who did. Their job is done, and so is yours. Let them go back to their shrouds; and get back to St Gregory's yourself.'

'I'm as cross as two sticks.'

'Nobody feels impelled, pet, once they've discovered the source. You could be hanged for a thing like that.'

'I couldn't kill a fly,' cried Edward, annoyed with himself for saying it, 'I'm no crusader for three dead women and they should know it.'

'Well, then?'

'I'm fed up with all of you. I've had the same breakfast every day since I came to London. I've been dropped into a state of depression, pitched about from pillar to post. Words have been put into my mouth; I've been hit on the face by a butcher, and threatened by Septimus Tuam, and called mad by practically everyone. I am not mad, Lady Dolores: I'd rather say the dead are in charge than that.'

'You cannot trust the dead.'

'They messed me up.'

'It's a disgraceful thing –'

'Devil take you, Lady Dolores!' cried Edward suddenly and with agitation. 'And devil take the dead. I've had enough.'

In the love department the air was thick with poetry and the scent of the typists, but in Lady Dolores' chill sanctum there were only the greyness of the filing cabinets and the gloom of the squarely-built woman who had never been classified as a dwarf. She would not see Edward Blakeston-Smith again; she would not see his pale hair or the blush of his cheeks. She would miss his innocence.

Septimus Tuam said:

'We'll be so careful in future, Blanche, that not even a fly on the wall would notice a thing. You see if we aren't.'

'Goodbye,' said Lady Dolores. 'Don't ever forget me. Don't ever forget the love department.'

'How could I?' cried Edward. 'However could I?'

Septimus Tuam looked away, and saw the youth in the telephone-box. The youth was standing oddly, as though he had suffered from a seizure, as though in a state of collapse.

'We'll be unbelievably cautious,' said Septimus Tuam, pleased that the wretched little private eye, or whatever he was, was dying in a telephone-box. 'You'll be surprised.'

Mrs FitzArthur was silent for a moment. Employing then a prepared formation of words, she said:

'I'm afraid there is to be no future for you and me, my dear. I came to this conclusion: that should I return to Harry Fitz-Arthur I should return with all my heart. You and I must say goodbye.'

Mrs FitzArthur held out her right hand for Septimus Tuam to receive, imagining that he would take it with a slow motion and raise it, possibly, to his lips: he had acted as elegantly before. But Septimus Tuam did not take the right hand of Mrs Fitz-Arthur. He recalled his own limb held out in a similar manner not fifty minutes ago in the Bluebird Café in Wimbledon. He saw from the corner of his eye the door of the telephone-box open and the youth who had given his name as Blakeston-Smith stagger ridiculously out. The youth stood peering at him, and peering at Mrs FitzArthur.

'That man's no good,' said Edward, coming closer. 'He'll send you to your grave, Mrs FitzArthur.'

Mrs FitzArthur opened her mouth to pass a comment on this, but in fact could think of no comment to pass. Feeling calmer, Edward walked away.

'What's that in aid of?' enquired Mrs FitzArthur, and then said she was sorry, referring to the news she had broken to her one-time lover. 'I'm truly sorry,' said Mrs FitzArthur. She proffered her right hand again, but Septimus Tuam only looked at it. He looked at it and then looked into Mrs FitzArthur's eyes.

'So you couldn't trust me,' he said bitterly. 'You had to go getting a private detective. And now you're giving out lies and slop.'

'Whatever do you mean?' cried Mrs FitzArthur.

This fat old bitch, thought Septimus Tuam. 'It'll sicken me to think of you,' he said, and he walked away without another word.

Edward, crouching behind a luggage-trolley in a corner, saw Septimus Tuam make his way among the travellers. He looked in the other direction and saw Mrs FitzArthur still sitting on the seat.

Septimus Tuam, in a fury as great as Edward's had been, walked in the rain from Victoria Air Terminal to the King's Road and on towards Putney. He walked with his umbrella up, cursing in his heart the whole of womankind. He had burnt his boats with Mrs Bolsover; Mrs FitzArthur had betrayed the trust he had placed in her. Together, these facts made Septimus Tuam bitter, as often before he had been bitter, for his life had not been an easy one. Tomorrow he would have to start again; he would be obliged to frequent pastures new, and he did not care for the thought. He had left on a seat in the air terminal the most generous woman he had ever experienced; he had left in a Wimbledon tea-shop a woman who might have suited for quite a bit yet, had she not been so foolish as coolly to inform her husband of the facts. He sighed in the rain, striding the anger out of his system, endeavouring to look ahead. With the flaw in his nature, he knew that he would try and fail, he would risk in-dignity and he would suffer it, he would be lucky not to suffer incarceration as well. Who would the next woman be, he won-dered, that woman he was destined to fail with? Tall or short, young, old, middle-aged, dark or fair? And who would the woman after the failure be? Would he strike one who was not as well-to-do as she looked? Or one who was given to violence, or drink, or had ugly finger-nails? He had experienced many, he reflected, as he strode ahead: the good and the bad, the generous and the mean, the meek, the foolish, the wise; women who had, for a time at least, been full of love.

Far behind him, wheeling his bicycle and carrying no um-brella, Edward was bidding goodbye to Septimus Tuam, follow-ing him along a street for old times' sake. He was leaving Septi-mus Tuam to Lady Dolores, and the three dead women could like it or lump it. In a minute or two he would jump on to his landlady's bicycle and ride away from this large city, from the enemies of love, and from London's lovers. He would turn on the lamp he had bought for the bicycle and he would ride out into the night, with no hat upon his head, to the south coast of England, to St Gregory's by the sea.

Edward wondered if anyone at all would kill Septimus Tuam in the end; perhaps, he thought, Lady Dolores would. He shook his head over himself, marvelling to think that he had ever feared that against his desires he might do the wicked man to death, driving home a bullet or strangling him with telephone wire. Perhaps it was true what Lady Dolores had said, that three dead women had met in their after-life and had picked him out as a suitable candidate for the work; however it was, it didn't much matter now. As he pushed his bicycle along the streets, seeing the umbrella of Septimus Tuam far ahead of him, he remembered the fuss he had made about the posters and the odd state he had found himself in when he had confused the people of the posters with Goths and Visigoths. 'Strain and overwork; impelled by the dead. I'm a mixed-up kid,' said Edward. He stood in the rain and made up his mind 'I shall take rest and tranquillity again and I shall bring them in my time to others. St Gregory's is my resting place: I am scheduled to become Brother Edward.' Many faces came into Edward's mind then, including those that might well have belonged to the three dead women. They were nodding at him, pleased with him, implying that he had done well. 'So we part on good terms,' said Edward, 'even though I have not done a deed.' He looked ahead and could see no sign of the thin form of Septimus Tuam. 'I have lost him for the very last time,' said Edward, and laughed and jumped on to his landlady's bicycle. He felt cold with all the rain on his clothes and stopped by a café to have a cup of tea.

'You're damp,' said the woman who handed it to him.

'I am truly damp,' replied Edward, and drank the pale beverage without taking off his gloves that were beginning to cling uncomfortably to his fingers. 'Goodbye,' he said, and left the café. Crouched over the handlebars, firm on the saddle, Edward prepared himself for the long journey. He was anxious now not to waste time: he wished to see, as soon as was humanly possible, the kind countenance of Brother Edmund and the hands of Brother Toby moving the draughtsmen on the board.

But as he moved ahead the faces appeared again in his mind, and then the face of Eve Bolsover came and banished all the others. There were tears on her cheeks, the tears that had flowed in the Bluebird Café. Her face remained until Edward said, 'I shall call in on Mrs Bolsover, to tell her I'll pray for her marriage.'

He pedalled fiercely, causing buses and motor-cars to hoot their horns at him. The rain fell heavily on his bare head and soaked through his clothes. He could feel it on his back and on his legs. In Putney he pulled the wash-leather gloves from his hands and threw them on to the street.

A man, seeing something fall, shouted after Edward, imagining that the gloves had been dropped in error. He darted into the street himself, to rescue the pale objects, still shouting at Edward, hoping to return his property.

A taxi-cab, moving fast, swerved to avoid this man and, since it was moving faster than its driver imagined, mounted the pavement.

'What d'you think you're doing,' shouted the angry driver, peering from his cab through the rain and the twilight, 'running into the road on a night like this? You could have caused an accident.'

'I'm terribly sorry,' said the man, holding Edward's gloves in his hand. 'A chap on a bike dropped these. I thought, you see, they might have been something valuable.'

'I don't see at all. It's bloody improper, that.'

'Well, no harm done,' said the man. 'And these turn out to be only a pair of gloves.'

'What's he mean, no harm done?' cried the shrill voice of a pedestrian from the other side of the taxi-cab. 'Look here at this lot.'

Edward pedalled hard up Putney Hill, panting a bit. He cycled on, past the house in which he had observed, through a window, Mr and Mrs FitzArthur emotionally involved in their drawing-room. He bore to the right, and drew up eventually in Crannoc Avenue.

'Mrs Bolsover!' cried Edward. 'Mrs Bolsover! Mrs Bolsover!'

He called her name as he dismounted in a hurry from the bicycle. He ran towards the hall-door, shouting it still. He rang the bell and banged on the wooden panels, and in the end the door was opened, and Eve stood in front of him.

'Yes?' she said in a calm voice. 'Yes?'

'Don't you know me, Mrs Bolsover?' As he asked the question in an excited way, Edward remembered saying the same thing on the doorstep of Mrs Poache. He thought about Mrs Poache, and decided not to call on her. Eve said:

'I cannot help you if you are a detective. You were kind today, but I would rather not.'

'I was employed a while since in a love department. You, I'm afraid, were a payer of debts.'

'One lives and learns, God knows.'

'I'm sorry, Mrs Bolsover. I am terribly sorry.'

Edward seized her right hand and shook it up and down. 'I'm going back to St Gregory's,' he said. 'I'll never forget you. I'm going to become Brother Edward.'

'I'm afraid I don't understand anything of what you say. You're soaking wet.'

'I'll remember your face, Mrs Bolsover. You have great beauty: you are a lovely thing.'

'You haven't a coat,' said Eve, opening the door wider. 'Come in.'

Edward shook his head. 'I'm going to cycle ninety miles,' he said, 'in the rain.'

'But you can't. Look –'

'No, Mrs Bolsover. Pause only to assess the damage. I'll pray for your marriage: I've come to tell you that. I'll pray for your marriage every day of my life.'

'But I've never known you. I don't understand.'

Her children, in a bath, were calling for her attention, laughing and seeming to be happy. Tears came into her eyes as she heard the noise and looked at the young man standing there, saying he was sorry for her and speaking of prayer. Septimus Tuam had said this young man was mad: she supposed he was right.

'Don't go into a decline, Mrs Bolsover. Try and keep your pecker up. I'll pray every day, at eight o'clock in the morning.'

'Please come in –'

'I'm exchanging innocence for wisdom, Mrs Bolsover. I am

in that process. Love falls like snow-flakes. It conquers like a hero.'

Eve, puzzling over these sentiments and the choice of their expression, saw the young man run off, dripping wet. He mounted a bicycle and rode away, down Crannoc Avenue.

25

That night, lying snugly in her bath, Lady Dolores thought of Edward. She guessed that Edward was cycling towards the south coast in the rain, and when she thought of him she thought too that the rain would match his sorrows. She knew that because she had come to know Edward: she herself found rain a happy thing, and always had.

Edward passed Guildford, noticing the bulk of the cathedral on a hill. He saw some of the poster people, like ones he had seen in London. He felt pain in both his feet, but pedalled on.

Lady Dolores stood up in her bath and dried her short body with an orange-coloured towel. She wrapped the towel around her and poured herself some whisky. With a glass in her hand, she sat down on her bed and looked into her file on Septimus Tuam. It contained all that Edward had reported, and all the letters that the women had written to her about Septimus Tuam over the years.

Lady Dolores poured more whisky. She sipped it as she absorbed again the details of the information that Edward had carried to her. She learnt some of it by heart, closing her eyes and repeating the sentences with her chin lifted. She compared a phrase here and there with something in the letters from the women.

Lady Dolores had no intention of employing the hard-headed man that Edward had imagined: there was no need to. Edward in his innocence had noted all the evil of Septimus Tuam; he had not overlooked a single thing: he had written a book about the creature.

Lady Dolores removed her glasses and rubbed them with a corner of the orange-coloured towel. She put on a night-dress and took the file to bed with her, repeating what she read over and over again, speaking loudly in the stillness of her bedroom in the love department. She dreamed, while still awake, of her meeting with Septimus Tuam. She walked up the stairs of the house in which he lived, and knocked with her knuckles on the panels of his door. 'My old friend has sent me,' she said. 'A lady you have known. You breed bulldogs, I understand?' Septimus Tuam said no, he did not breed bulldogs. He had had a bulldog as a child, he admitted; he was fond of the animals. 'What a silly mistake!' said Lady Dolores. 'How on earth can it have come about?' Septimus Tuam said he didn't know. 'Come in,' he said, 'since you're here.'

Edward smelt the sea and cycled towards it. He brought the bicycle to a stop on the sea front, and left it there, propped against a lamp-post, while he walked on to the sand and onward to the sea. He took his shoes and socks off and crept with his bare feet into the foam of the sea's edge, letting the salt sting his blistered soles. It was the place where he had seen the children playing soldiers and, remembering that, he pretended to be a soldier too, moving alone in the hazy light of the dawn, feeling good to be alive. He wheeled the bicycle to St Gregory's, and pressed open a kitchen window.

Lady Dolores slept for an hour, from six until seven. She rose then and bathed again. She ate a little cake, dressed herself expensively, and arranged for a taxi to convey her to Putney.

In the early morning the drive was pleasant. People on the pavements moved speedily to work, or stood at bus-stops. They were people who didn't waste time, as later in the morning they might, talking to one another or looking at the goods for sale in shop windows. There was a briskness about all movement; nobody was passing away the time of day.

The taxi crossed Putney Bridge and moved into a web of back streets. 'About here, I imagine,' said Lady Dolores to the driver, taking from her purse a ten-shilling note. She secured a cigarette in her holder and applied a match to it. 'Thank you, madam,' said the taxi-driver. 'I need change,' said Lady Dolores.

Septimus Tuam's name did not feature among the names beside the bells at the door of the rooming-house, a fact that did not greatly surprise Lady Dolores, since she imagined that he was careful over the displaying of that name.

'Can I help you?' said an elderly man to her, coming out of the house. 'For whom are you looking, madam?'

Lady Dolores repeated Edward's description of Septimus Tuam. 'I am looking for him,' she said. 'Do you know which room?'

'Are you his mother?' said the man in a respectful voice, taking off his hat.

'I am not his mother,' returned Lady Dolores, 'nor ever have been. Which room?'

'Madam,' said the man.

Lady Dolores frowned, thinking that this person was a bore. She said, 'Never mind if you cannot help me. Don't let it worry you.'

Lady Dolores smiled, but the man said:

'Madam, may I offer you the condolences of a stranger?'

'Why condole? What are you on about?'

'I am on about a dead man,' said the elderly stranger. 'In the hands of the Blessed Lord since half past five yesterday afternoon.'

'No. You have mistaken me. The man I am seeking is a live one.'

'The one you describe, madam, has been in heaven since half past five yesterday afternoon. Slaughtered by a motor-car in Putney High Street.'

Lady Dolores fell over. She dropped to the street and lay in a faint at the feet of the elderly man. 'Madam,' exclaimed he, bending and blowing in her face. 'Here, come and help me,' he called to some people who were walking by. 'A woman's passed out.'

'Why,' said one of these people, 'that's Lady Dolores Bourhardie. I've seen her on the telly.'

Another person agreed with this opinion, and added:

'Fancy this in Putney!'

Lady Dolores was lifted and propped against the wall of the house in which Septimus Tuam in his lifetime had resided.

'Isn't she stout?' said one of the passers-by. 'I'd never have thought it.'

'She's to do with the fellow that copped it,' said the elderly man. 'She was asking about him when suddenly she folded up. She's O.K., is she? It's not a double death?'

'Double death in Putney,' said one of the others, speaking facetiously.

But Lady Dolores, as if to dissipate these fears, rose to her feet. She had never fainted before, either in public or in private. 'I'm so sorry,' she said.

'You're a national figure,' said one of the people who had helped her. 'Lady Dolores. You fix people's troubles.'

'I'm extremely sorry,' said Lady Dolores. 'I had business here. It is now not necessary. I was taken aback.'

'Poor fellow,' said the elderly man. 'He was walking along the pavement, proper as could be. I'm afraid you'll have no further business with him, madam.'

'What happened?'

'He was hit by a taxi-cab. He was strolling along with an umbrella up, it being raining stair-rods.'

'The taxi swerved,' another person said, 'to avoid a man who ran out into the road. It seems a guy on a bicycle dropped some article which this second party thought was a dog and so ran to the rescue.'

'No,' said the elderly man. 'The second party thought it was something valuable. He was retrieving it for the cyclist. It was, in fact, a pair of gloves.'

'What?' said Lady Dolores.

'A pair of gloves caused all the trouble. Yellow things.'

Lady Dolores frowned. 'This cyclist,' she said. 'What became of him?'

'Rode on, oblivious. The cyclist didn't know a thing.'

'Didn't know a thing,' another voice confirmed. 'Rode on.'

There was a long gap in the conversation while all considered the facts of the accident.

'So a cyclist's gloves,' said Lady Dolores ponderously, 'have caused the death of a man.'

'It is strange enough,' agreed the elderly man, 'when you put it like that.'

'The cyclist rode off,' said a woman who had not spoken before. 'The cyclist was innocent.'

246

'You cannot blame the cyclist,' said another.

Lady Dolores went away as the voices continued. The people stood by the house where Septimus Tuam had lived, and talked on for another five minutes about the death of a man and the fainting of Lady Dolores on his doorstep.

Although she greatly disliked walking, she walked now. She was aware of a flatness of spirit, and she was still incredulous. He had been there on the pavement with an umbrella, and now he was dead. An accident had taken place in the rain. She thought of Edward Blakeston-Smith on his bicycle, and found the thought ironical: Edward Blakeston-Smith pedalling in the rain, throwing away his wash-leather gloves before quitting the city. 'Oh, my dear,' said Lady Dolores. He would not know, she imagined; he would never return to the love department, he would never be told. He had prepared for her a revenge that was as sweet as it could be; he had put her into a position of unassailable power, and she herself had given him the gloves. 'I thought you bred bulldogs,' Lady Dolores whispered. 'Imagine my thinking that.' And Septimus Tuam stood before her, shaking his head. 'Well, at least we have met,' said Lady Dolores, and she reached out a hand and took the arm of Septimus Tuam and dominated him completely. She called up her powers, the gift she'd been given: she had a way with people. 'You have a way with you,' said Septimus Tuam, and she smiled at him and still held his arm, and asked him to lend her two pounds ten, which Septimus Tuam did not hesitate to do.

'What good is death?' cried Lady Dolores on Putney Bridge, looking over the parapet. 'Death is no good to me.'

'Now,' said a Sikh bus conductor who was passing by. 'Do not do that, lady.'

'I have fallen in love with you,' said Septimus Tuam. 'I cannot do without you for a second of my day.'

They went together to restaurants and rode about in taxi-cabs. They drank coffee and whisky, and talked the hours away while Septimus Tuam paid out his money for every single item. 'I cannot understand it,' he said. 'I have a way with people,' said Lady Dolores.

'No,' repeated the Sikh bus conductor. 'Honestly.'

'What?'

'You spoke of death, lady.'

'There is a great emptiness.'

The Sikh bus conductor, a kind man, did not know what to do about this woman with spectacles who was speaking of death and looking into the Thames. He wished to comfort her, but felt a shyness.

'You do not know me,' said Lady Dolores, 'but he would have come to know me well. He was to have turned to me and said one day, "I have no money left, I'm skint." And then I would not have hesitated. "No money?" I'd cry. "No money left?" I'd run a lipstick over my lips. "Cheerio, Septimus Tuam," I'd murmur. And his room would be filled with the wailing of the defeated and the gnashing of teeth of an evil man cut off in his prime. And the tears, sir, would be the tears of a broken heart, of a damaged organ that would never mend while the River Thames flowed, while the trees grew in the parks of London. Septimus Tuam on his knees would make confession. He would cast himself down before the face of God, abasing himself in his guiltiness.'

The Sikh bus conductor paid attention to these statements and considered their import. The streets of this city were strange in that people spoke strangely on them. I know her face, he said to himself.

'And he would lie there an hour, or maybe three hours,' said Lady Dolores in a singsong voice, thinking of the holy language of Edward. 'He would lie on the boarded floor of his room, while his sins rose high before him, filling out all the room. And the faces of the women would appear unto him, the women from the roads and the avenues, the streets and crescents, the luxury lanes, the parks and the squares. The faces would come weeping as he was weeping, and the tears of the women would flow over the penitent and cleanse him as best they could. He would rise up in the end and wipe his eyes, and see that it was dusk. He would leave that room, turning over a new leaf in his life. He would go to a sandwich bar and eat good food, and for the rest of his days he would perform honest duties.'

'I have seen you in my house,' said the bus conductor. 'You've been on the box: an advertisement for Scottish oats.'

'Not Scottish oats. No, not that. I am Lady Dolores Bour-hardie, well known in my way.'

'I have seen your face.'

'It appears in the homes of this country. It is the face that God gave me; I have never complained.'

'You are as your God has made you,' said the Sikh bus conductor. 'For me it is different.'

'I sit alone, pet. I read the letters and compose replies. The girls clatter their typewriters, the young men sing. And when they have gone their way, I sit alone in the love department and think of Septimus Tuam. Now it seems I may think no more. I have been robbed of victory; and in an ironical way.'

Lady Dolores, her face pale and her deep eyes dead within it, left the Sikh bus conductor. 'I think I shall never weep again,' she said as she walked away. 'I shall mourn his death until kingdom come.' She hailed a passing taxi and said to the driver, 'I have been robbed of my fair victory,' and told him then to take her to the love department. That taxi-driver, having seen the Sikh bus conductor in conversation with the woman and noticing that he now remained on the pavement glancing after her, grimaced amusingly, his eyes indicating Lady Dolores. But the Sikh bus conductor did not return this grimace. He stood in perplexity on Putney Bridge, reflecting again that the streets of London were full of strangeness.

26

James bought many gardening books and read them all from cover to cover. He read about fuchsias and fritillaria, convolvulus, immortelles, wisteria, pinks, plume poppies and toadflax. He sat alone at night in the empty house reading about the cultivation of flowers and shrubs and all domestic vegetables. *Though the gooseberry*, he learnt, *will grow on the poorest soil, it will not produce really fine fruit unless planted in a deep, rich, well-drained loam, and treated generously. Fresh air and sun are essential to the gooseberry.* James planted gooseberry bushes five feet apart, and cut the bushes back to a moderate extent. He planted them in well-drained loam, and hoped for the best.

He had employed two men to help him. 'Never seen the like,' the two men said, and appeared to enjoy marvelling over the neglected garden. 'Some rare stuff here,' they remarked, examining old Mr Bolsover's shrubs, not knowing, really, whether they were rare or not. When it was dark, James read the gardening books and wondered how long it would take to get the place into shape again. He wandered from room to room, as he had wandered after his father died, and as he had again with the estate agent. He looked at the place where the estate agent had screwed his heel into the rotten board, and wondered what to do about it.

Late one afternoon, while clearing some ground for asparagus beds, James heard the sound of a car, and looked up and saw his wife. She came towards him and stood on a path that the men had recently tidied.

'Hullo,' said James.

He showed her all that had been happening in the garden. He showed her all the gooseberry bushes, and where sweet-pea was to grow and lily-of-the-valley, and cauliflowers, cabbages, Brussels sprouts, broccoli, celery and celeriac, broad beans and early carrots. 'There'll be strawberry beds,' said James, pointing. 'The men are in the greenhouses.'

Eve walked through the house with him, from one large room to the next, looking up at the ceilings. He showed her where the estate agent had damaged the floor-board. 'All have to be re-done,' said James.

As he laboured in the gardens, James often thought about the eight fat men in the board-room. He heard their voices and saw the sun glint on their spectacles. Clinger talked on about door-handles, Mr Linderfoot strolled still about the corridors, eyeing the young girls, the Captain slept, the others talked and drank gin with tonic water in it. They would proceed thus for ever, James imagined: he saw them dying in the board-room.

For the time being, though, and as James imagined, the men continued in their ways. They ate their lunches and talked of minor matters; they returned by night to their wives in their houses, who saw them coming and prepared the room for them, switching on a television set. 'It is the way of the world,' said Lake. 'Life has its ups and downs. One must take them in one's stride.' He smiled in his shame, cutting his losses and seeking advancement elsewhere. He became, eventually, the manager of a tobacconist's shop in Wandsworth. Miss Brown married an architect.

'These wallpapers have been up for thirty years,' said James. 'What colour, I wonder, were they in the first place?'

Eve suggested colours that seemed suitable, and added that wallpapers nowadays didn't fade as easily. James said:

'The elderly don't notice much.'

'No,' said Eve, shaking her head. 'I don't suppose they do.'

'How's Septimus Tuam?' said James. 'How's he getting on these days?'

They were standing in the centre of the drawing-room when James said that. The furniture, Eve thought, was uglier than she'd remembered it. She walked away from James. She spoke with her back to him, looking through the window at an ash-tree.

'He came one morning, the day after that dinner party, and

he helped me in his peculiar way with the housework. He had damaged my stocking with the tip of his umbrella in the button department of Ely's: he came to give me other stockings instead.' Eve related these details because she had not spoken of them before. She told James all there was to tell, how Septimus Tuam had captivated her, causing her to imagine scenes in a country of the Middle East, and Arabs who danced in celebration.

'I find it hard to visualize the chap,' said James agreeably. 'Well, well.'

'I behaved like a schoolgirl of fourteen.'

'I would have thought not. Do schoolgirls of fourteen take on lovers?'

'I meant I was as silly.'

'You are thirty-seven. It's an age of discretion, Eve.'

'James, could we come here? The children and I?'

James explained that he had set the machinery of divorce going. He said that a housekeeper would come to the house in time, and the children could come too. 'You've got Septimus Tuam,' he said, 'in his low-slung motor-car.'

'I haven't got Septimus Tuam.'

'Well, don't blame me. Why haven't you?'

'He went off. I gave him three hundred pounds.'

'You've been taken in by an adventurer,' said James. 'Shall I light a fire?'

'Do as you wish. I know about being taken in.'

'They are two a penny,' said James Bolsover.

On the lawns of the hotel the Bolsovers had strode together, hand in hand. They had cut a cake, and a bearded photographer had darted about with a camera. It was dim in Eve's mind now: she could hardly make out the details. 'Let's begin again, James,' she cried, as she had cried on the night of the dinner party, while he slept in an armchair.

'You're as bold as brass,' said James. 'You've got no shame.'

Eve said she had shame in plenty, and added that even as she had made the suggestion she had felt it to be brazen.

'It's a pig in a poke,' said James, 'if ever there was one.'

'There was love that let us down. Now at least there is less to lose. And love may come again.'

'May it?' said James Bolsover, and struck a match and lit a fire.

'It may,' said Eve after a moment. 'Who can tell about a thing like that?'

'Some was my fault,' said James. 'I am generously admitting it.'

'No.'

'I think so. It doesn't matter now.'

'I had too little understanding. I wanted too much. I was stupidly romantic.'

'A ridiculous name for a man to have,' said James. 'I've said that before.'

'Well?'

'A debt is owed to him: one must be fair.'

Eve turned her back and walked away from her husband. She felt empty of everything. She said:

'Are you going to grow verbena?'

'I may,' said James. 'Yes, I suppose so. Though at the moment, I confess, what you are saying interests me rather more. Why should we set up again, since success is in the lap of the gods and failure already a proved thing between us? Wouldn't it be better not to?'

'There are the children.'

'A marriage, you said, should not be bridged by children. Or some such phrase. You were quite right.'

'What then?' cried Eve, feeling that James was being unduly difficult and yet not quite blaming him. 'What else is there?'

'Other people have stuck by one another for the sake of children: it's the modern thing to do.'

'If Septimus Tuam hadn't come along we'd have stuck by one another and never questioned it.'

'Will you forget him?'

'I shall remember him with bitterness.'

'Perhaps we might come alive. You never know. Growing verbena together and being the best of pals, while you get over your bitterness.'

James knelt down and blew at the fire with his mouth.

'A young man is going to pray for us,' said Eve. 'He is going to pray for this marriage every day of his life.'

'Pray?' said James, looking up at his wife. 'What young man?'

'He came to our house on the night of that dinner party. He arrived with the old man. He came to see me again, to tell me about his praying.'

James rose to his feet and regarded Eve earnestly. 'A friend of Mrs Hoop's,' he said. 'Wasn't he? There was some talk also about his being the Poaches' son.'

'He was neither, as it turned out. He said he had been employed in a love department.'

'But isn't it odd? Don't you think it's odd? I remember his face. What on earth's a love department?'

Eve said she didn't know.

'Well?' she said.

'There's a small chance for us,' said James. 'I suppose there is. It isn't much.'

The Bolsovers stood in silence, watching the fire begin to burn. Then they walked again about the house and saw fresh signs of damp and decay, or signs they had missed before. Watery sunlight spread over furniture and floors, revealing much that was amiss. The Bolsovers were nervous in the house, and felt it correct to be so. They walked gingerly together, in silence until James said:

'Why ever should he pray for a marriage? I don't get it.'

'You have forgiven me with kindness,' said Eve. 'I must thank you for that.'

'He must be crazy,' said James.

27

'You are required on the telephone,' said Brother Edmund to Edward in the garden of St Gregory's, interrupting a game of draughts.

'Mind you come back,' said Brother Toby, and laughed and looked around for his pipe.

'Who's that?' said Lady Dolores. 'Am I speaking to Blakeston-Smith?'

'You are,' replied Edward. 'How are you getting on, Lady Dolores?'

'The dead have gripped me,' cried Lady Dolores. 'I thought you'd like to know.'

'I have left all that behind, Lady Dolores. I'm on my way to becoming Brother Edward.'

'Septimus Tuam's as dead as a door-nail,' said Lady Dolores. 'A taxi-cab took his life.'

'What happened?' asked Edward, and Lady Dolores told him. She told him everything she knew, but she did not mention the wash-leather gloves.

'That is not all,' said Lady Dolores. 'The dead –'

'I cannot accept that stuff about the dead, Lady Dolores: I must tell you that. I am exchanging my innocence for wisdom and insight; I can't agree that dead women impelled me to the love department and on to the tail of Septimus Tuam. In the calm air of St Gregory's there's not a chance at all for a theory like that. Strain and overwork fired my imagination; hadn't I already seen Goths and Visigoths on the posters?'

'The dead are as slippery as circus seals. Watch out for what you say about that crowd.'

Edward laughed with suitable restraint. 'Did the three dead

women impel that old taxi-driver to knock off Septimus Tuam? Are you going to tell me that?'

'Mr Blakeston-Smith?'

'Yes?'

'I see no sign of wisdom and insight: you're as innocent still as ever we knew you. What kind of a funeral d'you think our friend had?'

'Quiet,' said Edward.

Two days before, the body had been burnt and the ash disposed of without much ceremony. A name, not the name by which the women had known him, had been found, written in his own hand, on a piece of card in a wallet. It was followed by the address of his room in Putney, in which a relevant document was discovered: a paper giving the simple instruction that when he died his body was to be reduced to ashes, which were in turn to be thrown away. On the back of this paper was the valid will of the man who had been killed in Putney High Street: it had been witnessed by two milkmen, and it left his money and his chattels to the Royal Commonwealth Society for the Blind.

The title of the dead man was noted in bound ledgers and on numerous lists: all records were brought up to date. The Royal Commonwealth Society was grateful, and enquired if there happened to be a next of kin so that appreciation might be passed on, but there was no next of kin that anyone could discover.

No woman who had known Septimus Tuam knew that it was he who had suffered in an accident in Putney, and no woman at all had looked upon the casket that contained his remains. At the hour of his death, Mrs FitzArthur spoke the words her husband had wished to hear. 'He is a scoundrel and a ruffian,' Mrs FitzArthur intoned. 'If we saw him now, Harry, I would ask you to kick him in the pants.' Mrs Poache read of the accidental death of a man with a name that was not Septimus Tuam, and remarked to the Captain that taxis were a scourge. For many years afterwards she noted the contents of obituaries, and perused with close attention items headed *Man Found Dead* or *Foul Play not Ruled Out*. A month or so before her own death she came to the conclusion that the young man who had called on her had been practising some form of esoteric humour, or else that she had completely misheard him.

'Well,' said Edward, 'so that's the end of that.'

'End? Are you away in your head? I tell you, the dead –'

'Lady Dolores, I must ask you not to utter any further insinuations about my sanity. I am in St Gregory's now, in a quiet atmosphere. I have altogether finished with people who think I am a certified lunatic. As well as which, you may talk about the dead until the cows come home and I'll not accept that the souls of three women from the Wimbledon area met up in their afterlife and did what you say they did. They'd never be allowed, Lady Dolores. You know that well.'

'I know no such thing,' shouted Lady Dolores. 'Will you listen to me, pet?'

Edward could smell the lunch cooking. Brother Edmund had said at breakfast that he intended composing a rich stew for lunch. 'Would you mind going round to the butcher,' he had said to Edward, 'and asking for two pounds of succulent braising steak?' Edward had done that and on his return had observed Brother Edmund carve the steak up in an expert way, and cut up as well a number of onions, carrots, parsnips, and a small green pepper. Beside him, in a bowl, were freshly-made dumplings, Brother Edmund's speciality.

'I am listening,' said Edward, 'but I cannot help smelling the lunch cooking. We're going to sit down to a stew.'

'I will tell you a story,' said Lady Dolores, 'before you sit down to anything. I'll tell you a story about the dead.'

'Now, look here, Lady Dolores –'

'Are you there?'

'I have great respect for you, Lady Dolores. You've taught me a considerable amount. But I'll not be talked to about the dead. The dead have a province of their own. I'd be obliged if the dead could be left out of this.'

Brother Edmund, passing by with a tin of condensed milk for a lemon pudding, inclined his head in an agreeing way. 'A province of their own,' he whispered, 'is putting it aptly.' He descended to the kitchen and said there that Edward was coming on.

'You are talking to me brusquely,' protested Lady Dolores, 'when I'm only trying to tell you something. Why fear the dead, Mr Blakeston-Smith? We're in this together.' For a moment, Lady Dolores wondered if she should oblige Edward to listen to her by placing before him the facts about the wash-leather gloves in Putney High Street. She resisted the temptation, not wishing to ruin the youth's life. 'Well, then?' she said.

'Go ahead,' said Edward, deciding not to listen to a word. He had already resolved that every day of his life he would pray, not for the Bolsovers' marriage alone, but for Mrs Hoop and the man called Lake who had ill-treated a woman. It had come to him firmly that the enemies of love needed what prayers they could get. He had resolved that until the day he died he would not forget the letters he had read in the love department and that he would never allow them to cease to shock him. He would recall with pain and concern the bewilderment of women, and Odette Sweeney, whose husband had brought home a doxy. And whenever he recognized in himself a single prick of conceit he would remember the accosting of Mr FitzArthur and the blow he had received from the butcher in Wapping. He had accused Mr FitzArthur of sins against women in cinemas; he had caused horror and confusion, and scenes on the streets of London. Edward guessed that he would remember for ever Mrs Poache asking him what message it was he had brought to her, and the weeping of Mrs Bolsover in the Bluebird Café, and old Beach murmuring after a woman on the make. He would not forget. He would pray for the preservation of love within marriage, and for married women everywhere. Already he had dreamed of being handed a thing like a halo and being given to understand that they had made him the patron saint of middle-aged wives.

'Who are you?' said the voice of Lady Dolores in Edward's ear, and Edward said that he was Edward Blakeston-Smith.

'No, no,' came the shrill voice back. 'I am telling you what I said to him. You cannot escape the dead, and there's no use hiding your head and saying you can. Three dead women, and now this other. I'm surprised at your arguing, Mr Blakeston-Smith. What do they teach you in that place?'

'I will pray for you, Lady Dolores. I will add you to my list.'

'Be careful with that, pet: don't go upsetting anything. Don't tell any tales about what these dead are getting up to.'

'I wish you'd consider getting that out of your system, you know. Love is a healthier subject to talk about. You had great wisdom there, Lady Dolores. "Love falls like snowflakes" was one of the first things you said to me.'

'I never said any such thing,' snapped Lady Dolores.

'Ah yes, now –'

'I'll sign off, Mr Blakeston-Smith. I have shown you my heart.'

'We've been good friends,' began Edward.

'We're the wanton prey of the dead, the two of us. You have your evidence in that they went into a decline and matched up their notes –'

'Lady Dolores –'

'They winkled you out of St Gregory's and laid you before me, and, to tell you the truth, I nearly had a fit. Three dead women, average age fifty-one and a half.'

'I cannot discuss the dead with you in this way. It's far from proper for me in my present vocation. In any case, I find it upsetting.'

'Are you there, Mr Blakeston-Smith?'

'I am saying goodbye now.'

'As for the other, you must take my word for that. I have given you the final scene: I have opened my innermost thoughts to you.'

It occurred to Edward when he heard these words that, having closed his ears to her story about the dead, he had missed as well, apparently, something that was close to Lady Dolores' heart. He had not meant to be as discourteous as that.

'Look,' said Edward.

'Goodbye, pet. Take care what you say in those prayers.'

'Wait, Lady Dolores –'

'We'll be dead when next we meet, Mr Blakeston-Smith.'

'Lady Dolores –'

'I'm signing off now.'

'I'll definitely be praying for you,' said Edward quickly, 'and for the soul of Septimus Tuam.'

'I'll tell him that,' said Lady Dolores.

Edward stood by the telephone in the hall of St Gregory's. He replaced the receiver slowly, his eyes on the polished linoleum of the floor. The smell of the stew was greater now, for Brother Edmund had lifted the lid of the pot to inspect its contents. 'I did not listen,' said Edward. 'I should have.' He waited, and the voice of Lady Dolores echoed in his mind, and the story she had spoken disturbed his consciousness.

Edward saw the love department again. He saw the typists rising from their seats and powdering their faces, about to leave for home. The clerks tidied away their jotters and the letters they had recently read; they said some final words and went their way. The silence in the hall of St Gregory's became the silence of the love department, for only Lady Dolores was left there, in her grey sanctum, raising a glass of whisky to her lips, looking at a chocolate cake.

Lady Dolores remained at her desk for many hours, reading the file on Septimus Tuam, unhappy because the man had been snatched from her. 'It was a Tuesday night,' said the voice of Lady Dolores. 'It was ten minutes to midnight.'

Edward saw Septimus Tuam enter the love department. He saw him walk through the typists' room and then through the clerks' room, beneath the frieze by Samuel Watson. 'Who are you?' said Lady Dolores. 'Who are you and what do you want? It is ten to twelve.' And the man advanced and said he was Septimus Tuam, come to enter her life. 'I had planned,' said the voice of Lady Dolores, 'to seek him out on the pretext that he was in the dog business. But when he came to me dead there was no need for that. I'll tell you now: I didn't ever mention dogs to Septimus Tuam.'

Edward moved softly across the linoleumed hall, thinking that Brother Toby would still be waiting for him, while the voice of Lady Dolores continued to speak in his mind. It was a low voice now, softer than he had ever heard it, and he knew by the sound that Lady Dolores was opening her innermost heart, and so he stood still. He was aware that the smell of the cooking had caused him to feel hungry; and he was aware of this dead man. Septimus Tuam stood before Lady Dolores' desk and gazed at her without a smile. He projected a beautiful face, the still features of a saint, and the eyes of an animal with a soul. Returning that gaze, Lady Dolores swooned and shivered; she noted a trembling on the man's lips; blood thickened in her veins. She realized then that he was about to say the words that she had never heard: he was about to address her as no living man had ever thought fit to address her. There was a haze around her, which touched her and warmed her, and her pulse was sluggish. There was an explosion that was soundless in the love department, and her ears were filled with the words she had read about. 'I love you,' said Septimus Tuam.

Edward sat down. For a moment he thought of picking up the telephone and talking again to Lady Dolores, confessing that he had not listened while she had been speaking, explaining that the story had caught on to something in his brain and had returned to him in full later. There were things he might say in a gentle way, but when he turned towards the telephone he sensed that he should not use it. 'He is to rise from the dead repeatedly and often,' said Lady Dolores in Edward's mind. 'He is a penitent, Mr Blakeston-Smith: you can think of that.'

Edward saw her waiting with bleary eyes, emptying her whisky bottle in the middle of the night. He saw her lonely in her love department, seeing what she wished to see. 'Love will go on,' she said, 'a magic that is sometimes black.' Edward knew that love would indeed do that: it would go on for other people, drawing them together for a reason of its own, now and again betraying them. And in a shoddy way it would go on for her: she would receive as her share the words of a dead pedlar, and she would be thankful for it.

'A really beautiful stew,' said Brother Edmund, passing through to the garden. 'Brother Toby's waiting for you.'

Edward followed him slowly. He felt the love department invading St Gregory's completely: the scented flesh of the typists, the murmuring clerks, the ferns and the palms and the rubber plants. 'His dog prowls,' said the murmuring clerks. 'Now, red mechanic!' they cried in unison. He looked on the face of Lady Dolores and she remarked that they'd meet when they were dead. 'You have said to me things that women have written to you,' exclaimed Edward in a whisper. 'You have spoken the same kind of stuff.' And she nodded her head and said she was a woman too.

Edward closed his eyes and spoke to her. He agreed with her most vigorously that the dead were everywhere, coming to see people, talking and impelling, as slippery as circus seals. He should not have argued, he confessed that now: he had been wrong, and she had been wholly right. As he spoke, attempting to be kind, his whisper rose to a gabble and his words began to trip one another, tumbling without form from his mouth. He tried to say that he was sorry for failing in that world he had walked into, and for throwing away the gift she had given him, and for failing to see her as she was. In his distress, his voice had none of the gentleness he had intended it to have, and he felt himself defeated. He stood in silence, waiting for a change, seeing her hair like the mane of a horse, and her teeth smiling at him. When calmness came to him, he turned away. He left the grey sanctum and walked through the love department, and found himself in the garden of St Gregory's.

'We thought we'd lost you again,' said Brother Toby, and laughed.

'Lost?' said Edward.

'Well, you know. Gone for a walk.'

Edward shook his head. He sat down and brought his eyes to bear on the draughts-board, and did not entirely understand the state of the game. 'A farce in a vale of tears,' he said.

The sun shone on the garden of St Gregory's, warming the backs of Edward's hands. It shone on flower-beds that were empty of blooms and on the face of Brother Toby and on the printed page of Brother Edmund's newspaper. It shone on the black and white squares of the draughts-board, causing them to glisten, bringing out the contrast. Edward sat still and made no move on the board before him. A cat, a long way off, walking carefully on the grass, crossed his line of vision but did not enter his thoughts. Nor did anything in the garden, not Brother Edmund, nor Brother Toby, nor even the garden itself. Edward saw himself dying, a man of eighty-seven whose hair had turned brittle, whose jaws had forgotten their function; and he felt himself remembering still, at that great age, how once he had

ridden a bicycle through suburban roads, how he had read letters and listened to a woman in a place peculiarly titled. There
would be no forgetting. He would remember for ever the facts
of love as he had seen them played before him, and he would feel
a sadness.

Edward closed his eyes and felt the sun on his face, and opened
them again and saw the cat still creeping on the grass and
Brother Toby's dark clothes and the figure of Brother Edmund
moving away to attend again to his stew in the kitchen. He
noticed the draughts-board and the black draughtsmen awaiting
his attention, and the white kings of his opponent intent upon
victory. He sat for a moment longer like a statue in the sunshine,
and then he stretched out a hand and moved a black disc
forward.

READ MORE IN PENGUIN

In every corner of the world, on every subject under the sun, Penguin represents quality and variety – the very best in publishing today.

For complete information about books available from Penguin – including Puffins, Penguin Classics and Arkana – and how to order them, write to us at the appropriate address below. Please note that for copyright reasons the selection of books varies from country to country.

In the United Kingdom: Please write to *Dept. EP, Penguin Books Ltd, Bath Road, Harmondsworth, West Drayton, Middlesex UB7 ODA*

In the United States: Please write to *Consumer Sales, Penguin USA, P.O. Box 999, Dept. 17109, Bergenfield, New Jersey 07621-0120.* VISA and MasterCard holders call 1-800-253-6476 to order Penguin titles

In Canada: Please write to *Penguin Books Canada Ltd, 10 Alcorn Avenue, Suite 300, Toronto, Ontario M4V 3B2*

In Australia: Please write to *Penguin Books Australia Ltd, P.O. Box 257, Ringwood, Victoria 3134*

In New Zealand: Please write to *Penguin Books (NZ) Ltd, Private Bag 102902, North Shore Mail Centre, Auckland 10*

In India: Please write to *Penguin Books India Pvt Ltd, 706 Eros Apartments, 56 Nehru Place, New Delhi 110 019*

In the Netherlands: Please write to *Penguin Books Netherlands bv, Postbus 3507, NL-1001 AH Amsterdam*

In Germany: Please write to *Penguin Books Deutschland GmbH, Metzlerstrasse 26, 60594 Frankfurt am Main*

In Spain: Please write to *Penguin Books S. A., Bravo Murillo 19, 1° B, 28015 Madrid*

In Italy: Please write to *Penguin Italia s.r.l., Via Felice Casati 20, I–20124 Milano*

In France: Please write to *Penguin France S. A., 17 rue Lejeune, F–31000 Toulouse*

In Japan: Please write to *Penguin Books Japan, Ishikiribashi Building, 2–5–4, Suido, Bunkyo-ku, Tokyo 112*

In Greece: Please write to *Penguin Hellas Ltd, Dimocritou 3, GR–106 71 Athens*

In South Africa: Please write to *Longman Penguin Southern Africa (Pty) Ltd, Private Bag X08, Bertsham 2013*

BY THE SAME AUTHOR

The Collected Stories

'The finest living writer of short stories' – John Banville

Originally published in separate volumes as *The Day We Got Drunk on Cake*, *The Ballroom of Romance*, *Angels at the Ritz*, *Lovers of Their Time*, *Beyond the Pale*, *The News From Ireland* and *Family Sins*, this volume also contains four stories not included in these collections.

Whether they portray the vagaries of love, the bitter pain of loss and regret or the tragic impact of violence upon ordinary lives, these superb stories reveal the insight, subtle humour and unrivalled artistry that make William Trevor the contemporary master of the form.

'A rollcall of excellence ... Again and again you wonder how does he achieve such consistency and variety ... a book to buy and treasure' – *Irish Times*

BY THE SAME AUTHOR

Elizabeth Alone

'He is a master of regret, betrayal and intimations that things will never again be as they were' – *Sunday Times*

'Comfortable, amiable Mrs Aidallbery – Elizabeth – is in hospital for a hysterectomy. So is Sylvia Clapper, with false teeth and bleached hair . . . she lives with a slippery Irishman: no children yet and now no chance. Likewise confined, devout Miss Sampson . . . and Lily Drucker, after repeated abortions, is in for childbirth . . . And there is William Trevor, taking relays from flies on a hundred walls, snipping, linking, shaping his material with delicate understanding, respect and a sparing trickle – just enough – of humour . . . A finely observed, gently sensitive comedy, delightful to read, like lived experience to remember' – *Daily Telegraph*

Mrs Eckdorf in O'Neill's Hotel

'A small work of art' – *The New York Times Book Review*

What was the tragedy that turned O'Neill's Hotel from a plush and prosperous establishment into a dingy house of disrepute? Ivy Eckdorf is determined to find out. Yet it is Mrs Eckdorf alone who is the victim of the truth she seeks to exploit, for the elusive mystery of O'Neill's Hotel turns out to be her own.

BY THE SAME AUTHOR

Other People's Worlds

Julia is very happy. Safe in her old stone house, drowsing in the sun, she is soon to be married to Francis. Doris is not happy. Sprawled among the grime of her Fulham flat, she gropes behind the breadbin for the vodka that keeps her going and waits endlessly for Francis. And Francis, dreaming of Constance Kent driving the knife deep into the child's throat, smiles . . .

The Boarding-House

By selecting carefully, William Wagner Bird filled his boarding-house with people that society would never miss – even if it noticed they were around. But then he made a fatal mistake. He died.

The Old Boys

Intrigue and skulduggery surround this year's election for the President of the Association. For the Old Boys, at seventy, the election revives the dormant conflicts that had tormented them as schoolboy adolescents. But now, being old, they possess a fiercer understanding of the things of life that matter – power, revenge, hatred, love and the failure of love.

BY THE SAME AUTHOR

Excursions in the Real World

'He's that rare thing, a writer who writes best out of love; and there are wonderful portraits here, as in his fiction, of failures, misfits, oddities ... William Trevor writes autobiography just as well as fiction ... keeping a watchful eye on life' – Carole Angier in the *Spectator*

Two Lives

'*Two Lives* offers two superb novels in one volume ... as rich and moving as anything I have read in years' – Glyn Hughes in the *Guardian*. '*Reading Turgenev* is one of the most beautiful and memorable things he has written ... a drift of enchantment is evoked ... it stays in your memory – like Turgenev' – Hermione Lee in the *Independent on Sunday*. '*My House in Umbria* is a brilliant examination of the mechanics of delusion, seen from within' – James Saynor in the *Observer*

BY THE SAME AUTHOR

Fools of Fortune

Willie Quinton lived a pleasant, cossetted life in County Cork, un-touched by the troubles . . . until the soldiers came and took a terrible revenge . . . Spanning sixty years, William Trevor's tender and beauti-ful love story has at its centre a dark and violent act that spills over into the mutilated lives of generations to come. 'To my mind William Trevor's best novel and a very fine one' – Graham Greene

The Silence in the Garden

Winner of the *Yorkshire Post* Book of the Year Award

'The silence in the garden has hardened and grown cold before Will-iam Trevor's novel begins. It opens in 1971 when Sarah Pollexfen, the last witness to one family's secret tragedy, has died and her diary is about to be read . . . Trevor's grave and lucid prose weaves recollections and the present together, and his measured compassion fuses the several narrations . . . spare and moving' – Nicci Gerard in the *Observer*

The Children of Dynmouth

A small, pretty seaside town is harshly exposed by a young boy's curiosity. His prurient interest, oddly motivated, leaves few people unaffected – and the consequences cannot be ignored . . . 'A very fine novel. It is the work of a master craftsman and a deep creative talent . . . The bare bones of its structure are stark, simple, and stunningly subtle . . . simple yet brilliant . . . Without doubt he is one of Britain's finest novelists' – Peter Tiniswood in *The Times*

BY THE SAME AUTHOR

Felicia's Journey

Winner of the 1994 Whitbread Book of the Year Award and the *Sunday Express* Book of the Year Award

'You're beautiful,' Johnny told her and so, full of hope, seventeen-year-old Felicia crosses the Irish Sea to England to find her lover and tell him she is pregnant. Vividly and with heart-aching insight William Trevor traces her desperate search through the post-industrial Midlands. Unable to find Johnny, she is, instead, found by Mr Hilditch, pudgy canteen manager, collector and befriender of homeless young girls.

'A book so brilliant that it compels you to stay up all night galloping through to the end . . . exquisitely crafted' – Val Hennessy in the *Daily Mail*

'Immensely readable . . . The plot twist – a characteristic mix – is both sinister and affecting, and so skilfully done that you remember why authors had plot twists in the first place' – Philip Hensher in the *Guardian*

also published:

Ireland: Selected Stories
Outside Ireland: Selected Stories

forthcoming:

Miss Gomez and the Brethren